The Singularity series:

Redshift
The Observer Effect
Uncertainty Principle
Quantum Entanglement
Event Horizon
Point Singularity

Prequel
Ani, or, the care and feeding of your great tree-
dwelling venomous tentacled land-devil

EVENT HORIZON

R.M. OLSON

ISBN-13: 978-1-990142-28-4

Cover by MiblArt

To Riverdog, for keeping me sane

"… and around a black hole, there is an area from which no light can escape, because the escape velocity exceeds the speed of light. This boundary is called the event horizon, and beyond this boundary, all events will inevitably be pulled further inside the black hole's gravity. Escape is no longer a possibility."

-From a physics textbook, Sao Martim University, Vila Nova do Sol, Colorida

1

"Aran." Istvay's voice was barely louder than a whisper, their arm tightening around Aran's waist. And for a moment, Aran was almost overwhelmed by the sheer, unbelievable, unimaginable luck of it. That after everything—after Istvay's kidnapping by a hostile raider crew, after Aran's desperate flight across the galaxy after them and the raider battle that had almost killed him—he had Istvay again. That Istvay was beside him, right now, their brown eyes staring into his, their black hair mussed and falling loose from its ponytail over their familiar sharp cheekbones and prominent nose, the light brown of their skin stained with a faint flush of exertion, the comfort of being with them the only home Aran had ever needed.

"Aran, would you please wipe that damn grin off your face?" There was a familiar worry under the exasperation in Istvay's tone. "I'm pretty sure that thing outside has figured out we're here by now, and if it has, we and everyone else in this damn cave are going to be turned into shish kabob in about thirty seconds."

Aran tore his gaze off Istvay's face reluctantly, and glanced around at the damp cave where he and Istvay and the raider hunting party was gathered, and then down the long, pebbly slope that stretched out below them.

They were a good thirty metres onto the shore, huddled into a shallow cave at the highest point on the small island, but Istvay was right—whatever had chased them here seemed perfectly capable of lunging far enough onto shore to make short work of him, Istvay, and the half-dozen raiders crouched in the cave behind them.

It was only days since the raider leadership war had ended in a draw, with the two main contestants, Krevai and Sharda, agreeing to a truce. Only days since Aran had been all but cut in half by a raider in his attempts to rescue Istvay, and fixed up by some raider technology that had left him alive and only slightly sore. Only days since he and Istvay had finally, somehow, figured things out between them, admitted, finally, that they loved each other—which would have been, probably, irrelevant to anyone but him and Istvay, except that the purported reason Krevai and Sharda had agreed to a truce was that he, one of Krevai's crew, and Istvay, who'd been coopted into Sharda's crew, were mates, and, by longstanding raider tradition, captains whose crew were mates were bound to an unofficial truce for as long as it lasted.

And now the two captains had called in every raider ship in the vicinity to resupply, in anticipation of the real reason for their truce: a full-fledged war against the yibo.

Aran was still trying not to think too hard about the implications of that.

Dessi was back on Captain Krevai's ship, running analyses of the data she and Aran had gathered in order to find the cure for the genetic defect that was killing Istvay, and Aran had asked to come along on the resupply mission because he was about to drive himself mad with impatience. Besides, this was an absolutely perfect opportunity to examine the flora and fauna of this planet.

And based on his examination, the fauna of this planet appeared mostly interested in eating them.

The water below was eerily silent, lapping against the grey rock beach.

And then it exploded in a massive, fountaining wave as a creature with mottled blue skin—scales? Probably, but so far it hadn't held still for long enough for Aran to be sure—burst upward, its wide mouth gaping open in its thick, heavy head, set with teeth longer than Aran's arm.

Aran watched in complete fascination. It was clearly an aquatic creature, but its flippers seemed well-suited to shoving its bulk forward over the rocks in a thrashing, serpentine motion that was surprisingly efficient, and the glitter of the dull sun on its scales—they were almost certainly scales, now that he could see them more closely—seemed almost too precisely calculated to blind or confuse prey to be an accident.

"Dammit ..." Istvay shoved Aran backwards and tumbled on top of him as the beast's thick forehead crashed into the mouth of the cave, sending rocks and debris showering to the ground around the huddled group of them. Aran landed heavily against the muscular bulk of one of the raiders, who yelped something that was probably a raider curse. He yanked Istvay forward, and the creature's teeth clicked shut millimetres from their boot.

The beast thrashed against the entrance, its bulk blocking out the dim light of the sun, and then it slid back down the beach, the water swallowing it with hardly a splash.

Aran sat up and grinned at Istvay, a little shakily. "See? I told you it wouldn't get in here."

"Which is just fine, except for the part where you almost damn well got your face taken off by that thing's teeth," Istvay grumbled, brushing themself off.

Aran rolled his eyes. "I was fine. I'd calculated the distance. It wouldn't have got me."

Istvay sighed. "Good hell, Aran, it looks like I survived Sharda just so you could kill me with a heart attack. I feel a hell of a lot better about these expeditions when you have Ani with you, since she, at least, seems to feel some actual concern about you getting back in one piece." They closed their eyes, and for just a moment, Aran could see the residual strain and the exhausted relief in their slumped shoulders. "I almost lost you just a few days ago," they whispered. Their fingers slid up into his hair, and they tipped their forehead against his. "I don't think I can handle doing it again. So please, for my sake, put a couple more centimetres into your safe calculations?"

Aran leaned into the touch, fighting back the small sting of tension the mention of Ani had brought up. "Yeah. Sorry." He paused. "Anyways, judging from its previous attack patterns, we should have at least a couple of minutes before it tries again, and we saw the route it took up the beach. I'm almost sure I'd have enough time to plant a couple of sensors that could give us some good baseline information, which we could use to—"

"Aran ..."

"Humans." Landru stepped forward, shoulders hunched and head ducked carefully to avoid braining herself on the cavern's low roof. She was Captain Krevai's second-in-command and in charge of the hunting expedition, and to her credit, none of her raiders had been killed. Yet. "I've hunted salyans before. It will keep trying until it tastes blood, or until we kill it." She grinned, the sharp canine teeth peeking from beneath her lips lending menace to the almost human shape of her face. Her blood-red eyes and ice-pale skin almost glowed in the dim light, a sharp contrast to the thick black sheet of her hair that fell past her hips. "We'll have to make a break for it. It will get one or two of us before we reach shore, likely, but that's only to be expected on hunts like this. And perhaps the rest of us will get a chance to kill it as it feeds."

Her expression manifested a disturbing amount of unconcern at the prospect of death.

Aran glanced behind the raider woman.

There were four raiders from Krevai's crew in the cave, as well as three from other raider crews who'd stopped by to resupply at the same time.

She followed his glance.

"Krevai or one of the other captains could send out a rescue team," she said, lowering her voice. "But it won't get here before the salyan manages to break in. And if it gets in far enough to trap us, none of us will come out alive. I've seen a salyan feed. It's not a pleasant death."

Aran nodded, trying to recall everything he'd observed of the creature. "I imagine it doesn't kill immediately, just tears off strips of flesh while the victim is alive, yes?" he said absently.

Landru raised an eyebrow. "Have you seen it feed?"

He shook his head. "No, but judging from its mouth and the set of its teeth, that would make the most sense." He paused. "Listen, what if we—"

Landru shook her head decisively. "I'm sorry, human. We're not going to be able to leave here without bloodshed. If the Ani was with us, perhaps I'd reconsider, but ..." She shrugged, and turned over her shoulder. "Krevai's crew, to me. We'll go out and create a distraction to let the humans escape, since they're naturally more weak and stupid than raiders. The rest of you, I suggest you either come with us, or bring up the rear. Unless you need the humans to protect you."

She turned forward again, teeth barred in a grin. "Are you ready, humans?"

Before Aran or Istvay could answer, she ducked out of the cave and started at a brisk jog for the water, pulling out her butcher knife as she ran. The four raiders from Krevai's crew fell into step behind her, and two of the other raiders joined them.

Ripples spread ominously at the base of the pebble beach.

In the distance, across a shallow sandbar, lay the relative safety of firm ground, but Landru was right—there was no way all the raiders would make it across.

Aran turned to Istvay, whose face was pale and set. "Pishti, we can't just let them die! And they'll probably kill the salyan, too, it's not its fault its hungry. We have to—"

He grunted and stumbled forward as something hit him from behind.

Istvay turned, frowning. "What—"

Whatever it was slammed into Aran again, hard enough to knock him to the ground. Istvay cursed, and Aran rolled over just as the last remaining raider in the cave grabbed him by the arm and shoved him into the wall where she'd already pinned Istvay.

"What the hell—" Istvay began furiously.

The raider smiled. It was a small, unsettling smile, as if she'd heard of the concept of smiles, but had never had a chance to practice until now.

"Humans," she purred. "I think that raider left me to protect you, yes?" There was something off about her tone, a strangeness that

Aran couldn't quite place. "Let's go, then."

"Let go of us," Istvay snapped, teeth gritted. "We can protect ourselves."

The raider ignored Istvay. Still smiling that disconcerting smile, she dragged Istvay and Aran, stumbling after her, out of the cave and into the open air.

Below, Landru and her crew had reached the water. Landru stepped cautiously in and beckoned the others forward. "It'll come for us first. Vasha, you get across, and then we'll get the humans over. The rest of you, stay with me to hold it back." She glanced over her shoulder at the raider holding Aran and Istvay and beckoned with a jerk of her chin. "Get them down here, but wait until Vasha starts over. We'll only have a minute."

Aran glanced uneasily at Istvay as the raider dragged them down the beach at a deceptively quick pace. "Listen," he said, struggling to turn in her grasp. "If you'll just—"

They'd reached the edge of the water.

Landru turned towards them, frowning. "I told you to wait until we'd—"

The water in front of them split around a massive, plough-shaped head and a gaping mouth packed with long, needle-sharp teeth, and the raider holding Aran and Istvay flung them forward, directly into the thing's path.

Aran landed in water up to his waist and scrambled upright, blinking and spitting foul-tasting muck from his mouth and looking franticly for Istvay. There were shouts from the raiders behind him, and the sounds of a fight breaking out, but he didn't have the time to worry about it right now. "Pishti! Where are you? Are you alright?" His eyes caught on Istvay a couple of metres away, struggling to their feet. Their face was sick with horror.

It was only then that he realized the heavy, fishy smell that coated his nostrils wasn't just the leftovers of the oily water in his mouth.

He half-turned. Then he dived out of the way as far too many teeth snapped shut on the leg of his trousers, ripping through the fabric like paper.

"Dammit ..." he choked as his face broke the surface again, his feet scrabbling for purchase on the slimy lakebed. He could hear, indistinctly, Istvay swearing, Landru shouting something, but most of his attention was caught by the creature bearing down on him, jaws gaping wide. Its motions were smooth and powerful, its ungainly appearance on land more than compensated for by the easy grace of its movement through the water.

He had to drag his mind away from admiring how its physique was so perfectly suited to its mode of hunting, and back to the urgency of the matter at hand. He threw himself clumsily to one side as the creature struck, but it spun in the water, movements lightning-quick, and he barely had time to shove his knapsack in front of him as the jaws snapped shut again.

The attack gave him his first glimpse of the side of the creature's face, and for a moment, he stopped in pure wonder. "Look at you," he murmured, grinning despite himself. "You've got gills for water, and oxygen-absorbent skin patches for when you're on land. You clever thing!"

The fish shook its head, and the knapsack tore down the middle, spilling the roots and berries they'd gathered earlier into the water.

"Aran!"

He just had time to register the terror in Istvay's voice before the fish's attention turned from the food in the water—now mostly demolished—and fixed once more on him.

"Aran, just hold on—"

The fish struck, mouth wide.

Aran gritted his teeth and dived past the snapping teeth and into the gaping mouth as it snapped shut, yanking the remainder of the knapsack in with him.

He was completely enveloped in the dark and the smell, his senses choking with it, and he had to clench his teeth against the heart-pounding terror that always seemed to accompany closed-in spaces.

"Sorry, sweetheart," he whispered through his gritted teeth. "I know you were looking forward to this, but I promised Pishti. And I'm sure you'll find something else to eat, a lovely, clever thing like you."

The sharp barbs on the fish's tongue scrapped against his body, shredding whatever fabric or skin they caught on, and Aran offered a quick, silent prayer of relief that he'd thought to wear a jacket. He wriggled to get out of the way as it pushed him forward towards the long spikes of its teeth.

"I was right," he gasped. "You use your teeth for tearing, don't you, and I'm too big for you to swallow."

Its mouth opened again as the fish tried its best to expel him, and for an instant he caught a glimpse of Istvay splashing through the water towards him.

He swore under his breath.

"Okay, sweetheart, we're going to have to come up with a new plan," he muttered, yanking his foot back just in time to avoid having it neatly nipped off. He braced himself against the bony edge of the creature's jaw and fumbled in his now nearly empty supplies pouch.

A flare would work, but something that hot set off inside the fish's mouth would injure it badly, if not kill it. As would bracing its mouth open with anything with sharp edges—he'd seen enough of the intricate web of skin and gills that allowed the thing to survive above water to hunt to realize the devastation cutting through it would have.

But he couldn't exactly let it eat Istvay, either, and from the look on his friend's face, they were fully intending to let themself get eaten if it meant getting Aran out.

And then his fingers caught on something, and he breathed a quick sigh of relief.

The inflatable emergency marker he and Istvay carried in case one of them got caught in an avalanche—large enough and buoyant enough that it would push its way up through the still-soft settling snow and carve out a breathing space while they waited for help.

"Sorry," he murmured as the creature's rough tongue shoved against his back, pushing him towards the teeth. "This won't feel good, but it'll only be for a minute." He yanked the small device free of the supplies pouch and tore off the tab with his teeth, shoving the device towards the back of the salyan's mouth.

The inflating emergency marker expanded with explosive force, and Aran was slammed up against the back of the creature's teeth, hard enough that it emptied the air from his lungs. And then the salyan's teeth were shoved apart, and Aran tumbled free, landing face-first in the lake.

He sucked in a lungful of the oily water before someone grabbed him by the shoulder and hauled him upright, and he coughed and spat and blinked his eyes open to see Istvay, their face sick with worry, dragging him bodily towards shore.

"I don't know what the hell you just did, but let's get the hell out of here while it lasts," they hissed as Aran struggled to get his feet under him, and finally succeeded. "Come on!" And then they were both stumbling through the knee-deep water towards the sandbar.

He had to catch Istvay twice to keep them from falling, but

Landru and her crew were already splashing out towards them, and behind him, the fish, now distracted by the massive inflatable sphere that blocked its mouth from closing, thrashed madly in the shallow water.

"Don't worry," Aran gasped, "its tongue is covered with barbs, it'll be able to get a hole in that in a minute or two. I don't think there'll be any lasting damage."

"How the hell do you always misinterpret so badly what I'm actually worried about?" Istvay muttered.

"Come on, humans! Back to the sandbar! I'll kill it for us, and then we can get to shore," Landru called.

Aran dug his heels in, stopping both himself and Istvay abruptly. "No," he shouted, "don't kill it! There's … I mean, what kind of battle would it be if it can't even fight? Better to, um, give it time to recover, I think." He glanced surreptitiously over his shoulder, willing the creature to move its thrashing deeper into the lake.

He could already hear the high-pitched hiss of pressurized air escaping from the inflatable.

A movement from the pebbly beach behind him caught his eye, and he turned. It took a moment for his brain to make sense of what his eyes were seeing. And then his entire body went cold with dread.

The raider who'd thrown him and Istvay into the water was standing on the shore, that incongruous smile still on her face, and something in her hand that Aran recognized from his battles on Krevai's ship.

A stun-bomb. Powerful enough to knock him and Landru and every other raider off their feet and unconscious, which, as soon as the fish got its mouth free, would be a death sentence.

She was clearly waiting for just that. And—he glanced over his shoulder again at the salyan.

The whine of air through the tortured material of the inflatable was clearly audible now.

"Landru!" he shouted, yanking his arm out of Istvay's grip. "Landru, get down!"

Behind him, there was a loud *bang* as the inflatable burst.

The salyan's jaws snapped shut.

The raider started down the beach towards the sandbar, her odd smile showing her sharp canines.

Aran shoved Istvay towards where Landru was waiting on the sandbar, then scrambled away from safety and back towards the rocky beach of the small island they'd just escaped.

He reached the beach, the pebbles slippery under his wet boots, and slammed into the raider woman just as she drew her arm back to throw. She stumbled back with a startled curse, the stun-bomb slipping from her hand, then turned and backhanded Aran. He landed on his back on the rocks, the air knocked from his lungs.

And then there was a wet slithering sound, and the sky around him went momentarily dark.

There was a long, horrifying scream that he was pretty sure wasn't coming from him. He couldn't breathe, and there was pressure everywhere, and the rocks were cutting into his back and something heavy pressed against his chest and the thick smell of fish and slime and blood was all around him, and someone was screaming and screaming …

And then, with a wet squelch, the pressure was gone.

He shoved himself into a sitting position, gasping and disoriented.

Someone grabbed him, slinging him over their shoulder, and after a panicked moment he recognized them as one of Krevai's raiders, and he caught from the corner of his eye a glimpse of someone doing the same with Istvay. And then the whole group of them was splashing across the narrow sandbar at a sprint, back towards land and safety.

They reached the shore just as there was a soft *woosh* from the stun-bomb back on the island, and a sudden, sucking pressure. The entire group of them tumbled to the rocky ground, but they were far enough from the explosion that they didn't suffer any more ill effects.

Aran glanced at Istvay, and then back at the beach, where the raider who'd tried to kill them had stood.

There was nothing left of her now except a few bloody scraps.

And in the distance, he could see the quick flash of a tail as the salyan disappeared into deeper waters, nothing to mark its previous presence but a few floating fragments of the inflatable.

He drew in a deep breath and pushed himself shakily to his feet. Around him, the raiders were doing the same.

"Aran. Are you alright? You're bleeding." Istvay was standing over him, holding out their hand. He took it and pulled himself to his feet. For a moment, the two of them stood there staring at each other.

And then Istvay pulled him into an embrace, and Aran leaned in and kissed them, and he momentarily forgot about everything else in the sheer, utter, glowing relief that he *could*.

"I'm fine," he said, when Istvay finally pulled back and he'd caught his breath again. "It was nothing, it's just the salyan had a barbed tongue." He paused. "Actually, I wonder if …"

"Aran. Let's wait until we're back on the ship." Istvay's voice was fond and rueful. They hesitated, then pulled something out of their pocket. "I … had a scanner going. I thought you might want to have some data to look at, assuming either of us got out of that alive."

For a moment, Aran was completely speechless. And then he grinned, so wide his face hurt.

Istvay chuckled and put their arm around his waist. "Alright, let's get back then." They glanced around them at the raiders, who were also pulling themselves to their feet, grumbling in a mix of Common Dialect and the raider tongue. "Landru?"

She turned. She, too, was grinning, although, Aran reflected, probably for a different reason than he was.

"Istvay! I'll tell Krevai all about you and your Aran's actions. He'll be impressed. Sharda will too, whatever she might say. The captain's right, it doesn't pay to underestimate you humans. All of us out without a casualty that mattered."

Istvay sighed. "That's what I wanted to ask about. What the hell was that? I thought Brigga's crew had sworn under Krevai and Sharda's command."

Landru shrugged. "I don't know. There're always a few captains after a leadership struggle who think things should have gone differently. But I'll tell Krevai and Sharda to look into it—if it's a ship-wide thing, we'll have to wipe out her whole crew, likely."

Istvay shook their head slowly. "I don't think it was, though. Because I was there when Brigga met with Sharda. If she was planning a challenge, I'd be willing to swear her crew didn't know about it. So why this?"

Landru raised her eyebrows, considering. At last, she shrugged again. "I don't know. They've been out in deep space for a while now. Perhaps it was just space-madness. It happens on every crew once in a while."

Aran frowned.

Space madness, whatever that was, could be the answer.

But there had been something about how their would-be murderer had spoken, how she'd smiled. Something that he was pretty sure couldn't be attributed to simply too long in space.

Something much, much too intentional.

He glanced at Istvay, and read on their face the same concern he felt.

And then his communicator crackled, and he slapped the button, his heart suddenly pounding much too quickly. "Dessi?" His voice almost cracked.

"Aran, you and your Istvay should get back here." The raider scientist's tone was triumphant. "My analyses finished running, and I think both of you will be very interested in what I've found."

2

Alba

Alba watched the three men sitting across the small table from her.

The contrast between them couldn't have been sharper—Yosip, her former diplomate aide, with his shaved grey hair and weathered brown skin, the wrinkles on his face those of laughter and good humour and a hint of the usual irrepressible twinkle in his eyes; her old clerk Feliu, a good ten years younger than either she or Yosip, but the pink skin of his face tightened with scowl-lines, less from bad temper than from worry, although she had to admit it was at least partially the former—there had been a reason that she and he had worked together so well, and it was mostly because he was irritable enough to stand up to her; and Jair, the youngest of them by at least a couple of decades. His close-cropped black hair had only just begun to grey, and his brown face had the tight muscles and clean lines of a man not much past his prime, his bearing tight and military, but there were lines cut across his face as well, lines of pain and worry that hinted of things Alba could only guess at. She'd never asked him about what it had been like when the yibo had, decades previous, destroyed the Labarinto System, where Jair and most of the humans in this system had been born, and he'd never volunteered the information. But she could see it in the planes of his face and the creases around his eyes and mouth.

But as much of a contrast as they made with each other, the three men's expressions were all variations on a single theme—worry.

It had been a matter of weeks since Alba and the others had arrived through the portal, although it felt like a lifetime. And when she and the ragged remnants of the diplomatic corps had sabotaged the mechanism that had opened the portal between the two systems, in order to protect their own system from invasion, Alba had resigned herself to the cold, hard fact that she'd live out the remainder of her life in this strange, hostile place, although she'd been kept so frantically busy fighting for her very survival since then that she'd barely had the chance to let the implications of that sink in.

And then she'd learned from Jair that the yibo Synod had other portal mechanisms. And yesterday, after they'd managed to rescue the remaining survivors of the diplomatic ship from the Nativist yibos, whose dearest wish was to rid the system of humans entirely, and who the former captain of the diplomatic ship, Mattin, had been negotiating with in secret, Alba had learned something else. A captive human soldier had spat out that General Eniko Cavaco, one of the two remaining Joint Heads of Government and one of the most powerful men in the Joias System, was planning to use her disappearance to seize power back in Joias.

And since then, she and Feliu and Yosip had spent almost every waking moment discussing the implications of this.

"You see, Madam, how he could have taken effective control of the Council," Feliu was saying, gesturing at the diagram. "If he's managed to turn enough of the judicial committee ...”

"I doubt the judicial committee is as easily bought-off as all that," Alba snapped. Then she sighed. "But you're right. If he plays his hand well, he can certainly use this."

Cunning, intelligent, and a ruthless purveyor of power, General Cavaco was someone she and everyone else in the Joias System who'd been paying attention had watched with concern over the course of the past decade, as he'd slowly amassed more and more power to his branch of government by incremental, seemingly insignificant means. The man who, the day the portal through to the yibo system had opened, Alba had planned to defang permanently.

Instead, she'd only managed to give him warning of the danger. He'd outmaneuvered her, forcing her into coming along on the diplomatic mission as head diplomat in exchange for agreeing not to respond militarily to the unknown potential threat.

And her mistake, she thought bitterly, was in not realizing how far he'd be willing to go to avoid the quiet retirement she'd so carefully planned out for him.

A mutiny on the diplomatic ship. A back-door negotiation with the yibo to sell out the Joias System in exchange for consolidating his hold on power. An instruction to his people to ensure that Alba and her diplomatic aides wouldn't return to Joias alive.

Perhaps she was finally beginning to feel her age. She'd always prided herself on being as sharp at seventy-three as she'd been in her forties, but perhaps this had always been inevitable, and she'd simply missed it.

She sighed, and pulled her attention back to the diagram.

More likely, what was catching up to her was less age than the soul-grinding, body-crushing exhaustion, physical and mental, that they'd all been wading through since the break-up of the diplomatic ship.

Feliu nodded. He looked even older and more tired than she felt. But he'd always shown the strain more than she had.

She sighed. "Even if the Council agrees to declare martial law, there are safeguards." She paused. "But ... it's not impossible that Cavaco could try to seize power in Joias, should we not return in time to prevent it. He was able to place far too many things into position in far too short a time for something like this to have been entirely unplanned."

"What do we do now, Madam?" asked Feliu, his voice quiet.

She took a deep breath, forcing down the exhaustion. "I don't know. But before anything, we must find a way to convince the Synod to open a portal to the Joias System. And we must do that without risking our system's extermination by either the Nativists or the raiders. And that, I think, is enough to occupy us at present." She pushed herself upright, her joints twinging painfully at the movement and the inevitable aches and pains jolting through her muscles as she steadied herself on the edge of the table. "I have requested a meeting with Karri this afternoon, and I intend to bring up the matter with her, if she'll listen."

"I've asked around, as you requested," said Jair in a low voice, glancing behind him as if worried about being overheard. "There are ... at least a small percentage of humans who survived the destruction of the Labarinto system who'd be willing to travel to Joias, if they were promised refuge and safety. It's not all of them, or even most, but it may be enough to convince the yibos that opening the portal would rid them of enough of their unwanted guests to make it worth their while." There was a bitter undertone to his words.

Alba forced herself to smile at him, although the expression felt foreign on her face. "Thank you, Jair. That gives me something to bargain with, at least." She paused. "I understand the risk you took in doing so," she added quietly. "Truly, I am grateful."

He nodded, looking up at her with a brief smile, then pushed himself to his feet as well. There were dark bags under his eyes, and a weariness to his posture that matched her own.

He'd lived in the yibo system for decades, married and had children, worked as the human liaison to a yibo military general. Helping her could have put at risk not only his job, but the fragile political compromise the coalition of them had worked out with the yibo days earlier, to give the humans in this system some degree of autonomy and self-governance.

And he'd done it anyways.

He glanced down at his communicator. "They'll be expecting you in the Advisory Chambers shortly. We'd best get going. I've called us a transport."

"Thank you," she said again, although she knew the words weren't nearly enough. Then she followed him out of the small room in their cramped refugee compound, and into the busy streets outside.

3

Savina

Savina woke to something warm and wet dripping onto her cheek, and a familiar voice whispering her name.

She struggled to open her eyes, but they felt far too heavy. Her head ached, and at even the suggestion of movement, bile rose in her stomach.

She clamped her teeth together, but that hurt too, and she barely managed to tip her face to the side before she vomited, the bitter acid taste of it burning her throat and setting her coughing.

"Savina!" There was an arm under her shoulders, lifting her, and she moaned.

The arm tightened, holding her steady.

She tried again to open her eyes, and this time when she did, it was to the blurry outline of a face, closer than she would have expected.

She blinked, and the face swam into focus—dark skin, sharp, elegant features, sensuous lips and piercing grey-hazel eyes, framed by black hair growing in spiky and rough from a half-shave on one side, falling to the woman's shoulders on the other.

Reka Soler.

And then she remembered.

Their flight from Kachik's warships in the battered attack pod, already damaged from yibo military shots. The way the tendons in Reka's hands stood out as she gripped the controls, her entire body tense as she fought to get them away and to safety.

The air around the pod burning as they plunged down through the atmosphere of the small moon, fire licking up to surround them, the strain in Reka's face. Reka shouting something, voice tight with despair, a wave of pressure that felt like a wall of concrete, slamming into Savina's entire body at once.

And then ... nothing.

"Savina." There was something cool and hard against her back, propping her upright. Reka's arm slid from around her shoulders, but lingered on her arm. "How are you feeling?"

She felt drained and empty, her head throbbing enough that she didn't have the energy to swear at the objectively stupid question. She closed her eyes for a moment, taking stock.

Besides the throbbing in her head, she wasn't as badly injured as she would have expected.

She reached up to brush the wet from her face, and brought her hand in front of her, forcing her eyes open again.

Blood. Which wasn't a surprise, if her memories were accurate.

What was a surprise was that she was alive at all.

"What happened?" she rasped.

Reka's face came into focus more easily this time. She was wearing a grim expression, but it was the small, dangerous spark of anticipation in her face that told Savina more clearly than anything the danger they must be in.

"The ship was damaged, and it depressurized as I brought us in. It put you out cold, but I managed to hit the landing sequence before I passed out. Not the prettiest landing I've ever done, but ..." She shrugged eloquently, glancing over her shoulder.

Savina followed her gaze.

The pod was a charred wreck of metal, strewn across a stretch of broken trees and torn-up vegetation. There were a couple of small fires still smouldering in the undergrowth.

She glanced behind her, wincing at the sharp pain in her neck at the movement.

The cockpit had been torn clear of the rest of the ship, and had skidded to a stop against a stand of thick trees. The force of the impact had flattened the entire back of the cockpit, and split the front wide open, and Savina shuddered as she realized how easily both she and Reka could have been crushed to a pulp in the landing.

"We need to get out of here," Reka whispered, lowering her voice. She hitched a small emergency knapsack higher up on one shoulder. "The yibo military ships followed us down. The crash site won't be hard to find. The farther away we can get, the better our chances."

Savina nodded, and then had to swallow hard against the vomit that was trying to rise in her stomach.

"Let me help you up. Can you stand?" Reka's voice was warm with concern, her hand on Savina's arm steady.

Savina leaned against her, and somehow, between the two of them, she managed to get to her feet. She tried her balance, and when she was sure she'd stay upright, she let go of Reka's arm and took a cautious step.

She stumbled, cursing, as her ankle gave out, but Reka caught her easily, lifting her back to her feet before she had time to fall. "Lean on me," the woman said tersely, glancing over her shoulder into the trees behind them.

Savina wanted to snap something about not needing help, but it wasn't true, and both of them knew it. So, with Reka supporting most of Savina's weight, the two of them started forward into the spreading shadows under the trees.

They struggled on as the sun passed its zenith and began its slow descent. The heat of the day left trickles of sweat dripping uncomfortably down Savina's face and dampening her hair. Reka hardly seemed to take note of the discomfort, her movements as smooth and confident as always, but Savina was leaning on her, and she could feel the way Reka's muscles trembled a little each time the woman had to pull both of them up a steep incline or over a fallen tree. Reka was taller than she was, and seemingly built of solid muscle, but Savina had never exactly been a lightweight.

Already, there were sounds of pursuit behind them, the distant shouts of yibo soldiers, the sound of booted feet crashing through undergrowth.

"They're not trying to be subtle, are they?" Savina muttered through her teeth as Reka half-carried her over yet another fallen log caught in a tangle of brush.

"They don't need to be." Reka's tone was short. "They have tracking devices, and they know we're alone and injured. There's nowhere for us to go."

Savina leaned sharply back against Reka's supporting arm, bringing them both to an abrupt halt. "What are we doing, then?" she snapped, catching Reka's gaze. Her heart was pounding with the exertion, every muscle in her body aching with exhaustion and strain. "They can track us. They're going to kill us. There's nowhere for us to run, you just said so yourself. Joska said she'd come find us, but there's no way she gets here in time, and even if she did, there's nothing she can do against the yibo military. So what the hell is all this for? Why can't we just stop?"

Her voice almost cracked on the words.

Reka stared back, eyes narrowed. The exhaustion in her face was more apparent now, cracks of pain showing through her usual stoic expression. "We're going to keep running until we can't run anymore. And then we're going to find a place to make a stand, and we're going to fight them until we have nothing left to fight them with." Her tone was hard and dispassionate.

"Why?" Savina's voice was almost a sob. "Why the hell do you always have to be a damn hero?"

Reka tipped her head to one side, studying Savina, and again, Savina had the disconcerting feeling of being *seen*, in a way no one had ever actually seen her before.

In a way no one was ever supposed to see her.

"Because I can't just let them kill you," Reka said at last, her voice ragged with weariness.

She turned away, leaving Savina gaping, and jerked her chin to the right. "I think I saw a rise in that direction. That's as good a destination as any."

She started forward again, not waiting for a response, and Savina had to stumble after her or lose her footing.

By the time they reached the top of the low hill, it was dusk. The yibos' footsteps were close enough that now that Savina could make out the sound of individual soldiers moving, the low mutter of whispered commands. Her head ached, and the stabbing pain that shot up her leg at every step had now blended into a solid bar of agony that stretched from her ankle to the middle of her back.

She didn't realize Reka had stopped until she practically stumbled into her. Reka caught her, one hand on her arm, one on her hip, just in time to keep her from falling on her face.

She stood there a moment, staring dully at Reka's hand on her crumpled yibo tunic. When she glanced up, Reka's normally stoic expression was overlaid with a tight worry.

"We're not going to make it much farther," Reka said quietly.

She should probably argue, Savina knew. It was what a hero like Reka would do. But she couldn't find it in herself, so she just nodded. "Are we going to give ourselves up? Or try to make a last stand?" She was almost too tired to form the words.

Reka gave a small, tight smile. "I have one more surprise for them. It might buy us some time."

Savina blinked at her, trying to force her tired brain to translate the words. "And then what? You honestly think we'll get away?"

Reka shook her head. "Not much chance of that." She was looking over Savina's head, back into the forest behind them. "But we may be able to take some of them down with us."

Savina glanced over her shoulder, following Reka's gaze. There was a sharp, hot undercurrent of anger burning even through the fog of pain and exhaustion. Anger that she was going to die. Anger at every hellish thing she'd gone through so far on this journey, most of it to do with the yibo.

Anger at the knowledge that Reka was going to die too, even after everything they'd both done.

It was a thought she was too tired to parse, so she let it pass. Instead, she just nodded. "What do you need me to do?"

Reka rummaged in her small knapsack, and pulled out a small container of—something, Savina wasn't certain what. She flashed Savina a small smile. "Ship fuel. Highly explosive. You stay here, cover me if any of the soldiers get too close. You still have a weapon,

I imagine?"

Savina glanced around quickly, opening her mouth to protest, but Reka was right—she'd be nothing but a liability right now if she tried to help. And from the top of the small rise she had a good view of the terrain around them, and there was enough undergrowth to give her cover.

Reka helped her over to the base of a tree and eased her down beside it. Savina pulled out her pulse pistol, checking it carefully to make sure that it hadn't been too badly damaged in the crash. It was battered, but it seemed functional enough not to explode when she pulled the trigger. That was probably all she could ask for at this point.

And then Reka slipped away, a ghost in the shadows.

Savina let her eyes track any telltale rustle in the undergrowth that could mark Reka's progress, but those moments were surprisingly rare. With the rest of her attention, she watched for the yibo soldiers.

It couldn't have been more than a few minutes before Reka appeared out of the undergrowth beside her, silent as a shadow. She lowered herself down beside Savina, a small controller in her fingers. There was a smile on her lips and a tension to her expression that told Savina everything she needed to know about what awaited the first few yibo soldiers who made it up the hill.

Savina glanced over at her, ready to force herself upright again, but Reka shook her head. "Let them come to us."

Savina leaned her head back against the tree trunk and closed her eyes for a moment. Every muscle in her body was humming with strain, and she found herself starting at the slightest sound. Below them, the muffled noise of soldiers pushing through brush was getting more and more distinct.

Reka was poised and alert, her entire posture broadcasting

readiness.

The sounds were closer now, and Savina could make out whispered curses or commands through the dark of the evening air.

They must be almost at the top of the hill now. Almost within sight.

The first yibo soldier broke through the undergrowth at the rim of the hill. Savina saw his eyes go wide, and he turned to shout something over his shoulder.

Reka tapped the controller in her hand.

A wave of heat and sound rolled over the edge of the hillside, the sound almost too loud for Savina's brain to comprehend. There were screams from below them, frantic, incoherent shouting.

Reka didn't move, her whole body tight, her hands ready on the controller, but the knife-sharp smile on her face had widened a fraction.

The soldiers tried twice more to reach the top of the hill. Twice more, Reka tapped the controller, and a circle around the top of the hill burned.

By the third time, it was full dark.

Savina and Reka waited where they were, huddled close together for warmth. Even with Reka's body heat seeping into her where they were pressed together, Savina was shivering.

At last, when the silence had stretched for what must have been half an hour at least, Reka let out a small sigh, her posture relaxing. "I doubt they'll try it again until morning," she whispered. "Just as well—I'm not sure how much longer that would have held them." She glanced at Savina.

Savina clenched her teeth in a futile attempt to keep them from chattering.

Reka gave her a small smile of mingled concern and amusement.

"Let's warm up, eat our rations, since I doubt we'll be alive long enough to worry about conserving food. And then, I suppose, we should figure out how many of them we can take with us when they come for us in the morning."

4

Aran

When Aran and Istvay reached Krevai's ship, half a standard hour's hike across the small resupply planet from the beach where they'd almost lost their lives, Aran could barely force himself to pay attention to Landru's enthusiastic retelling of their adventure to the captain, or to the grinning clamour of the crew, followed quickly by hissed whispers to "Keep the noise down, our Aran doesn't like it," guilty looks, and mumbled apologies.

"Where's Dessi?" he asked, cutting off another of the raider crew who'd come to say something congratulatory.

The raider frowned. "She's in her lab, I think." He stepped back courteously to let the two of them pass as Aran strode off down the hallway towards the makeshift lab, Istvay trailing behind him.

Istvay turned to Aran with raised eyebrows as Aran tapped at the door. "You certainly earned their respect."

Aran sighed. "No, it's—it's nothing like that, they just—they're probably just worried that Dessi is going to yell at them if they're too loud."

Istvay shook their head fondly. "I've been watching them—they don't treat you like that because they're afraid of Dessi. They respect you. And they respect your boundaries, which is a hell of a lot more than I can say for most of the people we worked with back in do Sol."

Aran managed a reluctant grin at them before the door swung open.

Dessi's outfit was rumpled and looked slept in, her short black hair tangled, and there was an almost fanatic expression on her ivory-white face. She seemed completely unsurprised by their appearance, and Aran realized he probably didn't want to think too hard about what that meant about what she'd expected to happen to him on the supplies-gathering trip. "What took you?" she said. "Come! You need to see this!"

Aran followed her, the dread and excitement bubbling together in his stomach strong enough to make him nauseous.

Dessi stopped at one of the lab tables, fiddled with the unfamiliar machine sitting atop it, and pulled up a screen on her data pad. "Here." She ran her fingers down a small diagram on the screen, and Aran leaned over it, his breath tight in his chest.

It was two diagrams, side by side, two genomes mapped out— human, and raider.

"That's your blood sample, Aran, human DNA without the genetic abnormality," she said, expanding the screen to zoom in on one section of the diagram. "And this is from my blood sample, raider DNA without the abnormality. Now—" she swiped the screen, and another diagram popped up. "This is your Istvay, and this is Krevai. You can see here, I've highlighted the genetic abnormality in yellow, and in red, all the potential genetic differences that the program was able to conclude impacted the genes in question. I've narrowed it down to these." She swiped the screen again, opening a page with several dozen gene clusters highlighted. "And then I ran the program again, trying to isolate how each of these genes might affect the others." She tapped the screen, and it spread out into a spiderweb of interconnecting lines. She swiped several more screens in rapid succession, the spiderwebs expanding and contracting as she did so. "I won't bore you with details, but I was running more analyses in the background, and a master-program to consolidate the data. And it looks like if we were to splice this gene in place of this one—" she zoomed in the screen to two particular highlighted clusters, "it should neutralize most of the negative effects of the genetic abnormality without causing major repercussions in other areas. The test-program is running now to check for unwanted side-effects and all the potential ramifications of a gene transfer, but I think ..." she glanced up, and he could see the thrill of excitement in her face.

"We may have found our answer," Aran finished softly. He was clutching the edge of the lab table, a feeling somewhere between disbelief, and euphoria, and a sick, overwhelming happiness twisting his insides so tight that for a moment he thought he was going to break down in tears.

Istvay glanced between him and Dessi worriedly. "Listen, Dessi, Aran is going to need—"

"He needs a few minutes to collect himself, I know." She peered at Istvay. "I understand from Aran that there are humans like you, who are ... he called them—allistic? People who aren't autistic, I mean. I hope I'm not making you uncomfortable, but from what Aran told me, allistic people are common enough that you would have at least met other people like yourself. I gather that people with your particular neurotype are not as sensitive to stimuli, and so perhaps would need less time to recover after a moment like this?" She paused. "Of course, I'm sure there are benefits to being allistic that would help make up for the deficiencies created by your unique neurotype …"

"My … unique—" Even from the hazy, distant place he was in right now, Aran could hear the amusement in Istvay's voice. "What, exactly, has Aran been telling you?"

Dessi shook her head briskly. "Not nearly enough, I'm afraid— I'm fascinated by this allistic neurotype in humans, and I'd love to study it, but unfortunately, Aran and I have been exceptionally busy with our current project." She glanced over at Aran again. "You may as well take your Aran back to your rooms. I'm running an analysis right now to narrow down the most effective way to utilize our discovery and turn what we've learned into an effective cure, but until I get a full analysis of the data, we won't be able to predict which method of administering the cure will be most effective."

"Yes. Of course." There was a sudden subdued note to Istvay's tone that told Aran just how desperately his friend had been trying not to consider the implications of what Dessi was saying, and how suddenly and thoroughly they had just lost that battle.

Aran nodded, swallowing hard and straightening. It should be Istvay losing their crap right now, not him. "Yeah," he managed.

Istvay tried to smile at him. "Dessi's right—we may as well get back to our room and clean up." There was strain in their voice, despite their light tone.

Neither he nor Istvay spoke as they walked through the corridors towards their cabin. Aran kept casting quick glances at his friend, but aside from the tension in Istvay's posture he couldn't read what they were thinking.

Istvay pushed the door to their and Aran's cabin open and

followed him inside. The door swung shut behind them, and for a moment, the two of them just stood there, staring at each other.

"Pishti," Aran whispered, not really trusting his voice. "See? I told you there had to be a cure. And there is. We found it. You're—you're going to be—" He squeezed his eyes shut against the hot ache of tears, then Istvay had him in an embrace. Their arms were trembling, and Aran leaned into them, and they dropped their head on his shoulder.

At last, Aran took a deep breath and pulled back, wiping it his eyes. "Anyways," he said, clearing his throat, "I should go check on Ani."

Istvay nodded and let go of him. "Yes, you'd better do that. I don't think she really wants to talk to me right now." They gave him a rueful grin.

Aran grinned back and made his way back to the small storage cupboard that Ani had taken to hiding in. "Hey, sweetheart," he whispered, tapping at the door.

For a moment, nothing happened. And then a tentacle tip emerged through the crack under the door, unlatching the outer lock, and Aran pushed the door open. He could have unlatched it himself, but he'd decided that as long as she wasn't somewhere she could get hurt, Ani deserved her privacy.

She crept out of her hiding place, the set of her bulbous body radiating sulkiness.

"Hey, sweetheart," he whispered as she twined herself around his arm and pulled herself up to her usual perch on his shoulder. "How are you feeling?" He stroked her gently as he spoke, and she purred, a little grumpily, and settled into his arms.

He turned over his shoulder to Istvay. "Pishti, come check—do you think she's warmer than usual?"

Istvay sighed and crossed over to them and reached out a hand warily. Ani grumbled with discontent as they ran a hand over one of her tentacles, and huddled down on Aran's shoulder.

"No, she feels normal to me," they said at last. "Maybe a bit warm, but I'd expect that if she was hiding in her cupboard all morning." They paused. "Especially considering she's stolen two of your shirts, a pair of socks, and my pillow to put in there over the last two days."

Aran nodded absently, checking Ani over carefully for injuries or lumps or any abnormalities. "What do you think is wrong with her? She doesn't act sick, but I've never seen her like this before. And she didn't even throw a fit when I told her to stay here this morning, in case she was coming down with something and being out in the water would be bad for her."

Istvay shook their head ruefully. "She's been out of sorts since I got back."

Aran sighed. "This could be a stress reaction, I suppose. Maybe she was worried about you."

Ani gave a pathetic little chirrup, winding her tentacles around him, and he tugged them gently away from his face and rubbed her head affectionately. "Were you worried for Pishti, sweetheart? I'm sorry, I was worried about them too. But look, they're right here. And they're alright. They're going to be—" His voice choked off.

Ani turned an irritated look on Istvay and tightened her grip on Aran, and Istvay let out a snort of amusement. "I was thinking more along the lines of jealousy."

"Okay, sweetheart, go on, I'll get you some food," Aran whispered.

Reluctantly, and with many a backwards glance at Istvay, Ani detached herself from Aran, catching the wall with one tentacle, and swung herself back to her cupboard.

He reached into the storage compartment next to her and brought out a handful of dried meat snacks, and she took them delicately with the tip of a tentacle, pulled herself inside her nest, and slammed the door closed after her.

Aran shook his head again and glanced at Istvay. "You really think she might be jealous?"

Istvay grinned. "I mean, you've certainly given her something to be jealous of."

Aran blew out a long breath, closing his eyes and running a hand over his face. "Maybe you're right. Maybe I should—"

"Maybe you should what?"

Istvay's voice was teasing, and much closer than it had been. Aran opened his eyes to find them standing right in front of him. There was a mischievous grin on their face as they leaned forward, bracing their forearm against the wall beside his head.

He blinked at them, trying to recapture his train of thought in the giddy disorientation that always flooded over him at seeing Istvay this close.

They leaned in closer, still grinning. "Maybe you should what?" They threaded their free hand through Aran's tangled hair and tugged gently.

Aran's voice seemed to have deserted him completely. "Maybe I should—maybe—" his words came out in a horse croak.

Istvay's gaze ran down Aran's body with a leisurely, possessive air that made Aran's mouth go dry and his stomach tighten with desire, hot and heady. "Hell, Aran," they whispered. "It's not actually fair that you look like this after being just about eaten by whatever the hell that thing was. No wonder everyone on Colorida was desperately in love with you."

"I—" Aran managed.

"You what?" Istvay's hand trailed down his spine, sending shivers through his entire body.

"Damn it, Pishti," he gasped, and grabbed them by the back of the neck and dragged them forward into a kiss.

By the time the two of them drew apart, gasping and breathless, they'd maneuvered themselves over to the small bed. There was a look in Istvay's eyes that was making Aran almost dizzy, but they managed to pant, "I thought you said you wanted to stop making Ani jealous."

"I changed my mind," Aran growled, shoving them onto the bed. Istvay fell backwards, laughing, and pulled Aran down on top of them.

Istvay already had Aran's shirt off and was fumbling at the fastenings on his trousers when there was a sharp tap at the door.

"Aran?" came Dessi's voice.

Aran jerked up, glancing around frantically for his clothing. "Just —just a sec," he managed, untangling himself from Istvay and snatching his filthy shirt from the floor. He shrugged it over his shoulders as he crossed the cabin, and he pulled the door open with one hand, fastening his buttons with the other.

Dessi stepped inside, glancing curiously between the two of them. "Ah," she said at last. "I apologize for interrupting your sex." She paused again, a delicately inquiring look on her face that Aran recognized far too well.

"No!" he said. "No, you—this isn't something you can study. It's —a human custom. To, um, to ... do sex in private."

"I could just attach sensors to the two of you, to measure your hormone levels and pulse-rate and—"

"No!" said Aran firmly. "It's ... against our traditions."

Dessi looked mildly disappointed. "Of course, I don't mean to disrespect your customs." She perked up a little. "But that's not why I came. Look."

Aran came closer, peering over her shoulder at the data pad, and scanned the text quickly. Then he frowned. "You need something that's coded specifically to Istvay's genetic makeup."

Dessi nodded. "I don't know how gene therapy in your system works. But here we code it directly to the recipient's DNA, working off a personalized template, then we program the corrected genetic template into a catalyst solution and inject it into the recipient. If this was for a raider, we could get something put together in a day, maybe two. We already have the baseline raider genetic code template, and we'd just have to run some schematics. But humans are different enough genetically that I think we'd have to start by coding for a base human genome, and then refining it to your Istvay's specifics."

"And … how long will that take?" Aran kept his voice quiet, and somehow refrained from glancing over his shoulder at Istvay, who was now sitting up in bed. But he couldn't keep the memory of them stumbling in the water just a few hours before, or the growing hollows under their cheeks, the way they had to stop to catch their breath after even the most minor exertion, from replaying over and over in his head.

Dessi shrugged. "I've already got it started. By the time I run all the tests and analyses … two months? Three, if we're being cautious."

Aran closed his eyes, sucking in a steadying breath. Again, he forced himself not to look over his shoulder at Istvay.

He didn't have to.

"We need something faster," he said in a low voice. "Istvay

doesn't have that long." He paused. "Listen, we do gene surgery back on Colorida. We don't use exactly the same procedure as you do, from the sounds of it, but in the research lab in Sao Martim University they're working on developing a new procedure that sounds fairly similar—at least, they need a background genetic template to make it work. I'm sure they have a human DNA template you could use, or at least something similar enough to what you need that you could work with it. If I could get you that—"

Dessi raised her eyebrows. "In that case, it would be on par with my estimation if we were doing this for another raider—a few days at most."

Aran nodded distractedly. His mind was already chewing over the problem. "Alright, so we've got to find a way to get back through the portal."

"The portal?" Istvay had come over, and they placed a hand on Aran's shoulder, leaning in to see the screen.

Aran turned to them. "Dessi was just telling us what we need to finalize the cure. It'll take too long for her to create an entire working template for human DNA from scratch. We'll need to get her that gene program they work with at Sao Martim's—you know what I'm talking about?"

Istvay nodded slowly. "Yes. But ..." they glanced up at Aran. "You do remember that the raiders just declared war on the yibos, and the yibos are currently the only ones we know of who have the technology for making a portal? Not to mention that if we did open a portal and sent a ship full of raiders through, it would mean the end of our entire civilization as we know it."

"I know, I know. But—" he shook his head. "I don't see another good option."

"Aran. I'm sorry, but your Istvay's right," said Dessi. "Even if we weren't at war, the yibos would never agree to open a portal at our request. Even if we could convince them, by the time we finished wrangling out details, it would take at least as long as creating the template." She paused, frowning at Istvay thoughtfully. "The yibo suffer from a viral disease that causes similar symptoms as your Istvay has been exhibiting, and I believe they've come up with medical technology to preserve life in those cases for long enough to cure the viral infection—a few months to a year, I believe."

Aran felt his body slump with relief. "Then we'll just …"

He caught the look on Istvay's face.

"The virus doesn't affect the raiders, so we've never had a use for that type of technology." Aran could tell from Dessi's tone that she was trying to break bad news gently. "The yibos are the only ones who have it, and as your Istvay pointed out, we're currently at war with them. They're not going to agree to help an enemy's crewmember. Even if Krevai was willing to try to work something out, he's allied with Sharda now. He can't make those decisions on his own. And I doubt you could convince him anyway—he's far too set on the idea of making a show of force to the yibos, and he's made promises to the crews who followed him."

Aran shook his head impatiently. "I'm sure we can figure something out, if we can just …"

There was a loud crash from outside, and then a scream, abruptly cut off. An alarm began to wail.

Aran and Istvay stared at each other. "What—" Aran began.

There was a loud pounding on the door to their cabin. Aran reached over automatically to unlatch it. Before he could pull it open, it swung inward, slamming against the wall, and Krevai burst through.

"Dessi. Landru said I'd find you here." There was a grim look on his face, and it was a moment before Aran realized what he was dragging—the bloody body of a raider. Aran assumed the raider was dead, but then the body stirred, eyes still closed, and laughed. It was an odd, high-pitched laugh that reminded Aran, suddenly and chillingly, of a few hours ago on a pebbly beach, and the raider woman shoving him towards the gaping jaws of the salyan.

Dessi's face had gone even paler than usual. "Is it … it's not an infestation. Is it?"

"I was hoping you could tell me." Krevai heaved the body through the door and dropped it on the floor, and Dessi bent over it. "Landru told me about what it happened back on the beach. We all assumed that Brigga's crew had simply changed their loyalty. But when I sent people over to check, the entire crew were tearing each other apart."

Dessi had already pulled on a pair of thick gloves and restrained the arms and legs of the raider on the floor, and now she was tapping their chest with a small sensor. Their body arced with what looked like an electric shock, then arced again. And then the body went limp.

Dessi stared down at it for a moment, then felt for a pulse. At last, she looked up. Her face and Krevai's wore identical expressions of horror.

"Was Brigga's ship sealed off?" asked Dessi, getting to her feet and brushing off her knees. "If they just came in from deep space, there's a chance we may be able to contain it."

Krevai shook his head. "There's no chance of that. Her crew went out with the others on supply runs, and the ship doors have been wide open this whole time. If it wanted to get out—"

"If it wanted to get out, it already has," Dessi finished quietly.

"What is it?" Aran asked, glancing back and forth between the two of them.

"Charaks," said Dessi shortly. "They live in deep space, and if you spend too much time out there and aren't careful, it's possible to get an infestation on a ship. And if an infected ship comes into contact with another ship before they either get it under control or it kills off the crew—" she broke off, shaking her head. "The worst part of it is, they're almost impossible to find. They mind-meld with their victims and take control of them, and you have no way of knowing who's infected until they turn on you. And the charaks can sometimes control the body for a few minutes even after death, if they've got a strong enough hold on it—that raider was already dead when Krevai dragged her in here. They can control multiple victims at once, and they can control them from a distance, so there's no real way of knowing how far an infestation will spread, or where the charak itself is hiding."

Aran raised his eyebrows, interested despite himself. "Wait, so these are actual creatures?"

"They are." Dessi shot Krevai an irritated glance. "The captain caught one to keep as a pet once. It turned out about as well as you'd expect, but since at least we knew where it was, we could kill it to stop the mind-meld effects before things got too far out of hand."

Krevai was looking at the ceiling, a faintly guilty expression on his face.

"Aran …" Istvay put a hand on his shoulder, their tone wary. Aran was too excited to pay much attention, his mind suddenly spinning.

"Is this going to affect your war with the yibos?" he asked abruptly, turning to Krevai.

Krevai frowned. "The war will go ahead. But this will make things much more difficult—as Dessi said, we have no way of knowing who was infected and who wasn't. A skin-to-skin touch with a person whose mind is being controlled is enough to allow the infection to spread. I doubt there are more than a few charaks on board the ship—even if there were an entire nest of them, it would only be between seven and ten—but that's more than enough to cause problems, since they can mind-meld with more than one raider at once. We may have to quarantine off some of the crews, and that won't be good for morale. You and your Istvay should be safe enough at present, because you're a different species. It would have to observe your habits for a while before it could take over your mind properly, I imagine."

Aran nodded. He was grinning, he realized absently.

"Aran? What are you thinking?" Istvay sounded distinctly nervous now. Aran ignored them.

"Listen, Krevai. If Istvay and I were able to figure out some solution—study these things, maybe find a cure for someone who was infected—"

Krevai raised his eyebrows. "I'd tell you that's impossible," he said at last. "But if anyone could do it, it would be our Aran." He paused. "If you could do this, you and your Istvay—you'd have the gratitude of all the raiders."

"Enough gratitude that I could ask for a favour?" He had neither the time, the energy, nor the attention to worry about sounding polite. "I need access to yibo medical technology to keep Istvay alive while Dessi and I prepare the cure. It's the only way to save their life."

Krevai frowned. "That is a large favour indeed, considering our current relations with the yibos."

"But think of the advantages of having a solution for a charak infestation," said Dessi, from behind Aran's shoulder. "It would make up for the political headache, don't you think?"

"Perhaps," said Krevai slowly. Then he chuckled. "Here you are, Aran, inserting yourself into raider politics again."

Aran shook his head impatiently. "I don't care about politics. I just need access to that medical technology for a few months."

"Yes, well, politics seem to care about you." Aran could have sworn there was a hint of wryness in Krevai's tone.

"Listen," he said. His voice was shaking a bit. "I don't care about who's in charge, or any of that. I just—I need to save Istvay. I can worry about everything else after that. I can deal with the consequences then. But I need to save Istvay."

Krevai was studying him, considering. At last, the raider captain turned to Dessi. "Well, at the very least, we know if our human wants something badly enough, there's no power in the system that will stop him going after it." His tone was a mixture of amusement and resignation. He turned back to Aran. "I'd have to talk to Sharda. But I think I can safely predict that, if you can do what you're telling me, she'll agree. You find a cure for us, and we'll find a way to get you the medical tech to keep your Istvay alive."

Aran blew out a long breath, his legs going weak with relief. "Thank you," he managed. "I'll—we'll get started on it right away."

When Krevai and Dessi at last left the room, deep in conversation and dragging the dead raider between them, he turned to Istvay.

Istvay was watching him with that familiar look of fond resignation. "A new species with a new and interesting way to kill us, and studying it is the only way to get what you've been looking for your whole damn life," they said, shaking their head. "This is every dream you've ever had come true, isn't it?"

5

Reka had a small, portable heater in her knapsack. She pulled it out and set it up, its bright, smokeless flame sheltered by the bushes around them. "No point in freezing," she said over her shoulder as she worked. "They know where we are already."

Savina watched dully, her entire existence narrowed to pain and cold and exhaustion.

It wasn't until the fire had been burning for long enough to pull the chill from Savina's muscles and melt the exhaustion from the surface of her deep into her bones, that she finally felt alert enough to sit up and look around.

"Here." Reka turned back to her, an emergency rations pack in her hands. "How are you feeling?"

"Like it would've been a hell of a lot easier if I'd just died in the crash," Savina grumbled, taking the food. Her stomach rumbled at the smell of it, unappetizing as it might normally have been.

Reka grinned, her teeth shining white in the light of the flame. The breeze swaying through the tree branches above them cast dancing shadows over her features. "Now I know you're feeling better," she said, making no attempt to hide the humour in her voice. "When you were too tired to complain, I started to worry."

Savina scowled reflexively. Reka laughed, and the sound was much more comforting and familiar than it had any right to be.

"Serves me right for being stupid enough to team up with a Mystery-damned hero," Savina muttered.

Reka sobered, her gaze dropping to the smokeless fire as if she were avoiding Savina's eyes. "Savina," she said quietly. "I understand you're here because of me. This isn't a situation you've chosen on your own. So—"

Savina leaned forward. "We've had this discussion before. If your plan involves me running away while you let the soldiers kill you, you may as well save your breath." She'd meant the words to be harsh. Instead, they came out in a husky half-whisper that felt far too intimate in the quiet, warm space carved out by the fire and the shadows of the trees.

Reka looked up, studying her, but Savina refused to look away. There was something compelling in Reka's gaze, something about the quiet of the night and the desperateness of their situation that made everything feel almost too close, too real.

Reka held her gaze for a few heartbeats. "Well. I know better than to try and talk you out of something once you've decided," she said, dropping her eyes at last. "So if that's the case, I suppose we'd best make a plan for tomorrow. Once it gets light, we won't have much time before they come for us again."

Savina glanced around her. The woods were dark, but in the distance she could see the small lights of the soldiers' campsites surrounding the hilltop where she and Reka had taken refuge.

"They'll have us tracked in their sensors, even if we could get around them in the dark," said Reka, as if reading her thoughts.

Savina nodded. "Then let's figure out how to kill as many of them as we can before we go." Her voice shook a little, but the overwhelming terror that should have accompanied this moment was … muted, somehow. Perhaps after the relentless terror of the past few weeks, she'd simply grown accustomed to the idea of dying.

Reka smiled at her and leaned back against the tree where she sat, wincing. Savina watched her from under her eyelashes.

Reka couldn't have come out of the crash entirely unscathed, but she hadn't breathed so much as a word of complaint in the endless hours of trekking through the thick forest, and she'd been practically carrying Savina the whole time.

Savina shook her head, a flash of unaccustomed fondness accompanying the thought. "You're completely crazy, you know that?"

Reka gave her a sardonic smile. "So I've been told."

They were silent for a few minutes.

"We can use the remainder of the ship fuel," said Reka at last. "We can carry it under our jackets, hold out here as long as we can. Then, when we're taken in, we wait until we're in the middle of the camp and then ignite it."

Savina took a deep breath, waiting to be sure her voice would be steady. "Alright," she whispered. "That's probably our best plan."

"I'm sorry," Reka said in a low voice. The shifting light danced off her face, casting her features in shadow. "I'm sorry it had to end like this."

Savina rolled her eyes. "You can't fool me— you've been trying to die gloriously ever since I met you." She'd meant for the words to be humorous, but Reka's answering expression was solemn.

"Perhaps," Reka said. "But believe me, Savina—I truly did not mean to drag you to a glorious death with me."

Savina dropped back against the tree and closed her eyes. "Don't flatter yourself," she said without opening them. "You couldn't drag me anywhere I didn't want to go. I guess stupid heroism is catching."

Reka chuckled softly.

The cool of the night, contrasting with the warmth from the small heater, was trickling a soft sort of relaxation through Savina's tired muscles.

She heard Reka stir, but she didn't open her eyes.

"Let me look at your leg, at least." Savina could tell by Reka's voice that she'd gotten to her feet. "It will be easier for us to walk to our glorious deaths if it's bandaged and not infected."

Savina opened her eyes to find Reka crouching in front of her.

She was very close, Savina realized in a dreamy, detached sort of way, close enough that their bodies were almost touching. The white light of the artificial fire reflected off Reka's dark skin, drawing out the shadows under her eyes, the sharp definition of the muscles in her shoulders and arms, and Savina was hit with a shock of tangled memories, of all the many times she'd been this close to Reka. Of all the times she'd wanted to be this close to Reka, and hated herself for it.

Reka reached out, taking Savina's injured ankle gently between her hands, and Savina sucked in a sharp gasp of pain.

"Easy." Reka's voice was soothing. "I'm going to check to see if it's broken. If it hurts too much, let me know." Her hands were warm, her grip firm, and she held Savina's injured ankle steady in one hand as she rotated Savina's foot with the other.

Savina winced, but it was more in anticipation of pain than from the pain itself. Reka's movements were surprisingly gentle, and she found that if she simply relaxed into the movement, it hardly hurt.

"Not broken, I think," Reka said at last. "Just a bad sprain. I'll wrap it and give you something for the inflammation, and you should be able to at least bear some weight on it by tomorrow morning." She placed Savina's foot gently back on the ground and stood, turning back to her knapsack, and Savina felt a quick, unexpected pang at the sudden absence of the touch.

She forced herself to breath in, then out again.

They were about to die. None of this actually mattered.

Reka returned in a moment with a small medic kit. She dropped a couple of anti-inflammatory tablets into Savina's palm. Savina swallowed them, and Reka sat down close in front of her, taking Savina's leg between her hands and laying it in her lap as she wrapped the bandage. The shadows flickered around them, the small space formed by the firelight warm and immediate and intimate. Reka was frowning down at her hands on Savina's ankle, but Savina could sense the attention in her posture, feel the smallest hint of strain in her strong fingers.

"Savina. Do you remember the kill you made five years ago? The businesswoman?" Reka said at last. Her voice was quiet, but there was a thick emotion behind her words.

Savina nodded, frowning.

Reka's fingers brushed against Savina's skin as she wrapped the bandage, snug, but not tight enough to hurt. Her hands were warm, the calluses on her fingers rough, and her touch sent a jolt up Savina's skin, like a sparkle of electricity.

"Cavaco sent me in to prevent it. But we were too late. You managed to outwit us, fool the people he sent with me into setting off an explosion that killed half a dozen innocent people. Cavaco pinned it on me. I was young and I had no connections, no proof, no one who dared to stand up for me. My … my family was dead by then. Even if they hadn't been, they'd never had any sort of political power. So he got away with it. I was left with nothing. Everything I'd sacrificed for, everything my family had sacrificed to get me there, all gone in an instant."

"I'm … sorry." Savina's voice came out odd and unsteady.

She'd never stopped to wonder, before, what had happened after she'd pulled her jobs. What had happened to the people left behind.

She'd never cared, before. She'd always assumed they deserved it.

Reka raised her head. Her eyes were so dark in the firelight that they pulled Savina in like gravity. Savina could feel the ghost of Reka's breath against her skin, the warmth of Reka's body, Reka's hands trembling a little on her leg. "I hated you, Savina. I swore I'd kill you, even if it meant I'd die doing it. And when we both ended up here, behind the portal—" Reka huffed a small, humourless laugh. "There's nothing for me back in Joias. My family is dead, I'm disgraced. There's no one to miss me, no one to care if I don't return. The least I could do was make sure you didn't return either."

Savina couldn't look away, even if she wanted to. That quiet intensity she'd always felt behind Reka's every word, every motion, was entirely focused on her now, and she wasn't sure she could remember how to breathe under the weight of it.

"I swore I'd kill you. I thought killing you would redeem me." Reka's voice was a whisper. She leaned in a fraction, removing one hand from Savina's ankle, and hesitated a moment. Then she reached up and ran the back of her fingers gently along Savina's cheek.

Savina was caught between one heartbeat and the next. When Reka's fingers left her cheek, she swayed forward, like a candle guttering towards a draft.

"Reka—" It came out hoarse and quiet, no louder than a whisper.

She wasn't sure what she'd been planning to say after it. Maybe nothing. Maybe she'd simply needed to say Reka's name.

Reka reached out again and brushed a strand of hair behind Savina's ear, and Savina's entire body shivered in response to the touch.

But they'd both be dead tomorrow, and in this moment of trapped time between life and death, none of the rest of it seemed to matter.

Reka's hand traced gently down the line of Savina's chin, lifting it slightly. Her lips were parted, dark and soft in the firelight, her face so close to Savina's that they were sharing breath, a vulnerability in her eyes sharp enough it was almost pain.

And then she dropped her hand abruptly and drew back, something shuttering over her gaze. "Keep your ankle elevated tonight, that will help." Her voice was rough and not quite steady, and she turned away, gathering the medical supplies neatly back into the med kit.

Savina closed her eyes and slumped back, breathing for the first time in far too long. She shivered, a cold that had nothing to do with the night air creeping through her limbs.

Reka stood and crossed over to her knapsack, crouching beside it to replace the medic kit. She took longer than she probably needed to, and Savina could see the tightness in her shoulders as she worked. At last, she returned with an emergency blanket.

"Here," she said, her voice cool and steady once more. "You may as well use this, you're shivering."

"I'm fine," Savina snapped. "Anyway, since you're the only one of us who can walk right now, both our lives might depend on you not being too cold to move quickly."

Reka hesitated, an unfamiliar uncertainty in her posture. At last, reluctantly, she lowered herself down beside the tree trunk next to Savina, taking care not to meet Savina's eyes. "We'll sleep back-to-back, then," she said. "Probably the best way to keep warm anyways."

Savina nodded, resolutely turning her head away.

After a moment, she felt the solid warmth of another body pressed up against her back.

"Here." Reka's voice came almost in her ear.

She reached over to take the corner of the blanket Reka held out, forcing her breath to stay steady. She probably didn't succeed as well as she wanted to, and she could feel the tension in Reka's back where it was pressed up against hers. But she was tired enough that even that couldn't keep her awake, and she was asleep almost before she had time to process the thought.

It was the unfamiliar cool on her back that woke her, and it took her a moment to realize that it only felt cold because it had been warm a moment before.

"Reka?" she murmured, rolling up on her elbow.

The sky was still dark, but there was a hint of grey on the horizon, and she could make out Reka's silhouette against the faintly glowing remnants of the artificial fire.

"The soldiers will be coming soon," Reka whispered, tucking something into her belt. "Best get ready."

Savina pushed herself painfully into a sitting position, wincing as the movement sent a rush of blood through her swollen ankle, setting it throbbing.

When she looked up, Reka was crouched in front of her, her hand extended.

Savina hesitated, then took it. Reka lifted her to her feet, her calloused grip firm, and reached out with her other hand to steady her. "Are you alright?" she whispered.

Savina nodded. "I'm fine." She hoped the strain in her voice sounded like irritation, rather than fear. "It doesn't matter anyway—we'll both be dead before midday."

Reka studied her, then nodded, letting go of her and pulling something out of her pocket. "Strap this on, under your jacket if you can."

It was a small pouch attached to a controller—probably the remainder of the ship fuel Reka had salvaged yesterday.

Savina took it. Her hands were shaking a little, but if Reka noticed, she didn't say anything.

The grey in the sky was growing brighter incrementally, slowly enough that it was difficult to notice the change. But it was already noticeably brighter than it had been when Savina had woken.

"Remember, we want them to take us alive, if at all possible," Reka whispered.

Savina nodded silently.

On the hill below them there were the muffled sound of whispered yibo commands, the rustle of brush trampled by military boots.

Savina pulled out her pulse pistol, holding it loosely in her hand.

This was it, then. The end of everything.

She wondered, idly, if Nicolau was still with that interpreter girl. She hoped he was. They'd seemed happy.

Abruptly, the muted commands stopped, the rustling in the brush stilling. Some instinct, some soft sound or change of pressure, maybe, made Savina glance up at the horizon.

There was a flash of brilliant, blinding light, so bright that Savina almost stepped back, the silence of it almost eerie.

And then the thunderous roar of an explosion shook the forest, a cloud of smoke and debris and flame spewing up over the tops of the trees like a volcano and spreading in a thick cloud across the sky.

Savina stood stunned, not quite able to understand what had happened. Below them, the soft commands had turned into shouts of panic, the sounds in the undergrowth receding and leaving nothing but a silent forest in their wake.

"What the hell—" Savina whispered.

Reka just shook her head, lips pinched.

For several minutes, the forest was silent.

Savina stayed where she was, most of her weight balanced on her good leg, her pistol loose in her hand. Reka didn't move either, but her whole body looked poised for action.

There was a sound behind them in the trees, footsteps and the noise of someone not being particularly careful as they moved through the undergrowth.

Savina and Reka both spun, weapons raised.

Then a familiar wry voice came from the trees on the outskirts of their small camp. "Savina? Savina, if that's you, I'd be grateful if you'd hold your fire."

Savina stared.

A figure stepped through the trees, her face more careworn than Savina remembered, clothing torn and ragged, a familiar amusement in her expression.

"Joska?" said Savina at last, blankly.

Joska smiled, her face softening with relief. "You're alive. I was hoping we'd made it in time, but it was hard to be certain."

Nicolau stepped out of the brush next, Ines beside him. They were followed by Beni, their face creased in the familiar expression of concentration they always wore when picking their way over unfamiliar ground using no context but their wavelink's echolocator, and then Rafel.

"What the hell are you doing here?" Savina's voice was unsteady, and she wasn't sure if it was anger, or terror, or relief. "There's a damn army after us. What the hell were you thinking?"

Rafel scowled at her, but there was a twinkle of reluctant humour in his eyes. "We've spent too much time around you," he grumbled. "We know what a bad idea it is to leave you to your own devices."

Joska was looking out over the valley, and there was a small, grim smile on her face as she watched the rising cloud of debris. "Hopefully, that will have made them more concerned about how they're going to get back without one of their ships than about the two of you for the moment," she said, turning back to Savina and Reka. "But it won't last forever. I suggest we make ourselves scarce." She paused. "Savina? Savina, what's wrong?"

Savina shook her head. She couldn't seem to stop the tears that were gathering in her eyes and spilling down her cheeks.

Joska came closer, laying a comforting hand on her shoulder, and she sagged into it, and for a moment, made no effort at all to stop her sobs.

When she looked up at last, wiping her eyes, the others had gathered around her and Reka. Nicolau was hovering next to Joska with a look of abject concern on his face, his hand half-stretched out as if he wasn't completely certain whether the benefit of his comfort would be worth the risk of getting his hand sliced off at the wrist if he touched her.

Savina managed a watery laugh. "You're right," she said, swallowing. "We should probably go."

Reka was already gathering up their meagre belongings and

packing them neatly into the knapsack, and a moment later, she'd joined them.

"That was you, was it?" she asked, gesturing towards the site of the explosion.

Joska nodded. "We made a distraction first, to ensure there wasn't anyone on it when it went up. But Rafel served in the military long enough to know how to put together a decent sabotage job."

"I'd call that more than decent," said Reka, a small smile on her lips. She turned to Savina. "Are you alright to walk?"

"I'm fine," she said, testing her weight experimentally on her injured ankle.

It hurt, but it was better than it had been the previous day.

"Lean on me," said Joska. "We'll want Reka's hands free, in case we run into anything."

Savina nodded, and the small party of them started down the hill.

When they were far enough away that Reka judged it safe to rest for a few minutes, Joska helped Savina to sit, then sat down a short distance away, her back against a tree trunk, and closed her eyes. It wasn't until then that Savina recognized the exhaustion in the woman's face.

"When did you get here?" Savina asked, turning to Beni, who'd come to sit beside her.

Beni frowned. "A few hours ago. We set the explosives, and then we took the *Dolphin* this way, following your trail."

"Speaking of that ..." Joska had raised her head, and was watching Savina. "There's ... a bit of a complication. We intercepted some of the yibos' internal communications when we were on the ship. It was military code, but our friend Ines was able to translate it for us." She hesitated. "When Kachik's government realized you'd landed on this planet, they didn't send the ships only after you. They wanted to keep anything similar to what happened with the refugees you saved from happening somewhere else, apparently. There's a decent-sized human settlement on this planet, and their instructions were to make an example of it." She paused. "They … plan to destroy it. Completely."

Reka's breath hissed in through her teeth, and Savina didn't even need to look over at Nicolau to picture the horror on his face. He was the type to be horrified at something like that no matter how long he'd had to process it.

"The *Dolphin's* close by," continued Joska. "We could get ourselves away, I think. And once we're back in the Synod's airspace, I doubt Kachik's people would follow. But the rest of the humans here …" She didn't finish the sentence.

Savina glanced over at Beni. Then she almost groaned aloud.

Beni wore the expression Savina had become much, much too familiar with over the years of working with her sibling. It was that concentrated half-scowl that most people thought meant Beni wanted to kill someone, and Savina knew meant that her sibling was completely unconcerned. Unworried about whatever situation the two of them had found themselves in, because they knew Savina would fix it.

She closed her eyes.

There was a tight knot in her stomach, and she wasn't sure whether it was from the pain of her injured ankle, or from whatever the hell had almost happened last night between her and Reka, or from the residual terror of the prospect of imminent death—or if she was, in fact, as horrified as the others at the thought that the humans on this planet would be slaughtered, through no fault of their own, because of her and Reka.

"Vina—" It was Nicolau. He sounded worried, and frightened,

and almost sick.

She opened her eyes at last, straightening with an effort. "Well, Joska," she said, with a twinge of bitterness. "You've done it. Congratulations. You've made me into a good person after all."

Joska's lips twitched at the corners. "I don't know if I'd go that far."

"What do you—What is she saying?" Nicolau had turned to Joska as well.

Savina shook her head and sighed heavily. "I'm saying," she said, "that I suppose we're just going to have to stop this."

And she tried, very hard, to ignore the quick glow of admiration in Nicolau's eyes, the quiet pride in Joska's face, and worst of all … the fact that Reka didn't even look particularly surprised.

6

When she'd made it through the security protocols and into the open, greenery-lined hallways of the now-familiar yibo government building, Alba forced herself to straighten and put the measured purposefulness into her stride that had always marked her, back in Joias, as someone to be listened to.

If she'd learned anything in her years in politics, it was that the impression of competence was at least as important as the competence itself. Perhaps more so.

At the very least, it was enough that she wasn't interrupted by irritatingly polite security officers on her way to Karri's office.

She tapped sharply at the door, and a moment later, an entrance opened up in the translucent wall, and Alba stepped through.

The yibo woman inside looked up at her entrance. She was wearing a typical yibo tunic, the brown fur surrounding her eyes on her lemur-like face shot through with traces of grey—a sign of age among yibos, Alba had learned, as much as among humans. Her tail was tucked neatly over one arm, and her long, prehensile fingers were paused above a long list of notations on the holoscreen in front of her. "Alba," she said in accented Common Dialect. "I suppose congratulations are in order. Your friends from the diplomatic ship that we rescued from Kachik are settled in?"

Alba nodded. "They are. I appreciate your concern."

Karri gestured to a seat on the opposite side of her desk, and Alba bit back an internal curse when she saw the woman had procured one of the ubiquitous hard stools that yibo seemed to associate with human culture.

It was a gesture of politeness. And at this stage, with relations between yibo and humans what they were, she'd take any gesture of politeness as a good sign. Still, she had to bite back a wince as she lowered herself onto the proffered seat.

If she never saw one of these Mystery-damned stools again, it would be too soon.

"I suppose with that crisis past, you have other things to discuss with me," the yibo woman continued when Alba was settled.

Alba nodded wryly. "I do. However, I'm optimistic that my proposal will be as much to your benefit as it is to mine."

Karri hummed in amusement. "If you'd said anything different, I should have known you as a pretender. Refugee or no, you are nothing if not a politician, Alba." It wasn't entirely clear whether the words were meant as a compliment or an insult.

Alba sighed. "Perhaps. Nonetheless, if you believe my proposal is one you can support, I would request that you sponsor me into the Advisory Chamber to submit it for discussion."

Karri tipped her head to one side a fraction. "I assisted you on the previous proposal because you were able to convince me that leaving two hundred humans to be slaughtered by the Nativists for no viable reason was unconscionable. But I hope I haven't given you the impression that I am someone who will blindly advocate for human interests, regardless of subject or cost." She twitched her tail in a neutral gesture. "Either way, it will have to wait until tomorrow. The Hierophants have called an urgent meeting of all the Advisors, and I won't have time to consider any additional proposals until after I know what they've brought us to deal with." She looked at Alba's face and sighed. "I suppose it wouldn't hurt for you to come along to observe. You're a familiar enough face in the Advisory Chambers by now anyways. And I understand your human friend, the aide-de-camp to General Riit, will be there as well."

Alba fought back the sudden concern tightening her chest.

Jair hadn't said anything about this, which meant it had likely come up suddenly. And her experience in this system told her that whatever it was, it was probably not good news.

"Thank you," she said. "I'll follow you, then."

When they reached the chambers, the tiers of seats lining the walls were already mostly full. Karri left Alba in the public chambers and ascended to her seat near the top of the tiers of seats, tipping her head in greeting to the other advisors as she passed them.

Alba stood amongst the press of yibo bodies of those who'd come to witness the proceedings, supporting herself against the railing. Her breath was coming short and tight in her chest. There was an air of nervousness and anticipation throughout the chamber, she could see it in the twitching of tails, the nervous jerk of heads, hear it in the undertone to the whispers.

At last, a large doorway opened in the back of the Advisory Chambers, under a thick trailing vine that Alba had assumed covered nothing more than a decorative wall.

Seven yibo stepped through it in a loose company.

Their robes were made of fabric finer than any Alba had seen before, and pure white, and they held themselves with the dignity of people who knew the deference their appearance would elicit, and expected it as their due. They were followed by a military escort, and Alba recognized Jair standing near the back, his taller human stature noticeable against the backdrop of yibo soldiers.

He glanced around quickly, and when he noticed her, he gave a nod of greeting. His face, though, was as grim as she'd ever seen it.

The seven members of the highest yibo governing body were more varied than Alba would have expected. She wasn't certain in her ability to tell yibos' ages, but there were two who couldn't have been more than early middle-aged, and there was a marked diversity in their fur colour and body-types. The looks on their faces, though, were an almost identical grim stoicism.

And Alba had spent enough time in the yibo system to recognize the emotion under the stoic expressions: stark fear.

"Advisors," said the man who seemed to be the oldest of the Hierophants, stepping forward. His voice carried, through some form of amplification that Alba couldn't see from where she was standing. "We have called you together to inform you of an event that is, perhaps, the gravest threat we have faced in my lifetime. I am confident in our ability to meet this challenge; however, it will take all our combined attention and will." He was speaking yibo, but the translator set into Alba's wavelink translated the words effortlessly.

The Hierophant glanced up at the towering rows of seated advisors.

The tension in the room was palpable.

"We were able to successfully navigate the situation with Kachik through peaceful means. For that, I commend you. However, I find myself now forced to announce that despite your efforts—we are now at war."

Alba sucked in a quick breath. Around her there were rustles of surprise, little gathering ripples of shock spreading outward throughout the room.

"The backdrop to our negotiation with Kachik was, as you know, a raider leadership war," the hierophant continued. "The leadership war, it appears, was decided with a truce—Krevai and Sharda together have claimed leadership of the raiders, and they've been accepted by the majority of crews." He paused, as if unwilling to finish the sentence he'd been leading up to.

"And their first act as leaders," he continued finally, "has been to declare open war on the yibos."

Alba caught Jair's eyes across the crowded hallway as the ripples of shock around her turned to terror.

She saw in his face the same realization as the one tightening her chest.

A war with the raiders would take every drop of yibo concentration until it was over. It would be a struggle for their very survival.

This wasn't only a death-blow to her hopes for a reopened portal. Considering the raider preference for human flesh, and the precarious place of humans in this system, combined with the desperation of their yibo allies—this could mark a death-blow to the survival of this system's humans as a species.

The noise of the crowd, their panic and terror, the press of people trying to simply *get out*, perhaps to warn loved ones, perhaps simply an unconscious need to escape what was coming, was almost overwhelming. Alba had to suck in a long breath, pulled back, for a moment, onto the deck of a dying diplomatic ship—people pushing and shoving, trampling each other to get to the escape pods before the hull cracked and the icy vacuum of space sucking the life from their bodies as casually and dispassionately as it would suck the air from their lungs.

"Alba!"

She looked up, pulled out of her spiralling terror, to see Jair her pushing his way across the floor towards her.

She let out a steadying breath and lifted a hand to make herself visible over the crowd. He must have seen, because he turned and came towards her.

She closed her eyes, fighting back the sick taste of fear.

It was alright. This wasn't the diplomatic ship, and they weren't suffocating, yet. There was still time to figure something out.

Jair made his way around through the security gate and into the public balcony to join her. He glanced around at the frantic crowd, and gestured with a jerk of his head.

"This way." He was almost shouting to be heard over the noise. "There's a place we can talk, I'll have access with my security clearance."

Alba nodded mutely and followed him as he pushed his way through the crowd. They reached what looked like a solid wall, although Alba could make out the telltale discrepancies on the surface that told her this was where a door would open, and he slid his finger along it as Alba had seen the yibo do.

The wall parted, and Jair stepped through, gesturing her to follow.

Inside was a small sitting room. The handful of yibos inside, talking in whispers, looked up in alarm at their entrance, but a quick glance at Jair in his military uniform seemed to reassure them, and they went back to their conversations.

Alba found a seat in the corner and sank into it, and Jair took the seat beside her. His naturally brown skin was paler than usual, and there were deep worry-lines across his face.

"I suppose this means asking for a portal is no longer a winning proposition," said Alba, with a weak attempt at humour.

Jair shook his head grimly. "This isn't good for any of us." He paused. "We found out about this only a few minutes before you did, but there's already talk in the military—Kachik's generals have contacted ours, and whether or not they were openly threatening, they may as well have been. They're 'strongly suggesting' that we put aside our differences for the duration, and have made it clear that this means if we don't send our forces to protect their cities, while turning a blind eye to whatever they see fit to do to the humans in their jurisdiction, it won't be only the raiders we're fighting. The Nativists are gambling, rightly, I think, on the assumption that when the raiders do launch their full-scale attack, it will be on the larger metropolises, not one of the Nativist-controlled cities."

Alba nodded, ice forming in her stomach. "And I assume that with the threat of the raiders at hand, his proposal is not nearly as untenable as it might otherwise have been."

Jair ran a hand wearily over his face. "They're already talking about the difficulties of trying to keep the human settlements safe during a raider war. I doubt they'll take much convincing."

Alba closed her eyes and slumped back in her seat.

"The human settlements here are places of last resort," Jair's voice was quiet. "As I'm sure you've gathered, the status of humans in this system is never better than uncertain. Legally, we're supposed to have some protection. But it's not much, and it's not always given, and much of it is dependent on the goodwill of whichever local politician is over the district. When there are too many humans in a place that is utterly unbearable, and they aren't permitted to resettle into another district because no one wants the added liability, the yibos have very kindly permitted us to form our own settlements. Using, of course, the resources that we have earned ourselves." The smile on his face was bitter.

"There's some government assistance, yes, but not nearly enough. They're shantytowns at best, and they're far-flung across the system. Even in a war with someone like Kachik we'd be hard-pressed to get the government to guarantee protection for them. The best we could likely hope would be the current arrangement of allowing refugees to flee to the larger centres. But from the sounds of it, one of Kachik's conditions to join forces with us will be that the government put an end to taking in human refugees. Which means thousands, hundreds of thousands maybe, either hunted for food by the raiders, or slaughtered by Kachik's Nativists."

Alba drew in a long breath.

She was exhausted, and terrified, but those two emotions had become almost a dull underpinning to her life after the long trail of disasters that had led them to this point—routine and unpleasant, but expected.

"Perhaps, then, it would be helpful to take stock of our position," she began in a tone that somehow came out measured. "What—" She broke off.

Jair was frowning, his expression gone suddenly vacant, as if listening to a voice she couldn't hear.

She waited, and at last his eyes refocused, his attention coming back to the room. "I'm sorry," he said. "I just received a communication. Military alert."

Alba raised her eyebrows.

He shook his head. "I'm not sure the significance. We got word

that one of the Nativists' troop carriers has been destroyed, which …
could mean the raiders have already begun their attacks. But our
sources say there was no sign of raiders in the vicinity. The last ship
they were able to verify approaching the moon where this happened
was an unfamiliar one, but certainly no raider vessel."

Alba frowned. "Where did this happen?"

Jair gave her a questioning look, but pulled a starmap up on his
communicator and let it hover in the air between them. "There," he
said, pointing out a small green moon.

Alba stared at it for a moment, her mind suddenly racing. "And—
do you know what the Nativist military was doing on this moon?"

"We don't know," said Jair, still watching her. "We assumed it
may have had something to do with the refugees who escaped, as it's
not far from their position when we sent our escort ships out, but …"

Alba's stomach was tight with excitement. Joska hadn't been
exactly forthcoming about her plans, but Alba was almost certain
she recognized the location Jair had pointed out. "I think," she said
slowly, "that I have a good guess as to what happened. That's where
Joska and Rafel were headed to meet up with Savina and Reka. The
ones who got the human refugees out of Chrr."

He was still watching her, his expression sceptical. "You think any
of them could have been responsible for this?"

Alba had to restrain herself from a small, incongruous snort of
laughter. "Oh, I think between the group of them, they'd be more
than capable. Reka is a top government agent, and Savina is an
assassin. And then there's the cargo ship's crew, Rafel, who is ex-
military. I'm sure he's been taught basic sabotage." She paused.
"Jair. Is the reason the yibo military is so anxious to ally with Kachik
because they need his weapons, or because they can't afford an
additional enemy?"

"The latter, I think," said Jair, frowning. "Why?"

"And do you think, perhaps, that if we were able to demonstrate to the yibo military that human technology and human ingenuity, especially coming from a system whose military strategies they've never studied, would be able to assist them to win the war against not only Kachik, but the raiders—it might cause them to rethink their calculations? If we could prove that humans were an asset, rather than simply a liability, would they be more willing to prioritize human lives?"

Jair was still staring at her, but she could see realization dawning in his face. "Do you really think that's possible? Do you really think these friends of yours could pull off a demonstration like that? Because if we want to convince the Synod, we'd need solid evidence, not just our suppositions."

"I can't promise anything," said Alba briskly, but there was a tinge of excitement bubbling in her chest, and a hint of something that might have been hope. "But I'm comfortable telling you I believe it is possible." She pushed herself to her feet. "Will I need your security clearance to get back into the audience foyer, or will it open for me?"

"Where are you going?" he asked.

"I'm going to have a conversation with an assassin and a cargo ship captain," Alba said grimly. "And after that—" she turned back to face him. "I shall need to ask you to get me an audience with the yibo war council."

7

Aran stood in front of the force field surrounding the abandoned raider ship, Istvay beside him. He was trying very hard not to look as excited as he felt, although honestly, Istvay could probably tell.

Dessi had led the two of them here, after giving them a thorough briefing: charaks were organic life forms, were not oxygen-dependent, but were adapted to live in oxygen-rich environments, and could be killed. They seemed to only infect mammalian creatures, and only those that regularly ventured into their territory. But they were translucent, more or less invisible to the naked eye, had no detectable heat signature, and were able to disguise their scent such that finding them was more a matter of chance than anything.

Add to that their ability to mind-meld with any mammalian creature that had been in physical contact with them or with someone they were currently infecting, and hunting for them was not really a viable option. Apparently, they fed on something produced by the rotting corpses of their victims, and since they didn't have the physical means of killing their prey, they had evolved a way to force their prey to hunt and kill for them.

Normally an infected crew would be quarantined until the infection had run its course, and either the crew had killed itself out, or had found and dispatched of the charaks. That was no longer an option in the current circumstances—there was no way of telling how far the infection had spread, and the charaks could easily have moved location to a new ship .

Dessi had looked mildly concerned when Aran mentioned that he and Istvay had been in contact with the infected raider on their hunting trip, but after making Aran go back over the events several times, she'd given a decisive nod. "It sounds like she didn't touch your bare skin, so you should be alright. Besides, I've never heard of them infecting humans, likely because your species doesn't venture out far enough. I'm sure they could, but they would likely need a longer, more sustained contact to be able to learn enough about your mental processes and biology to take over your mind."

Istvay had looked distinctly uneasy at this, but Aran hardly cared —he'd happily put himself in a situation with much worse odds if it meant saving Istvay. And Istvay seem to realize it, because despite the worry in their face, they simply sighed when he suggested they go examine the ship.

"No, I don't like this," they'd said. "But as you say, we've probably done more dangerous things, between the two of us."

And so here the two of them were, standing in front of the ship, geared up from head to toe in oversized raider protective gear, which was still, somehow, much more comfortable than the gear he and Istvay used back on Colorida.

Ani had deigned to come along this time, although she was clinging firmly to Aran's shoulder and had grumbled at Istvay when they'd reached out to hold Aran's hand.

Aran grinned a little despite himself. "Listen, Ani," he said gently, stroking her head. "I know things have changed a bit, but you're still my little sweetheart. That isn't going to change."

She grumbled again, but there was a certain smugness to her posture when Aran took his hand out of Istvay's for a moment to pet her.

Istvay made a small, amused sound. "We're going to have to talk this out with her at some point."

Aran sighed. "I know, I know. But it'll probably be easier when she's a little less stressed."

Istvay chuckled, then sobered, glancing at the empty ship ahead of them.

It was standing alone on a bare-rock clearing among the planet's rocky cliffs. It had been cordoned off with a force field barrier, and there were nervous-looking guards standing some distance from the perimeter, watching each other with almost as much wariness as they were watching the ship.

Dessi must have spoken with them, because despite the unease clear on their faces, they waved Aran and Istvay through when the two of them approached.

The force field flickered, a small opening appearing in the surface.

"Shall we?" said Istvay after a long moment.

Aran was too excited to trust his voice, so he just nodded. Istvay gave him a rueful smile and shook their head. "A fascinating scientific opportunity, I know," they said. Then they and Aran stepped through the opening together.

The force field snapped shut after them, closing them inside.

The ship squatted in the centre of the quarantine area, the hatch gaping open like a wound. The ground around it bore marks of a struggle, and was liberally splashed with dark stains that Aran was pretty sure he didn't want to look at too closely. Dessi had assured them that the dead bodies had been removed and burned, so they shouldn't stumble across any rotting corpses, at least. Aran was grateful—there was a stink to rotting flesh that lingered in your nostrils for far too long.

The complete, eerie silence gave the scene a supernatural air, similar to the feeling Aran remembered from when his foster parents would drag him to the Orthodox church on feast days—the uncomfortable sense of something unseen and unseeable, watching you.

He swallowed hard. Istvay caught his gloved hand in theirs and gave him a small smile. Their face was pale, and their grip wasn't nearly as firm as it should be, their fingers trembling just a bit. And there was something about the unfamiliar weakness in their grip that turned the twisting fear in Aran's chest into a rod of solid determination.

He gritted his teeth and started up the gangplank.

Istvay walked beside him, stun-pistol in their free hand, and the two of them ducked through the hatch and into the shadows inside the ship.

Lights flickered on as they entered, with a high-pitched hum that Istvay probably didn't even notice. Ani tensed on his shoulders. She seemed as affected by the eerie atmosphere as Aran was, growling uneasily and peering around her with bulbous eyes, her posture rigid.

Aran checked the sensors on his belt, and Istvay did the same.

"I've set it to scan for every detectable variable I've got," Istvay said in a hushed whisper as the two of them made their way cautiously down the abandoned corridors. "We don't even know if the thing is still on the ship, though."

Aran nodded. "If charaks live in deep space, they should carry traces of radiation. I mean, unless it can metabolize radiation, like Ani does. Which would actually be an amazing—" He cast a guilty glance in Istvay's direction and cleared his throat. "I mean, but with any luck, there'll be traces of it left even if the creature itself is gone."

Istvay sighed uneasily and nodded. "Let's hope," they whispered back.

Aran understood their reluctance to speak out loud—the corridors he and Istvay were passing down were completely deserted, the silence odd and unsettling. Like stepping into a homey farmer's cottage in the Rim Mountains, walking into the kitchen, and finding pots and pans abandoned on the stove, dishes left on the table, hearth fire still burning—but no one there.

There were still signs of the ordinary daily life of the ship around them—an abandoned jacket, a bowl of food, half eaten, spilled across the floor. And in and around those little markers of daily life, more sinister signs—walls dented, belongings strewn about, a dark smear of what was probably blood along one of the walls.

Ani's uneasy growling increased in volume, and she tightened her tentacles down on Aran's shoulder. He couldn't blame her. The tension ached through his own muscles, and he could feel a stress headache starting at the base of his skull.

The three of them continued through the ship, Aran checking the heat sensor before they stepped into any new room. There was nothing unexpected in any of the cabins, but something about the uncomfortable, unending sameness of it gnawed at Aran's nerves.

"Listen, we've covered most of the ship," said Istvay in a low voice, leaning close. "That's about as much as we can do, I think. Dessi told us we wouldn't be able to see them, so it'll just be a matter of looking through the data we gathered, and—"

Istvay and Aran both jumped as a door beside them, already partly ajar, creaked open a few more centimetres. Ani puffed up, hissing in surprise, and Aran's hand was already around the butt of his pistol … but nothing moved.

The three of them watched it for a long, tense moment. And then, just as Aran was beginning to relax, Istvay gave a shout of alarm, lunging forward between Aran and the door. Something hit them, knocking them back against Aran as Ani launched herself at whatever the hell it was. Aran caught sight of it as Ani landed, sinking her tentacles spikes into the creature's body—a small, rodent-like creature, a little larger than a rat, that he vaguely remembered seeing once or twice in the corridors of Krevai's ship.

"Space louse," he said in a shaky voice, turning to Istvay. "It must've been—"

He staggered sideways as Istvay shoved him out of the way.

The creature hit the wall where Aran had been, then turned, its beady eyes honing in on him. Its small teeth were bared, and its eyes glittered in a strange way that was somehow horribly familiar. Ani, who'd stepped delicately off the creature, jumped for it again, but it paid her no attention, dragging her behind it as if she weighed nothing.

Istvay yanked out their pulse pistol, and at the sound, the creature's head snapped towards them. Aran grabbed Istvay's wrist and pulled them backwards as the small rodent sprang. "Ani bit it, it's not alive, your pistol won't do anything! Remember how Dessi said charaks can still control things for a few moments after death?"

Ani hung on to the thing grimly, and he could already see the creature's joints loosening as her acid began to dissolve it from the inside, but even still it was trying to get at them. It caught the cuff of his trousers and began a jerky scramble up his leg, its movements increasingly disoriented, but enough to let it slide free of Ani's grasp, then braced itself, as if to leap across to Istvay.

"No you don't," Aran muttered. He snatched it out of the air by the scruff of its neck as it leapt and flung it away from him. It landed on the floor, staggered to its feet … and finally collapsed in a boneless, liquifying heap.

For a long moment, Istvay and Aran stood where they were, breathing heavily.

Aran cast a quick glance at Istvay. Their face had gone an ashy grey from the exertion, and they were leaning heavily against the wall of the ship, as if standing unaided was beyond their current ability. "Alright, Aran," they said at last. They straightened with an effort and gave him something that was probably meant to be a grin. "If we didn't get enough of a reading from that, we're probably not going to get anything better. Shall we head back?"

Aran forced a smile of his own. "Yeah. Our sensors should have picked up readings from anywhere on the ship we didn't get to." He paused. "And," he added, with a slightly guilty look at his friend, "I managed to get my sensor running while the thing was trying to attack us, so——"

Istvay stared at him for a moment, then shook their head. "Of course you did," they grumbled, but they were smiling a little. They pushed themself off the wall, and Aran grabbed for their arm as they swayed. "Well then, let's head back and look at our data."

Ani, having thoroughly satisfied herself this time that her prey was not going to move again, slithered along the floor and pulled herself up Aran's trouser legs, settling herself with offended dignity on his shoulder. He stroked the top of her bulbous head. "It's alright, sweetheart, that wasn't your fault," he whispered. "You killed it, it just wasn't following normal rules."

Ani still looked offended and deeply suspicious, but she relaxed gradually, and Aran, one arm still supporting Istvay, turned back the way they'd come.

He stole another glance at Istvay as the two of them walked.

The fact that Istvay hadn't protested him helping them was more worrying than he really wanted to admit. He hadn't been exaggerating to Dessi—Istvay was almost out of time.

Politics or no, mind-melding alien creatures or no, he'd make this work somehow. It was simply a question of how. And in the meantime, he'd just have to do the best he could to keep Istvay from overexerting themself unnecessarily, and make sure they got a bit of rest before anything else happened.

Before he mentioned, for instance, the small tear in his glove, the slight tingle in his hand from where he'd touched the creature when he'd grabbed it by the scruff to toss it away from Istvay. The small, sibilant, whispering touch against his mind, soft as a snowflake, but somehow much, much more invasive, sliding across his consciousness like an oil slick over still water.

If he told Istvay now, they'd insist on staying awake to help him figure out what it was, and with the state they were in he couldn't afford that.

He shivered. From everything Dessi had said, it might not even be able to infect him. And even if it did, it would take some time before it could do anything to him. In the meantime, as long as he was still in full control of his mind, his touch wouldn't spread the infection. So he'd just have to make sure that he figured it out before he was a danger to anyone.

He tapped a quick message to Dessi through his communicator when Istvay wasn't looking. The message he got back was … well, more or less what he'd expected: *Aran. With all due respect, that is the thing I'm worried about least at the moment. We probably have two dozen infected raiders walking around right now, and we don't know who they are. Just watch yourself for any sign of infection.*

By the time they got back to the cabin, Istvay was sagging against him. They pretended they were fine when he asked them, and he pretended he wasn't worried as he helped them strip out of their protective suit and supported them over to the bed. They slumped down onto it, their eyes already closing. "Just—just give me a little," they mumbled. "I just need to rest a second."

"No rush," said Aran with forced cheerfulness. "You get some sleep, I'll work on the data and come to bed in a bit."

Istvay nodded. They looked like they were already half-asleep.

When their body finally went limp, Aran stood, carefully tucking the blankets around them. Ani was still grumbling on his shoulder. "Alright, sweetheart," he whispered. "I'll get you some food. You're probably hungry after all that, especially considering the fact that you emptied out the supply cupboard again this morning. At least you have an appetite, I guess." He glanced at the sleeping Istvay, and then down to where he was running his hand absently across the edge of his shirt, as if the space louse's touch was something he could simply wipe off. "And I suppose we've just given ourselves an even tighter timetable than before," he added ruefully.

8

Savina

Savina glanced over at Reka, crouched beside her. There was a dark sheen of excitement in Reka's eyes, that reckless look she always got when they were doing something that might kill both of them.

But this time, it wasn't just the two of them.

Savina was uneasily aware of the small group behind them—her baby brother, Ines, Beni, and Joska and Rafel.

Of all of them, Beni was the only one that Savina trusted to be able to take care of themself.

She couldn't help a quick look back.

Reka followed her gaze, and gave her a small smile. "They took out a yibo military ship yesterday, remember?" she said, her voice little more than a whisper. Then she half-stood, gesturing to the others, and they crept forward through the small hole in the force field that Reka had made with her stolen yibo military equipment.

The small, dirty town looked more like a desperately poor Rim Mountain village than anything the yibo had built. The streets were packed dirt, the buildings ugly things constructed of a slapdash combination of materials, logs from the surrounding forest built onto shelters that looked prefabricated and generic. Even here, though, there were signs that the inhabitants had tried to make the place beautiful—the brightly coloured holocurtains that hung in the windows and the braided mats outside the doors, done in unfamiliar patterns, spoke of people who were doing their best to make a home with what little they had.

The Labarinto elements of the town were odd, in their mix of familiarity and unfamiliarity—a group of people with a shared language and a shared history and five centuries of difference between them and the Joias System. The people were taller than what Savina would have expected from Joias, and most of them had coppery hair, regardless of the colour of their skin.

Savina and the others drew a few curious stares, but everyone who noticed them looked away quickly and hurried on. Perhaps not the most promising sign, but at least no one was shooting at them.

Which hadn't been a given, honestly.

Savina glanced around, looking for someone old enough to be able to help, and young enough not to be too offended by the interruption.

At last she saw someone who looked around Nicolau's age, striding purposefully down the street. She stepped forward, putting a hand on his arm to get his attention.

"Excuse me, sir," she began. "I'm looking for your majordomo."

He stared at her, incomprehension written on his face.

She tried again, a little slower, smiling up at him innocently and trying very hard to mask her irritation.

Reka, who'd been watching in amusement, stepped forward. "Let me," she whispered, and turned to the young man. "Hello. We're new here, and we need to speak to the head of the village. Is that possible?"

Savina stared.

Reka had spoken in perfect Mountain Dialect.

Savina probably could have spoken it if she needed to badly enough, but it had been drilled into her head, over and over, from the time she was old enough to speak, that she was never to speak Mountain Dialect outside the compound.

And she never had. Her time outside the compound had borne out the wisdom of it, especially after the Council had passed laws discouraging it. Speaking Mountain Dialect marked you out, and not in a good way.

And Reka, of all people …

The man was still looking at them in confusion, but his face had cleared a little at Reka's words.

"You want to go to the building over there," he said at last, enunciating his words slowly. His words were … not Mountain Dialect, exactly. But closer to it than Savina would have suspected.

This must be the Common Dialect that the humans here spoke, although it was slightly less formal and archaic than the Common Dialect the yibo spoke when they were communicating with humans.

The young man gestured. "You may as well follow me."

Savina fell in beside Reka as they started after the young man. "I didn't know you were from the Rim Mountains," she whispered.

Reka glanced over at her, but didn't say anything. Still, there was a tension to her posture that told Savina that she was not as nonchalant about her history as she wanted Savina to believe.

They hadn't been walking long before they reached the building that must belong to the village majordomo, or whatever they called them here. It was a large structure, at least by the standards of the place, formed from two or three of the portable shelters thrown haphazardly together and a bulky rectangular addition constructed of unpeeled logs.

The young man tapped at the door, and a moment later the door was pulled open. A middle-aged woman, Joska's age or a bit older, stood in the entrance, looking distinctly unimpressed.

"What do you want?" she said, turning to them, when the young man had finished explaining—whatever he'd been explaining.

Reka stepped forward. "We just arrived here, and we wish to beg shelter," she said in Mountain Dialect.

The woman studied them suspiciously. She must have decided that the group of them didn't look likely to pose a threat, because at last she sighed and stepped back, giving them room to pass inside. Savina nodded her wide-eyed thanks, and both Joska and Reka shot her warning looks as they passed.

She blinked at them innocently, which did nothing to quell the suspicion in their gazes. But they didn't say anything out loud, which was just as well—for once, Savina wasn't, in fact, contemplating anyone's murder.

The inside of the wooden structure was rough and uncomfortable, but clearly some effort had been put into making it habitable. There were the low stools that Savina's mind had begun to instantly associate with humans scattered about the place, as well as matching low tables. The woman gestured, and the small group took their cautious seats.

For a few moments, the woman and the newcomers watched each other in silence. At last, the woman said, "You're the ones who came through the portal, aren't you?" It was phrased as a question, but from the look on the woman's face, it was more a confirmation of fact.

Joska nodded. "Yes. We're from the Joias System."

The woman frowned at her. "The Joias System? Our system had contact with yours, then. Until—" She trailed off.

"Yes." Joska paused. "We … heard about what happened. I'm sorry."

The woman's mouth tightened. "Not as sorry as we are, I promise you."

There were a few moments more of silence. At last, the woman said, "I assume you're not here just to commiserate. Are you truly seeking refuge, or is this something else?"

Joska sighed and leaned forward, resting her elbows on her knees. "I wish that was all it was. We've learned that the yibo military intends to destroy your settlement as a message to the other human settlements. We came to warn you."

The woman frowned, her gaze moving from one of them to the other, as if searching for a hint of a lie.

Then she slumped. The movement wasn't much, but the desperate hopelessness in it was far, far too familiar to Savina, after the last few days.

"What do they want from us?" The woman's voice was low and despairing. "What else can they possibly take from us, more than what they have already?"

"This was our fault."

Savina looked up at Reka, surprised.

"I'm sorry. It wasn't our intent, but they came to this moon hunting us. I think they hope that by destroying you, they can prevent anyone else from giving aid to the humans they wish to kill."

The woman turned to glare at Reka, sharp hostility forming in her expression. "So why are you here? Shall I feel sorry for you as I watch my people get slaughtered for your sins?"

Reka gave her a weary smile. "No. We have no desire for anyone else to suffer the consequences of our actions. I think enough people have already."

"Then why did you come?" There was despair under the anger in the woman's tone. "Do you think I can evacuate these people? Do you think we have somewhere else to go, somewhere that the Nativists won't hunt us down? Believe me, I know Kachik's views on humans. You think hiding in the woods would save us?"

Reka leaned forward, the compelling intensity of her gaze seeming to catch and hold the village majordomo as easily as it had caught Savina. "No," she said quietly. "We don't intend for you to be killed at all. We intend to give Kachik's soldiers a taste of their own supper." She smiled, a grim, dangerous smile that was as sharp as one of Savina's knives. "We intend for him to learn that a war against humans is just as dangerous for him as it is for us. I'm a government agent from Joias. Savina Moya is a world-class assassin. Rafel is ex-military. And the rest of us have been surviving Kachik's attempts to kill us off since we arrived."

The woman was staring at her, disbelief warring with the smallest trace of hope in her expression. "And if this doesn't work?" she asked at last.

Reka shrugged, still smiling that small, dangerous smile. "Then at the very least, there will be seven more of us to die with you."

9

Alba

"Alba. How did it go?"

Alba sighed at Yosip's worried expression, and stepped through the door he held open for her into the refugee compound. The cramped, dark entranceway was a stark contrast to the airy, light-soaked halls of the yibo homes and offices. "What Savina and Reka and those others did to the yibo military ship was enough to catch the interest of the Advisory Body. And there are hints through military intelligence that the group of them are helping defend the human settlement on that moon against Nativist forces. However, even if they succeed, it will take more than that to convince the yibo that humans are worth saving—the anti-human cohort is already starting a narrative that, if Savina and Reka win this, it will be because Kachik wasn't expecting pushback, not because of any inherent abilities or strategic expertise. We've got to come up with a way to convince the military that humans could make a difference in this war, and then we have to prove to the Advisory Body that it's possible."

Yosip nodded, coming in behind her and letting the door swing shut.

"I've spoken with the people from the diplomatic ship." It was Feliu this time. He'd come over to stand beside them, so quietly Alba almost hadn't noticed.

"And are they willing to help?" Alba's voice was unintentionally sharp. But after all, this was yet another aspect of the plan she wasn't certain of her footings on.

The terrified, exhausted refugees had barely arrived, barely escaped prison and the horror of being offered to the raiders as prey. And here she was, asking for their help once again. Help without which, she'd lose any possibility of saving their lives, and the lives of the tens of thousands of humans from the destroyed Labarinto system scattered through the yibo settlements.

Important goals, certainly, but—she was the one whose assurances had brought these refugees from Joias through to the yibo system in the first place. And although she wished she could lay the responsibility of persuading these people to help on Yosip, or even Feliu—both of them more practised than she at life outside of the halls of politics—she couldn't. Because the yibo politicians' relationship with humans would go through Alba, whether she liked it or not, and everyone knew that. If the rest of the human refugees weren't willing to trust her, they wouldn't give her the information she needed: not to her face, and not through Yosip and Feliu.

"Are they ... what?" Feliu sounded puzzled.

She took a deep breath. "I assume, then, that the answer is no. In that case—"

Yosip's eyes sparkled in sudden understanding, and he stepped forward, chuckling. "Alba. They were all but falling over each other to help. The biggest difficulty we had was explaining to them that we couldn't use everyone."

Alba stared at him. He smiled back. "After what you did to save their lives—fighting for them in the yibo Advisory Chambers, strong-arming the yibo politicians and the yibo military to escort them in and save them from the Nativist soldiers—you're a folk hero, at this point."

"After I put them in danger in the first place," she snapped.

It should feel flattering, she supposed. But it didn't. It felt uncomfortably like guilt.

She looked up to find Yosip and Feliu still watching her. "Well," she said tartly. "I'm glad you were able to talk them into helping."

Yosip's smile broadened. "As I said—there really wasn't any talking-into involved. The most difficult part was turning down all the people who wanted to help who we didn't have room for."

Alba managed a small smile in return.

There was an understanding in Yosip's eyes, as he watched her, that reminded her suddenly how perceptive he could be under his friendly, kindly demeanour.

She closed her eyes for a moment, bracing herself.

Then she made her way down the narrow corridor and into the open main room of the refugee compound that had become their home over the past weeks.

The wide, boxlike area, lit more by artificial lights than windows and furnished with low aluminium tables, was crowded—almost two dozen men and women were gathered into the space—and Alba noted the looks on their faces as she stepped in. Relief. Camaraderie. Respect.

Something caught in her throat.

She'd always taken respect as her due, and camaraderie as foolishness.

"Thank you," she said at last. "Thank you for agreeing to help. As I'm sure Yosip and Feliu have explained, our task is somewhat urgent—we must convince the yibo that protecting the human refugees and human settlements in this upcoming raider war is worth the cost. I think it likely you know much more intimately than I what our failure would mean. And to do that, it appears, we must demonstrate to them that we can make a tangible difference in this war—enough to offset the potential hostility from the Nativists."

"What are we working with?" The man who'd spoken looked to be in his early sixties, his face grim, with a haunted look to it that she'd come to expect from the refugees who Savina and Reka had, against all odds, rescued.

"We are … working with less than would be ideal."

There were some wry chuckles around the room. "That's been the story since we got here," said a woman.

Alba sighed. "You are entirely correct." She paused. "We're working with the following: Savina and Reka, who you are already familiar with, the captain and crew of a cargo ship, and our diplomatic interpreter, who have between them managed to take out a yibo military ship—if they're willing to help us, of course; a handful of yibo politicians who've indicated they're friendly towards us; and whatever experience and expertise we have gathered in this room. Aside from that—" she shrugged helplessly.

"From what I saw of Savina and Reka when they were helping us escape the Nativists, they're quite competent at killing things," said a woman dryly. "Reka is impressive, and, I'll be quite honest with you, Savina scares the living hell out of me. I pity anyone who has to go up against either of them. But I'm not sure how we can contribute. We were put together as a diplomatic team, not a fighting force. I can't see that we would make much difference in a fight against the raiders, or even the yibos."

"It's not your fighting abilities we need," Alba said. "We need strategies and tactics that the raiders, and possibly the yibos, haven't seen before, something that without us, the yibos would find difficult to replicate. And considering that none of them have been to the Joias system, I think between all of you, we might just have that."

The man nodded slowly, his forehead furrowed in thought. "Strategies, then."

"Strategies and technology," said Alba. "Anything we have that the yibos currently do not. Anything that we can use to convince them of the tactical value of human lives."

"And what assurance would we have that they wouldn't take our technology and our ideas, once we offered them, and leave us to be eaten by the raiders?" the man asked.

Alba sighed. It was a fair question, and one she'd asked herself more than once.

But in the end—

"We shall simply have to trust in the assurances they have given to me in the course of our negotiations," she said. "And while I can't guarantee, personally, their trustworthiness—I don't believe we currently have a better option."

At last, the man nodded. "If you advocate for trusting them—" he shrugged. "I'm willing to go along with it. The Holy Mystery Itself knows you've proven your judgement."

She nodded brusquely, trying to hide her discomfort at his words. "Thank you. Now, with that in mind—" She pulled up a holodisk and set it in the centre of the table. "Let's discuss potential strategies."

Jair joined them sometime later. His face was grim as he settled into a seat one of the others hastily pulled up.

"Jair, thank you for coming," said Yosip, with his usual smile. "I assume you have news for us?"

Jair sighed, and was silent a moment. At last, he said, "I just got back from the latest military briefing. It appears the Nativists are set to attack another settlement, a yibo settlement, nominally, but it's at least fifty percent human. And we don't have any ships close enough to help."

Alba's stomach tightened in unconscious dread. "And why are you bringing this to us? Did the military decide to ask us for help with strategies after all?"

He shifted a little in his seat, shaking his head. "No. But I checked the star maps—if what you've told me is true, your human friends may be close enough to do something."

She stared at him. "Savina and Reka? Against an entire Nativist attack force?"

"I understand it's not ideal." Jair's tone was still grim. "But at this point, we don't have time to wait for the ideal. And this is what we're working with. I understand it's more dangerous than what we'd originally talked about. But—" he sighed. "If you're looking for a chance to convince the Advisory Body you can do this, here it is. No one will be able to argue that our expertise isn't valuable." He paused, then continued in a lower voice, "And at this point, it's the only chance that settlement has to avoid being slaughtered."

Alba closed her eyes.

It was too many 'if's—their plan depended on far too many variables that were each far from certain. But Jair was right. They didn't have the luxury of picking and choosing their battles. They'd have to work with whatever they were handed, and hope it was enough.

"How much time do we have?" asked Alba at last.

"Judging by the current trajectory of the Nativist ships, we estimate they'll arrive within a cycle, a cycle and a half at most," said Jair.

One of the engineers glared at Jair, then sighed and turned to her neighbour. "Tell me again what type of technology this cargo ship would be likely to be carrying?"

The discussion went late into the night. Even after they'd finally retired to bed, Alba lay awake for a long time, staring at the ceiling.

She wasn't sure if it was nervousness over the proposed course of action, or the discomfort of realizing that the people here were following *her*—not Yosip, not Feliu, but her—and that now, she was finally coming to understand the full burden that carried with it.

10

Aran woke in groggy disorientation. His back ached, and his neck was impossibly stiff, and it took him a moment to realize why—the surface underneath him wasn't the soft of the cot, but the hard top of the table.

He groaned internally. He must have finally just fallen asleep where he sat. Which meant he was almost certain to have a sore neck for the rest of the day, on top of having to explain to Istvay why he hadn't come to bed last night. It wasn't infrequent that he got so caught up in his research that he forgot about sleep, but it always stressed Istvay out. And the last thing they needed right now was additional stress.

He tried to sit up, and felt a brief jolt of panic as his muscles didn't respond. He slumped, biting back another groan.

He was definitely, definitely going to be sore.

Bracing himself against the pain, he tried again.

Nothing happened.

It was as if his muscles were frozen.

A small swell of panic started to rise in his stomach.

There was no reason why he shouldn't be able to move. No matter how stiff he was, he should at least be able to sit up, even if it hurt.

The uneasy memory of the creature he had grabbed the day before flashed in his mind, but there was nothing about touching the thing that should have affected his ability to move …

And then he felt again that small, whispering sensation in the back of his head, the feeling like tiny, cold fingers running across his consciousness. A sibilant sort of a whisper, just outside the realms of hearing, not recognizable as words or language of any sort, but as an emotion. Curiosity, perhaps. Interest.

And then—a quick swell of something that felt like satisfaction.

Aran's entire body went cold with horror.

"Ani," he tried, but he couldn't make his mouth move, or force the air through his vocal cords.

Blind panic swept over him like a wave.

He'd been infected. And whatever this charak creature was, it was controlling him completely. He couldn't even breathe without its permission. If it wanted, it could simply … stop his lungs, refuse to draw in air, and he would die, suffocating, choking, unable even to scream out for help—

He shoved the panic back with every bit of practice he'd gathered over his years in the field, and before that, in university, and before that, in foster care.

That, at least, wasn't true. It clearly couldn't simply stop his breathing or his heart—already, he could feel his pulse coming more rapidly as the adrenaline spike from his panic attack washed through him. It would be voluntary muscle movements the thing could control, not involuntary. So for now, he was alive.

And he tried very hard not to let himself think about all the many things that something controlling his voluntary movements could do to ensure that wouldn't last long.

He forced his brain to slow and his mind to calm.

The first element of the periodic table was hydrogen, which had an atomic number of 1 and a valency of +/-1. The second was helium, atomic number 2, valency 0. Lithium had an atomic number of 3, and a valency of +1.

As always, forcing his brain into something comfortable and familiar helped, at least enough to allow him to think through the terror. Even so, he almost tipped over into panic when his body moved without his permission, his arms pushing him unsteadily to a sitting position.

Beryllium had an atomic number of 4, and a valency of -1. Boron had an atomic number 5, with a valency of +3.

Panic was clawing at the inside of his brain now.

He just needed to watch, to observe from inside his own mind. As objectively horrifying as this was, it was—well, probably the best chance he'd ever get to understand and study these creatures.

The thought pushed back the upswelling panic, replacing it with a tinge of scientific curiosity.

Istvay would be furious, of course, but still—he really couldn't have asked for a better opportunity, all things considered. Because there probably wasn't a way to get a closer view than to have a charak inside his mind, controlling his body. And presumably it was the fact that he was human, not raider, that was preventing the thing from entirely short-circuiting his thought process—it must have a weaker hold on him than it would on a species it was accustomed to. Honestly, now that he thought of it, this was really actually a fascinating set of circumstances in which to make some observations.

Assuming he survived long enough to make any sort of use of his observations, of course. But then, it seemed like that was never really as much of a given as he'd like.

He felt his muscles tighten, and the charak, using his arms and legs, pushed back the chair and stood. He swayed for a moment, and was caught, briefly, with the terrifying sensation of being off-balance with no way to correct—and then his body straightened and caught its balance, and he was on his feet.

Ani, who'd been cuddled by his feet, perked up groggily. Then her entire body stiffened, the pouches under her eyes puffing out. She growled uneasily and slithered backwards, watching him.

Clearly, she realized something was wrong. And clearly, she understood that doing anything about it would hurt Aran. She hissed and bobbed her head up and down, and then, at last, retreated to the safety of her cupboard and pulled the door closed behind her, only the tip of one tentacle and one round eye peering out.

He wished, desperately, that he could comfort her, but … that would have to wait until he'd figured a way out of his current predicament.

He turned his attention back to whatever the hell was happening in his brain.

The odd feeling of being a passenger in his own body was jarring. He observed his own reaction clinically—presumably, almost anyone would panic at a sensation like this. And presumably, their panic reaction would activate their amygdala, temporarily shutting down their critical thought and language centres, which probably made their bodies that much easier to control. So perhaps the induction of panic in their victims wasn't just an unfortunate side effect of a charak infection, but an intentional technique of these creatures, to give them easier access to their victims' higher brain functions.

It was actually quite brilliant, now that he thought about it.

His first few involuntary steps across the cabin were unsteady, and more than once he was sure he was going to fall flat on his face. But he didn't, and soon his unsteady steps became more sure.

He tried, once or twice, to put forth some bit of control—change the length of his stride, move his fingers—but each time he did, the sibilant whispers in his mind grew sharper, tinged with a feeling of unmistakable irritation, and the uncomfortable, choking sensation, that feeling of being smothered while you were still able to breathe, grew thicker until he stopped.

He shivered despite himself, and gave up trying. It didn't seem to be any use anyway, and the feeling of something touching his consciousness was almost too viscerally horrifying even for the periodic table to do any good.

He couldn't even take a deep breath—the creature controlled any voluntary movement of his lungs—and so he settled back into the small hollow of his consciousness, gauging the creature's reactions and emotions with absolute fascination.

Within a surprisingly short amount of time, he was walking normally—or, the creature controlling his movements was walking normally—and he was just trying to calculate how long it had taken when a stirring of movement from the far corner of the room jolted him out of his concentration.

Istvay.

They were going to wake up any moment now ... The thought brought with it a jolt of worry, the picture of the small research table, Aran's chair pushed back. Where Istvay's eyes would go first to look for him, and where, if they didn't see him—

There was a sharp glitter of interest from the thing inside his head.

He cursed internally.

The thing didn't seem to be sensing his thoughts, exactly, but the emotions behind them. That was what seemed to attract its attention.

And of bloody course, he couldn't think about Istvay without a jolt of emotion—love, concern, relief, desire. Or, like right now— horrified, abject terror.

Issstvay, the thing hissed in a sibilant, triumphant whisper. Aran almost choked, panic flooding his brain once more, too strong for research, or the periodic table, or anything else to push back.

The pressure squeezing on his consciousness tightened.

Istvay, it whispered again.

He needed to stop panicking. His panic was giving them access to the parts of his brain that were shut off during fight-or-flight reactions—language, memory, executive function. But the raw, hot horror at the thought that he might inadvertently hurt Istvay—infect them, or worse—was far, far too visceral for any rational thought to penetrate.

The creature's movements in his body had gained a confidence that they lacked before, and he swore viciously in his head and desperately fought back the panic. Like he'd had to so many times in the past few weeks, when he hadn't known whether Istvay was alive or dead, and he was the only one who could help them, and he was utterly, abjectly aware of his inability and of the fact that Istvay might pay for it with their life.

At last, slowly, he clawed back enough control of his emotions that he could push the sibilant, whispering thing back a little. He felt its jolt of annoyance and disappointment as he did so.

But—

He groaned internally, trying to cling onto his enforced calm.

His panic, apparently, had already done its work. He could feel how the creature had entwined itself through his consciousness, pulling out the bits of him that it needed.

And now Istvay was sitting up on the bed, rubbing their eyes.

They looked over at him with a small, sleepy grin. "Up already? Or did you just not go to bed last night?"

He could feel the creatures spark of interest at his flash of guilt, and again he cursed himself, cold sweat beading on his skin as he fought back panic.

It could sense his emotions. It would react based on his emotions, and it could react very naturally indeed, now that it had access to his language. And damn it, there was no way in hell he would ever be able to think of Istvay without the brightest, most brilliant emotions glowing through every part of his consciousness like a signal beacon.

"Sorry, Pishti," he heard himself mutter.

Istvay shot him a look. "You didn't, did you?"

Another flash of guilt, seized on by the thing in his head. He felt himself looking away, not meeting their eyes, and, to his horror, grinning sheepishly. "I—guess I must have fallen asleep looking at the data."

He felt sick to his stomach. This thing sounded just like him—his own voice, his usual mannerisms. Not even a stutter of hesitation.

"Find anything interesting?" Istvay stretched, then grimaced. "Ooof. I never would have imagined I'd be sore from fighting a space louse."

Aran heard himself chuckle as he turned, against his will, and crossed over to Istvay. His entire consciousness was seizing with horror, but he kept hold on his panic with an iron grip.

He couldn't touch Istvay. He couldn't infect them, they were on the brink of exhaustion as it was, there was no way they could stand up to something like this.

As he neared the bed, the charak held his hand out, as if to help Istvay up.

Aran *shoved*, with every bit of force in his mind.

He stumbled, knocked off balance, and caught himself on the edge of the bed, still a good metre away from Istvay.

"Are you alright?" Istvay pushed themself to their feet, face creasing with concern.

The thing in Aran's brain tightened mercilessly, his muscles once again fully under its control, and he could hear his own voice mumble, "Sorry, I tripped."

Istvay looked at him a little more closely, and he strained to put something in his expression—some emotion, a warning, something

—

But he couldn't make his features move even a millimetre.

Istvay gave him a rueful grin. "Yes, staying up all night will do that to you. You didn't get hurt yesterday on the ship or something?"

Aran heard himself laugh. "I thought I was the one that was supposed to be worried about you. I'm fine."

Again, he swore internally—his emotions around Istvay were apparently so easy to read that the creature could pick up every nuance.

"Come on, I'll show you what I found," he heard himself say. The inflection was perfect—the tinge of excitement in his voice, but muted, as if he was trying very hard not to sound quite as eager as he felt.

Istvay chuckled. "Alright," they said. "Let me get dressed, at least. And then you can show me what you found in your all-night research session."

They stripped out of their clothes and changed into a clean pair of trousers and a ragged button-up shirt, and for once, Aran couldn't exactly complain about the direction that the creature was pointing his eyes.

And, of course, within about two seconds, it was very aware of the absolutely absurd depths to which Aran was physically attracted to Istvay.

He gave a resigned internal sigh.

That, of course, was probably inevitable, all things considered.

Istvay glanced over, saw him looking, and rolled their eyes, but they were grinning that lopsided grin that made Aran's involuntary bodily reactions erase any possible doubt of his physical attraction.

Istvay shook their head and rummaged through one of the supply cupboards to pull out a package of the dried ship rations that the raider crew stocked for their longer runs. They held out a package for Aran, and Aran's arm reached out to take it, his fingers almost close enough to brush Istvay's—

Aran shoved against his own mind again in sheer, blind panic, and again he stumbled, barely catching himself on the wall of the cabin.

Istvay frowned. "You sure you're alright?"

Aran give a rueful grin. "Just tired. I guess I should start listening when you tell me that I'm going to regret these late nights."

Istvay was still frowning at him, and he willed, with every spark of willpower he could muster, for his face to show something—

But the thing clamped down even harder on his consciousness, hissing with displeasure.

At last, Istvay turned away. "Well, I hope whatever you found was worth it," they grumbled.

The sound of it made Aran's chest ache, even through the iron grip he was keeping on his panic.

He couldn't hurt Istvay. He couldn't.

And he wasn't sure, anymore, how long he would be able to prevent it. The thing's grasp on his mind was growing stronger with every passing moment.

Istvay pulled up a chair and dropped into it, grimacing, and scooted it up across the table from where Aran's notes and the sensor readouts lay scattered. Aran crossed to his own seat. For a moment, he felt a sick wave of relief as the creature controlling his body made no attempt to brush by Istvay's chair. And then he felt himself sit, smoothly, and he realized—

There was nothing to trip over, when you were sitting down.

Istvay had pulled some of the notes across the table, and was studying them, their forehead creased in a frown.

Maybe, if the thing in his head tried to move his hand, maybe he could … maybe he could push his muscles so it would look like he was trying to … hit them or something, maybe that would be a warning enough … He could feel the sweat gathering under the collar of his sleep-wrinkled shirt.

His hand didn't reach out to take the notes from Istvay though—he simply sat where he was, elbows on the table, chin in his hand, watching them. He could feel the soft, fond smile on his face.

He felt like he was going to throw up.

Istvay looked up after a moment and caught him watching them. They gave him a small grin. "You going to show me what you found?"

Aran felt himself lean forward over the table, exactly like he would have, probably, if he'd been controlling his own muscles. If this entire thing hadn't been his worst possible nightmare.

"I've been thinking—maybe you're right. Maybe I should head to bed." His words came out playful and teasing.

Istvay raised an eyebrow.

He cocked his head at them, grinning. "Watching you just now convinced me of the error of my ways. I'm sure I'd feel much better after some rest." He reached out his hand, and inside his own brain, clamped down to the point that he felt like he was suffocating in earnest, Aran prepared himself to do … something, he wasn't sure what, but something, anything, make some last, desperate attempt, even if it bloody killed him—

But the creature must have been expecting it, because he felt his hand pause halfway across the table, waiting for Istvay to reach the rest of the way.

Istvay was still watching him, eyebrows raised, a small, amused smile on their face. Aran wanted desperately to look away, wanted desperately not to see what would happen next. But he couldn't, because he couldn't damn well control even that.

Istvay reached across the table, and their hand hesitated, just a few centimetres away from Aran's.

Aran almost wasn't breathing. He wasn't sure how much longer he could hold back his panic, he wasn't sure he'd actually survive this, wasn't sure he'd survive being the one who hurt Istvay, after everything—

"Come on, Pishti." His voice was still teasing, showing no trace at all of his utter terror. "I thought you said you'd do anything for me."

Istvay's smile widened, just a little. And then they looked up, directly into his face.

"No," they said, their voice still calm and pleasant, but now with an edge to it. "No, actually, you're mistaken. I would do anything in the world—anything in this system or any other—for Aran." They leaned forward, and he realized that, while he'd been watching their hand on the table, they'd pulled on a heavy glove over the other.

Before the thing in his head could react, Istvay caught Aran's wrist in their gloved hand. The look on their face was so cold, so bleakly furious, that Aran couldn't help a sudden, involuntary shiver.

"And so," they said, their voice still mild, "I would advise you to think very, very carefully about what you say in these next few sentences."

Aran heard himself give a nervous little laugh. "Pishti? Pishti, what's—"

Istvay's hand tightened on his wrist. "You do not get to call me that," they hissed. "Now. What have you done with Aran?"

Now Aran could feel the unease sparking through the suffocatingly tight grip on his mind. "Istvay, it's—it's me. What are you—what's wrong? What are you doing?"

Istvay leaned back in their chair. Their grip on his wrist wasn't tight enough to hurt, but it was as solid as a steel clamp. "I don't know very much about you," they said in a conversational tone. "Aran and I were trying to study you, that's how you infected him, isn't it? He probably touched that thing that attacked us yesterday when I didn't notice, and he probably didn't say anything because he didn't want to worry me. And he probably thought he had enough time to figure things out, because of what Dessi told us. I don't blame him. In his position, I might have done the same thing. He and I may disagree about the relative amount of risk he subjects himself to, but he's not stupid." They were still talking as if having a polite conversation, but there was a cold menace to their voice that made Aran shiver again.

He'd never actually seen Istvay like this.

It was terrifying. And also, if he would admit it—well, it was kind of hot, honestly.

"He didn't get too far, from the looks of his notes here—he probably only had time to jot down a few of his thoughts before you did … whatever you did to him." Their voice had taken on an even colder edge now. "But Aran is a bloody genius. And I would wager that his notes are going to be very, very useful. I know Aran cares about creatures that I quite frankly would just as soon throw into the damn Void, and so, for his sake, I'm going to tell you this:" They leaned in closer, staring directly into Aran's eyes. "Get. Out. Of. Him." Their words were so quiet Aran had to strain to hear, but they were chipped from sheer steel. "Get out of him right now. Because if you don't, I will find you. I will hunt you down, and I will find you, because I know you have a corporeal form somewhere. And I will take that corporeal form, and I will pin it to the damn wall with a rusty bush-blade."

From behind them, Aran could hear the door opening, hear Dessi calling, "Aran? Istvay? I brought you some food, I thought we could measure—"

Dessi's voice went suddenly silent.

Istvay didn't even react, their eyes still fixed on Aran's. "I will find the part of you that feels the most pain, and I'll use that to hang you with. And then, I will strip the skin from you, piece by piece, while you're alive and bleeding and screaming. I will peel you slowly, bit by bit, and I'll keep my sensors running so that I can ensure that you're alive and conscious the whole time, and that you feel every second of that pain. And then, when I'm tired of that—"

The presence in Aran's mind had been growing more and more panicked the longer Istvay spoke. Finally, with a wriggle that felt like a swamp-eel bursting out through the mud—it was gone.

Aran slumped against the table, gasping. His muscles were so shaky that he could hardly move, even now that his body was back under his control.

"Aran?" Istvay's voice was frantic.

He looked up into their face, a wave of his previous terror washing over him. "Pishti," he croaked. "Stay back, I—I don't know if—if that *thing* is hiding somewhere—"

Then Istvay had grabbed him by the shoulders, pulled him to his feet, and wrapped him in their arms like they thought he might dissolve if they let go. "Aran," they whispered in a choked voice. "Aran, are you alright? Are you hurt? Are you—" their words cut off, and they buried their face in his shoulder, their entire body shaking almost as bad as Aran's was.

"Pishti?" he managed at last, pulling back a little. "How ... how did you know—"

Istvay gave a choked, wet little laugh, blinking back tears. "I've spent the majority of my life madly, ridiculously, stupidly in love with you. Do you honestly think I wouldn't be able to tell if something was off?"

"Aran!" Dessi's voice was thick with admiration. "No wonder you were so intent on finding your Istvay!" She turned to Istvay. "What did you do to the charak, exactly? Just threaten it? I imagine that, since you are humans and it was still trying to get used to you, it likely hadn't settled in quite as firmly as it normally would have, or I can't imagine it listening to your threats." She paused, a considering look on her face. "Or," she added slowly, "it was just enough integrated with Aran's mind and emotions that it realized that not only were you telling the truth, but that you were perfectly capable of doing what you were threatening to do." She turned back to Aran, grinning. "I'll take a scan, but it appears to have let go of you for the moment, thank God." She shook her head. "You're probably still infected, so you'll have to lock yourself in your cabin at night I think, but as long as it's not controlling you, you won't be able to infect anyone else."

Aran stiffened, but Istvay tightened their hand on his shoulder. "It's alright, Aran. I glanced through your notes, and I think you've got the start of a way we can keep it out of your head, at least temporarily. You noted that it seems to affect bioelectric signatures, and we can work with that. We just need to figure out details."

"I have to say, you chose well with your Istvay." Dessi laid the tray of food on the table and pulled out her scanner. She checked his eyes, asked him to do a few basic tasks that probably could have been used as sobriety tests, honestly, then turned back to the door. "I'll get Krevai in here, I'm sure he'll be interested in this. Occasionally people will break an infection, but it's not common. Well done, Aran!"

"I didn't—it wasn't me, it was Istvay, they—" Aran began, but Dessi had already turned and started down the corridor.

Aran sighed, his entire body so weak with relief he wasn't sure how long his legs would hold him up. Istvay caught him by the arm, pushing him gently back into the chair. "Are you sure it didn't hurt you?" they whispered. Their voice was still tight with worry. "Did I hurt you, grabbing your wrist? I was trying to be careful, but—"

The door slammed open, and Krevai stepped through, Dessi behind him. "Aran!" he bellowed, laughter in his voice. "Dessi told me what happened. We'll get you some rest and some food, and you'll be back to yourself in no time. But I'm impressed! You chose your mate well. I knew you were a clever one. Your Istvay is quite fierce!"

The shaky fear and terror and the strain of the entire morning had pushed Aran's nerves to the very edge of their endurance, and now he straightened abruptly, glaring at Krevai. "They're not 'my

Istvay,'" he snapped. "I don't damn well own them. They're their own damn person, and they're a damn, bloody genius, and I'm just … I'm lucky to—" he broke off, not sure he could continue without his voice breaking.

For a long moment, there was silence in the cabin.

"I'm sorry, Aran," Krevai said finally. "I didn't mean to upset you and your—" Krevai shot a quick glance at him and broke off guiltily.

There was another moment's silence. Aran could feel the tension practically vibrating in his bones.

"Aran?" Istvay whispered.

He managed a short nod. Istvay slid their hand up his arm and around his shoulders, and his entire body relaxed at the familiar touch.

Then Istvay winked at him and glanced over at Krevai. "Aran's brilliant, but it so happens that this time, he's wrong. I am, in fact, his Istvay."

Aran turned, startled, and they leaned in to kiss him gently. "I've been yours since the first day I met you," they whispered. Aran just blinked at them, and they smirked. Then their expression turned grim. "And," they said, that unfamiliar edge of steel back in their voice, "I'm going to make damn sure that whatever the hell that thing was, it isn't able to hurt you ever again. And if it tries, I'm going to make sure it's either dead, or wishing it was."

Aran shivered, but again, something about the sight of them like this sent a pleasant tingle down his spine.

"Now," Istvay said, pushing themself to their feet and reaching out a hand to help Aran up.

Aran's legs were still shaky enough that he needed it.

"Krevai's right. Let's get you something to get your blood sugar back up, and then you need some actual sleep."

"I don't need to be coddled," Aran grumbled, trying to sound irritated.

"Of course you don't need to be coddled," Krevai said soothingly. "Now, your Istvay can help you to bed, and Dessi will bring you some food, and we'll make sure you have enough blankets and are nice and comfortable. We'll lock the door to be safe, but it looks like your Istvay is very well positioned to warn us if the charak starts to regain control."

Aran glared at him. Istvay had turned away, hiding their face in the crook of their arm, their shoulders shaking suspiciously.

"Why can't anyone in this damn place bloody listen to me?" Aran muttered at last, shaking his head.

Istvay took a deep breath and turned back to him, clearly fighting down their amusement. He could still see the laughter in their expression, but their eyes were deadly serious. "Aran," they whispered. "You may as well accept that there are a lot of us here who care about you, because it's not going to change any time soon. Now. Bed, and I'll wake you up when I find something."

11

Savina

The yibo military ships made no secret of their approach—it seemed they were unconcerned by the potential of resistance.

"Are we ready?" Savina whispered.

Reka glanced over at her, a small smile on her face. "If we're not, we'll all find out soon."

Savina scowled.

If she'd admit it, her scowl had less to do with Reka's infuriating calm than it did with the sharp worry twisting in her chest.

This was no longer just about her, or even just her and Reka. Everyone she loved was out there, right now, and there was a good chance that none of them would survive the next few hours.

And it would be her fault. She'd agreed to this. She could have made some excuse, told them that she was hurt too badly and that they'd have to come back later when they were better prepared.

And she hadn't.

Reka's hand touched her shoulder, and Savina jerked her head up, startled.

"They'll be alright, Savina. Joska knows what she's doing."

Savina gave a short nod and turned to face ahead again.

But she didn't shrug Reka's hand off her shoulder, and when Reka moved away, her hand slid down Savina's back in a gesture that felt oddly tender.

Savina shivered, and turned to glance at the people standing in a huddled cluster behind her, makeshift weapons in their hands and tension in their faces.

Reka was right—if they'd miscalculated, they'd all find out very soon.

And then they'd die.

She glanced back out at the bright shape of the yibo military ships approaching.

Presumably, the idea had been to simply bomb the village into oblivion—even with a force field, the kind of firepower two yibo military ships could bring to bear would be more than enough. They likely weren't even planning to disembark troops.

They were almost within firing range now.

Savina realized she was holding her breath.

Then, from the direction she'd left her siblings, there was a brilliant white flash through the trees. Savina blinked quickly, opening up the ship communication lines Beni had tapped into.

Through it, there were panicked shouts and barked commands in yibo. As Savina watched, the nearest ship teetered unsteadily in the sky, and then dropped, in the precipitous manner of an emergency landing. The other ship faltered as well, and then it, too, lowered to the ground, a little less urgently than the other.

Savina let out a long breath, her shoulders dropping in relief. There were whoops of triumph from the small group behind Savina, and even Reka's posture softened, just a little. Over Savina's wavelink, Beni said, "Rafel was right. Who knew they wouldn't have protection that'd work against the *Dolphin's* EMP tech?" There was a steel to their voice that Savina hadn't heard there in a very long time.

She raised her eyebrows. Apparently, spending time with Joska and Rafel had done her sibling some good.

"It won't take them long to disembark," she said. "Get your people to lead them towards us a soon as they do."

"They're on their way." Beni's voice was still calm and businesslike. The line clicked off, and Savina looked up to find Reka watching her.

"Ready?" Reka whispered.

Savina gave Reka her brightest smile. "Of course! I'd hate to keep our friends waiting."

Reka smiled back, a touch of fondness in the expression, then turned to the hand-picked group behind them, her face slipping back into its usual severity. "Move out," she whispered. "Let's get into position."

She started forward at a half-crouch, Savina beside her, and the others followed.

The forest around the village had been mostly cleared, and as they crept through the thin trees, stepping over roots and scrambling over fallen logs, Savina was unpleasantly reminded how exposed they were. Still, as long as they moved faster than the yibo soldiers, it shouldn't matter.

Reka slipped through the trees like a ghost, and Savina did her best to follow, scowling in irritation at the effort. There was a reason she worked the way she did, and most of it had to do with the fact she bloody hated this sort of thing. The humans behind them were also moving with impressive stealth, and Savina remembered, uncomfortably, the words of the village majordomo. This clearly wasn't the first time these people had been forced to protect themselves or die.

At last they reached the lines they'd laid out hours earlier, and at a silent gesture from Reka, spread out.

"They're on their way," Nicolau's voice hissed over their communicator lines. "Maybe two kilometres out."

Savina glanced over to where the others were hidden. Even knowing they were there, it took her a moment to pick them out. Then she ducked down behind the shelter of a tangle of fallen logs, Reka beside her.

They didn't have long to wait—within far too short a time, Savina could hear the soft tread of boots, the hissed commands in yibo that sent a quick surge of remembered fear up her spine.

She gritted her teeth.

This time, she wasn't injured and helpless.

This time, she and Reka weren't alone.

And these bastards deserved what was coming to them.

She caught sight of the first of them through the trees. Reka must have seen them at almost the same time, because Savina could feel her stiffen. "Hold your fire," Reka whispered through the communication lines. "Wait for my command."

Savina closed her eyes a moment, willing her hands steady on her pistol. Then she dialled in her sights, pulling in a long, steadying breath.

There were so many soldiers. And they just kept coming.

The first of them had almost reached the line, their boots only a few paces from the thin demarcation on the ground, when Reka hissed, "Now!"

Savina let out the breath she was holding and squeezed the trigger.

Shots hissed from the trees around her as the rest of their small group opened fire, slamming into yibo soldiers and knocking them back.

The yibo captain shouted a command. The soldiers scrambled for cover, and within a few moments, the air was thick with answering fire.

Reka glanced over a Savina with a grim nod, and Savina grinned back, then slipped out from behind the shelter of the fallen tree. She palmed her knives and crept forward, slipping from cover to cover until she was around and past the fighting front. The yibo soldiers' full attention was caught on finding the source of the weapons fire around them. They clearly didn't have any to spare for a frightened human girl, obviously not a soldier, hiding in the trees, even if they had noticed her.

When she was far enough past the shooting that she could slip in without attracting attention, Savina pulled her hood down to shadow her face, and, with a quick glance around, straightened and stepped out among the rear ranks of the pinned-down soldiers. They hardly took any notice, all their attention focused on pinpointing their attackers and getting a temporary barricade in place so they could bring up their larger weapons.

Savina scanned the soldiers quickly, keeping her head down. After a moment, she grinned to herself.

She'd found the captain.

He was wearing an armoured suit, like the rest of his soldiers, his helmet pulled low over his face. But she was used to working with armoured suits by now. She made her way towards him inconspicuously and waited until the yibo soldiers beside him stepped away, leaving him momentarily unguarded. Then she grabbed him by the wrist. He jerked around, opening his mouth to shout something, and she slipped her knife through the thin space between his helmet and his collar, slicing neatly through his jugular. He slumped, choking, and she lowered him carefully to the ground and stepped quickly back and away, fading into the crowd.

Now, to cause as much chaos as she could in the few remaining seconds before she was discovered.

She grabbed another soldier by the elbow, and as he turned, shoved her bloody knife up through the joint in his armour, twisting it neatly between his ribcage and into his heart. He collapsed, and she grabbed for another at random.

She managed to kill three more before someone noticed the dead captain. There were shouts of alarm, and far too quickly, heads began to turn towards Savina.

"It's a human! They've got through our lines!" Savina's wavelink translated the panicked shouts, and she dived out of the way as a shot dissolved the ground where she'd been standing.

"Where did she come from? Get the force field up, now! We can't risk more getting in."

Shots hissed around her as she scrambled to her feet, limping heavily on her injured ankle, and ran. Her foot caught on a tree root and she stumbled, swearing. Already, she could see the beginnings of the force field flickering ahead of her.

If she didn't make it, if she was caught inside—

Someone caught her shoulder, yanked her upright, and shoved her through the flickering field just as it solidified. She landed on her back on the hard dirt, gasping, Reka on top of her.

"Are you alright?" Reka hissed.

Savina nodded, without the breath to answer, and Reka rolled to her feet as gracefully as a cat, hauling Savina upright after her. "Now!" she shouted through her communicator,

Another force field slammed into place over the first, neatly trapping the soldiers within.

"You got it?" Savina gasped, leaning up against a tree.

Reka grinned and held out a yibo force field controller. "They won't be taking down their force field anytime soon—as long as we have access to one of their controllers, Beni's modifications should take care of that. And they can't take down our force field from inside their own."

"So they're trapped. It worked." Savina could hardly take in the words, her brain still spinning at the lack of oxygen and the bright rush of adrenalin and the pain from her twisted ankle.

Reka grinned at her. Her eyes were lit with a dangerous joy, and there was something sharp and fierce in her grin that held Savina's gaze like a magnet. She realized she was staring, still breathing heavily from the run, skin tingling with the remembered pressure of Reka's body on hers.

Then Reka drew back, turned away, and was gone.

Savina stared after Reka, and it took an embarrassingly long time before she felt in control of her body enough to straighten and start after her.

By the time she reached the agreed-on gathering place, most of the rest of their small force had already trailed in, and Reka was moving from one group to another, assessing the damage.

Savina blew out a breath and shook her head to clear it, and started over to help.

They'd lost a couple dozen to yibo weapons, and twice that number injured. But considering the alternative, they could hardly complain.

"Rafel?" Savina whispered through her wavelink. "How are you and Joska doing?"

There was a distant, muffled series of explosions, and black smoke drifted up from the direction of the grounded yibo ships. "Ships guns are down," came Rafel's voice a few moments later, a grim satisfaction in his tone. "The only thing these ships'll be good for now is letting the military run back to Kachik with their tails between their legs."

It didn't take long to negotiate the yibos' surrender. A few hours trapped under the double-layered force field shields were enough to persuade the yibo commanders who were still alive that surrender was their best option, and in the interim, Joska and Rafel led the teams quickly and efficiently stripping the yibo ships of any technology that the human village might find useful. They had talked, at one point, of keeping the yibo soldiers hostage, but the small village didn't have the resources to hold them, and Joska had firmly refused to be party to a plan that involved killing anyone who'd laid down their weapons.

Even so, it was well past dark by the time Savina and the others gathered once more in the village town hall, oil lamps burning on the walls and casting flickering shadows over the faces of those in attendance.

"Thank you," said the village majordomo. Her tone was weary, and in her face Savina saw the weight of the lives lost in the attempt.

For the first time, she felt a pang at the thought.

She hadn't even considered them. In the thick, dizzying relief that her siblings and Reka and Joska and Rafel were safe and uninjured, she hadn't spared a thought for those who weren't.

This village was already small and struggling. Perhaps the two or three dozen lives lost were hardly enough to count, in comparison to what the yibo had planned for the village. But it might be enough to put the remaining villagers' very survival at risk.

She shoved back the guilt. It wasn't like she or Reka had asked for this. And they'd done more to help these people than anyone should have expected of them.

More than Savina would ever have considered a few weeks ago, a small, uncomfortable voice in the back of her head whispered.

She pushed it away.

"We can't be sure the soldiers won't come back." Joska's voice was weary as well. "But at the very least, they know you have army-grade weapons and technology to protect yourself now. Hopefully that will be enough to convince them to think twice."

"Kachik isn't going to forget this," said the Majordomo.

"I know." Reka straightened from where she'd been leaning against the wall. "He won't. But you've bought yourselves time to prepare."

Savina's head pounded dully, still aching from the crash of yesterday, and her ankle throbbed with a sharp pain. She was trying to keep her mind focused on the conversation, but her thoughts were sluggish, and she didn't realize she was swaying on her feet until she felt Reka's arm slide around her waist, steadying her.

"Is there a place we can sleep for the night?" Reka's voice was brusque as she turned to the Majordomo.

The woman paused, considering. "There's space in the back of the hall," she said at last. "We'll bring some blankets and bedding, if you don't mind sleeping on the ground. I'm sorry I don't have anything better."

Reka nodded. "That will be acceptable." She paused. "We'll leave tomorrow, before we can bring any more trouble."

Savina closed her eyes at the sudden, unexpected rush of relief.

She hadn't realized, until it was over, how much strain she'd been carrying since … well, since they'd come through the portal. Every moment since then had been a desperate battle for survival. The thought of being somewhere safe—somewhere she wasn't being hunted, for once in her life—was almost unimaginable.

She woke the next morning to sun seeping in through cracks in the heavy blinds. Her entire body was stiff, and her ankle felt like it had swollen to at least twice its size, and it took her a moment to piece together where she was.

At last she sighed and pushed herself up into a sitting position.

The others were asleep on the floor around her, and she smiled a little, watching them.

Nicolau was sprawled out, his blankets kicked off, one arm tossed over Ines, who was curled up beside him. Beni was asleep in one corner, their head tipped back against the pillows, short hair forming a silky halo around their head. The black in their hair had mostly washed out by now, and the dark auburn colour of it reminded Savina of childhood, before she and her sibling had been forced to hide every trace of who they were. Not far away, Joska slept with one arm over her eyes, her body relaxed, face slack with exhaustion, and Rafel snored softly under his pile of blankets near her feet.

And Reka …

She frowned. Reka wasn't there.

"Savina."

She jerked in surprise, half-spinning to see Reka crouched behind her. She hadn't even heard her approaching.

Reka chuckled softly as Savina put a hand to her chest to slow her racing heart. Then she put a finger to her lips and gestured Savina to follow.

Wincing, Savina rolled to her feet, trying to avoid putting weight on her ankle. Reka crouched beside her, her hand half-outstretched to catch Savina if she needed it.

It was odd how comforting the gesture was.

She made it upright with only a few hissed curses, and limped after Reka out of their makeshift sleeping quarters and into the main room of the empty village hall.

When they were far enough away not to be overheard, Reka turned to her. "I … received a call on my wavelink from the Chief Justice yesterday. I received another this morning."

Savina stared at her, fighting back the surge of blind, instinctive terror.

Reka laid a calming hand on her arm. "Both times I explained to her I wasn't acting as her agent anymore." She paused. "She didn't sound exactly surprised."

Savina managed a small smile.

"The first time she called, it was to get an update on our situation," Reka continued. "The second time … she asked me for help. I told her I wouldn't make any decisions without speaking with you first, and she told me she had guessed you wouldn't be willing to take her call without some reassurance. She asked me to assure you that she had no ill intentions towards you or any of your friends, she simply wants to talk. I told her I'd pass the message on, and leave the rest in your hands."

Savina closed her eyes. Her heart was pounding, and the thought of Alba still left the sour taste of fear on the back of her tongue.

Damn Alba to hell. Damn her to the Void. This whole nightmare of a journey had been Alba's fault to begin with.

At last she opened her eyes and blinked to activate her wavelink.

"Call Alba," she muttered into it.

The wavelink buzzed a moment before Alba answered.

"Savina." Her voice was cracked with age and weariness. "Thank you for calling."

"What do you want?" Savina probably shouldn't have snapped, but something about the genuine gratitude in Alba's tone made her viscerally uncomfortable.

Alba drew in a long breath. "I need your help."

Savina closed her eyes, and tried, very hard, not to swear.

"Savina?" asked Alba after a long moment. "Can you hear me?"

"What the hell do you need my help with?" Savina's voice was so flat that she noticed, from the periphery of her vision, Reka glancing over at her in concern.

There was a pause on the other end of the line. "The yibo here were … impressed with how you dealt with Kachik's forces," she said at last. "The Advisors are debating handing the humans in this system over to the Nativists in return for safety, and this is the first thing that's given them pause. But …" she paused again. "It's not enough."

Savina sucked in a breath through her nose. "Not enough?" she snapped. "What the hell would be enough, then? Fighting off a full-scale Nativist attack?"

There was another moment of silence. "Yes," came Alba's voice at last. "There's a settlement that appears to be Kachik's next target. I had hoped … I called to ask if this was something you believe the group of you can do. There's not much I can do to aid you from here, but the best strategists I've been able to put together from the diplomatic ship and from the survivors from Labarinto will be working to help you."

Savina blinked the wavelink offline, and for a moment, she stared blankly ahead of her, her mind refusing to give Alba's words meaning.

It was too much.

This whole thing was too much. It was impossible. What Alba was asking was completely impossible, and completely unfair. She'd never signed up for this! She'd never volunteered to be some sort of hero, she'd never meant to save anyone, except for Beni and Nicolau. And then Joska had somehow become someone she'd risk her life to protect, and stupid Rafel, and then Nicolau had fallen for Ines, and so Savina had to worry about her, too, and then Reka, and now this …

Her ankle ached, and her entire body hurt, and the only thing she wanted to do was curl up in a blanket and sleep for a month and forget about the yibo and their stupid war and this entire damn system.

She just wanted to be *home* …

Something choked in her throat, a ridiculous half-sob, because she couldn't go home, she didn't have a home, she had nothing at all to go back to …

And then there was an arm around her shoulders. "Savina, what's wrong? What happened?" Something in Reka's whispered tone that told Savina she wouldn't be the only one swearing at Alba in a moment.

"I'm … I'm fine," she mumbled, squeezing her eyes closed as hot tears tried to leak out. "It's—"

Reka's thumb brushed across her cheek, catching a tear that trickled down her face.

Savina blinked her eyes open in shock.

Reka's hand cupped the side of Savina's face, warm and steady, and she was staring into Savina's eyes, her face creased in concern. "Whatever she asked you, Savina, you don't have to do it. I'll take care of it. You need some rest." Her voice was low and compelling.

Savina couldn't drop her gaze from Reka's, and the warmth of

Reka's hand on her cheek, the intimacy of the gesture, seemed to have robbed her of the ability to think.

"Tell her I'll do it," Reka whispered, her eyes still fixed on Savina's. "You take Joska and your siblings and find somewhere safe. I'll meet you there afterwards. Alright?"

She shouldn't be tempted by the offer. She *shouldn't*.

No, she shouldn't be hesitating. Why was she hesitating? She should have agreed before Reka had finished speaking. Saving people was Reka's job, not hers.

Reka's hand was still cupped around the side of her face, and she found she was leaning into it unconsciously.

She didn't take her eyes off Reka, just blinked to bring her wavelink back online. "I won't speak for the others," she said, in a voice that managed to come out mostly steady. "But … send me the details. Reka and I will find a way."

She blinked twice to shut down the communication.

Reka was still watching her, and there was worry in her face, and a hint of bewilderment, and something that was horribly, hideously tender.

Savina turned away quickly. "I guess we'd better wake up the others and let them know their options," she mumbled, trying to inject sarcasm into her tone.

"Savina …" Reka's arm tightened around her. And just for a moment, Savina let herself sag against her, closing her eyes, and just for a moment, she didn't let herself think about what they were up against next, or how impossible the task ahead would be.

She only let herself think about how warm Reka was, and how natural Reka's calloused hand felt, cupping Savina's skin, and how much easier it was to stay on her feet with Reka holding her up.

12

Alba

The yibo advisory hall had been busy for as long as Alba had been here, a chaotic bustle of people, advisors and aides alike, hurrying up and down the bright, sunlit hallways, focused on whatever business they were about. But now the hallways were filled with a different type of preoccupation, a sort of existential dread that Alba could feel in the marrow of her bones, and the faces of the people she passed as she made her careful way down the hallway, past the plants that climbed the walls and hung down from the ceilings, were grim and terrified.

"Alba." Alba turned to see Karri waiting for her in the corridor outside her office. The yibo woman opened a door in the wall as Alba made her way over.

"Alba," Karri said again once they were both inside, and the opening shut behind them. "I received your message. I must say, I have my doubts as to the wisdom of your proposal." The tip of her tail twitched, and Alba could see the lines of concern in her face. "You truly want to gamble everything on the ability of these friends of yours to hold their own against Kachik and his Nativists?"

Alba sighed. "I understand this is not ideal. But you saw what they did to the Nativist forces at the human settlement. I truly believe they stand a chance. And that is more than can be said for us if we can't convince the Advisory Body and the Synod that humans are worth protecting."

Karri's expression was sharp. "If you can pull this off, I think it will make a significant difference in the attitude of the advisors towards humans," she said. "However—" she tipped her head to one side in an uneasy gesture. "If I propose this, and your friends fail …"

Alba gave a brusque nod. "I am aware of the risks," she said. "Unfortunately, I do not see an abundance of feasible alternatives."

Karri tipped her head to the side again. "As you say. I will, at your request, present this to the advisory body. But I must warn you, Alba—I am not convinced of the wisdom of this course."

Alba sighed. "If I had a better option, believe me, I would have used it before this."

Karri studied her for a long moment. "Then I suppose we'd best hope that your trust in these friends of yours is justified."

The shock from the assembled advisors at Karri's proposal was no more nor less than what Alba had been expecting. It was, objectively, an absurd idea—that a motley group of human civilians could succeed in holding off a full attack by the Nativist army.

Alba did her best to allow her posture to convey a confidence that she in no way felt.

"And your human friend believes that her compatriots will succeed?" There was no attempt to disguise the disdain in Tika's words. Alba watched him from the corner of her eye.

Ever since she'd gone behind his back in order to save the human survivors of the diplomatic ship—something he had viewed as a betrayal of the highest order—he'd been looking for any opportunity to undermine her reputation in the Advisory Body. She'd hoped that even if he never actually forgave her, at least he'd become caught up enough in other affairs that he wouldn't have the time to focus his hostility on her.

That hope, however, appeared to have been in vain.

"She informs me she is entirely confident."

It was, Alba had to admit, impressive how calmly Karri was able to speak the lie. Alba wasn't sure, even with all her experience in politics, that she would have been able to do as well.

Still, as much as Karri seemed to genuinely sympathize with humans, she wouldn't feel the effects of failure in the same urgent way that Alba certainly would.

"And if the humans show they can help us in the war, what then?" one of the advisors asked at last. "What are they asking in return?"

Karri tipped her head to Alba, who drew in a deep breath. "Honoured advisors," she began. "We are not asking for more than what you have been willing to do in the past—that you inform Kachik that you will not agree to bargain the lives of sapient creatures in order to gain his favour, and that you provide the human settlements with the same level of protection as you do the yibo. We understand your concern at Kachik's threats. Therefore, my friends wish to demonstrate that we can assuage any potential disadvantage of this course of action by the knowledge and skills we can contribute to the war effort—indeed, that assisting the humans within your borders is not simply fulfilling a moral obligation, but gaining you a practical advantage."

"Very good," said another advisor, "but as you recall, Kachik has made us an offer that would put us strategically in a much stronger position against the raiders than we are currently. And any moral obligation we may owe to human settlements must be balanced against the obligations we owe to our own people."

"That is precisely the point," said Alba. "Kachik seems to be under the impression that without his assistance, you will be helpless in the face of the raiders. I wish to demonstrate that this is not your only option. As you have no doubt heard, my friends have already shown that Kachik is not as strong as he wants you to believe."

There was more quiet murmuring through the advisory chamber. At last, the Master of Readings said, "Advisor Karri. Please read your proposal in its entirety so that we may discuss it and present it for a vote."

Karri glanced at Alba, her expression giving Alba a last chance to back down. The proposal as written staked the fate of the humans on the success of a plan that was far from certain, and they both knew it.

Alba gave a small nod, trying to appear more confident than she felt. If she was the only one nervous about the fate of the system being placed on the shoulders of an unwilling assassin and an unremarkable cargo ship captain, at the very least she wasn't going to show that unease in front of the yibo.

Karri stood and read out the proposal.

Alba tried to keep her face steady as the advisors debated and the votes were cast.

If it didn't pass, at least she could go back to the others and tell them they'd need to think of another plan. But she knew well enough there was very little downside to the proposal for the yibos. If the humans won, then the yibos had a new weapon against the raiders, and they'd simply have to reopen negotiations with Kachik on different terms. If the humans lost—well, then there was no moral argument against abandoning them to their fate. After all, the humans themselves had agreed to it.

"The vote has passed in favour of Advisor Karri's proposal," the Master of Readings said at last. "Come forward with your discussion of implementation."

By the end of the day, the nagging headache at the back of Alba's skull had transformed into a pounding migraine. She forced herself through the motions of explaining to the others waiting back at the refugee compound what had happened, and then through the wavelink call to Savina and Joska, explaining the circumstance and adding any additional suggestions that the human strategists had come up with over the last few hours.

She was used to working through physical discomforts, but she caught the looks Yosip and Feliu were casting in her direction— either she had become less skillful at disguising her discomfort, or both of them knew her intimately enough to be able to see through the façade.

She wasn't completely certain which of the two options made her more uncomfortable.

It couldn't have been more than a couple of hours after she'd finally stumbled to her cot and fallen into an exhausted sleep that she was dragged back into wakefulness. It took her a few groggy moments to realize the sound was a call coming through her wavelink, and another moment to gather her wits enough to answer.

"Yes?" she croaked at last.

"Alba, I'm sorry to disturb you, but—I have news." There was something about the grim tone in Jair's voice that made Alba come suddenly wide awake, her stomach tight with dread.

"Yes?" She tried to keep her voice steady. "What is it?"

"Are your friends already on their way to the settlement?"

"Yes." She cleared her throat and tried to push down the irrational panic. "You know that as well as I. What's happened?"

The pause on the other end of the line went on for so long that, for a moment, Alba wasn't sure if he'd answer at all.

"There's been a change in the information we're working with," he said at last. "It seems that Kachik has pulled his forces back."

Alba closed her eyes in a sudden, sick relief that was shocking, even to her.

Yes, this disrupted their plans. But Savina and Reka and Joska and Ines ... she wouldn't be responsible for their deaths, if anything went wrong.

"I understand that isn't what we've planned," she began, "but surely—"

Jair cut her off. "You don't understand. They pulled back, because it turns out the raiders have chosen the settlement as a target instead. Even Kachik doesn't want to face that."

For a long, long moment, neither of them spoke. At last, Alba said quietly, "I'll tell them. I'll recommend they pull out."

"If they pull out, Alba—we made a commitment. We staked the humans' lives on this."

"I know!" she snapped. "But the circumstances have changed!"

Jair blew out a long breath. "I understand that. But Tika is looking for an excuse, you know that. These are your friends, you don't want them hurt. But we're talking about every damn human in this system!" She'd never heard his tone so sharp, but she could hear the despair under the anger.

"It's not because they're my friends," she said, although she wasn't certain, anymore, if that was true. "The Holy Mystery knows

I've sacrificed my friends to politics in the past." She couldn't keep the bitterness from her voice. "But this is hopeless. They can't win against the raiders. And if they lose, we've lost our gamble anyway."

Jair was silent, but she could picture his expression.

"I'll ask them," she said at last. "I'll ask them, and if they're willing, I'll speak with everyone here to come up with a plan. But our chances of success …"

"I know." Jair's voice was heavy. "But it's a chance, at least." He paused. "Thank you, Alba." There was a thickness to his tone that could have been weariness, or could have been despair, or could have been tears. She was too tired to analyze it.

"Don't thank me. Thank our friends in the cargo ship, assuming they agree. But … I shall do my best to convince them to help."

The line went dead, finally, and Alba closed her eyes and swore under her breath.

No wonder she'd always tried to keep the personal and the political separate. Because she no longer had any confidence in her own impartiality in the face of danger to people she'd grudgingly come to care for.

And yet, she'd have to ask them to sacrifice themselves regardless.

13

The village Alba had sent them to was a small fishing village, perched precariously on the edge of a massive, foreboding body of water.

Savina scowled down at it from the loading ramp of the *Dolphin*.

The village must have been warned about what was coming, because it currently looked like an ant's nest that had been stepped on—people, yibo and human both, running around in panic, doing … well, whatever you could do, with the threat of a raider attack on the horizon.

The thought of the raiders sent a fresh spike of ice down Savina's spine.

She still wasn't sure why she'd agreed to do this.

No, she knew. Because when Alba had mentioned the raiders, she'd seen the horror on every face in their small group. She'd seen the way they'd turned to look at her, the blind confidence on Nicolau's face, the glimmer of desperate hope in Joska's.

She wasn't who they thought she was. She wasn't some hero, like

Reka. But somehow, to her absolute disgust, she couldn't seem to bring herself to disappoint them.

Not even for the raiders, even though they scared her so badly she could hardly breathe when she thought of them.

She'd only been close to the creatures a few times. But each time, she'd felt, gut-deep, how fragile her survival really was. They could kill her, and not even think about it. Track her, like prey, for food, or for the simple enjoyment of killing. And when they were done with her, there'd be nothing left but bone-shards.

"The yibos have evacuated everyone they could on short notice." Joska's voice at Savina's shoulder was grim. "And of course, that didn't include the humans. The yibos don't have any additional ships in the area, and even if they did, there's not a chance they'll get here before the raiders do."

Savina nodded, clenching her teeth to keep from shivering.

She didn't care about any of the damn humans in this system. But even so, the thought of them watching as their yibo neighbours were evacuated, and they were left to the mercy of the raiders, made bile rise in her throat.

"How much time do we have?" she asked, making her voice sharp to disguise any emotion that might try to creep in.

"I've been in contact with Feliu," said Reka, coming up beside them. "He says the trackers indicate we have maybe … five standard hours."

Savina closed her eyes, trying to push back the sick in her stomach.

It wasn't enough time.

But then, there would never be enough time to prepare for a raider attack. The entire yibo civilization had been built around fear of the raiders. And even then, from everything Savina had seen since she arrived in the system, they were far from confident in their ability to defend themselves.

"Well, I guess we don't have time to stand around talking, then, do we?" she snapped.

Joska gave her a small smile that told her the woman hadn't been fooled in the slightest, and nodded. "You're right. We should get down there."

They disembarked onto sharp, black volcanic rock and made their way towards the village, the pounding of the ocean waves against the high cliffs a dull, monotonous background noise, the taste of salt and the scent of fish hanging heavy in the air.

The village majordomo was waiting for them at the entrance to the force field. Rafel stood next to the man, leaning against the wall to a building and rubbing absently at the place where his prosthetic joined to the stump of his leg.

"I have people bringing in the yibo military weapons you brought in with you under Rafel's direction," the man said as they approached. "But it's going to take time to get them into place and powered up."

Savina glanced at Reka, and took a deep breath. Then she turned back to the majordomo with her brightest smile. "Of course. We've taken that into consideration." She paused again, and she wasn't completely sure if she was hoping to talk herself into, or out of, what she was about to say next.

It didn't matter, though—it was far, far too late for second thoughts at this point.

"Joska and Rafel are going to work with you to get the ground forces set up. Beni will work on the technical aspects—we have yibo military tech, and Joska's ship has Joias weaponry with a basic destabilization design that Beni will use as a template, as well as the yibo military weapons we installed after the last battle. Nicolau and Ines will work with Joska and Rafel, and you will listen to them like you'd listen to the damn Mystery itself, or I will personally put a knife through your spinal cord. Do you understand me?"

The majordomo's face had gone from a ruddy pink to a sickly white, but he nodded.

"Savina," Reka murmured, although she sounded more amused than disapproving.

"And in the meantime," said Savina, forcing the words out in the same pleasant tone, "in the meantime, Reka and I will keep the raiders occupied for long enough that you can set things up."

Joska turned quickly, frowning. "Savina—"

"It's our best option." Reka's voice was low and perfectly steady, as if the thought of being hunted by raiders frightened her not at all. "I've worked with the raiders before. I understand how they think, at least better than any of the rest of us here. And if the rumours are correct about Sharda being one of the two raider war captains … anyone flying under her command will be very motivated indeed to kill Savina, considering the blood-price she's put on Savina's head. Savina and I spoke with Alba's strategists, and they agreed this may be the only thing that will give you the time you need to get ready."

Joska let out a long breath. "Well, Savina, I suppose I can't complain about you being too selfless, after everything I've said." The wry humour in her voice did nothing to mask her concern. "But when I said I wished you'd start caring for someone other than yourself, I wasn't envisioning you attempting to sacrifice your life to the raiders on such a regular basis."

"Be careful what you wish for," said Savina, shooting the captain her brightest smile.

She could tell from Joska's expression that the woman wasn't fooled in the slightest, but she sighed and nodded. "I can't very well forbid you. But call in if you need help. Please." Her eyes caught Savina's before Savina could turn away, and the genuine affection and worry in the captain's weathered face was enough to make something tighten in Savina's chest.

"Yeah," she muttered. "I will."

Joska held her gaze a few moments longer, then, at last, nodded and reached out a hand, squeezing Savina's shoulder. "I'm proud of you," she whispered, her voice catching just a little. Then she turned back to the majordomo. "Alright. We'll have to work fast if we want any chance of success." She drew Rafel and the majordomo and the two or three people he'd brought with him into a small huddle just inside the force field, speaking quietly enough that Savina couldn't follow the conversation.

Savina swore softly to herself as she turned away. No wonder she'd gone her whole life trying to keep everyone at arm's length.

She'd always known loving someone could hurt. She'd had no idea that being loved could hurt even worse.

"Are you alright?" Reka's voice was soft, and damn it, this wasn't helping.

"I'm fine," she snapped. "Let's go."

The villagers had provided Savina and Reka with a transport, small and rickety, but it was better than walking.

Marginally better than walking, Savina thought uncharitably as it jerked and sputtered along above the black volcanic rocks that made up the landscape.

"The raiders hunt mostly by scent," said Reka as she steered the craft. Her tone was matter-of-fact, but there was a grimness underlying it that told Savina that she wasn't looking forward to renewing her acquaintance with the raiders either. "And they enjoy a challenge. I doubt they'll see the village as much of one, if they don't know what Joska and the others are doing. So I suggest we radio in to their ship and let them know who we are and where we are." She shot a glance at Savina in the seat beside her. Savina nodded wordlessly, and Reka turned back ahead to the trackless expanse of black rock. "I spoke with the majordomo, and he said the ground here is solid, but the rock is sharp. So any misstep on our part will leave a blood trail. But that still gives us a better chance than trying to escape in this thing." She made a disparaging gesture at the transport. "I'll call in, and then we'll land, send out our coordinates, and abandon the transport. And after that ..." She shrugged eloquently. "The hunt is on, I supposed."

Savina closed her eyes and squeezed her fists tightly to stop her hands trembling.

"This is Reka Soler, paging the raider ship." Reka's voice rang through the inside of the small craft. "Reka Soler, paging the raider ship. I have a proposition for you."

There were a few long moments, where Savina half-hoped that the silence would be their only answer.

And then a raider's voice crackled through the transport's communicator. "Reka Soler. We were on the verge of making a bargain last time we spoke, were we not? And do you still have Savina Moya with you?"

Savina let out her breath in a quick rush and leaned forward. "I'm here," she said brightly. "If you want me ... come get me. But be warned, you'll have to be a little faster than you were last time. I don't plan on waiting around."

She hit the communicator off, her breath coming short and sharp.

And then the raider's voice. "We came for the yibo fishing

village," he said. "But that's your bargain, isn't it? Come after you instead of them, and give them a chance to prepare?" He laughed, a low, amused sound that sent shivers down Savina's back. "I accept. I'd rather go after a village if it's a bit of a challenge after all—that's the one thing Captain Sharda didn't think through quite enough, how easy all this would be. So we'll hunt you down, and when we've got you, we'll eat your friends at the village, knowing that maybe some of them will have found a way to evacuate in the meantime. I think when I tell Sharda who you are, she'll find it a worthy trade."

The communicator crackled off.

Reka hit a button on the controls. "There," she said. "They have our coordinates." She turned to Savina, a sharp glint of anticipation in her eyes. "Best strap in. We may have a rough landing."

The 'rough landing' consisted of the transport bouncing along the sharp black rock, the whining screech of tortured metal almost worse than the bone-rattling series of impacts.

The ship finally ground its way to a stop, the sudden silence almost jarring. Savina's nerves were singing, every muscle in her body on edge, but even so, it took her a moment to adjust to the shock of the sudden stillness.

And then she jerked a knife out of her belt and slit the harness straps, and was at the exit hatch at the same time as Reka.

They glanced at each other, Reka still grinning that small grin, and then Reka gestured Savina out ahead of her. "Get away from the transport," she whispered, ducking back inside. Savina stepped gingerly out onto the sharp volcanic stone and took a few steps back.

There was a moment of silence.

And then the craft jumped forward. Savina gave a small scream of surprise and started towards it at a run, ignoring the pain in her ankle, as the transport lurched its way toward the long, sharp cliff that loomed out over the rough sea far below.

She'd never reach it, she'd never be on time, what the hell had possessed Reka … and then Reka's lean figure dived out of the craft as it teetered on the edge, and she rolled over her shoulder and came to her feet as the rickety transport plunged over the drop.

Savina reached her a moment later and grabbed her by the arm, jerking her around. "What the actual hell were you thinking?" she ground out between her teeth. "What the hell were you playing at? Next time you want to pull some stupid stunt like that, for the love of the Holy Mystery tell me first, damn you to the void!"

Reka stared at her blankly for a moment, almost like she was … surprised. Surprised that Savina had been worried.

"Come on," Savina hissed, shoving down her discomfort at the thought. "Let's go."

Reka's expression went businesslike once again, and she gave a short, sharp nod. Savina drew in a quick breath, fighting back her terror, and the two of them started forward across the knife-sharp rocks.

Savina's ankle was still tender, but she forced herself not to limp— at least, not while Reka was watching. But Reka stepped up next to her and offered her arm anyways. And when Savina glared at her, she sighed and said, "If you can't walk, we'll both be killed. So think of this as a favour to me, if that makes it easier to swallow."

Savina nodded grudgingly and allowed Reka to slip an arm around her waist. She leaned into Reka, ignoring the shiver Reka's touch sent through her body, and they set off at a half-jog across the flats.

They'd hardly made it half a kilometre before they caught a glimpse over their shoulders of the raider craft, flying low over the area they'd crashed their transport.

"They haven't seen us yet, or they'd be on top of us," Reka whispered, and it was only then that Savina realized how much she'd unconsciously tensed up at the sight.

She sucked in a breath and forced herself to keep going.

But when she glanced over her shoulder again, blinking to let her retinal screen enhance her vision, she could see the figures of the raiders, tiny with distance, stepping out of their ship. And she caught the moment one of them lifted their head, like a valley-wolf catching a scent.

The raider turned to beckon to the others, and then they started forward, following her and Reka's trail. Their movements were sure and unhurried, the deliberate steady lope of predators settling in for a long chase.

"Joska. We've got them following us. How long do you need?" Savina whispered into her wavelink.

"We need at least a standard hour." Joska's voice was grim. "We're still setting the tech up."

Savina blinked the wavelink off and glanced up at Reka. "An hour."

Reka grinned, that small, knife-edge grin that always sent a shiver up Savina's back. "I think we can manage that."

Savina nodded, and they stumbled on.

It couldn't have been much longer than half a standard hour before they could see the raiders behind them, without even the need for Savina to zoom in her retinal screen. She swore and picked up her pace, wincing at the pain jolting up her ankle and into her hip at every step. Reka was still supporting her almost effortlessly, her eyes scanning the rough ground ahead of them.

"Up there," Reka said, indicating a small series of ledges ahead of them with a jerk of her chin. "That's where we'll make our stand, I think."

Savina nodded, too out of breath to answer.

It served her damn well right for teaming up with Reka, she thought sourly, glancing at the woman beside her.

Reka, of course, didn't look as if she even felt the exertion, although she must still be injured from their crash and their desperate flight only days before. Then again, she'd managed to look fresh, cool, and calm days after almost dying from a gut-shot from Savina's pulse pistol, so Savina could hardly expect a simple ship crash to do any worse.

By the time they reached the place where the table of black rock thrust upwards from the barren plain, the raiders were close enough that Savina could hear the crunch of their heavy boots on the rocks.

She shivered, and forced herself not to look back.

If this didn't work, she and Reka would be nothing more than the opening course for an orgy of violence that would destroy everyone Savina loved. But on the bright side, she probably wouldn't be around to feel bad about it.

She looked up when Reka came to a halt, almost startled to see the rock ledge looming over them. Reka bent, making a step of her hands. "Step in, I'll hoist you."

Savina gritted her teeth, but stepped into Reka's cupped hands. Reka lifted her easily, and Savina's scrabbling fingers caught the rough lip of the ledge. The sharp rock cut into her flesh, even through the sleeves of her jacket she'd pulled down over her hands, but she gritted her teeth and pulled herself up. Reka swarmed up after her, and was up and surveying the plain behind them before Savina managed to push herself shakily to her feet.

"How close are they?" Savina whispered, trying to keep the irritation from her tone.

"Maybe five minutes, at the pace they're going. They'll start shooting soon, I imagine." Reka's voice was still cool and detached, but her posture exuded a dangerous excitement. "Best get down."

Swearing under her breath, Savina shrugged out of her jacket and dropped it onto the ground, then lowered herself gingerly down on top of it, pulling out a pistol. Reka crouched beside her, the small disrupter they'd taken from the *Dolphin* held casually in her palm. "You cover me," she whispered. "Do you want the rifle?" She was screwing in the assembly pieces to the disrupter as she spoke. It had taken some modification to bring the cargo-ship device up to approaching the power-level that the Joias military used for crowd control, but between Reka's skills and the help of the engineers from the diplomatic crew, they'd managed. At least, Savina hoped they had.

Reka put the device down for long enough to clip her rifle to the sighting tripod and hand it to Savina.

Savina sighted the weapon in. Her muscles were shaky, and a cold fear had taken root in the pit of her stomach, but this, at least, was something familiar.

She held her aim steady on the leader of the raider party, waiting.

She wasn't going to kill him—the very last thing they needed right now was for the raider crew to form a blood-feud against the fishing village. Their entire plan hinged on Joska and the others convincing the raiders that the settlement was more trouble than it was worth. Savina killing one of them would only make them angry, and that much less likely to leave without enacting revenge. But she didn't need to kill him to make him damn well regret his choices.

She drew in a steadying breath.

He was in range.

She breathed out gently and squeezed the trigger.

The raider staggered backwards, and for a moment Savina almost choked on the sudden horror in her throat—it had been a long-distance shot, maybe she'd miscalculated, maybe she had killed him, and doomed the village—and then he straightened, and with her vision amplified through her retinal screen, she could see the red burn-mark across his face and upper chest, brilliant ruby against the ice-white of his skin.

But he didn't look frightened in the least. He was grinning, the sort of grin that promised pain, and a thorough enjoyment in inflicting it.

He grunted a command to his followers, and they started forwards at a run, pulling down armoured visors, half-crouched to make smaller targets.

Savina sent a volley of shots into the middle of them, but with the armoured suits and the armoured visors, the best she could do was knock them back a pace or two.

She glanced over her shoulder, to where Reka was still working on the disrupter, a look of studied concentration on her face. Then Savina pulled the rifle back, adjusted the pulse settings quickly, and sighted in a few steps ahead of the leader. The black volcanic rock crumbled and split at the pulse-wave, sending the raider to the ground on hands and knees. Savina smiled grimly and swung the barrel, firing at the feet of another running raider.

It took the raiders only moments to realize what Savina was doing and adjust, and soon they were tracking her shots, springing sideways or over the crumbled ground with hardly a break in their pace.

"Dammit, Reka, I hope you're just about—" Savina began through her teeth.

And then Reka snapped, "Brace," and Savina hit her stomach,

clutching at the sharp rock around her as Reka tossed out a handful of small, heavy spheres and hit the controller.

The ground around them shook, sending the raiders tumbling to the rocks. As they scrambled to their feet, Savina pushed back up on her elbows, pulled the rifle barrel around, and started shooting, sending the raiders back into confusion.

At last the raiders managed to stumble to their feet, despite the heavy fire, and Reka hit the controller again. Again they went sprawling, and again Savina began shooting.

But this time, there were shots coming back. They hissed harmlessly over her and Reka's heads, but it was clear it wouldn't be long before the raiders would have their weapons sighted in, disrupter notwithstanding.

Reka hit the controller again, sending the raiders stumbling, and Savina aimed and fired, and fired, and fired.

The shots were getting closer now, hitting the rock around them.

She glanced over. Reka's face was grim, her knuckles white on the controller.

"Joska, how much longer?" Savina hissed through her wavelink.

"We've got the tech working." Joska's voice was grim. "Get clear of the raiders' ship. We're going to send an energy blast."

"We're clear," she snapped.

"Good."

There were a few moments' pause.

And then there was a brilliant jag of light that burned the corners of Savina's vision.

She half-turned on instinct, just in time to see the raiders' ship turned a momentary glowing white.

The curses of the raiders as they scrambled to their feet took on a much more urgent tone, and as Savina blinked against the white scar across her vision, she could see them starting back the way they'd come, apparently deciding that the time it would take to kill her and Reka would be better spent killing whoever had dared to damage their ship.

"They're on their way," Savina hissed through her wavelink.

"Good. Hold tight. If this works, we'll come find you after they're gone and we've cleaned up. It may be a few hours." Joska's voice cut off.

Savina was left staring in the direction of the village, as if, if she looked hard enough, she'd be able to catch a glimpse of them.

She felt a hand on her arm, and she jerked around, cursing.

Reka stood there, a small smile on her face.

Savina pushed herself to her feet, swore, and almost collapsed as she tried to put weight on her injured ankle. Reka caught her, and Savina leaned against her, still swearing through her teeth.

She hadn't had the attention to spare for it earlier, but between their long march earlier and her awkward position on the rocks, she could barely put her foot on the ground.

She sucked in a few long breaths through her nose, and followed Reka's glance to the bright rim of the sun slowly disappearing behind the horizon, silhouetting the retreating group of raiders.

"There's no more we can do from here," Reka said at last. "We may as well make ourselves comfortable. The others won't be able to come for us until tomorrow morning at the earliest. There are some caves not too far distant, I saw them when we climbed up. Do you think you can make it that far?"

Savina slumped against Reka for a moment, then, with an effort of will, forced herself to straighten. "Let's go."

The trek across the few hundred metres of sharp rocks in the rapidly darkening night took what felt like an eternity. By the time they reached the mouth of the small cave, Savina was barely able to drag one foot after the other.

"This should do." Reka's voice echoed strangely in the shallow space. "The village majordomo said there are no predators large enough to worry about on the rock flats." She stooped to lay her jacket carefully out on the rocky floor, then helped Savina to sit. The floor and walls of the cave, at least, were mostly smooth, and Savina leaned back and closed her eyes, too exhausted to feel guilty for not helping Reka set camp.

Soon, the artificial fire was glowing in front of them. Reka pulled some packaged emergency rations from her pack and handed one to Savina. They ate in silence, side by side, the glow of the artificial fire a brighter reflection of the fading glow from the horizon outside. Savina shivered involuntarily at the cool breeze blowing in from the ocean, flavoured with salt, and Reka moved closer, shrugging out of her jacket and draping it over Savina's shoulders.

"What? Aren't you cold too?" Savina had meant the words to be sarcastic, but the quiet of the cave and the shiver in her voice made them come out far, far too vulnerable.

Reka smiled, just a little, without looking at her. "I'll be fine. I'm not the one who's hurt."

Savina closed her eyes and leaned her head back against the cave wall, pulling the jacket around her.

The strange electricity that always seemed to gather in the air when she was alone with Reka was building up around them, and she could feel it humming across her skin. It was quiet enough in the cave that she could hear the soft sigh of Reka's breath, the whisper of fabric against rock as she shifted position. Reka's body, pressed up against her side, was warm, and the brush of Reka's arm against hers was somehow both much too intimate, and not nearly intimate enough.

"Savina?"

She felt Reka's hands on her shoulders, and when she blinked her eyes open, Reka's face, in the flickering firelight, was so close to hers that she could see the dancing light reflected off the cave walls in her dark eyes.

She shifted, and she wasn't sure if she was trying to pull away, or move closer. Reka's eyes flicked down Savina's body in a way that seemed almost involuntary, and Savina shivered.

Reka looked away quickly and cleared her throat. "Let me see your ankle. We should wrap it, before the cold makes it worse." She shifted so she was kneeling in front of Savina, and Savina found herself leaning forward unconsciously, like she and Reka were tied with an invisible thread.

She shook herself, and forced her body to relax back against the wall.

Reka ran her hands over Savina's ankle gently, unwrapping the tattered bandage and rewrapping it with a clean one she'd taken from her pack. The dark brown of her hands stood out against Savina's skin, and Savina found herself unable to look away. Her entire body remembered, viscerally, the feeling of those hands, the countless times Reka had caught her, held her, grabbed for her—violence and mockery and tenderness and care, all twisted together in a confusing jumble of desire and hate.

Reka finished wrapping the bandage and ran her hands up Savina's calf, checking for injury. Her grip was firm, her hands warm, and Savina could feel her muscles relaxing into the touch, and a warmth gathering in the pit of her stomach.

Reka's hand cupped behind Savina's knee, and she paused, attention singing through the lines of her body. At last, she raised her head. The firelight glittering in her eyes lent them a depth that made Savina feel, suddenly and illogically, that she'd drown if she looked for one moment longer. Reka pulled in an odd little breath, as if she wasn't sure she remembered how. Their faces were close in the warm darkness, and Savina's eyes dropped to Reka's lips. She could taste the memory of the drunken kiss from weeks previous, the way Reka's mouth had softened under hers, her lips parting.

"Savina—" Reka's voice was hoarse, her pupils dilated larger than normal in the dark. Her hand slid higher up Savina's thigh, and Savina's entire body shivered in response. Reka reached up with her other hand and traced the line of Savina's face, cupping her chin. "Savina," she whispered. "Tell me to stop."

"Why?" Savina's mouth was so dry she almost couldn't make the word come out.

Reka's fingers tipped Savina's chin up as she leaned in. "Because I'm your enemy." Her eyes were dark, and the intensity in them sparked a hot surge of something in Savina's blood that could have been desire, or could have been fear. "Because I tried to kill you. Because you hate me." Her voice was thick with a pain that Savina had never heard there before, and her next words were whispered almost into Savina's lips "Because if you tell me to stop, Savina—I will."

Savina felt that same nakedness, the same open, shivering vulnerability she felt every time she met Reka's gaze like this, but this time some reckless, self-destructive, stupid part of her thrilled to it. Reka's touch thrummed through her body, a bow caressing the strings of an instrument.

"I know," Savina whispered. "That's why I won't."

Something in Reka's expression shattered like shards of glass. She closed her eyes. "Mystery forgive me—" Her words were choked and desperate and aching with desire.

And then she leaned forward, closing the last millimetres between them, and the touch of her lips against Savina's was like a spark on dry tinder.

Savina gasped into the kiss, breathless, desperate, her entire body thrilling to the touch, and Reka leaned in closer, pulling Savina against her with one hand, her other hand following up the lines of Savina's body. Savina's breath caught, her body humming with desire, and she tangled her hand in Reka's tattered uniform and pulled her closer, greedy and wanting.

There was a part of her, still, that knew that this was dangerous, that she could never trust Reka, not now, not ever … but she didn't care. Even if everything fell apart tomorrow, this one desperate, tender moment would be caught in her memory like a fly in amber, and it would be worth whatever it cost.

Savina slept that night curled into Reka's arms on the rough stone of the cave floor. Her body felt loose and wrung out and glowing, and even the pain from her twisted ankle had dimmed. Reka's body pressed against hers made a wall, blocking out the rest of the world, her soft, steady breathing lulling Savina into a sleep more peaceful than any she'd experienced in a very long time.

She couldn't remember the last time she'd felt like this. Protected. Cherished. Safe.

She woke to a soft buzzing in the distance, and jerked her head up, only then registering the weight of Reka's arm across her stomach, the warmth of Reka's body pressed up against her back. It must be almost morning—through the cave entrance she could see a hint of grey on the horizon, the first traces of light creeping across the black of the landscape.

Reka leaned in, brushing the tangled hair off Savina's forehead, and kissed her gently. "Shhhh. It's alright, it's friends. Joska called me this morning on the wavelink."

Savina relaxed back into the circle of Reka's arms. A smile had spread itself across her face, and there was an effervescent lightness inside her that left her feeling giddy and almost drunk, Reka's touch an intoxicant she couldn't get enough of and couldn't regret.

Reka smiled down at her, and there was a softness to her expression that Savina had never seen there before. "How are you feeling?"

Savina tried to scowl, but she couldn't seem to wipe the smile off her face. "I'm fine. I've been hurt worse before."

"That doesn't make it better." Reka's face tightened into a frown, and the sight made delicate birds flutter in Savina's chest. "You stay here and rest, I'll pack up the camp." Reka got lightly to her feet, tucking the blanket around Savina, then leaned down and kissed her again before turning to her work. The casual intimacy of the gesture took Savina's breath away, almost as much as the hot, heady desire of the night before. She pushed herself gingerly up into a sitting position and leaned back against the cave wall and watched Reka's swift, sure movements as she broke camp.

She was still smiling. She looked like a complete idiot, and she knew it, and she probably was objectively being a complete idiot— but she couldn't seem to help it.

Reka had their meagre camp packed away by the time the ship put down outside the cave entrance, and she helped Savina to her feet as Joska stepped cautiously inside.

The captain's grim expression relaxed as she saw them, her gaze lingering on Savina's smile and the protective way Reka held her. She raised an eyebrow, a small, amused twitch at the corners of her lips. "I'm glad the two of you made out alright while you were waiting," she said, her tone impressively deadpan.

Savina did manage a scowl this time, but it didn't last.

Joska's smile faded quickly as well. "With the combination of the Joias System tech from the *Dolphin* and the amplification from the yibo tech, we were able to chase the raiders off," she said quietly. "No lives lost."

Reka's arm tightened around Savina's waist instinctively, and Savina felt herself droop with relief.

Joska shook her head. "It's a victory, certainly. But I'm afraid the rest of my news isn't as good." She paused, and there was something in her face, as if she was trying to figure out how to say what she needed to say, that made a sharp shard of ice form in Savina's chest.

"What—" she began. "Is Nicolau …"

Joska managed a small, grim smile. "Nicolau and Beni are fine. But … while we were busy here, it seems the raiders attacked somewhere else as well. A yibo village, three times the size of this one. I didn't see the vids, but I … heard rumours." The tone in her voice made Savina suddenly certain that she did not want to see the vids.

"I'm sorry," said Reka at last. "But I'm not sure how that impacts us."

Joska glanced over at her. "It appears that Kachik learned somehow that we'd be defending the village, and leaked our location to the raiders when he pulled his forces back. And then …" she paused. "And then he leaked word that the yibos' attention would be focused here, and that there were other nearby settlements that would be completely unguarded. He apparently wants to show the Synod that humans really aren't valuable enough to be worth saving."

There was a moment of silence as Savina and Reka took in the implications of the news.

"He …" Savina stopped, closing her eyes.

The pain from her ankle, the strain and worry of the last few days, running from Kachik's ships, fighting Kachik's soldiers, and then this, only to find out it had been nothing but a distraction, coalesced in her chest into a hard, white-hot surge of rage.

"Savina?" There was concern in Reka's voice.

She took a deep breath, and when she was sure she'd be able to talk, she opened her eyes and smiled up at Joska.

There must have been something in her face, because Joska's expression went suddenly wary. "Savina …"

She smiled wider. "I guess we're not quite done yet, then."

Joska frowned.

Savina blinked at her innocently. "You can do whatever you'd like, of course. But I will be damned to the Void before I let Kachik think he can get away with that."

"What are you thinking, Savina?" There was still that note of concern in Reka's tone.

Savina turned to her, and this time she let a hint of steel into her voice. "We're going to take that bastard down. Forget running and hiding and waiting for him to decide who to pick off next—we're going to make him sorry he ever thought about starting a fight with humans."

14

"Aran?" Krevai was standing in the doorway. His face was creased in concern, and there were weary lines under his eyes, but he managed a quick smile. "I just came to see if you've made any progress." His voice was rough, as if he hadn't slept well in a while. "We just found out that Morthiri's crew was contaminated, and we had to quarantine them all separately. The survivors, that is."

Aran frowned. "The—"

Krevai gave a humourless laugh. "Unfortunately, we didn't realize until half their crew was dead." He paused. "Your Istvay will be back soon, Sharda's almost done talking with them. But I wanted to come check on you, make sure that nothing else had happened since—" he waved his hand vaguely.

Aran tried to smile. "I'm fine, I promise."

Krevai nodded. "Well, I'm glad to hear it." There was a forced jovial tone to his voice. "In that case, I'll leave you to your science. But—if you do find something—"

Aran nodded. "I'll let you know the moment we have a solution."

Krevai nodded and stepped out the door, and Aran watched after him, a spark of concern in his chest.

He'd known Krevai for long enough to know that it took a lot to worry the raider captain. But something about this threat to his crew, and to all the crews under his command, seemed to have sobered even the generally cheerful raider.

Aran's mind flashed back for a moment to the horrifying sensation of something else in his mind, something foreign controlling his muscles, his speech, his expressions.

He couldn't blame Krevai, honestly. If Dessi was right, the only reason Aran had gotten away so easily was the fact that the creature was unaccustomed to human physiology, so its grip on him hadn't been as strong.

He shivered.

He could have hurt Istvay. He could have killed Istvay, and Krevai, and Dessi, and been aware of what he was doing the whole time, and completely unable to stop it.

He closed his eyes and tried to force his pulse to steady.

He and Istvay had dealt with worse things before, and under worse conditions. Now that Istvay was back—

There was a creak from the corner where Ani had made her cupboard-den, and he glanced up to see her sidle out of her cupboard. She tiptoed diffidently over to him on the tips of her tentacles, and he smiled and held out his hand. "Hey sweetheart. How are you feeling this morning? I see you emptied out the supplies cupboard again. Are you hoarding food? You don't have to, you know—if you're hungry, you can just ask. Or are you just looking for attention?"

She made a disconsolate clicking with her beak, and his smile widened, despite everything. He held out his arm and she clambered up, resuming her usual perch on his shoulder.

"Starting to feel a bit more like yourself?" he whispered, stroking her.

Her discontented clicking soon smoothed into a soft, chirruping purr, and he drew in a deep breath.

He had Istvay, and Ani was getting over whatever fit of temper his and Istvay's new relationship status had put her in, and everything was going to work out, somehow.

He scowled down at Istvay's notations, pulling out his own palmscreen to check them, and slid into the chair they'd vacated.

He wasn't actually sure when Istvay returned—he was too caught up in the research, until they cleared their throat and he looked up to see them standing over his shoulder.

"Pishti," he said, with a rueful grin. "Sorry, I didn't hear you."

Istvay was watching him fondly. "I didn't actually expect you to." They slid into the chair beside him and glanced at the table. "What are you working on?"

Aran gestured to the line of equations on the palmscreen in front of him. "We're close," he said. "Based on our scanner readouts, an infection forces some change in bioelectric signatures. I think Ani could sense it—she didn't come out of her cupboard at all while that thing was in my head. But even if she can sense something, we can't exactly have her just wandering around hissing at people, because she hisses at anyone if she doesn't like them, and besides, I think half the raiders are more afraid of Ani than they are of the charaks."

Istvay chuckled. "I know I'll never get you to believe me, but some people would say their fears are entirely justified."

Aran turned to scowl at them, and they laughed and held up their hand placatingly. "Listen, Aran, I've spent the last three years of my life defending your murder-pet's honour to all and sundry. I'm on your side. I'm just saying that their fears aren't completely irrational." They dropped their gaze. "And—" they said, their voice a little embarrassed, "I may have brought her back a treat. To make up for forcing her best friend to fall madly in love with me."

At the word "treat," Ani perked up, and at last, with a mixture of eagerness and suspicion, she made her delicate way off Aran's shoulders and onto Istvay's. She took the treat from their hand, still making small, suspicious growls, then scuttled back to the shelter of Aran's shoulder to devour it. Istvay gave a long-suffering sigh and reached up to pet her, and this time she deigned to let them.

Aran smiled, watching the scene, and Istvay turned to him with a lopsided grin. "See? Even if Ani and I couldn't stand each other, I would do literally anything to see you smile like that." Their eyes were soft, and Aran had to clear his throat.

Istvay pulled up a chair across from Aran and straddled it, and Aran glanced back down at the lines of calculations. "So I was thinking—if we were able to measure the electrical impulses, that seems to be one of the few ways you can detect when a person has been taken over…"

Istvay frowned, scooting their chair closer. "You're right." Their voice held the same interest Aran was feeling. "I wonder—"

The two of them leaned forward over the table, and Ani leaned forward as well, doing an excellent job of feigning interest.

It must have been hours later, and Aran's eyes were sandy with exhaustion, when Istvay grabbed his wrist. "Wait a minute. I think if we can just … " Their voice was tense with excitement as they leaned in, correcting a number in Aran's equation. "There! If we're able to set each person's baseline bioelectric signature into the bracelet, and force it to recalibrate after the infection—it should, technically, keep the charak from being able to take over while the bracelet's on and powered up. It's at least a temporary solution, while we work on figuring out how to cure an infection completely."

Aran grinned, his shoulders dropping in relief. He hadn't realized how tight they'd been until just now. "It's a hell of a lot closer to a solution than anything else we've found so far," he said, leaning over on impulse to kiss Istvay's temple.

Istvay smiled, despite the weariness in their eyes. "You have no damn idea what you do to me, do you?" They kissed him back, then sighed. "Oof. And I think that's enough for me for today. Let's calibrate the test bracelet for you, then I'm going to bed."

Aran held out his wrist as Istvay measured his bioelectrical signature and set it into the thin metal bracelet, and the gentle hum of it shuddered up his arm.

"There. You can stop worrying about accidentally killing both of us in our sleep now." Istvay was smiling, but their face was drawn with exhaustion, and they looked almost dead on their feet.

Aran jumped to his feet and helped them up. "You go to bed, Pishti, you're exhausted. I'll be there in a bit. Krevai will want to know what we've found."

Istvay nodded, holding onto the edge of the table. Aran slipped an arm around their waist to support them, and they gave him a brief, weary smile, but didn't try to make any excuse for their weakness. Despite the worry tightening his stomach, Aran was glad that at least he wasn't going to have to argue them into getting some rest. "It's been a long day," he said instead. "Lean on me, let's get you to bed."

Istvay had to stop and rest twice, leaning heavily on Aran, even in the short distance across the room. When they finally dropped onto the cot, they couldn't hold back a small gasp of relief.

Aran tried to keep the worry out of his face.

He should have been paying more attention. He couldn't afford to let Istvay get too tired, he should have been watching them more closely.

"'Night, Pishti," he whispered, leaning over to kiss them.

They barely managed a mumbled reply before they were asleep.

Aran stood looking down at them for a few moments, fighting the tight panic in his chest, then stepped quietly out, closing the door behind him.

Ani deigned to accompany him this time, and she perched on his shoulder, one tentacle winding around his arm, as he walked down the deserted corridors of the raider ship. The silence was almost unsettling. He'd grown to expect the loud, rowdy shouts of the crew, cut off with comical abruptness as they caught sight of him—a display that was almost as irritating as it was endearing. But these days, all the crew were keeping close to their quarters if they weren't on active duty. No one said it, but the fact was, if you were infected, the only way that you might keep from killing your friends was to be somewhere easily contained.

He heard Krevai's voice from inside the cockpit as he reached it. He paused, bracing himself for the inevitable booming greeting, then pushed the door open and stepped through.

Krevai glanced up and smiled at him. "Ah, our human! Glad to know that you're not dead yet!" There was a strain under his expression, though, that belied his attempt at cheerfulness.

Aran crossed the cockpit to stand beside the raider. "Captain. I think Istvay and I found a solution—or at least, not a solution, but something that should buy us time until we figure out something more permanent."

Krevai's expression went sharp with sudden interest.

Aran managed a small grin. "It's a temporary fix, at least. Which means—"

Krevai looked puzzled, then his face cleared. "Of course. Your Istvay." He grinned. "Don't worry, we'll get your Istvay their medical treatment the moment we've finished with these yibos. And once you have a permanent solution for the charaks, it will make things that much quicker."

Aran frowned. "When you've—"

Krevai chuckled. "As I said, I have every intention of following through on my promise. Sharda has assured me she will as well—you may not know to look at her, but she's very fond of your Istvay."

"Listen," said Aran through his teeth, his heart was beating faster now. "Istvay doesn't have much time. It's not going to do any good to get them medical treatment in a month or two!"

Krevai raised his eyebrows. "Who said anything about a month or two? All we need to do is give these yibos enough of a defeat, let the crews hunt a bit, and they'll do whatever we tell them." He chuckled. "Honestly, I think our biggest obstacle might come from your little human friends. Word is, a handful of humans from your system managed to fight one of our raider crews off a yibo and human settlement. You always manage to surprise me."

Aran stared, feeling suddenly sick to his stomach. "A human settlement?" he repeated.

Krevai laughed. "They might not be that strategic to the yibo, but I've told you how much we raiders love human flash. And if nothing else, you and your Istvay have convinced us that you're worthy foes, not mindless livestock like we used to think. I even hear rumours that there are humans from your system helping the yibos with their war strategy! Maybe one day, they'll speak of this war not as our war against the yibos, but as our war against their human protectors." He grinned at his own joke. "But at any rate, it's not all bad—while your human friends were occupied with a fishing village, I sent a raider crew to another yibo settlement. Take a look at this."

The holoscreen over the map table flickered to life.

Aran stared at it, transfixed by horror, as the pictures flickered across the scene. For a moment, he thought he might vomit.

"Aran?" Krevai's voice seem to come from far away.

"You … you can't—" He could hardly recognize his own voice.

Krevai chuckled. "Aran. These are just yibos. They tried to kill you all, didn't they? I can't imagine you have any friends there. And a few more attacks like this one, and they'll be begging to surrender to us." He grinned. "We won't accept, of course, until we have enough food stores to last all the crews for a while. Yibos don't taste as good as humans, but they'll do, and there are enough humans in the system that I'm sure we'll get enough of them to go around. Once you give us a solution to the charaks and we can start attacking the bigger cities, it'll be a matter of days, at most."

Aran was still staring. There was a cold numbness in his chest that even Ani's soft, concerned chirrups didn't seem able to penetrate.

He'd spent enough time in nature to be intimately aware of how predators hunted. But this wasn't just hunting. This was war. And he'd seen it on the raiders' faces, as they ripped open the bodies of the terrified, fleeing yibo in the settlement—a sort of vicious, hungry triumph.

This was how Krevai was planning to save Istvay. This was what Aran and Istvay's research would be used for.

"Aran? Are you alright?"

"I'm—I'm a bit tired, I think," Aran managed.

He stumbled out of the cockpit and paused for a few moments outside, leaning against the corridor wall. He couldn't let himself think too hard about what he'd seen, because he honestly was going to throw up. At last, he made his slow way back to his cabin.

When Aran dropped down onto the cot, Istvay stirred. "What did Krevai say?" they mumbled sleepily.

They must have sensed Aran's mood, because they blinked and rolled up on one elbow. "Aran? What's wrong?"

Aran ran his hand down his face. "We can't do this."

Istvay frowned, and Aran shook his head. "Pishti, he's killing people. Humans, yibos—they attacked a human fishing village, and our friends managed to fight them off somehow, but in the meantime the raiders wiped out another entire yibo settlement. Krevai and Sharda are planning to use our charak solution to win the war. You traveled with Sharda. You know what that means— how many people they'll kill."

Istvay was watching him, sympathy in their eyes. "I thought you said you didn't want to get involved in politics," they said at last.

"I don't!" Aran snapped. "I've never wanted to bloody be involved in politics, I just wanted them to leave me alone! But they're not going to bloody leave me alone, are they?" He saw the small, sad smile on Istvay's face, and sighed. "You knew this all along."

Istvay shook their head ruefully. "Here's the thing, Aran—you tell me, all the time, that you don't understand why people won't leave you alone—reporters, politicians, other scientists. It's because you're bloody brilliant. You're brilliant, and you're kind, and you're much, much too compassionate and moral for most of the people who do involve themselves in politics to understand. They can't conceive of someone genuinely caring about things like you do. So they find a way to justify using you. They want what you have—your expertise, and your knowledge, your fearlessness in the face of a whole bunch of things that I kind of wish you were a little more afraid of—and they don't want to pay a fair price.

"And you don't want to hurt anyone else like they've hurt you, so you let them do it. You let them walk all over you, take what you can give them and treat you like garbage in return. You let them, because you think that's all you're worth, because that's how they've made you feel your whole life. You feel like you owe them for the smallest kindness or respect, and that's exactly what they want you to think." They reached up, running their hand down the side of Aran's face. "They don't deserve your help half the time, but I've known you for long enough to know you won't stop giving it to them if they need it. So I'm not saying you should. I'm just saying that you have every damn right to insist that at the very least, you do it on your terms instead of theirs."

Aran stared at Istvay for a long moment. But there was no hint of joking in their expression. And this wasn't something they would joke about, anyways.

Istvay chuckled without humour. "See? You still don't believe me."

Aran shook his head and blew out a breath. "I don't. Krevai is my friend, and I do owe him. I owe him your damn life, and that's more important to me than anything else in the entire system. I don't want to see the raiders turn on each other because of this charak infestation. But I can't … I can't let people be slaughtered like that. I can't."

"So? What do we do?" asked Istvay.

Aran tried to smile back at them. "I … I guess you're right. I guess we figure out how to talk Krevai and Sharda out of their damn war."

Istvay's smile in return was a little more genuine. "Well. So much for staying out of politics."

Aran sighed. "So much for staying out of politics."

15

Alba

Karri's small office was crowded far beyond its capacity. It had been meant to hold a few yibo at most. Now Alba, Yosip, Feliu, Jair, and a handful of others were packed into the tiny space, peering over each other's shoulders in an attempt to see the holodisplay on the politician's desk.

Alba had been given a seat in the front—it had been billed as an act of courtesy, and likely was, but she couldn't help but realize that it had also been a pointed nod to her age and fragility.

She sighed, and accepted the courtesy regardless. As nervous as she was, she wasn't entirely sure her legs would have held her up anyway.

"How can it possibly take this long to hear back with the news?" Feliu muttered, voicing Alba's own feelings.

The logical part of her mind, of course, knew that even if everything went perfectly, it would take some time for the tiny, embattled settlement to reach a point where it had the leisure to call out with news of their victory. The illogical, impatient side of her brain, the part that understood how desperately important this was to every living human in the system, was screaming with impatience.

And then, at last, the screen flickered with an incoming transmission.

Alba held her breath, unable to force herself to look. Instead, she watched Yosip's face. There was no particular reason why she chose him, rather than anyone else, except that somehow it felt more bearable.

His eyes widened as he read, and there was a moment where she thought her heart might actually stop.

And then he smiled, a giddy, relieved smile, and Feliu gave an audible gasp, and then everyone was cheering, and some of the younger members of the group were dancing around the confines of the office, dizzy with joy. Alba slumped back in her seat, relief flooding through her so strongly that she was shaky with it.

The update had been a brief one—a quick note informing them that the raiders had left, and the village was still standing. They'd have to wait for the full report to learn what the victory had cost. But for now—for now, Alba could simply sag with relief.

She felt a hand on her shoulder, and knew, without having to look, that it belonged to Yosip. "They did it," he whispered, his voice choking a little. "Alba, they did it!"

Alba nodded, blinking back tears of her own.

After a brief debate, it was decided that Alba, Jair, Feliu, and Yosip would stay to wait for the full report, while the others went back to get some sleep—it was, after all, close to the middle of the night. No one dared suggest that Alba leave, although she saw the uncertainty in a couple of faces. She would have refused if they had, though, and they were likely aware of it. Karri stayed as well, at least in part because it would have been a shocking breach of protocol for her to allow humans in her office completely unsupervised, but Alba was profoundly grateful nonetheless. She wasn't sure she could have borne waiting until the next day to hear the details.

The information trickled in slowly over the next few hours—there had been no casualties on either side, which was a good thing, considering that further antagonizing the raiders had never been part of the plan. The defensive strategy that they'd developed and Joska and the others had modified had been effective, and it proved that the raiders could be beaten by something other than overwhelming force. That, of itself, was more information than they'd had going in.

Another transmission lit up the screen, and Alba frowned. It wasn't from anyone at the village.

"Excuse me," Karri murmured, reaching forward to tap the screen. Her eyes flicked across the incoming transmission, and her expression tightened suddenly.

"Karri? Is everything alright?" Yosip's tone was still somehow gentle.

Karri silently turned the screen so they could see. The message was written in yibo, but thanks to Ines's translator, Alba could decipher it. She read it through once, then again, to be sure she hadn't misread.

Then she sank back heavily in her chair.

Yosip looked as grim as she felt. "He used Joska and Savina as a decoy to let the raiders take another settlement," he said quietly, and she could hear the horror under his words.

"At least this isn't any better for the Nativists than it is for us," said Karri at last. "If Kachik wants to force us to face the raiders on our own to teach us a lesson, he'll put himself in the same position."

Feliu shook his head slowly. "Except—he won't. He doesn't have to win the war. He only has to sit back and watch, hamper your forces when you're trying to stave off a raider attack. Eventually, the Synod will sue for peace. I very much doubt Kachik is worried about his cities getting attacked before that happens. If my understanding is correct, they are likely much farther down the raiders' list than any city the Synod would be comfortable losing." He pushed the transmission screen back across the table to Karri. "And see here? Our friend Tika has already added a comment—he intends to place the blame for this squarely on the humans. When news of the destroyed settlement is broadcast, there will be enough panic that he may well succeed. If anything more goes wrong in the war against the raiders, anything at all, it will give him the excuse he's looking for to pass a proposal and call a vote."

Karri scanned the communication once more, her expression grim. At last, she nodded, glancing up at Alba. "I suppose we both knew this was coming," she said brusquely. "You will simply have to ensure that nothing else goes too badly wrong."

Alba, Feliu, Yosip, and Jair didn't speak on the transport back. There wasn't much they could say, honestly. Karri was right—their only viable option was to ensure that nothing else happened that Tika could blame on the humans, and Alba knew well enough how unlikely that was.

Jair left them at the entrance to the refugee building, and they made their weary way past the yibo guards situated at the entrance.

"Madam Chief Justice, a moment—"

She turned at the voice. It was a nervous looking young man, from Joias by his accent. One of the junior engineers, if she remembered correctly. She searched her memory for his name.

"Yes, Samso?"

Her use of his name left him looking completely shellshocked, and she had to bite back a smile.

"Madam Chief Justice," he stammered, recovering himself with an effort. "I—I thought I should warn you. I'm in charge of the security for the refugees and I … saw someone today. Outside the refugee apartments."

Alba's thoughts weren't as quick as they should have been after the strain of the day, but when the meaning behind his words sunk in, she frowned in sudden concern. "What do you mean?"

He cleared his throat, looking even more nervous. "Someone was trying to get into our apartments, someone I didn't recognize. I asked for the name, and they gave me the name of one of the refugees, but I know her, and it wasn't her. They must have realized I was suspicious, because they backtracked and said actually, they were friends with her and were coming to say hi. I was suspicious at that point, so I told them that she was out, and I'd have to wait until she got back before I could let them in. They said that was fine, and I went in to talk with my superior officer, but when we came back, they were gone."

"You didn't recognize them," Alba repeated.

The young man shook his head. "Not at all."

"Did they have an accent?"

The young man frowned. "No?" His tone was uncertain.

Alba looked at him sharply. "You're from do Sol yourself?"

He nodded. There was a vaguely terrified look on his face, like he wasn't certain whether he'd made a mistake, but was coming quickly to the conclusion that he had. Alba sighed, and made a conscious effort to lighten her grim expression. "You did nothing wrong," she said shortly. "I'm simply considering the implications of what you told me."

From the look on his face her words had not entirely reassured him, but at least now he looked less utterly terrified. He muttered an apology under his breath, then scuttled off at Alba's nod of dismissal.

"Alba?" Feliu sounded concerned.

She managed a small smile as she turned to him. "It seems Kachik has not entirely given up on us. It appears someone from do Sol tried to gain access to the building. Someone our guard didn't recognize, and who lied about why they were there."

There was a moment of silence, as Feliu and Yosip processed this information.

Yosip shook his head. "It certainly doesn't sound good."

Feliu's lips were pinched in concern. "In light of what happened with the raiders, Madam, we'd best prepare for the worst. Kachik was willing to sacrifice an entire yibo village. He and Captain Mattin both seem willing to do anything in their power to turn the yibo against us—I doubt he'd hesitate to use Mattin's remaining soldiers to cause trouble here. And any human implicated in any disturbance, even if they're one of Mattin's, implicates us all. It's not going to be enough that we show the yibos that humans can be an asset in the war. We'll have to figure out what trouble Kachik is planning. We'll have to be on our guard."

Alba closed her eyes wearily. "You're right, of course. Please advise Jair to be on the alert the moment you're able to speak with him."

Feliu nodded, and he and Yosip turned away to their own rooms.

Alba stood where she was for a few moments. At last, she made her way through the common room and back towards her own quarters. If nothing else, she could at least change out of the clothes she'd been wearing for the previous twenty-four hours.

When she reached the door to her room, she paused, something unnamed and uneasy crawling up the back of her spine.

A few months ago, she would have shaken it off.

A few months ago, she couldn't have imagined the horrors she'd face, over and over, the people she'd watch die. The bruises on her neck, healed by time, and the bruises on her psyche that would likely never heal.

She reached down into her pocket, wrapping her fingers around the small pistol she'd taken to carrying with her. Even the feel of it made her hands want to tremble, but she refused to let them.

Sucking in a deep breath, she pushed the door open a careful crack, listening for any sound from inside.

There was none, and she pushed the door wider, glancing around quickly.

Nothing inside seemed to have been disturbed. But … somehow, that didn't make her feel any better.

She turned the light on, her heart pounding far too fast.

The window was open, but only a crack, and the fastening was still intact, the space too narrow for someone to have come in through, and there was nothing on the floor underneath.

She walked slowly over to the windowsill, forcing her feet forward. When she reached it, she braced herself, and then looked out.

It took her a moment to see it, but when she did, it was hardly a surprise.

Footsteps, clear and distinct in the mud outside her window. The depth of them suggested that whoever it was had spent some time out there, observing.

She couldn't breathe. Her heart beat in an odd, painful rhythm, every muscle in her body tensing in remembered panic.

Hands around her throat, something pressed over her face. Struggling for breath, her scrabbling fingers finally finding the cold weight of a pistol.

A shot.

Blood soaking through her thin nightdress, hot and sticky, the wet fabric clinging to her skin.

It was far too long before she managed to force her fingers to let go of the windowsill, force her legs to stumble back until she dropped, at last, onto the edge of her bed. She was breathing heavily, as if she'd been running, her muscles tight and shaky.

It shouldn't affect her like this. She'd lived through so many horrific things. But something about that moment back in Kachik's city, hands wrapped around her throat as she choked for air, the cold, heavy weight of the pistol in her hand after she'd pulled the trigger—it had done something to her that felt irreparable.

She couldn't afford this. She couldn't afford this awful, thought-stopping panic, the way her muscles froze and her body tensed and her mind lost its capacity for rationality.

But she wasn't sure how to fix it.

She forced herself to breathe, long and slow, until she felt somewhat in control of herself again.

And then she sat there, staring blankly ahead of her.

She should do—something. She should tell someone, let them know that this may have already gone farther than they'd anticipated. But she wasn't sure, at the moment, that she would be able to force her mouth to form the words.

She would, though. She would, eventually, when she could talk again. When she could think again. She would go out and tell Jair and Yosip and Feliu. And then—

And then they would do nothing. Nothing more than they were already doing. Because they were already doing everything they could. Now it was just a matter of finding out whether that was going to be enough.

16

Aran

Aran was jolted out of a sound sleep by the blare of an alarm and Istvay's muffled swearing. He tried to sit up, smacking his chin hard against Istvay's shoulder, who'd apparently been thrown on top of him by the jolting of the ship, and mumbled a half-coherent apology as he tried to disentangle himself from both Istvay and the blanket, which was wound round his legs and pinioning his arms.

By the time he'd managed to slide out of bed, Istvay was mostly disentangled as well, and sitting up. Aran glanced down at their pale, wan face, and refused to let his mind slide down the track of memories of before, when Istvay was always up before he was, their mischievous grin as they'd shake his shoulder and whisper, "You planning to stay in bed all day, sleepyhead?", because that way lay madness.

He had the cure. He just needed time. And then …

The ship rocked again, and Aran stumbled, barely catching himself on the wall.

"What the hell—" Istvay began, still sounding groggy.

Then there was a pounding on the door, and Aran grabbed for his trousers, pulling them on as he staggered across the room to answer it.

Dessi waited outside, her expression tight. "Good," she said when she saw him. "I was worried about the two of you and your Ani. No one was hurt in the disturbance?"

Aran shook his head ruefully. "We're not really all that fragile," he tried, but Dessi cut him off.

"I'm not losing my test subjects, not after everything I've been through," she snapped. "Come on, get your Ani and let's get you somewhere safer."

"What's happening?"

She sighed. "A yibo military squadron stumbled across our position. We're under attack. Krevai and Sharda are running the counter-attack."

"Alright, give me a sec," said Aran. He closed the door and glanced back at Istvay.

They'd made it to their feet, and were steadying themself against the wall in a gesture that was clearly meant to look more casual than it was. Aran crossed the room to them quickly, grabbing a spare set of clothing as he went and tossing it at them. "Get dressed, Dessi isn't going to leave us alone until we're in her lab. I'll get Ani." He waited surreptitiously until Istvay had dropped back down on the bed to dress before he turned to Ani's self-appointed nest. "Hey sweetheart," he whispered. "Let's go. I don't want you getting lonely and wandering around the ship looking for us. I don't know how the raiders will take that—they're still a little nervous around you, I think."

Istvay snorted loudly, but Aran ignored him. "Come on, girl," he coaxed. "It's alright, we're just going on a little walk." He glanced over his shoulder, and bit back a grin. "And I'll bet if you ask nicely, Pishti will find a treat for you."

At the words, one of Ani's bulbous eyes peeked out from the dark inside of the storage cupboard, followed by the tips of a couple of her tentacles.

"You're teaching her to beg," grumbled Istvay.

Aran held out his hand, and after a moment's hesitation, Ani swarmed up it to perch on his shoulder, her large eyes honing onto Istvay. Aran grinned. "Only from you. Besides, I thought we were going to try to help her get over her jealous fit."

Istvay rolled their eyes, but they were smiling reluctantly. "Fine. I'll get her a treat, although last I checked, she's been helping herself to the supply cupboard whenever she feels like it. But if she swears at me one more time …"

Aran shook his head, stroking Ani's bulbous body. "She means it affectionately. Anyways, you do the same thing. Don't they, beautiful?"

Ani nuzzled against his chin, purring, and he rubbed her head.

"I have no damn idea what you're talking about," Istvay grumbled, turning to rummage in their supplies pouch. "Here, she can have an energy bar." They held it out. "Happy?"

Ani took the offering delicately with the tip of a tentacle, and then the ship rocked again, and Aran staggered and barely caught Istvay before they hit the floor.

Dessi pounded on the door again. "Come on!"

"Coming," Aran gasped, and dragged Istvay over, pulling the door open.

"We'd better get you somewhere safe," Dessi began.

And then Landru came sprinting down the passageway towards them. "Dessi, wait!" she called. "I need the humans! Sharda said she wants to talk to her Istvay, and Krevai said best bring our Aran and his Ani along."

"Tell Krevai he's not putting my damn humans in danger again!" Dessi snapped, her voice sharp with exasperation.

Landru grinned. "He said you'd say that. He said to tell you that he'll protect them with his very life, although he doubts he could do any better than the Ani, all things considered. But Sharda's convinced that her Istvay will have some ideas, and Krevai didn't want to separate the mates any more than necessary."

Dessi sighed, glancing between Aran and Istvay. Aran knew the look on his face was probably the one that Istvay usually described as "I'd rather try to convince a damn rock wall to listen to me than you when you look like that, I'd have more chance of success," but in fairness, this time it was true. He wasn't letting Istvay go anywhere without him again, probably for the rest of both their lives.

"Fine," said Dessi at last, speaking through gritted teeth. "But tell that idiot that if either of them comes back with even one scratch—"

Landru slid her finger along one of her claws, drawing a bead of blood, and held her hand out. "He told me you could have his very life blood and eat his heart afterwards if he sends them back damaged." She turned to Aran and Istvay. "Come on, humans, I'll take you to the cockpit. Aran, Sharda has a line open with Krevai, so we won't have to take your Istvay off the ship." She chuckled. "Between you and your Ani, I doubt we could have if we'd wanted to. Come."

She turned and strode off, and Aran, with a helpless glance back at Dessi, followed, with Istvay behind him.

Aran slowed as their small group reached the cockpit door, bracing himself, and Istvay put a sympathetic hand on his shoulder. The inside of the cockpit wasn't the wild, shouting chaos he'd expected, though. The raiders inside it were talking in low whispers and gesticulating in what appeared to be at least three different dialects of sign language. Krevai glanced up as Aran stepped in, and gestured him and Istvay over with an exaggerated motion. "See?" he whispered loudly, tipping his head at the surrounding raiders with a grin. "I told them to be respectful of our humans or I'd rip their heads off. Tell me if there's anything else you need so you don't get stressed and die."

Aran sighed, something between gratitude and extreme awkwardness knotting in his stomach. "Um. Thank you," he whispered back. "I—thanks."

Istvay looked like they were biting back a grin of their own. "Where's Sharda?" they asked, also in a whisper.

Krevai jerked his chin towards a seat in front of a large screen that was, now that Aran was paying attention, broadcasting an overlarge version of the other raider captain's furious face—or maybe that was just how Sharda always looked.

Istvay, at least, didn't seem particularly alarmed. "What do you need?" they asked as they stepped up to the screen, their voice businesslike.

"Is what Krevai tells me true?" Sharda snapped, also in a whisper. "Loud noises can kill humans?"

Istvay glanced ruefully over their shoulder at Aran, then sighed and turned back to Sharda. "For purposes of this discussion, I'm going to say yes. Loud noises stress Aran out, and I don't tend to be at my most reasonable when Aran's upset, and that's probably the equivalent of a death sentence on a damn raider ship."

Sharda watched them through narrowed eyes a moment, then nodded. "Ah. So human mates aren't all that different from raider mates. This is valuable information." She turned to Krevai. "You should probably tell your scientist this. She'd be interested."

Krevai bellowed a laugh, then clapped his hands over his mouth with a guilty glance at Aran. "Sorry," he mouthed, then turned back to Sharda. "Don't you worry, our little scientist has been keeping a very close eye on these two. Why do you think I insisted that both the mates come when you asked for the Istvay?" He paused. "Besides, I want our Aran's opinion on something anyways."

Sharda nodded and turned back to Istvay. "Alright, human. You're good at making things more efficient, and I don't want to waste any more time or attack pods on these yibo ships than I have to." The screen changed from Sharda's face to an open star map, with ships' locations marked on it in glowing lights.

"Aran," Krevai hissed. From the corner of his eye, Aran saw him make an abortive move to clasp Aran's shoulder, then cut himself off. "I'd like your thoughts on this."

Reluctantly, Aran turned from where his friend was now deep in conversation with Sharda, and over to a table with a glowing starmap projected over the top of it. There were small points of light that appeared to be ships' positions, moving slowly across the map.

Krevai gestured to a bright red point in the centre. "This is our ship, and here are the yibos' positions," he whispered, gesturing to two yellow points of light perhaps a half-cycle away. "They're going to send long-range missiles, I expect, and we'll be using our pods to shoot them down." He turned to grin at Aran. "I know you don't like killing things. I don't mind killing things at all, but I don't want to send my people into a full-on fight until we have this charak infestation dealt with. So." He tipped his head at the map. "If these yibo ships were some sort of deadly animal, what would you do?"

Aran frowned at the starmap, his heart pounding.

It wasn't that he was particularly fond of the yibos—they'd

seemed just as willing to murder him and Istvay as the raiders had, although probably less likely to tear out their hearts and eat them afterwards. But after the gruesome scenes of the raider attack he'd seen on the holoscreen, he couldn't bear to let any more of them get killed if he could possibly prevent it.

He glanced up. "Can you ask Istvay to come over when they're done?" he asked. "This'll be easier if we can coordinate."

Krevai raised his eyebrows, but nodded. "I'll tell Sharda to be quick, then, and leave the two of you to come up with whatever it is you're going to come up with."

Aran scowled down at the starmap as Krevai pushed himself to his feet.

He wasn't any sort of battle strategist, but if he thought of this in terms he was familiar with, imagined the ships as animals of some sort …

It wasn't exactly the same. He could predict, with some accuracy, the behaviour of animals, if he'd been given enough time to observe them. Creatures like yibos or raiders, who were disturbingly similar to humans, baffled him. But if he thought of the ships as a colony of insects trying to protect their hive, perhaps …

"Aran. What've you got? Krevai told Sharda to butt out until we're done." Istvay grinned and dropped into the seat next to him. "Believe me, it will never not be satisfying to hear him say that. Now." They pulled their seat close to Aran's, so their arm was brushing his, and leaned in. "What are you thinking?"

Aran hardly glanced at them, now completely engrossed in the scenario in front of him. "Pishti, listen. You told Sharda to arrange the attack pods like this, didn't you?" He pointed at a small burst of the tiny blue points that signified the attack pods, formed into an arrow formation.

From the corner of his eye, he saw Istvay nod.

"What if we used them as a distraction? What if we got the ships around behind the rim of the planet while the attack pods formed a big enough mass that the missiles come after them instead? And when the missiles get close enough, they can scatter and shoot the missiles down from behind." He turned to Istvay, grinning. "Krevai said the yibo aren't going to come in close if they can help it. That should mean Krevai and Sharda can get the main ships out of range. The yibo probably won't bother trying to shoot down the smaller ships, and they know there's no real point to shooting down any ships that aren't Krevai's or Sharda's."

Istvay was grinning back at him. "And if Sharda holds her attack pods in the arrow formation and Krevai keeps to the usual four-prong formation that the raiders use—I understand why they use it normally, but in this type of circumstance it's incredibly inefficient—it won't be immediately apparent that they're both attack pod formations. The arrow formation is much more tightly packed, and it's possible we could fool the yibos' sensors into thinking the tighter formations are actually a larger ship, at least long enough to get the main ships out of the way." They pushed back their seat. "I'll go tell Sharda, you can explain to Krevai, see if he thinks it's feasible." They stood carefully, bracing themself against the chair back, and Aran tried, yet again, not to let mindless panic wash over him at every damn hint of Istvay's growing weakness.

He cleared his throat and forced his eyes away from his friend, and a moment later, Krevai was beside him. "Your Istvay says you had a brilliant idea?"

Aran managed an awkward smile, and stumbled through an explanation.

By the time he finished, Krevai was grinning broadly. "Well. I don't usually like plans that don't leave the enemy dead, but—"

There was an ear-splitting *crack*, and Aran had to grab for the edge of the table to keep from being tipped out of his seat and onto the ground as the ship shook.

"What in God's name—" Krevai growled, leaping to his feet.

And then Aran saw what the captain had seen.

One of the blue dots had fallen out of line, turning its guns on Krevai's ship.

"Captain! It's one of Skanthu's pods!" The frantic voice of one of Krevai's crew came in through the communicators. "They broke formation and started firing!"

"We can't contact them," came a shout from another line.

Krevai leaned over behind Aran, glaring down at the combat map. Aran could practically feel the captain's tension. "Try signalling them one more time," he snapped at last through the communicator. "You too, Landru. See if you can reach them."

Landru nodded, her own posture almost as tense as Krevai's.

For a few breathless moments after her call, the room was dead silent.

"Captain Krevai!" The voice was faint, but there was an odd, familiar note to it that sent a shiver up Aran's back. "Captain, don't hurt us! Please!"

Another burst of shots exploded from the ship.

"Shoot them down," said Krevai in a low voice.

"Captain! Don't shoot!" There was that same strange note under the panic in the voice over the communicator as in their first message. "Please, Krevai! We swore loyalty, and you swore to protect us!"

Something stirred again in the back of Aran's brain at the voice, sluggish and thick, and he gritted his teeth at the sudden surge of panic.

He couldn't panic, that would only make it worse …

"Do it." Krevai's voice was grim.

"Captain …" began Landru. Then she closed her eyes, as if bracing herself, and relayed the order.

A moment later, the blue light blinked out of existence.

There was utter silence in the cockpit.

"They were compromised. Charak. They wouldn't have lived anyways, and who knows how many crews they'd have taken down in the meantime?" Krevai's voice was still gruff, but Aran could hear the pain under it.

He knew, first-hand, what an oath to protect meant to Krevai.

The *thing* in the back of his brain moved again, sluggish and mindless, and then he yelped at a sharp sting on his wrist. He glanced down, rubbing the bracelet and trying to force his breathing steady.

The Holy Mystery knew he had enough practice forcing himself to be calm, after Istvay had been kidnapped.

"Aran?" Istvay had made their way over to him, and their voice in his ear was low and worried. He shot them a look that he hoped conveyed that he'd talk to them in a minute, and glanced back at Krevai.

The captain, expression grim, was striding back across the cabin to his seat. "Landru! I'll tell you the general outline of the humans' suggestion, we'd best get moving if we want to make it work." He turned over his shoulder. "Aran, you and your Istvay can go with Dessi, I'll talk to you later," he said. "But I hope you can follow through on your promise about the charaks."

Aran blew out a short sigh, and then Istvay was pulling him to his feet. "Come on," they whispered. "We're not going to be able to talk to him right now."

When they were outside the cockpit at last, Istvay turned to Aran, their face tight with worry. "What the hell was that?"

Aran closed his eyes, rubbing absently at his wrist. "I … when the infected raiders called in, I … felt it. The thing in my head. I think the bracelet is still taking care of it—at least, it shocked the hell out of me a second later—but …" he trailed off. "Anyways, maybe I should sleep in a different room or something. Just in case."

When he opened his eyes, the concern on Istvay's face hadn't left. "No. We went through the specs for that bracelet, it should work. And I'm not leaving you alone, especially not now, with that damn *thing* in your head." They shook their own head tightly. "We're going to figure this out. I'm not letting that thing have you again."

They turned and started back down the corridor to their room, one hand on the corridor wall for balance. Aran started after them, but there was a tight knot in the pit of his stomach.

His mind kept playing, over and over, the look on Krevai's face when he'd ordered the ship shot down, the way Istvay had to grab for the wall to steady themself, the sluggish thickness in the back of his brain, barely shoved back.

The faces of the human diplomatic party, Alba and Yosip and Nicolau and Ines, presumably back in the yibo city.

Damn it to hell, Krevai was right—he wasn't cut out for damn politics.

Because he honestly had no idea how to deal with any of this.

17

Alba

The holorecording that had been broadcasting across the advisory chambers flickered to a close, and the entire assembly sat in utter, sick silence.

Alba felt as sick as any of them.

She'd known, with the sort of instinctual knowledge of a prey species, that raiders could be brutal. She'd known that from the first moment she'd seen one, grinning at her and her party with their long fangs and blood-red eyes, and speaking casually of killing and eating. But even then, her mind had shrunk from envisioning carnage on this scale.

It had just been one raider ship, like in the attack that Savina and Joska had foiled, and it had happened at the same time. But this settlement had had no time to prepare. And Alba knew she would hear the screams of parents and children, the crunch of breaking bone, the sick splatter of entrails on hard ground and the crackle of burning houses in her nightmares, probably for as long as she lived. And the sight of it—

She shuddered. She could only hope that one day the sick shock would erase the sights from her memory: the blood staining the raiders' fangs, the glee on their faces as they ripped out throats and tore open stomachs like rabid lions set loose on a pen of sheep.

Even after everything she'd seen on this nightmarish trip, she was glad she hadn't eaten that morning—she wasn't certain she would have been able to hold down her food.

At last, the Master of Readings stood. Yibo expressions were still something of a mystery to Alba, but even she could read the vacant shock in the woman's eyes. "Come forward with your discussion," she said, her tone oddly distant, and then she sat heavily back in her seat.

The silence stretched for a few moments longer. At last, there was a voice from far above her. Alba craned her head back from her seat beside Karri, but the moment she heard their voice, she knew who it was.

"We knew this was going to happen," Tika's voice was grim. "The raiders declared war, and they won't stop until we find a way to stop them. And right now—" he gave a bitter hum of amusement. "Right now, we're fighting with a fraction of our resources, because we're spending them, instead, on an unnecessary internal war to defend unwanted refugees who have no political allegiance to us. I can't say if having the Nativist forces would have prevented this. But if we were able to allocate the resources as we saw fit, our chance of preventing another atrocity like this one would be much more likely."

Karri glanced at Alba and tipped her head in silent permission.

Alba stood, clearing her throat. "Permission to respond?" Ines's translator in her wavelink echoed her words in her own voice, but in passable yibo.

The Master of Reading tipped her head in acquiescence.

"I share your horror at what happened," said Alba. "But how can we blame humans when, as far as our intelligence indicates, Kachik himself passed the information to the raiders that caused this attack? If he's willing to do that, how can we say that, had we given into his demands, the yibo settlements would be safer? There is at least one other settlement that was spared this exact fate precisely because you rejected Kachik's bargain. And rather than threaten or terrorize you into accepting their terms, my human compatriots have been risking their lives to protect your settlements. How can you take advantage of their assistance while counselling to sell them out behind their backs? Surely this is not behaviour that represents you." Alba sat with as much dignity as she could. She was clenching her hands, under the sleeves of her yibo robes, to disguise their shaking.

Everything she'd said was true. But what Tika had said had undeniable truth to it as well—at the end of the day, it was unlikely she could convince these yibo that the benefits delivered by a ragged handful of refugees was more than that that could be delivered by the Nativists, with their war ships and armies. There was no solid evidence that it had been Kachik who had passed on the information, and without solid evidence, she knew exactly how easy it would be for a politician to discount what information they had. If they convinced themselves that an alliance with the Nativists would save them, it would be easy enough to ignore.

The coalition she and Karri had sweat blood to assemble was held together at least as much on conscience and altruism as it was on practical politics. It seemed Tika knew this as well as she did. And it was very difficult, with memories of screaming yibo children spattered with their parents' blood in the front of everyone's minds, to be entirely certain of the relative morality of their position.

"We have no proof it was Kachik, only rumours. As far as we

know, it will come out that it was instead the humans who passed on information to the raiders, so they could come out looking the heroes." Tika cast a venomous glance in Alba's direction. "You saw what the raiders were doing. It was a small settlement this time— perhaps four times as large as the number of the refugees we angered Kachik by saving. But who's to say that the next settlement will be that small? Even if we were at full strength, we would be hard-pressed to keep off a squadron of raider ships. And, if you recall, they have declared full out war. You'd trade that for the help of a small group of humans?"

"You've seen what that small group of humans has done in the past few days," Alba snapped, pushing herself back to her feet. "They fought off a raider attack. And if I'm correct, you are using none of your military resources to fight this battle with the Nativists. That small, unimportant group of humans is running and coordinating the defence on their own. The only thing they're asking from you is that you not betray them." Her voice was shaking with emotion.

"And how many warships do the Nativist have? How many soldiers? How many additional settlements would we be able to protect if those assets were on our side, rather than arrayed against us?" Tika's words were sharp and bitter.

Karri rose to her feet as well. "If you recall," she said, "The Nativists were the ones who refused to help us. We at all times were willing to concede to their reasonable requests. Even leaving aside who passed information to the raiders on the undefended settlement, at the very least, there were Nativist forces in the area that did nothing to stop it. Someone who is willing to sacrifice innocent lives in order to force unreasonable demands on us is not someone with whom we can afford an alliance. Kachik knew as well as any of us what the likely outcome would be if he refused to aid us in our fight against the raiders. And he calculated that watching yibo children die, watching yibo parents' throats ripped out in front of their children and grandchildren, was worth the cost if it would coerce us into agreeing to his demands, and giving him permission to murder the humans under his care and protection."

She paused a moment. "I am as unhappy as any of you with how the negotiations with the Nativists played out. But I do not think we can lay the blame for that solely on the humans, when the unreasonable party to the bargain was a yibo, and one who has openly come out in defiance of the legitimate government and the will of the yibo people."

She sat. Alba cast her a grateful glance, then looked out over the assembled yibo advisors. Again, she cursed her inability to read their expressions, but there were nervous twitchings and stirrings from various parts of the assembly hall.

"Bring forward your proposals from the discussion," the Master of Readings said at last, when the silence had stretched. Alba cast a covert glance towards Tika.

He didn't stand to offer a proposal, and she allowed herself a brief moment of relief.

He may not be the most astute politician, but the lack of proposal meant that he, at least, believed he did not yet have sufficient support.

But looking out at the assembled advisors, and at the worried grimace on Karri's face, Alba wasn't certain that, if he had put forth a proposed advisement, the human-friendly coalition would have won.

The rest of the Advisory Chamber business took less time than usual—it seemed everyone was still shellshocked enough from the horror of what they'd seen that appetite for debate was not high. Alba and Karri were back in Karri's office much earlier than usual, and Karri gestured Alba to a seat.

"I don't think I have to tell you how perilous our position is," said Karri quietly.

Alba tipped her head in weary agreement.

"One more disaster like that—" the yibo woman twitched her tail in a helpless gesture.

Alba sighed. "I know. Savina and the others are doing all they can. But—" She shook her head. "There's only six of them. And we're already expecting miracles."

Karri leaned back in her chair. "And I am afraid that it will take at least a miracle for this to hold together."

It was almost the dinner hour by the time Alba dismounted from the dirty public transport that stopped in front of the refugee compound. Feliu always fussed when she took the transport, and probably rightly so—she was as good a target for assassination as any of them, and probably better than most. But there was also no reason why public transport would be more dangerous than walking alone down the crowded streets of the yibo city, and her aching muscles were too weary, sometimes, for the walk.

She showed her yibo-issued refugee card to the yibo guards on the outside, then again to the self-appointed human guards on the inside, but there was a tension to the guards' postures that set off a twinge of unease in the back of her brain.

"What happened?" she asked one of the guards, a young woman who couldn't have been older than Ines.

The woman shook her head, facing straight ahead and not meeting Alba's eyes, but her lips were pinched tight with worry. "I think better to go inside and asked that question," she muttered out of the corner of her mouth.

Alba frowned, the unease ticking higher, but she stepped past the young woman and into the compound.

When she got to the main room, Feliu was waiting for her.

"Madam." His wrinkled face was pale, and there was an unusual strain in his posture. "Thank the Mystery that you're alright. Please follow me."

She followed him down the corridors, and Feliu pushed open the door to one of the smaller makeshift first-aid rooms and beckoned her inside.

Once inside the room, Alba stopped short.

A man in his fifties who she recognized instantly as one of the top engineers from the diplomatic ship lay on the bed. His eyes were closed, and his brown skin bore a greyish tinge, an unnatural white around his lips. The bed around him was spattered with blood, and a dark red stain seeped through the white bandages wrapped around his bare chest.

"Who did this?" Alba's voice was almost a whisper.

"We're not sure." Feliu's voice in her ear was quiet and sick.

"I think he'll pull through." The woman who'd been leaning over him glanced up and caught Alba's eye. "But it was close thing."

Alba walked slowly over to the cot.

The man's eyes fluttered open at her approach, and he made a weak attempt to sit up.

Alba made a sharp gesture. "Rest, please." She paused. "Do you know who did this?"

The man shook his head. "I didn't see them." His voice was hoarse and weak. "They were waiting in the rooms when I walked in. I tried to fight back, but—" he trailed off helplessly.

She turned to Feliu. "Have you spoken with the yibo guards?"

"We tried. The guards insisted that we were being alarmist, that it was probably some fight that had gone wrong." Feliu's face was pale, his expression grim.

"Even after—"

Feliu shook his head. "Madam. It's not that they don't have the information. It's that they have no desire to believe that there is a problem." There was a weariness to his tone.

Alba stared at him for a moment, then, slowly, nodded. "I understand. I will see what I can do, but I can't promise that my voice will have any more effect than yours will."

There was a familiar flash of outrage on Feliu's face at the mention of the lack of respect with which the yibos held Alba's former position, but it was more instinctual by now than anything.

He knew as well as she did their status in this system.

She forced back the sick fear that was trying to freeze her muscles and choke off her breath.

Later. She repeated it in her head like a mantra now. Later. One day, somewhere in the future, she would have time to drop down on her cot and sob, let the terror roll over her in waves, like it had been wanting to since back in Kachik's city.

But not now. There was too much to do, and she couldn't afford it.

She straightened and turned and made her way out the door.

Jair was waiting at the entrance to the compound. He looked like he'd come straight from work, his clothing wrinkled, his face tight with worry. "Feliu sent for me. What happened?"

Alba tipped her head back towards the room she just left. She wasn't sure she felt entirely up to explaining at the moment. "I need to go talk to the guards. Feliu will fill you in."

Her conversation with the guards was just as ineffective as she'd feared—patronizing assurances that the guards were doing all they could, insinuations that the humans were lying, or the man had been in some sort of a drunken fight and was trying to avoid consequences, suggestions that Alba should control her peoples' unruly impulses, hadn't the yibos had to save them once already from mutiny by their fellow humans?

She bit her tongue so hard that she broke through the skin trying to hold back retorts that she knew would serve no purpose. Anything she did or said at this point would simply be taken by the guards as confirmation of their opinions.

She'd known it would be ineffective, but she had to try, anyways.

And she hadn't realized that, even as accustomed as she'd become to the disrespect, how viscerally wounding it was to listen to the sneers and insinuations and badly concealed mockery in the tones of the only people standing between her fellow survivors and utter destruction.

Jair was waiting when she got back inside. "I assume you didn't have any more luck than Feliu did?" he asked when he saw her face.

She shook her head wearily. "They're determined that humans are troublemakers, or liars, or both." Her tone came out more bitter than she'd expected.

Jair snorted. "That's been our last few decades, yes." His words carried a bitterness of their own. He paused. "Alba. I wanted to talk to you alone before I mentioned this to the others. Is he certain that his attacker was human?"

Alba frowned. "I am … not sure," she said slowly. "From what he told me, he didn't catch sight of them before they attacked."

Jair nodded, biting his lip. "We know that Kachik is likely sending some of Mattin's humans after us," he said at last. "But I took the liberty of looking up the guards' roster that they've posted for the refugee compound." He hesitated. "Some of them are Tika's people," he finished at last. "I don't want to alarm you, but I think it's best to understand what we're up against. It's entirely possible that Tika, or some of the other antihuman politicians, have their own interests in sabotaging the coalition. We'll have to put more effort into figuring out Kachik's plans, and Tika's. We can't afford any more accidents."

Alba closed her eyes wearily. At last, she opened them and tried to smile. "I appreciate the warning. I'll pass it on to the others."

"It's all we can do, in a system like this," said Jair quietly. "Look out for each other, because there's no one else who will." He turned away, brushing a hand wearily across his face. "But I'm going to head home now. My wife and children are forgetting my face."

Alba managed a small smile as well. "Give them our regards, if you please," she said.

Jair turned back to her, and again, the smile on his tired face was genuine. "I will."

He stepped out the door, and Alba watched him go.

And then she turned back to the room she'd left, bracing herself for another long night.

18

Savina glanced derisively over the small group of people in front of her. Their expressions were utterly horrified.

She turned to the human woman next to her. "This isn't going to work. These people are useless. Don't you have any … prisoners, or something?"

The human woman turned to her yibo counterpart, a helpless look on her face, and murmured something in a low tone.

"Preferably violent criminals, but thieves will do in a pinch, if they're good and they don't mind a little blood," Savina added brightly.

Both the human and the yibo were now giving Savina wary glances from the corners of their eyes.

Savina gritted her teeth in irritation and turned to Ines, standing beside her. "I don't know if I am properly conveying what I need," she said in her sweetest voice. "Would you please tell them, Ines, that I want a group of the most violent, disgusting murderers, thieves, and criminals that their village or any nearby village has produced, and I want them here." She smiled and widened her eyes. "And tell them not to worry about me. Even a little Rim Mountain girl like me can take care of herself in this sort of place."

Ines hesitated, then turned and repeated Savina's words in passable yibo.

There was a short argument, in low tones, with three or four other humans and yibos pulled in. And then, at last, the yibo man tipped his head reluctantly in acknowledgement and strode off, calling out commands.

Savina watched him go with some satisfaction.

She turned to find Reka watching her. "How's the training going, Savina?" There was humour in Reka's tone, and Savina found herself smiling back like a twitterpaited idiot. She tried to force her face into a scowl, but it was singularly ineffective. "Everyone here is far too moral," she grumbled. "When I suggested pretending to be lost and asking for directions, then slitting the person's throat when they turned to help you, they were so horrified I thought they were going to pass out on the spot."

Reka's expression flickered between amusement and alarm, and landed at last on something fond and rueful. "My bloodthirsty Savina," she whispered, running a hand down Savina's back in an inconspicuous gesture. "What in the system am I going to do with you?"

"We're supposed to kill people, that's the point of all this," Savina muttered, but she was leaning into Reka's touch.

Reka sighed reluctantly and stepped away. "You're right," she said. "We're both training people to kill. And I should go do my job."

She slipped away, silent as a shadow.

Savina stared after her, a stupid, soft grin on her face.

"Savina?"

She jerked around to see Joska watching her with badly disguised amusement.

"What?" she snapped, but she still couldn't stop smiling.

"I see you and Reka are getting along better now."

Savina scowled, but from Joska's expression she knew she was still wearing a residual stupid grin.

"I just came to see how you were doing." Joska paused, her face creasing with worry. "Rafel is training some of the villagers on explosives and Joias weapon tech, and Reka seems to be pulling her people into shape with frighteningly brutal efficiency, but ..." she trailed off, shaking her head. "The information I'm getting from Alba's people says we have days at most before Kachik makes a move."

Savina bit the inside of her cheek.

Joska was right. This was an absurdly short amount of time to train a guerrilla army. But Joska was also right that they didn't have much choice.

She gave Joska a bright smile. "I've asked the yibo to bring me their most violent criminals, so that should give us a bit of a start."

Joska stared at her for a moment, then huffed out a small chuckle, shaking her head. "One thing about working with you, Savina," she said dryly, "it's never dull." She turned away. "Let me know if you need anything, and I'll do what I can."

After a frustratingly long amount to time, a nervous-looking yibo man tapped Savina on the shoulder. He led her to a small, enclosed courtyard with grim looking yibo guards on the walls, to meet what were apparently her new students.

She glanced at the faces of the motley group of yibos and humans arrayed in front of her as she stepped through the gate, the hardened, sneering cruelty in their faces, and pasted on her most innocent expression. She waved a hand lightly to the guards on the wall. "I don't think I'll need you. I'm sure we'll all get along very, very well, won't we? I think we just need to understand each other." She turned her wide-eyed gaze onto the prisoners.

A human man at the far edge of the group smiled, a slow, predatory grin. "Oh, yes," he said, his voice jovial, but with an unmistakable hint of menace to it. "The little girl is right, we don't need guards. She and the rest of us will get along just fine."

He took a small step towards Savina. On the wall, one of the guards raised their weapons.

Savina blinked up at the guards, all innocence. "Don't hurt these people! Didn't you hear him? We just need to get to know each other."

The man took another inconspicuous step closer.

Savina turned back to him, her smile blindingly bright. "I'm so glad that you want to work with me!" Her voice was breathy and sincere. "I think we'll work together so well, I'm sure you're just misunderstood. And I'm sure you all know what will happen if this doesn't work."

"What will happen?" The man's tone was low, mocking and cruel.

He lunged.

Savina wasn't sure what he'd intended—to grab her, maybe, hold her hostage. Maybe he thought he could simply break her neck with his massive hand and escape in the confusion.

But he didn't. Instead, he stared down, eyes wide in horror, at the hilt of Savina's blade sticking out of his throat.

Savina stepped to the side to avoid the spray of blood as he collapsed slowly to his knees, then his face, his eyes still wide with shock.

"That's what will happen," she said, bending to retrieve her knife. She turned back to the rest of the prisoners with a charming little laugh. They were all staring at her now, the expressions on their faces ranging from grudging admiration to stark horror. "If you don't help, Kachik's people won't have time to kill you, because I'll get to you first." She batted her eyelashes at them. "So. Shall we get started?"

The training went surprisingly smoothly after that. Savina had half expected to have to kill at least a handful more, but either the graphic nature of their companion's murder, or the seriousness of the situation itself, was enough to ensure their cooperation. And, to Savina's gratification, the criminals between them had experience enough to contribute in helpful ways to Savina's overall suggestions.

Still, at the end of three days, she was exhausted.

She leaned against the courtyard wall as the guards led the last of her students away and back to their prison cells. When they'd passed, she sank to the ground, closing her eyes and tipping her head back against the cool of the wall.

When she opened her eyes, Reka was crouched in front of her, a small smile on her face. She reached out, brushing a stray hair from Savina's forehead, and pulled Savina to her feet, glancing around quickly to make sure they were alone. Then she shoved Savina up against the wall, her lips finding Savina's, her hands running down Savina's body in a way that made Savina feel giddy and drunk. When Reka finally pulled back, Savina swayed, her knees so weak she wasn't sure they'd hold her up. Reka caught Savina's waist, supporting her easily as she tried to recover her senses.

"Long day?" Savina managed.

Reka chuckled, a soft, low sound that made Savina's heart stutter.

"It was. I missed you."

Savina leaned against her. "You're ridiculous, you know?"

"Utterly ridiculous." Reka's voice was clearly attempting to be solemn. She ran her fingers lightly across Savina's cheek, then down her throat, hesitating at the hollow of her breastbone. "I think I'm ready for bed, after all that work."

Savina almost swore at the sudden hot rush of desire that flooded through her at the tone in Reka's voice.

Reka laughed. "Come on, you're done for the day, aren't you?"

Later that night, as Savina lay cradled in Reka's arms, she tipped her head back to look into Reka's face. "Joska said she expects a call from Alba tonight or tomorrow, telling us we're needed."

"I know." Reka tightened her arm around Savina, pulling her back down against the pillow. "Then we'd best get some sleep, I think."

Sure enough, Joska appeared at the door of the small, half-finished cabin assigned to Savina and Reka far too early the next morning. Her expression was grave, and she looked as if she hadn't slept more than a couple of hours the previous night.

"It's tomorrow," she said shortly. "The yibo intelligence has intercepted enough of Kachik's messages to be fairly certain. He's planning a military strike for tomorrow afternoon, and if we're going to stop him, it'll have to be there."

Something heavy and sick was forming in Savina stomach. "Tomorrow?" She blinked the remnants of sleep from her eyes. "That means we'd have to leave ..."

"We'll have to be on the ships by this afternoon at the latest," said Joska. "Are your people ready?"

"We don't have much of a choice, do we?" Savina snapped.

Joska managed a small smile. "I suppose we don't." She sighed and turned away. "I'll leave you to get ready. Beni and Rafel and I are organizing the others."

By some miracle, the entire motley crew of humans and yibo managed to crowd themselves onto the one yibo government ship they'd been grudgingly lent by the time the sun was barely passed its zenith. The yibo man and the human woman who shared leadership of the settlement strode down the ship's corridors, holoscreens in front of them, calling out questions or orders. Nicolau jogged up beside where Savina stood in front of the locked-off section of the ship, his face bright with a mixture of worry and excitement.

"I guess this is it, then," he said.

"I guess it is." It took an effort to keep the snappishness out of her tone. It wasn't Nicolau's fault that the thought of seeing him in danger made her stomach tighten with dread.

He paused, and she could see the worry under the excitement in his face. "Do you think we have a chance?" His voice was soft and vulnerable.

She forced a smile. "I doubt that Kachik has any idea what's coming for him."

Nicolau nodded, looking a little reassured, then started off down the corridor after Joska.

Savina sighed, and glanced at the small group of violent criminals behind her. "We should be there in just over half a cycle," she said brusquely. "You may as well get some sleep while you can."

They nodded, and shuffled off to their various bunks. There had been a compromise struck—a reduction in penalties in exchange for services performed—but both the human and yibo leaders of the settlement had insisted that Savina's protégés stay in a locked section of the cabins.

She couldn't exactly argue—there was a reason her students had taken to her teaching so well, and most of them clearly had various, and, in Savina's opinion, valid grudges against certain other people on the ship. But as much as she may sympathize with them, vengeance would probably be better served after they dealt with Kachik.

It seemed to take days instead of hours to reach the small planet with the Nativist military base.

Savina spent the time pacing restlessly, wandering in to check in on Nicolau and Beni until Ines pulled her politely aside, a terrified but determined look on her face, to ask if she wouldn't mind letting Nicolau get some sleep.

Since Savina couldn't exactly murder her little brother's girlfriend, she grudgingly agreed.

Beni put up with it for as long as they could, and then told Savina bluntly to go find something else to do.

At last, she ended up in Reka's cabin, which—was probably inevitable, really.

"They're not ready for this," said Savina through her teeth, pacing back and forth across the floor of the small cabin.

Reka glanced up from where she was cleaning her weapons, one eyebrow raised. "Your students?"

"No," Savina snapped. "Don't expect me to care about a bunch of people who I don't know and don't want to. I'm talking about … about the others."

Reka sighed and put aside the pistol she'd been dissembling. "Savina. I know you spent your whole life taking care of Beni and Nicolau. But—" she smiled a little. "I've been watching them. You did a good job. They know what they're doing, and they're not afraid."

"That's exactly the point! They should be afraid!" Savina turned away quickly, swallowing back something in her throat that could have been tears.

She heard Reka stand and cross the room towards her, then felt a hand on her shoulder.

"Savina," Reka said quietly.

Savina closed her eyes and clenched her teeth.

"I'm not going to tell you it's not dangerous out there," Reka's voice was quiet in her ear. "But you're not the only one watching out for them anymore."

Reka tightened her grip on Savina's shoulder and turned her around, so they were facing each other. "I swear to you—I will do everything in my power to keep them safe."

"I thought we were just a bunch of criminals." Savina's voice wavered, halfway between sarcasm and tears.

Reka watched her for a moment, her eyes dark and startlingly intense. At last, she leaned in closer and whispered, "And I thought I'd explained to you that didn't matter to me anymore."

Savina let herself sag against Reka, even though there was a small, guilty part of her that told her both of them had better things to be doing right now. And even though that was probably true, Reka held her, and stroked her hair, and murmured comforting things in her ear until finally she was able to lay down on the cot and sleep.

She woke to the jolt of the ship's landing gear engaging, and blinked awake as, around her, the ship came to sudden, bustling life.

Reka was standing at the door, tucking the last of the weapons into the various holsters in her armoured suit. She looked up at Savina's movement and smiled, and there was something in her smile that made Savina smile back, a quick, unconscious happiness that had nothing to do with what was happening around them. She slid out of bed and dressed quickly, and Reka waited for her at the door.

"I'll see you soon," Reka whispered, leaning in to kiss her, and Savina kissed her back, and tried to ignore how Reka's words made her heart jump.

Their landing site was a large, grassy, windswept plain surrounded by rolling grasslands with patchy copses of trees in every direction, far enough from the military base that they could be mistaken for a cargo ship supplying a nearby settlement—no point in alerting Kachik's guards to their arrival any sooner than they had to. However, that necessitated a transport ride of another few hours, and by the time they finally reached their destination in the rolling hills near the base, Savina's patience was wearing thin.

"Are you ready?" asked Joska, coming to stand beside her as the loading ramp on the transport was lowered.

"As ready as I'll ever be," Savina said shortly.

Joska gave her a small, amused smile. "Well, I suppose I don't have anything to worry about, then."

Savina rolled her eyes out of habit. "Aren't you going to say anything about killing people?" she whispered.

Joska sighed, and there was an expression on her face that told Savina that, as much is she'd meant it as a joke, it wasn't a joke to the captain. "Under the circumstances, I don't know that I have much moral high ground to stand on myself," she said dryly.

Savina wanted to say … something, tell the woman that she was the most stupidly, ridiculously moral person Savina had ever met, and that included Reka, which was a high bar—but she didn't have the words for it. So she just stood there, tongue-tied and guilty, as Joska laid a hand on her shoulder. "Good luck," she said, then moved away to check in with the next group.

And then they were on the ground, and creeping through the short grass towards the military fortification, staying low to keep their silhouettes hidden.

When they were only perhaps fifteen minutes' walk distant, Savina turned to one of her yibo prisoners, a hard-faced young woman with a long scar across one shoulder. "You know what to do," she said.

The yibo girl smiled, a thin, vicious smile that sparked something warm and comforting in Savina's chest.

These students of hers knew what they were doing.

And then she lay on her belly with the others and watched as her protégé started forward along the road, looking lost and pathetic.

Savina magnified her vision with her retinal screen and watched as the yibo approached the gate, her steps faltering. She couldn't hear the yibo girl's words to the guards from this distance, but they'd rehearsed it over and over.

She was lost. She was trying to get to the nearest city and her transport had broken down, and she just needed some directions, and maybe a ride…

Two or three other guards had sauntered out, and were now surrounding the yibo girl, their postures showing nothing but idle curiosity as the soldier she'd addressed bent over a holomap.

Savina smiled to herself as she saw the small glint of a knife in the yibo woman's hands. And then there was a spurt of blood, and a scream, and the guards were drawing their weapons—

And then they fell, shouting and screaming, as weapons fire from Reka's group dropped them with pinpoint accuracy.

19

Aran

Aran slept badly that night. He kept jerking awake, heart pounding, and moving his arm or twitching his leg to make sure he was still in control of his muscles. Istvay, draped over him like a blanket, mumbled sleepily each time, until at last they pushed themself up on one elbow and grumbled that if Aran didn't lie still, they'd call Ani over to sting him with a tentacle spike.

"Pishti …" he whispered.

Istvay sighed and ran their thumb gently down the line of his cheekbone. "Listen. You have the bracelet on. You convinced Ani to sleep at the foot of the bed, and she could tell last time when it happened. And I promise, Aran—whatever the hell that thing in your head is, it's not going to be able to impersonate you well enough to fool me. Okay? Get some sleep."

He was sure he'd never be able to sleep again, not until they figured out how to get the charak out of his head, and then convinced Krevai to negotiate with the yibos for their medical tech, preferably without slaughtering all the yibos in his path first, and

201

finally, *finally*, Istvay could be cured and he could stop worrying. But despite his racing thoughts and the heavy knot of dread in his stomach, something about the comforting warmth of Istvay's body against his lulled him, finally, into slumber.

When he woke again, it was to a pounding at the door to their cabin. After a frantic, desperate moment where he tried to move his hand but couldn't, and then realized it was because Istvay was lying on his arm, he managed to shove himself upright and stumble for the door.

He pulled it open a crack, still shrugging into his shirt. Landru was waiting impatiently on the other side. "Aren't you going to open the door, human?" she snapped.

He frowned at her. "I … I mean, yes, but I'm not dressed …"

She cocked her head, as if what he'd said made no sense. "You're …"

He sighed heavily. "It's a human tradition that we don't let people into our bedrooms until we have clothes on, okay?"

She was still frowning at him, as if puzzled, and he frowned back. "Landru? What did you want?"

She seemed to shake herself, and she grinned. "Ah. Yes, the captain wanted to speak with you and your mate. But he wants you to leave the Ani behind."

Aran cast a glance back at Istvay, who looked as puzzled as he felt. "Alright," he said, turning back to the door. "We'll be there in a minute. Did you … want to wait?"

She was still staring at him in that slightly unsettling way.

"Landru?"

She smiled again, showing her teeth. "No, I won't wait. Come as soon as you're ready."

He closed the door slowly.

Istvay was sitting up in bed. "Landru?"

Aran nodded, coming back over and dropping down on the bed to pull his trousers on. "She said Krevai wanted to talk to us, and not to bring Ani." He shook his head. "It almost sounded like there was something wrong, and she didn't want to say."

Istvay frowned and pushed themself out of bed. It seemed to require more of an effort than it should have, and they had to pause for a moment afterwards, bracing themself against the wall, but Aran pretended not to notice. "Any thoughts?"

"No," Aran said. "But we'd probably better …" He winced, rubbing absently at the metal bracelet on his wrist.

"Aran …" Istvay's voice was quiet with dread. "What are you doing?"

Aran glanced up. "I'm …" He looked down at the bracelet, and his stomach clenched.

He stared at it for a long moment, trying not to consider the implications. "It's Landru," he said at last. The words felt heavy in his mouth. "It must be, that's why she was acting so strange. The charak got her." He looked up, sucking in a quick breath. "Dammit, no one else knows! If it gets Krevai—"

Istvay was already into their clothing and shoving a pulse pistol into their belt. "If it gets Krevai or Sharda, on the bright side, we aren't going to live long enough to watch the entire damn system implode, because we're the first people they're going to kill," they snapped. "I'm positive that once they start rooting around in Krevai's head and figure out that he's counting on us to find a way to get rid of them, they're not going to wait around to see whether we succeed."

Aran snatched up his own pulse pistol and held out a hand for Ani. "Come on, sweetheart," he whispered. "We might need you out there."

Ani slithered up his arm to perch on his shoulder, her body puffed up in alarm and her bulbous eyes peering around suspiciously for a threat.

Aran glanced quickly around the cabin. Istvay was at the makeshift work table, scooping the wire and electronic equipment they'd used for Aran's bracelet into their supplies pouch. "We're going to need every damn bit of help we can get," they said grimly, when they saw Aran watching.

Aran gave a short nod, then hesitated. "Pishti," he said in a low voice. "If I … if the bracelet—"

"The bracelet isn't going to fail," said Istvay, coming over and laying a hand on his shoulder. "And if it does, I'll … get Ani to stop you."

Aran gritted his teeth. But that was probably the best he could expect from them, and if he was being honest, the best he could have expected from himself, had the situation been reversed.

"Alright," he said. "Let's go, then."

He almost expected to be jumped the moment he stepped out the door. But the charak who'd taken over Landru must have decided that it had bigger prey at the moment than two humans. Which was both comforting—since it probably meant Krevai was still alive and in possession of his own mind—and utterly terrifying, since Aran could very well guess what the 'bigger prey' might be.

The corridors of the ship were suspiciously empty. Aran's stomach was clenched tight with dread as he and Istvay made their cautious way towards the cockpit, their footsteps echoing oddly in the silent passageways. Up ahead, he heard a scream, abruptly cut off, and he swallowed down a curse and gestured with his head to a corridor that led away from the sound.

Warning Krevai and preventing the end of the system as they knew it had to be their first priority. Everything else would just damn well have to wait.

He and Istvay were almost to the cockpit, and Aran could feel his muscles relaxing for the first time since he'd woken up that morning, when he heard a soft sound in the corridor behind him.

He spun, grabbing Istvay's arm to pull them around behind him.

A raider stood at the end of the corridor. Aran recognized him as one of the bodyguards Krevai had sent with him back in the raider trading city, what felt like a thousand years ago. The raider's eyes were lit up, his expression oddly hungry, and again, Aran felt the sluggish thing in the back of his brain stir, felt the sharp twinge of the bracelet against the skin of his wrist.

"Jarath?" he said cautiously, stalling for time.

The raider didn't speak, just stalked towards him, motions smooth and fluid and every bit the predator. And it wasn't that Aran hadn't seen raiders hunt before, but he'd forgotten how it felt for them to be hunting *him*, specifically.

"Aran!" Istvay was tugging on his sleeve, and he half-turned to whisper something to them—

And then he realized why they'd been trying to get his attention.

Another raider stood at the other end of the corridor, eyes fixed hungrily on him and Istvay.

Ani shifted uneasily on his shoulder, and Aran swore under his breath. "Any bright ideas?" he whispered to Istvay.

Istvay sighed. "Pulse pistols aren't going to work, they've got their armoured hoods on. I mean, we could set Ani on them, and hope she kills them before they get to us, but …" They trailed off.

Aran closed his eyes a moment.

He could do that, yes. But these were people he knew. People he'd worked with, people who'd saved his life more times than once. And he wasn't sure he could bear just watching Ani kill them.

"I don't like it either," said Istvay grimly. "But I'm not sure how much of a choice we'll have."

Aran glanced back and forth between the two raiders, turning to put his back to the corridor walls. "I don't know if it'll work in time anyways," he murmured, laying a cautioning hand on one of Ani's tentacles as she bridled, a growling sort of purr starting in her throat. "They're staying pretty far back. As soon as Ani goes after one, the other will pounce. And I doubt even Ani will be in time to get both of them before one gets to us—they don't die right away, remember?"

"Well, unless you can think of something else—" There was a trace of irritation in Istvay's tone that told Aran exactly how worried they must be.

He could hardly blame them.

The raiders had both taken a few steps closer, movements still cautious, but gaining confidence.

"We could wait until they're right in front of us," he whispered. "That might be our best chance. And maybe I can convince Ani to just knock them out, rather than kill them outright."

Istvay snorted. "Good luck with that. If Ani thinks you're in danger, she'll take down the entire system and everything in it."

Aran swore quietly. Istvay was probably right. And he wasn't sure that even then they'd be in time.

"Alright," he whispered. "I have the bracelet, so I doubt it'll affect me much if one of them touches me. So the moment they get close, I'll set Ani on them, and you run. Get to the cockpit and warn Krevai."

Istvay's hand tightened on his shoulder. "No." Their voice was flat. "That's the smart thing to do, I get that, but I watched you almost die in front of me once. I'm not damn well doing it again, the system can go hang."

Aran swore again helplessly.

The raiders were almost on them.

He took a deep breath and pulled the pulse pistol from his pocket. The raiders both wore armour, but it might hold them back for a few moments at least.

Ani shifted again, her low growl turning to a hiss.

And then there was a shout from behind the first raider.

The raider spun in surprise, mouth open to shout—and then crumpled to the ground. The second raider sprang forward towards whatever had taken down his companion, and there was a muffled scream, and then a curse in a voice Aran recognized all too well.

He jumped forward, jolted out of his shock, and swung the butt of his pulse pistol against the back of the raider's head, wincing at the *thud* it made on impact. The raider staggered, and then Istvay was beside him, their face grim. They swung their own pistol with a good deal more finesse, and this time the raider crumpled.

Behind him, Dessi stood, pale-faced and grim, a long metal bar clutched in her white-knuckled hands.

Aran stared. "Dessi?" he asked at last. "Dessi, is that … I thought you didn't believe in violence."

"I don't." Her voice was shaky. "But after that idiot Krevai almost got himself killed to save me from Sharda, I thought I should return the favour." She looked them up and down. "You two are alright? Come on, then. We've got to get to the captain before they do."

Aran sucked in a quick breath and nodded, and the four of them, Ani still hissing on Aran's shoulder, turned and ran for the cockpit.

As they got closer, Aran could hear voices shouting and the sound of weapons. Dessi's face, already ghostly pale, paled further.

"We're going to help Krevai first, we can worry about the rest of the crew later," said Istvay grimly. After about one corridor, they'd finally given in and slung their arm around Aran for support, and now he was all but carrying them. "Mystery knows I'm not the type to prioritize the establishment, but if those things take Krevai or Sharda, every damn person on this crew is dead already, so I'll make an exception this once."

Dessi nodded, apparently too breathless to speak, and then they rounded the last corner to the cockpit.

The corridor in front of the cockpit doors was a mass of shouting, screaming, swearing bodies as former crewmates struggled to the death. One of the crew who'd positioned herself in front of the doors caught sight of them, and shouted over the noise, "It's our Aran and the Ani! Let them through!" She turned back to the battle, and Aran recognized, with a sick feeling, the raider she was fighting.

Landru leapt at her, snarling, teeth bared.

"Come on!" Istvay hissed. "We can't help her if we're dead, and we can't help anyone if they infect Krevai."

Aran sucked in a quick breath, and the small group of them shoved their way forward to the cockpit doors. The raider woman guarding the door jumped aside to let them pass, blood streaming down her face and staining her armoured tunic. Her face was set in a grim determination. "Don't let the captain come out until we have this under control," she whispered as they passed.

Dessi nodded, and then they were through, and the cockpit door slammed shut behind them and locked.

Aran gasped for breath as he let his eyes adjust to the dim light of the cockpit. He could hear a muffled cursing, and he let his eyes drift around the room, searching for the source of the sound.

Then he saw Krevai, gagged and tied to the pilot's seat. His expression promised immediate dismemberment and death to probably several members of his crew, but Dessi let out a gasp of undisguised relief. "Krevai," she said, striding briskly across the cockpit towards him. "Is there any chance you're infected?" She pulled out a scanner and made some brief measurements, then, cautiously, she cut the gag from his mouth.

"That damned Sharda," he growled, as soon as his mouth was free. "She set my pilot up to do this. Cut me loose, I'm going out there. I'm not sitting here letting my crew get carved up to protect me."

"The entire system will get carved up if you're infected and the charak starts giving orders through you," Dessi snapped. "I never thought I'd say this, but thank God for Sharda."

Aran had caught his breath by now, and he came over to join them, still supporting Istvay, who was by now stumbling with weariness. He helped them to a chair, which they dropped into with painful relief, then turned to Krevai and Dessi. "Listen," he said, holding out his wrist with the bracelet on. "Pishti managed to design this to keep the infection contained, and it's working so far. But it has to be set to your personal bioelectric signature, and all the designs we've tried short out when we simulate an initial charak infection, so what we have doesn't work until after you've been infected. And with what's going on out there—" He gestured to the cockpit door, shaking his head. "I somehow don't see Landru standing still to let Pishti or me measure her."

"Landru is infected?" Krevai's voice was sick. He jerked his arm, fighting against the restraints. "I've got to get out there. Dessi, cut me loose, damn you!"

Dessi shook her head, her expression tight with strain. She turned to Aran. "I do have baseline measurements on all the crew," she said slowly. "I took them earlier, because since I'm already out here, I may as well gather as much data as I can. But that isn't going to be enough, is it?"

"It's a start." Istvay's voice was heavy with exhaustion, but they'd raised their head to join into the conversation. "We can program the baseline data into the bracelets with that. But we would still need access to them for the fine-tuning. And in addition," they added wryly, "I somehow doubt any of the infected crew will agree to stand nicely still and hold out their hands for a bracelet. If we can even tell for certain who's been infected and who hasn't, which I'm not completely confident we can."

Dessi was frowning, chewing on the inside of her cheek with an expression that Aran had come to recognize as her working through an idea. "You're right," she said at last, looking up. There was determination in her face. "The only thing is to knock them all unconscious, then."

Everyone in the cockpit turned to stare at her.

She rolled her eyes. "God's sake, Krevai, I'm not suggesting killing them. I'm nonviolent, you know that." She turned to Aran. "You come with me. I have enough raw ingredients for a gas that, at the correct saturation, should knock everyone out, and we can sort things out from there. I'll make sure it doesn't vent into the cockpit or my lab, so Krevai and your Istvay should be fine, but I doubt I'll get back to my lab without your Ani."

Aran glanced at Istvay, who gave a grim nod. "Go on. If Dessi leaves me with the baseline data, I can get started on programming the bracelets."

Dessi yanked a data pad from a roomy pocket of her tunic and scowled over it for a moment, then handed it to Istvay. "I've got the data listed there. Everyone who's highlighted is still alive after the leadership war, and we have no idea what's happened out there, so best make one for each of them if you have the materials."

Aran pulled Ani gently off his shoulder as Dessi spoke, and cuddled her against his chest. "Alright, sweetheart," he whispered. "I'm going to need you to help me, alright? I need you to keep me and Dessi safe, but I really don't want you to kill anyone if you can help it. Alright? Guard, not kill. Can you do that for me, sweetheart?"

She blinked up at him with her wide, bulbous eyes, a trusting look on her face, and he smiled and rubbed her head.

She probably had no idea what he'd just said, but he'd spent the better part of last summer trying to teach her the difference between "guard" and "attack." It had never been particularly successful, and had been badly hampered by Ani's general attitude that her sense of when something should be killed was more accurate than Aran's—an attitude with which Istvay wholeheartedly agreed—but there was always the chance she'd remember, or at least decide to pay attention to him for once.

When he looked up, Dessi was watching him. "Are you ready?" she asked. She was clearly trying to sound businesslike, but he could hear the tremor in her tone.

This was the crew she'd grown up with. The crew that had been willing to sacrifice their lives to rescue her from Sharda. And she'd hit two of them with a pole, hard enough to probably cause traumatic brain injury, in order to save Krevai's life, and she couldn't possibly feel any better about all this than he did.

"I'm ready," he said, giving Ani one final squeeze before placing her back on his shoulder. "Let's go."

The desperate struggle to get out of the cockpit and back through the corridors to Dessi's lab was the stuff of nightmares—raiders that Aran knew by name grasping at them, teeth bared, as he frantically tried to keep Ani from killing them outright—but they made it out uninjured, and, thanks to Dessi's full-body hazmat suit and the fact that Aran was already infected, without serious incident. There were at least two raiders who, if they did wake up, would wake up in at least three days' time with a hell of a headache, but Aran was trying very hard not to think about that, and besides, Ani had been doing her best. He'd told her to stay behind at the cockpit doors, because the gas wasn't going to knock her out, and he couldn't bear to leave Istvay completely unprotected, and then he and Dessi pounded down the almost empty corridors towards Dessi's lab as fast as they could run.

At last they were inside, and Dessi slammed and locked the door behind them, then slumped against it. Her entire body was shaking, and she'd closed her eyes, and for a moment, Aran was worried she'd actually pass out. But she straightened, unfastened her hazmat suit enough to pull off the helmet, and beckoned Aran over to the lab. "Here," she said, turning to fumble through the neatly labeled bottles in her cabinet and handing one over her shoulder to him. "Take this. We'll want … five cc's per ten cubic metres of airspace. The ship specs are on the wall, but you'll need to subtract the air volume of the cockpit and my lab, since we're not going to vent it in here. I'm going to vent everywhere else, though, since we don't know where else someone who's been infected might have got into."

Aran nodded and pulled up his palmscreen, striding over to the specs sheet on the wall.

He wasn't entirely sure how long the uninfected raiders defending the cockpit would hold out, even with Ani to help, and yes, there was a security seal on the door that Istvay was holding the control for, but

… dammit, Istvay was in there, and Aran wasn't going to feel even a little comfortable until he was certain that Istvay wasn't about to get ripped to shreds.

By the time Dessi emerged a few moments later with three other bottles, he'd finished the calculations and poured the appropriate amount of the steaming liquid she'd handed him into a volumetric flask. Dessi jerked her chin to the wall behind her. "Get a gas mask in case something spills. Your Istvay is going to be catatonic if you get knocked out, and they're fragile enough right now as it is."

He grabbed for the mask as Dessi pulled her own mask back over her face and measured a powder and a second liquid into the flask. At last, holding it as far from her as she could, she unstopped the final bottle and poured the liquid into a fragile glass beaker, stopped it with a thin seal, then dropped it into the flask, the contents of which were already smoking. She popped a stopper into the flask and tightened it firmly, then handed it to Aran.

"We've got to get it into the air vents," she snapped, her voice muffled through the mask. "And we've got about the count of sixty before the seal on the beaker melts through and the gas pressure blows the top off the flask."

Aran glanced at Dessi's pale face and sighed. "Where?" he asked. "I'll take it."

Dessi was a good head and a half taller than he was, and half again as broad, but he could tell what it had cost her to hit the raiders who'd been trying to kill him and Istvay.

He didn't particularly enjoy violence himself, and Istvay had given him exasperated lectures on more than one occasion along the lines of, "hell's sake, Aran, you hit like you're afraid you're going to hurt someone, that's exactly the damn point of hitting them!" But it wasn't going to give him an existential crisis, like the one that appeared to be looming in Dessi's future as soon as the current crisis was over.

She gave him a relieved look. "There's an air vent just outside the door to the right, half-way down the hallway before it branches. Just get the flask in there before it blows, the gas will do the rest."

He nodded, took a deep breath, and grabbed the flask in both hands. "Lock the door as soon as I'm out," he said grimly.

She nodded, and he yanked the door open and slipped outside.

The corridor was suspiciously empty.

He gritted his teeth against the nausea rising in his stomach at the suspense and started towards the opening in the wall at a spring.

He'd made it three steps before a raider sprang from the shelter of a doorway, slamming him painfully into the corridor wall.

"Dammit," he gasped, blinking back stars.

The raider's teeth were bared, and she lunged towards Aran's neck. Aran ducked out of the way, struggling against her grip. Her claws dug into his shoulder, catching him as he tried to slip out of her grasp.

It had already been at least thirty seconds, and Aran could practically feel the liquid bubbling in the container in his hand.

The raider grabbed him by the throat and yanked him off his feet, and with a last, desperate effort, he hurled the flask towards the narrow air vent.

He couldn't breathe, and black spots were floating in front of his eyes. The raider's face was swimming in his vision, but he saw her tense, and flung up his free arm in front of his face on instinct. She snarled, her teeth sheering easily through the layers of armoured cloth and into the flesh of his forearm, and he hissed out a choked curse of pain.

From the corner of his blurred vision, he saw the flask tip over into the vent.

There was a *pop* and the sound of shattering glass.

The raider half-turned at the sound.

A moment later, the air in the hallway went thick and white.

The raider's expression didn't even have time to change. One moment she was snarling, her teeth fixed in his arm—the next she'd collapsed in a heap on the floor.

Aran landed heavily, gasping for breath, and lay there for a few moments as the world spun around him. His arm hummed with a sharp, clear, transparent pain that meant that a much worse pain was coming the moment his nerve endings had time to process the damage, and his throat ached where the raider had gripped him, his thoughts woozy from lack of oxygen.

"Aran! Aran, are you alright?" Dessi's voice was sharp with concern.

He braced himself, then rolled over, pushing himself up on one elbow. "I'm … fine," he rasped. "At least, relatively speaking."

Dessi was frowning down at the growing pool of blood. "Am I going to have to do another transfusion? Thank God I got the replicator going for the artificial human blood, at least, although I may have to speed it up if we're going to make this a regular thing."

He managed a weak grin, even though he felt a little like he was going to throw up. "No, it's not that bad, I think. She didn't hit any arteries."

"Good." Dessi sounded heartily relieved. "Let's get some compression on it, then, and go see how Krevai and your Istvay held out."

Aran needed no further convincing. He stumbled to his feet, waited impatiently for Dessi to slap a makeshift compression bandage over the worst of his injuries, and then he and Dessi took off at a run towards the cockpit.

Running down the hallways through the rapidly-clearing smoke, past the still bodies of the raider crew he'd spent the last several weeks living, working, and fighting alongside, should have been an eerie and unsettling sight, but he didn't have the energy to care right now, not until he knew what had happened to Istvay and Ani.

Ani met them at the door to the cockpit. She looked unhurt, but mildly offended, presumably that her prey had had the audacity to collapse before she could sting them into submission herself.

And the door to the cockpit was still closed.

"Ani," Aran gasped in relief, holding out his arm to her as he sagged against the corridor wall. "Ani, sweetheart, look at you, you're such a good, sweet girl."

She gave a slightly mollified chirrup and swarmed up his leg, pausing on his chest to peer into his face, as if to reassure herself he was alright. She took her place on his shoulder, touching the bandages on his arm with the tips of her tentacles and hissing in disapproval.

"I know," he said ruefully. "But it's not as bad as it looks." He glanced around to make sure the smoke had fully cleared, and pulled off his mask cautiously. The air still carried a slight chemical tang, but it wasn't enough to do more than make him clear his throat. "Shall we go see how Istvay's doing?"

Ani hunched on his shoulder, grumbling, and he chuckled, reaching up to stroke her head. "You're just going to have to get over this, sweetheart," he said. "I still love you, and Pishti does too."

"Krevai?" Dessi tapped on the door to the cockpit, the sound loud in the quiet corridors. "Captain Krevai, are you alright? It's Dessi and Aran and the Ani."

There was a moment's pause. "Aran?" Istvay's voice sounded

worried. "Aran, is that you?"

"Pishti—" Aran began.

Before he could say anything else, the door slammed open, and he could see Istvay in the doorway, leaning heavily against the wall, with Krevai behind him. Krevai was grinning, his teeth bared and a long knife held in one hand, but when only Aran and Dessi stepped inside and no one tried to attack anyone, he looked vaguely disappointed.

"Everyone is knocked out," said Dessi in a businesslike tone. "Istvay? Did you get the bracelets programmed as much as you could? I'm guessing we have about half a decicycle before they start waking up."

Istvay had grabbed Aran and was studying the makeshift bandage on his arm, their jaw clenched tight.

"Pishti, I'm fine," he said. "Just … a little misunderstanding with one of the infected raiders. Nothing serious."

Istvay's expression said that the two of them were going to have a long conversation later about what "nothing serious" meant, but at last they nodded, their eyes closing in relief, and ran a hand along the side of his face, tipping their forehead against his.

"Istvay?" Dessi's voice was sharp. "You and your Aran can do your sex or whatever later. This is important."

"They're not planning on doing sex, our Aran's shirt is still on," said Krevai importantly. "If his Istvay isn't unbuttoning it, they're not planning on doing sex for a while."

Aran almost choked.

Istvay shot him a rueful glance, then turned to Dessi. "I did everything I could from this end. Now that they're unconscious, I can finish up." They paused. "This won't keep anyone from being infected, if they aren't already. It'll just suppress the infection in those who already have it."

Dessi nodded. "I know." She turned to Krevai. "Come on, you may as well make yourself useful."

Aran turned to go after them, then paused, turning back to Istvay. "Pishti?" he said, taking their arm and helping them back to their seat. "How did you know I wasn't … re-infected or something?"

"I didn't." Istvay's voice was grim. "But I wasn't about to leave you out there, so I figured I'd make do."

Aran sighed and opened his mouth to say something, then closed it again when he saw the look on Istvay's face.

"You have exactly zero grounds to complain about that," they said. "Now go on, I'll get started in here. And then when we get back, we're going to take a look at your arm."

Aran leaned in to kiss Istvay, then turned and followed Krevai and Dessi out of the cockpit.

By the time Istvay had fine-tuned the last bracelet and Dessi and Krevai were fixing it on, the raiders were beginning to stir. Within a few minutes more, groaning raiders were pushing themselves to their feet, holding their aching heads and supporting themselves on the corridor walls.

It was … better than it could have been, Aran reminded himself as he and Istvay made their slow way back to their cabin, Istvay leaning on him so heavily that he was practically carrying them. It could have been much, much worse, even if Krevai hadn't been infected.

But there were five of the crew who'd been killed, and there were raiders who'd watched in horror from the prison of their own minds as their teeth ripped out their companions' throats.

The bracelets had worked, for now.

But he and Istvay didn't have to exchange any words for it to be painfully apparent that none of them could afford what would happen if the bracelets failed.

When they got back to their cabin, Istvay lifted their head. "Wait," they said, as Aran tried to steer them towards the bed. "I want to write down our observations first."

"Pishti," he said, worry tightening his throat. "Just ... get some rest first. Please. You'll think better after you get some rest."

Istvay shook their head stubbornly and turned to Aran. The circles under their eyes were permanent dark bruises now, their face shockingly cadaverous. But their expression was as stubborn as ever. "You're not safe until we find a damn fix for this, and that's not something I'm willing to risk. And there's no argument you can make that will convince me. So don't bother."

Aran sighed, squeezing his eyes closed.

He felt Istvay's hand on his shoulder. "Listen. It's going to be alright. Putting off my afternoon nap for fifteen minutes isn't going to kill me." There was a quiet bitterness to their tone.

Aran blinked his eyes open and tried to smile. "Alright," he said. "Alright, but at least let me help."

Istvay nodded, as if they were too tired for words, and dropped into the chair Aran pulled out for them.

Aran watched Istvay from under his lashes as the two of them worked on the notes.

His stomach was pinched tight with worry.

Things were moving far, far too fast. They still hadn't come up with an argument that would convince Krevai, but the situation with the charaks was becoming desperate. And he wasn't sure, anymore, how long he'd be able to keep ahead of disaster.

20

Savina

Savina leapt to her feet. "Go!" she snapped at the small group of murderers and thieves around her, and they scrambled to their feet and came after her.

At least, she reflected bitterly as she sprinted down the dusty road, she was damn well getting better at running.

And then, interminable minutes later, they were at the rendezvous point outside the walls. The front gate had already devolved into pure chaos, people screaming and shouting, weapons firing into the trees.

Reka was waiting for them, and she smiled when she caught sight of Savina. "Are you ready?" she mouthed. She turned without waiting for an answer and slipped under the cover of the shadows of the walls. Savina and the others followed her in a silent sprint for the small side gate.

The guards on duty were clearly distracted by what was happening at the front gate. Reka shot the first dead before he had a chance to even startle, and he fell with only the beginnings of vague confusion starting on his face. Savina took his companion down with a knife to the throat, and then Reka and Savina between them melted the force field controller and Reka's lock pick slid it open for them.

Once inside, Savina looked around quickly. They'd all memorized the map of the inside of the compound, but it still took her a moment to reorient herself. Soldiers were scrambling into their armour, drawing weapons as they poured from the surrounding shelters to confront the attack at their gates.

Savina stepped forward into the path of a tall yibo soldier. Before the woman had time to react, Savina grabbed her by the shoulder and slid her needle knife up through the woman's ribs. She hit the button that sent a quick pulse of electricity into the woman's heart, and the woman stiffened, eyes wide, then crumpled. Savina dragged the body quickly into the shadows, undressed it, and slipped into the yibo uniform herself. It was too tight, and a little too short, but enough that she should pass at a casual glance.

Then she stepped out, checking for danger before gesturing the others after her.

They reached the back gate without much trouble, and Reka pulled it open. Rafel and his group of saboteurs, Nicolau and Ines among them, were waiting outside, and they slipped inside the moment Savina and Reka slid open a gap in the force field.

"Let's go, let's go, let's go!" Rafel hissed, his tone bearing the sharpness of someone raised in the military. The motley group of humans and yibo stumbled through after him, and he jerked his head impatiently towards the weapons storage. "Group A to the weapons storage, group B with me to find the ships."

The two groups split neatly, one following Rafel towards a landing pad, the other following Beni towards the weapons storage.

Savina glanced over her shoulder and grinned sweetly. "And the rest of us," she whispered, "let's make sure we're the only ones they're watching."

Savina watched with satisfaction as the small group of ex-prisoners split up, perhaps not with the military precision of Rafel's group, but with more coordination than Savina had expected, and slipped into the crowd of soldiers.

It was only a moment later that they heard the first scream.

Savina glanced at Reka.

"Shall we?" asked Reka, with a gallant gesture. Savina nodded, and they started off into the compound.

The problem, Savina reflected, with spending your life killing without much fanfare, was that it was a hard habit to break. She and Reka had each killed at least half a dozen people before they made enough noise about it that someone noticed. Then Reka grabbed Savina by the shoulder and yanked her down as yibo guns sprayed the area where the two of them had been, vaporizing the bloody pile of bodies.

They scrambled behind a pile of supply crates stacked up near a wall, and Reka rose in a low crouch and shot four guards down in quick succession. Savina pulled out a handful of throwing knives, weighing them carefully in her hands. When the first of the soldiers burst around the side of the crates, she sent a knife through his throat, and he dropped instantly.

She swore, and Reka gave her an amused glance. "Too used to being efficient?" she whispered.

"Shut up," Savina snapped, but she was grinning a little. When the next soldier came through, Savina reminded herself of their actual intention—to cause the maximum amount of chaos possible —and carefully sent the knife into a point right below his collarbone

—enough to make him scream in pain and to send blood spattering across the rest of the soldiers as he staggered back, but not enough to kill him instantly.

Reka was firing steadily from the gaps between the crates, and she'd picked off another half dozen soldiers by the time a larger and much more cautious group of soldiers came around the crates and into view.

Savina waited until they'd be able to see her clearly, then jumped to her feet, sobbing, "Help me! Help me, this woman took me hostage!"

The guards paused, staring at her in confusion. Then three of them stumbled back, gasping in pain as her throwing knives found marks in their thighs or shoulders or one of the many other places that she'd learned over the years would cause immense agony, and not result in immediate death.

"What—" one of them gasped, her words translated through Savina's wavelink, and then Reka shot three others as they brought their weapons to bear. Savina took out the last two with pulse pistol shots to the face, since honestly, three or four left alive were probably all they really needed.

The injured soldiers staggered back under cover, but a moment later a shot hissed out, dissolving the wall beside Savina's head, and she cursed and dropped back to the ground.

Reka had crawled to the edge of their crates and glanced out into the courtyard, and now she turned back to Savina. "Things are about to get exciting here."

Savina gritted her teeth. "That's fine by me. Nicolau and Beni are in that munitions storage, and as long as the yibo are staying away from them, things can get as exciting as they like."

Reka rose up on her knees to spray off a quick round of shots, then dropped back down as a handful of the containers in front of her dissolved. "You might change your mind in a minute," she whispered. Then she cursed and grabbed Savina's tunic, yanking her bodily out of the way as another shot dissolved a portion of the wall behind where she'd been sitting. "Dammit, we've got to find other shelter."

From the compound around them Savina could hear screams and shouts, gunshots, the wet gurgles of people dying.

That had been, after all, exactly the plan—Savina and Reka were going to keep the soldiers' attention while their trainees killed, injured, and overall wreaked havoc.

But … Savina rolled over painfully and allowed herself a quick glance around the corner of the cartons.

They may have succeeded a little too well.

The entire courtyard in front of them was full of yibo soldiers, and she could already hear the thud of soldiers' boots running towards where they were hiding. She and Reka could take out a few —more than a few, probably—but not that many.

Reka was peering around, her face grim, her eyes that calculating calm that meant they were probably both about to be killed. "Can you climb?" she whispered to Savina. "If I boost you, can you climb the wall behind us?"

Savina looked up at the dirty and, to all appearances, perfectly sheer surface and groaned. "Unlike you, I'm not a Mystery-damned action hero!"

The first of the soldiers rounded the corner, and Reka dropped him. Savina dropped the one behind him, and Reka shot three more as they appeared. But there was too many. It was only a matter of time—

Behind them, there was a shocking, blinding, yellow-white spurt of flame, followed, a moment later, by an earth-shattering *boom*.

And, as Savina and Reka and the two dozen soldiers who had just stumbled into view all stood and stared, the munitions building went up in a fiery explosion that seemed to shake the entire planet.

When the noise died away, there was a moment of silence. And then, a series of smaller explosions echoed from the docks as, one after another, a dozen of Kachik's warships met the same fate.

The battle wasn't over immediately—it took a few minutes for the irrevocability of what had happened to sink in. In the end, the thing that took the longest was for the remainder of the insurgents, who'd pushed inside once the compound's force field had been taken out in the explosion, to find someone with whom they could negotiate a surrender.

By the time they'd done that, Savina and Reka and their group had killed at least two dozen more yibo soldiers. Honestly, Savina thought, as she looked out over the bloody mess of the courtyard, that had probably been Joska's main motivation to find the person in charge as quickly as she had.

But surrender the yibos had—weaponless, all but leaderless, with their fortifications down and unknown numbers of enemies at their gates, they hadn't had much of a choice.

It took much longer than Savina had expected to get everyone rounded up, secure the compound, and re-instate the force field in case Kachik tried to take the compound back. It was hard to be irritated, though, in the general air of celebration. The ragged group of humans and yibos were laughing, shouting back and forth to each other, and swapping increasingly exaggerated tales of heroics with a camaraderie that hadn't existed hours before. And Savina found she was smiling despite herself.

There had been a few casualties, but Reka had survived, and Nicolau and Beni, and Joska and Rafel, and the relief of it was a weight lifted off Savina's chest.

She'd finally given up fighting the fact that Joska was as much her family now as Nicolau and Beni. Rafel, too, as much as both of them may resent it.

"Rafel is in the generals' quarters. He'd like us to meet him there." Joska's clothing was sweat-stained and blood-spattered and covered in dust, and there was a haunted look to her face that made Savina's chest squeeze with a quick spasm of guilt.

But Joska had agreed to this, willingly. And perhaps they were all being forced to go against their own principles of morality—Savina, working with the Judge of Heresies to save people she'd just as soon let die; Reka, falling in love with a murderous criminal for whom she'd accepted a warrant; Joska, organizing people to kill so that they could save lives.

It had been a fairly bloodless capture, all things considered—of the two or three thousand yibo soldiers in the compound, less than a hundred had been killed. But Savina had been around Joska long enough to know that every one of those deaths would weigh on Joska's conscience, probably for the rest of her life.

She and Reka followed Joska down the torn-up streets of the military compound towards a large building in the centre. Rafel was waiting for them inside, and he led them into an inner room.

"Beni is working at the tech aspect, and Ines is breaking the communications code. Those two are good at what they do, so I don't imagine it will take too long to hack into the military database," said Rafel in his usual brusque tone. "I wanted you here so the moment we know what's happening, we can decide on our next move." Savina could see from the concern on his face as he watched Joska that he knew as well as Savina did how this would affect the captain. But he seemed to have realized, as much as Savina had, that they didn't have another viable option.

By the time they and the rest of the group leaders were settled around the large table, Beni and Ines between them had broken the communications code. Within a few minutes, lines of information scrolled out in yibo on a holoscreen above the table.

Savina blinked twice to bring her wavelink translator online, then once more to record—this would probably be useful information for Alba and her people back in the yibo capital—and scanned through the material. Rafel and a handful of others were already scowling over the information, talking in low voices.

And then Joska said, "Wait. What's that? The flicker in the corner of the screen?"

Beni lifted their head at her voice. "That'll be an incoming transmission. Give me a second."

Another screen appeared on the table as the blinking of the incoming transmission morphed into words.

Savina glanced over them, then frowned and read them a second time, more carefully. Something sick and heavy was growing in her stomach.

"What is it?" asked Rafel, looking up from his work.

Savina stood quickly. "We've got to get a hold of Alba, now. We've got to warn them."

Rafel frowned, glancing over at the screen.

"Looks like Kachik has information that the raiders are coming after a major yibo city." Reka's voice was grim. "It doesn't specify which, but considering the raiders' communication talks about taking out the government, and that Kachik's annotation indicates he's going to use this to try to seize power—I think we can all guess."

Joska had gone very pale, but her voice, when she spoke, was calm. "Beni, I'm sorry, but would you mind playing the video they mentioned in the transmission? The one documenting the previous attack on the other yibo settlement?"

By the time the video stopped, everyone in the room was silent.

Savina had never been squeamish about blood. But even she felt sick to her stomach at what she'd just seen, the pictures emblazoned across her brain.

A look at her sibling's face told Savina that, whatever the audio descriptor in Beni's wavelink had said, it had made the horror of what had happened entirely clear.

The yibo village chief pushed himself to his feet, leaning against the table. "The raiders have held off until now, whatever their reason for it. But once they have a taste of blood like this—they're not going to stop." He turned, so he was facing all of them. "Whatever time we had is gone. We're going to have to call your friend back in the city and tell her that her only option now is to take down Kachik's forces as quickly as possible. The raiders will be coming for the capital—we can't afford to let Kachik take the government in the confusion."

"We can't take down Chrr. There's no way." Beni sounded as horrified as Savina felt.

The human village chief shook her head. "We don't have a choice. If we don't take down Kachik so that the rest of the yibo forces are able to focus on the raiders—I don't know that there will be any survivors. And in the end, whether the raiders win or lose, if Kachik gains the upper hand, the result for the humans in the system will be the same."

Savina wanted to protest. But she'd seen the video, and she still remembered the vicious thrill in the eyes of the raiders who'd tried to kill her.

And she knew, gut deep, that the village chiefs were exactly right. Ready or no, they had days—hours, maybe—to take down the Nativists completely, or none of this would have been any use at all.

21

Alba

The news passed along by Savina and Reka had thrown the city into chaos, and in honesty, Alba couldn't blame them. They'd all seen the footage of the raider attack by now.

She found she could hardly sleep nights, waking from nightmares of raiders, and straining in the dark for imagined sounds from the door or the windows. Their daily strategy meetings went on long into the night, and every one of the small group of strategists and engineers was looking more and more weary with each passing day.

As they should, Alba thought grimly. Not only were they discussing strategy to help Savina and Reka and a small band of humans and yibo military take Chrr virtually on their own, now they were also being called in almost daily for strategic advice to protect the city itself. And that was even without addressing their desperate need for information on Kachik's schemes.

It was two full days before Jair was able to get away for long enough to escort Alba and Yosip to the prison to speak with one of the human soldiers, and as none of the refugees had the security clearance to go alone, she was forced to wait. But the third morning, he arrived at the gates of the refugee compound, his expression grim and posture sagging with weariness.

"I got away as soon as I could," he said when he saw her.

Alba herself was weary enough that she could hardly muster a smile. "Thank you. I know how difficult it must have been. I appreciate your assistance more than I can say."

"Believe me," he said grimly. "I understand what will happen to all of us if we don't figure out Kachik's next move in time to stop it."

The security at the prison was impressive—it took a good fifteen minutes for Alba, Yosip, and Jair to get through, even with Jair's security clearance. But at last they were brought to a small room in the prison and seated, to Alba's intense disgust, on two of the ubiquitous, uncomfortable stools.

Jair took his seat with every sign of comfort. Which, Alba thought sourly, only made sense, as it was likely that the stools had originated from his home system of Labarinto, before it was destroyed.

And then the door to their small room swung open, and two yibo guards escorted a woman inside. She was dressed in yibo prison clothes, a brilliant yellow tunic with cuffs of green that would be difficult to disguise outside of the prison. But she didn't look in the least cowed. She carried herself with the same military bearing that Alba would have expected in a military parade in Colorida, not from a political prisoner in an alien system.

"Madam Chief Justice." There was a sneer to the woman's words that was not unexpected, but was still, somehow, jarring. This woman didn't have the excuse the yibo had, or even the humans from the Labarinto system. As far as this soldier was concerned, Alba was still her legitimate government authority. And her posture made it clear exactly how little that meant to her.

At the very least, the past few months had taught Alba how to gracefully deal with disrespect.

She raised her eyebrow at the woman and gestured to one of the stools. "Soldier. You may take a seat."

The woman narrowed her eyes, and made no move to sit.

Just as well. There was some small, mean part of Alba that welcomed the thought that this woman would now have to remain standing for the entirety of the interview, or else end up looking the fool.

"I'm afraid, soldier, that I haven't time for niceties." Alba kept her voice cool. "Your master, Cavaco, instructed you to mutiny, and instructed you to hold your own negotiations with whatever you found on the other side of the portal, for Cavaco's personal benefit. We all know this now, so your silence aids no one." She leaned forward in her seat, her eyes boring into the woman. "What you do not, perhaps, fully comprehend is the peril in which that has placed every person from the Joias system—not only the general's political enemies, but yourselves as well."

The woman was still glaring at her haughtily, no sign in her face that Alba's words had had any effect. But this woman, along with all the soldiers in the yibo prison, had been sold off to the raiders by the very people to whom they'd pledged their loyalty. She and all of her fellow prisoners had been deemed expendable. And even if Captain Mattin had not personally come up with the plan to sell them off, he'd acquiesced to it.

"I don't see how that's my concern." There was still a sneer in the woman's voice, that hint of distain.

Alba raised an eyebrow. "It seems to me it is very much your concern. Because Kachik is doing everything in his power to put you, along with each of the rest of us, directly into the path of the raiders in order to force Synod compliance with his demands. And his demands are, to be allowed to kill any humans in this system whom he does not personally find indispensable." Alba let her words hang for a moment, and then added pointedly, "I understand he has already demonstrated on what side of that equation you fall."

The woman was still glaring stubbornly.

Yosip shifted in his seat, and when he spoke, his voice was soft. "Naia."

Of course he knew her name.

"I know how hard it is when someone you admire has made a wrong decision. I know you were working in what you thought was the best interest of the system, and I know you care for our system and want the best for it. We all have politics we disagree with." He leaned forward, looking directly into her eyes. "But we can't fix the Joias system by working with someone who wants to destroy it. Kachik sees humans as disposable. He sees you as disposable. He's already demonstrated this. And he won't suddenly change his mind when he's made it through to Joias. You have family there. I know you don't want to hurt them, but can't you see? That's exactly what you're doing." He glanced at Alba. "Whether you agree with Alba's past politics or not, the Chief Justice is doing everything she can to keep the Joias system safe. Any disagreements she and Cavaco have as to how best to do this are something to be worked out within our political system, brought before the people. Not like this."

"Brought before the people?" The soldier scoffed loudly. "The very people the Chief Justice was willing to sacrifice by refusing to approve a military response to this threat? And now that you finally recognize that it's a threat, you want me to feel sorry for you? You want me to sympathize with the woman who started all this to begin with?"

Yosip glanced at Alba, giving her a chance to formulate her response.

"I can understand your anger," said Alba at last, quietly. "I can understand why you would be afraid. I can even understand why you decided to do what you did." She paused, her eyes not leaving the woman's face. "But what I cannot understand is intentionally subjecting people that you love to death, based on the word of someone who has already sold you out once."

For a long, long moment, they stared at each other. Alba didn't drop her gaze, and nor did the woman.

At long last, however, the soldier took a deep breath and turned to Jair. "Is it true?" she asked bluntly. "Is it true that Kachik is bargaining to allow him to kill human settlements?"

Jair nodded.

"And I'm to believe that this woman—" there was a note of contempt in her tone as she gestured at Alba, "was trying to stop it? That she was taking even the slightest risk to her own power to keep nameless humans alive? Even people who were below her, and who couldn't give her anything in return?" There was so much bitterness in her tone that it took Alba aback.

It shouldn't have. Judging by the woman's accent, she'd grown up somewhere in one of the poorer Belt settlements. It was very likely that one of the reforms or bills that Alba had passed had hurt her, or her family, or someone she cared about. And how easy would it be for Cavaco to take the woman's anger and resentment, strip it of any useful purpose, and turn it to his own ends?

"Naia," Alba said at last. "I am in no position to pretend all my decisions have been good ones. And I understand that good intentions are not enough to make up for harms caused. But if I or the policies that I have championed have hurt you in the past, I would beg you to please take that up with me personally, or politically. Don't use it to hurt more innocent people."

The soldier didn't take her eyes off Jair.

"She did," said Jair quietly, his eyes not leaving the soldier's. "More than her political power—she put her life at risk to save you and the very people your fellow soldiers tried to sell out to the raiders, to save your own lives."

For a long moment, the soldier looked between the three of them. And then, at last, her shoulders slumped, just a little. "It hardly matters, anyway." Her voice was still sharp with bitterness, but there was a tinge of despair to it now. "You're not going to stop Kachik. I don't know much, but I know he's terrified of the Synod taking advantage of information or expertise from anyone from our system. He honestly believes he's the legitimate government, and that any action against the Synod is justified. If you think he's only after the humans, you're fooling yourself. He intends to take the Synod down. That has always been his goal."

Alba and Jair exchanged glances.

"That was even before he refused to help in the raider war?" asked Alba quietly.

The woman gave a sharp nod. "From the moment we began negotiating with him, his top priority was destabilizing the Synod. And if you believe that's changed because of what happened over the past few weeks—" she gave a short, bitter laugh. "Then I have no hope for your intelligence."

For a long moment, the four of them were silent. At last, Yosip stood, laying a hand on the woman's shoulder. She flinched, as if expecting a blow, but he just shook his head, his eyes kind and sad. "Thank you," he said quietly. "Thank you for your help." He paused. "We'll do our best to see that you and your friends are not mistreated while you're here. And with luck, we'll all survive long enough to get home."

The woman snorted, but Alba could see a small spark of something that looked like relief on her face at the kindness in Yosip's tone.

He squeezed her shoulder gently. "Are you being treated fairly?"

She scoffed. "Fairly enough, I suppose."

Yosip nodded, and the woman closed her eyes for just a moment. And for just a moment, Alba saw a trace of humanity there that she hadn't seen at all during the course of the interview.

She glanced at Yosip, once again in awe of what he did—how he brought the humanity out in people who had forgotten they had it.

How, if she was being truthful, he'd brought the humanity out in her, when she'd long forgotten what it felt like.

Jair pressed the communication button to call the guards, signalling that their interview was over, and the three of them were escorted out of the prison.

Alba was lost in her own thoughts, so much so that when Jair cleared his throat next to her, she almost jumped. When she looked up, she noticed that the transport had come to a stop, and they were once again in front of the refugee compound.

"I'll drop you here," Jair said. "I've got to get back. I'm on duty soon."

Alba hesitated, then reached out a hand. Jair took it.

"Thank you," she said quietly.

He nodded, but the worry creases in his face didn't fade. "I'll take what we've found back to my superiors," he said quietly. "But I am not sure the effect it will have. No one here is accustomed to treating the threat posed by Kachik as seriously as it deserves, and I doubt they'll take the word of a human prisoner as proof."

Alba nodded. "I'm afraid the politicians are not either," she said dryly. "I'll talk to Karri, but I'm not at all certain that she'll be amenable to my warnings.

"All we can do, I'm afraid, is our best," said Jair. Then he turned back to his seat as Alba and Yosip disembarked.

"Jair is a good man," said Yosip quietly, watching after him. "I doubt any of us would have survived without him."

"He is," said Alba. "Let us hope we haven't sealed his fate in exchange for his kindness."

It took much longer than Alba had hoped before she was able to arrange a meeting with Karri. When she reached the woman's office, the yibo politician already looked long past the point of weariness.

"I hear you've been stirring up problems with the guards," she said, with no preamble.

Alba sighed. "I was forced to make a decision between keeping the peace, and ensuring the security of the people who may hold the key to defeating the raiders. The only military strategies in the system that the raiders have not yet encountered are those from Joias. Considering there is someone who has a vested interest in our failure, and, we've discovered, has expressed his desire to divest you of those resources, I thought it best to take precautions."

Karri passed a weary hand over her face. "I know you mean well. But we're working day and night simply to allocate resources to keep our people alive. We have none to spare for Kachik, and, in large part due to your people's so-called brilliant expertise, we now have him to worry about. I was barely able to get those ships you requested to help your human friends at Chrr, even after what they did with Kachik's military base, and I got less than half of the troops they requested allocated. I simply can't afford to provide you the sort of protection that the guards tell me you're demanding."

"We are not demanding anything," said Alba, trying to keep the sharpness from her tone. "We're simply asking for permission to protect ourselves."

Karri looked up at her, her tail twitching in a gesture of incredulity. "Then you're asking my colleagues and their guards to allow a group of refugee humans, whose loyalties they have no assurance of, to arm themselves? I hardly see how that's significantly better."

"It's not only the refugees I'm concerned about," said Alba, catching the yibo woman's eyes. "Kachik has declared war, formally or not. His interest is in destabilizing you to the point that you agree to cooperate with him. I believe there is a significant security risk for you, as well, especially those of you who've been working with us."

"I appreciate the concern. But I believe we have the experience to manage our own security." Karri's tone couldn't quite be described as cutting, but it only just avoided it. She tipped her head to one side. "If you indeed wish to assist, I would suggest you and your friends find a way to stop the Nativists quickly. Because I will tell you this:" She leaned across her desk, catching Alba's gaze. "I've been working myself to exhaustion to hold our coalition together. If we suffer a defeat at the Nativists' hands, I'm not sure I will still be able to."

Alba closed her eyes.

"I'm sorry." Karri's voice was a little more gentle. "I understand this is not your fault. However, it is the situation in which we find ourselves, and as much as we may wish for it to be different—" she let her words trail off.

"I understand." Alba managed, somehow, to keep the despair

from her tone. "I shall pass the word along. And—" she paused, biting down her pride. "And I appreciate the effort you have made on our behalf. I understand it has been difficult."

Karri managed a small, dry hum of amusement. "It has. But I hope, were the situation reversed, you would do the same for me."

Alba tipped her head to the side in weary acquiescence and made her way out of the office.

She, too, hoped that had the situations been reversed, she would have been as willing as Karri to put her position on the line for her convictions.

22

Aran

Aran stepped into the cabin and glanced around quickly. Istvay was sitting in their chair, elbows on the table, scowling down at a list of data in front of them. They didn't appear even to have heard him enter.

They glanced up as he came over, and the look in their face when they saw him—the way their face relaxed, the small smile that tugged at the corner of their mouth—made Aran unable to keep from smiling back.

"I think I'm getting close," Istvay said, pulling over a chair for Aran and turning back to the table with that trace of excitement in their voice that always came when they were going through data that they found interesting. "It's a matter of setting something up to detect the baseline bioelectric signal, and extrapolate from that whether or not there is an infection present. If we combine that with your data analysis on the creature itself, it looks like there's a very narrow range of energy signatures it can tolerate. I expect that that has something to do with why it can't seem to infect Ani, and prefers mammalian creatures. I'm not certain about that part, we'd have to do some testing, but I suspect that if I can get this detection method working, isolate the unusual energy signature, and pulse a brief energy pattern through it, it will be enough to, if not kill it, at least break its hold on the host."

Aran stared at his friend, his eyebrows raised in admiration. "Pishti, have I ever told you you're a damn genius? Also," he took Istvay's face gently in his hands and tipped their chin from side to side, "how long have you been working on this?"

Istvay groaned wearily, and rubbed a hand over their face. "Not too long, I think," they said. "Although you're rubbing off on me—I don't actually remember anymore. A few hours, maybe?" They chuckled. "Long enough for Ani to steal another one of your shirts, and also empty out the supply cupboard again to stash in her little nest, anyways. Before you ask, she looked fine, just sulky."

Aran glanced over at where Ani had closed up her cupboard again and sighed.

Still, as long as she had an appetite, it couldn't be too serious. And he'd just have to deal with it when he had half a second to catch his breath.

He turned back to Istvay, shaking his head fondly. "You were always just as liable to get caught up in science as I was, it was just different science for you. Why don't you lie down for a bit? Krevai asked me to go up to the cockpit to check how everyone's bracelets are holding up, which I think is probably a good thing, but I can do that by myself. You get some rest."

He could see the struggle in Istvay's face—they'd always hated any reminder of their weakness, and the worse it got, the more they seemed frustrated by it. But at last they nodded reluctantly. "I'm really close. Let me just get this finished up, and I'll go take my nap."

There was a sharp bite of bitterness under the self-deprecation in their tone, and Aran tried to hide the way it made his chest ache.

He opened his mouth to say something about how they were almost there, that they'd have a cure soon now—but Istvay knew that already. And there were more uncertainties than Aran really liked to think about, because he wasn't sure he could think about them without sliding into abject panic. So instead, he just leaned down and kissed Istvay's forehead and tried to smile at them as he slipped out the door.

Krevai was waiting in the cockpit. "Good, good," he said when Aran came in, and waved him over toward Landru. "Hate to have my first mate turn on me while we're in the middle of a battle." He chuckled heartily, and Aran frowned as he walked over to where Landru was waiting, pulling out his sensor as he went.

"A battle?" he asked as he checked the energy signatures on the bracelet. Even at a glance, he could tell the metal was showing more signs of wear in the past couple days than his had the entire time he'd used it. He'd have to talk to Istvay about it—probably something they needed to recalibrate to account for the differences in raider and human physiology.

Krevai grinned at him. "Thanks to the security I could offer the rest of the crews from your little bracelets, we've finally decided to start the real war. We're heading towards one of the yibos' main cities now—and you'll appreciate this, we picked it because we heard some of your human friends were helping defend it, and our crews wanted a challenge. You have no idea how many of my crews you and your Istvay have won over, after they hear the stories—a few months ago, no self-respecting raider would have rated humans as more challenging than yibos."

Aran's hands stopped of their own accord.

Dammit, he'd thought they'd have more time to come up with something, he'd thought Krevai would at least wait until they had a cure …

"I … I thought you weren't going to attack for a while yet," he heard himself saying.

Krevai raised his eyebrows. "Aran. I promised to get your Istvay the medical treatment they need, and from what Dessi says, they don't have much time. This is the fastest option—destroy the yibos and give the crews that follow me a chance to feed, and then I won't get a mutiny when I send the two of you and my scientist down into a yibo city for treatment."

"I … that's not what we agreed to! Istvay and I didn't agree that you'd get them medical care by wiping out an entire yibo city!" Aran's voice was choked with horror. "I don't care if they're yibos or they tried to kill us, it doesn't matter! You can't just—You can't just kill them like that, you can't—"

Dammit, Istvay had always been better at this than he was. This should have been Istvay, not him.

"Aran." Krevai stood, crossing over to stand beside him. "I understand you're upset. But this is political. I can't simply stop a war based on the preferences of one of my crew, no matter how much I value that crew member." He reached out a hand, and paused. "May I touch you?"

Aran gave a stunned nod, hardly able to focus on the captain's words.

Krevai placed a heavy hand on his shoulder. "Sharda and I made a promise, and we intend to keep it. You find us a cure to our charak problem, and your Istvay gets access to whatever yibo medicine they need until you and Dessi finish up the cure. I know you hate killing things, you're like Dessi that way—but these are yibos, not humans.

We're going to kill the yibos anyways, this war has been in the making for a long time. The charak solution you're giving us just means your Istvay gets medical care faster, and there are fewer raiders killed in the process. Leave the politics to me, and you take care of your science, and everything will work out."

"I—" Aran began again, but he wasn't sure he could think, on the spot, of an argument that would convince Krevai.

He wasn't sure there was an argument that would convince Krevai.

He felt sick to his stomach, and his hands wouldn't seem to stop shaking, and his words were caught and jumbled in his head.

"Go on, Aran," said Landru, her voice a little gentler than Krevai's. "It's going to get loud in here soon, and we don't want you to die from stress."

"But … but I—"

Krevai had already turned back to his holoscreen and was barking out commands.

"Go on," Landru mouthed, pointing to the door. "He's not going to have time to talk until after."

Aran gave a stunned sort of nod and made his way out of the cockpit and into the corridors.

The door to the cockpit slid close behind him, and he leaned against the wall, eyes closed, swearing quietly.

He could taste acid in the back of his throat.

Damn it to hell.

This was his fault. He'd been the impetus for Istvay figuring out the bracelets, which meant the attacks on the yibos were his own damn fault.

And he couldn't do a damn thing to stop them.

He should have had some argument, some clever retort, some

brilliant idea that would convince Krevai to stop this stupid, pointless war. But he didn't. He didn't understand the politics, and he didn't know how to make a good argument, he'd never been able to. He knew science. That's what he knew, and it was the one damn thing he was actually good at, and he'd never thought it mattered if people used him for their own political ends as long as at the end of it they just damn well left him alone.

But this …

At last, he pushed himself to his feet and started back down the corridor.

Maybe Istvay would have an idea. Maybe Istvay would know what the two of them could do, something to say to convince Krevai not to go ahead with his attacks.

He was almost at the door to his cabin when he heard the sound behind him, something he might not have heard had he not been so used to listening for sounds that were almost inaudible.

He spun.

He barely had time to make out the raider's face before he was slammed into the side of the corridor, their hands clutching around his throat.

He gasped, choking, as the raider's hand tightened, lifting him off the ground.

In their eyes, he could see the familiar odd gleam that sent something unpleasant slithering in the back of his mind.

He kicked feebly against the walls to the cabin, trying to pry the raider's fingers from his throat for long enough for him to gasp in a breath. Why did they always go for his throat, dammit? He was going to have bruises on top of his damn bruises.

The raider's hand tightened, and black spots swam at the edges of Aran's vision. He fumbled in his supplies pouch for something, anything, and yanked out the first thing he could find—a mending kit, much used and mostly broken—and jammed the tip of a long mending needle into the cluster of tendons on the raider's wrist.

The raider gave a grunt of pain, and Aran winced in sympathy as they jerked their hand back, dropping him to the floor. Before he could run, they grabbed him by the nape of the neck with their free hand.

"We know who you are now," they said in that odd tone that screeched on Aran's nerves like a cheese grater on glass. "And this time we'll kill you."

The hand on his neck tightened, and Aran could feel his vertebrae grinding against each other—and then his grasping hand found what he was looking for: the raider's bracelet, corroded almost through at one point, still connected but probably not able to conduct a current.

"Wait a minute, damn you!" he gasped.

The raider paused, probably from shock at his audacity, and he yanked a flask from his supplies pouch by feel, hoping against hope it was the right one.

The raider snarled, tightening her hand again, there was a lightheaded, horrible moment where Aran thought his skull would actually separate from his spine—and then he managed to get the stopper out, and dumped the entire contents of the bottle over the raider's wrist.

The raider hissed in pain as the acid burned into her skin, but a moment later the bracelet was bright again, the corrosion completely burned away.

A moment after that, the raider had dropped him to the ground and was staggering backwards, staring at her own hands in horror. "Aran," she gasped. "Aran, I'm sorry, I didn't mean—"

"I know," Aran said through his teeth. "Keep your damn bracelet clean next time."

"The charaks are trying to get you and your Istvay," the raider began.

"I know!" Aran snapped. He yanked open the door to the cabin.

And then he froze in horror.

Two raiders had made it into the room ahead of him, and they'd both turned at his arrival. One of them had a weapon, and they drew it, leveling the point at Aran's head.

"Ani!" Aran called. "Ani, I need you!"

But there was no answer from the closed door of the small cupboard that Ani had made her home.

"Dammit to hell—" Aran choked.

And then he realized that he hadn't heard a word from Istvay.

He glanced over his shoulder to see them slumped against the table, and for half a moment, his heart almost stopped. And then he sucked in a quick gasp of relief. There was no blood, and no signs of a struggle.

They must have fallen asleep over their work.

The raiders had been planning to kill Istvay in their sleep. That's why they'd been so silent when he'd come in.

A surge of blind, helpless, furious rage crashed over him like a tidal wave, sweeping him along in its wake. He grabbed the pulse pistol out of his pocket and levelled it at the two raiders. "Stay the hell back," he snarled. "You're not damn well touching my Istvay."

One of the raiders smiled. "Don't worry," they said. "We'll let you go, just give us that one."

"You're not damn well touching Istvay." He'd been working his way around the desk as he spoke, and he'd finally reached one of the supplies cupboards. "Stay the hell back and get out of this room while you have the chance."

His hands were working feverishly at the lock.

He felt it open under his fingers as one of the raiders lifted their guns.

"If you want us to kill you both, then—" the raider began.

Aran yanked out an entire refill bottle of the acid he'd used earlier, and flung it in a sweeping motion so the contents doused both raiders.

They blinked, startled, and he could see the sudden pain in their faces as the acid set to work on their skin—then their expressions changed as the corrosion on the bracelets burned away.

He didn't wait for their horrified apologies. "Get the hell out," he snapped. "Get the hell out and go rinse off, find the rest of your damn crewmates and get them to clean their damn bracelets, got it?"

The raiders nodded, shamefaced, and the moment they were out of the cabin, Aran slammed the door and leaned against it. His heart was pounding, and every breath ached in his raw throat, bruises throbbing in the places where the raider's hands had caught him.

"Ani?" he whispered.

There was no answer except a muffled grumble from inside the cupboard.

Exhausted and sick, he pushed himself upright and made his way over to Istvay.

By some miracle, the chaos hadn't woken them, and he managed a small smile. "Pishti?" he whispered, leaning over them.

There was no response.

He shook them gently. "Pishti? Pishti, it's me. Let's get you to bed, you'll be more comfortable there."

Again, there was no response.

"Istvay?" His voice was sharper this time. He shook them harder, and their body moved at his touch.

It wasn't until they rolled over, their body sliding limply from the chair, that Aran realized what had happened.

What had been inevitable, probably.

His heart was pounding so hard he felt dizzy with it, and he couldn't seem to pull in a full breath as he knelt beside their still form.

Their pulse was there, but only just, weak and light and rapid.

The way he remembered Istvay's mother's pulse, in the days before she died.

They were breathing quick and shallow, and each breath seemed to take much more effort than it should have, and that, too, was far, far too familiar.

"Pishti," he whispered, choking on the words. "Pishti, no, please, we're so close. Just—Pishti, please …"

Istvay lay silent and unresponsive, and looking down at them, their hollow cheeks and the shape of their bones under pulled-back skin, the barely-there weight of them, he realized what he'd known, probably, since the two of them had arrived in the system.

Istvay had been holding on for dear life this whole time. Istvay was the most stubborn person he'd ever met, and through sheer, raw determination, they'd managed, right up to the end, to hold themself together.

And now even that wasn't enough.

Aran lifted them gently—they were so light it was hardly an effort —and carried them over to the bed, where he laid them down gently on the coverlet.

Then he dropped down onto the bed beside Istvay's unconscious body, and dropped his head into his hands, and stared at the floor as the raider ship shot towards its target.

23

Savina watched silently as the military transport hummed over the jungles on the planet that had become far too familiar to her over the past few weeks.

Chrr. The city they'd first made contact with the yibo. The city where she had almost died, more times than she could count.

Reka stood beside her, her hand on Savina's shoulder. She didn't speak, but Savina could sense the tension from her.

Reka had always been much more stoic in the face of death than Savina had. But there were things Reka cared about—people she'd sworn to protect—and she had almost lost them here as well.

"We're going to get some backup from the Synod military," said Reka quietly as the transport came down a little way outside the city. "Alba assured me that they'd send at least a few ships, although I doubt we can count on more than a thousand troops at the most. But if we can take the city, the Nativist threat will be neutralized once and for all."

Savina nodded tightly. She knew all of this, she and Reka had already discussed it. Reka was just trying to make her feel better, and she wasn't sure it was working.

"Come on," Reka said, tightening her hand on Savina's shoulder. "They're calling a meeting in the council room."

By the time they got there, the others were already gathered. Joska looked up as they stepped in, and she smiled a little, the tired creases under her eyes deepening at the expression. "Sit," she said, gesturing to two empty chairs. "We were just about to get started."

Reka pulled back a chair for Savina, then took her place beside her.

"We have some advantage here," said Rafel once they were seated. He glanced over at Reka and Savina. "The two of you are familiar with the government compound, or at least part of it. Ines has spent time there as well. There are also several of us who are familiar with the streets, Joska and myself among them. Between those two bits of intelligence, I think we can plot out our best route for the attack."

He pulled up a holomap of the city, and enlarged it so it hovered over the table. "I've marked our objectives on the map. I'll go over them again so we're clear. Our first and most important objective is to take out their capacity for air-based warfare. If they don't have the ability to launch ships, we've defused the greatest threat. The Nativists almost certainly have other ships already launched through the system, but cutting off their base of operations will seriously impede their ability to resupply or restock the ships. The last time we were here, we took down a number of the ships and caused significant damage to the infrastructure. They'll have started rebuilding it, but considering their need for haste, I doubt it's as secure as it otherwise would be.

"Our next objective is to disable their weapons technology on the ground. We're not going to attack civilians, leave that to the Nativists and the raiders. But any military infrastructure is fair game, and I've marked the command centres, here." He gestured it to a cluster of red dots some distance from the government compound. "I assume Kachik set things up like this to avoid losing all his capacity if there was a major strike. If we can hit both centres together, I doubt he'll recover. Remember, the object here is not to kill soldiers. The object is to incapacitate the Nativists' ability to fight. If we can take out the landing and launching pads, the ground weapons, and the command centres, and especially if we can take them out before the Synod warships arrive, there is a decent chance we can force a surrender. Even if Kachik isn't willing, we can probably persuade the rest of his makeshift government to at minimum concede to peace terms for the duration of the raider war. The rest we can work out later."

"Let's go over the plan one last time," said Joska. She glanced around the table. "I'd rather we were all on the same page to avoid any confusion. Especially considering the abbreviated amount of time we've had to get ready for this." There was a weariness to her voice that was much more pronounced than it had been days ago, and again, Savina felt that spark of guilt at the strain this was putting on the captain. "Just like last time, Savina and Reka are going to take their crew in and get the gates open for Rafel. Once Rafel's crew is inside, Beni, Nicolau, and Ines are going to secure the communications room, while Rafel and the rest of the saboteurs spread out to cause as much damage as they can to the loading docks and the military infrastructure. I'll be taking my crew to cause a distraction at the main government compound, which I think we can get them to believe is our main target. We'll attempt to get inside and hold it for as long as we can while Rafel and Beni get their people into position. In the meantime, Reka and Savina's main goal will be to take out everyone in charge of communications, and any major decision makers. I believe you already have a list." There was a grim look on Joska's face, as if the words tasted sour in her mouth.

Savina sighed heavily. "And I will suggest to my crew that they use nonlethal methods whenever possible, since our marks may have useful information."

Joska looked up, startled, and then smiled at Savina with a genuine affection that made Savina supremely uncomfortable.

"My crew will hold out until we get word from Rafel and Beni that they're in place," Joska continued. "At that point, they'll warn Savina and Reka's crew and set off the explosions. That will be the signal for the Synod military ships. Hopefully that will be enough."

There was a grimness to her tone that made it very clear that this was far from an ideal situation. But then, that had been the story of their lives since they arrived in this damn system.

There were nods around the table, the faces mirroring the concern Savina had heard in Joska's tone. One by one they stood, pausing to whisper instructions or exchange wishes of good luck as they filed out.

Nicolau paused in front of Savina as he left.

"I'd damn well better not see you heroically sacrificing yourself," said Savina, scowling at him. She turned to Ines. "Make sure he doesn't do anything stupid."

Ines lifted her chin defiantly, although she was clearly still terrified by Savina. "Nicolau knows what he's doing," she said, her voice shaking only a little. "I trust him to make the right decisions."

Nicolau turned to her, his expression disgustingly soft, and squeezed her hand tightly before he turned back to Savina. "Take care of yourself, Vina." His voice was suspiciously choked. "I—I don't want to lose my big sister, okay?" And then, to Savina's absolute shock, he pulled her into a tight embrace.

He was a good head taller than she was, and his arms enfolded her completely, and once again her brain stuttered, trying to reconcile this version of Nicolau—impulsive, reckless, heroic, incredibly stupid—with the laughing five-year-old that he'd been when she'd last seen him, the tiny, pitiful infant she'd rescued when she was hardly more than a baby herself.

"I love you, Savina." His voice in her ear was rough with emotion. "I—I'll never forget what you and Beni did to keep me safe." Before she had time to respond—before she had time to come up with a response—he stepped away hastily, brushing at his eyes. He cleared his throat, gave her a brief, tight smile, then grasped Ines's hand like it was his lifeline. Ines leaned her head against his shoulder, and they left, leaving Savina watching after them.

She turned at the soft sound of footsteps to find Beni at her shoulder.

She was struck, suddenly, by how much Beni had changed over the past few weeks.

Her sibling had always had the gift of appearing more intimidating than they actually were, but Savina had always been able to see beneath that hard exterior to the frightened uncertainty beneath, the sibling she'd always had to take care of, and protect, and shelter.

But Beni had grown into themself, it seemed. There was a quiet assurance on their face, a determination to their posture, an unfamiliar confidence in their stance.

She could still see the fear in their expression, but it didn't haunt them anymore.

"Good luck, Savina," they said quietly.

"Beni—" Savina began. She was certain her voice hadn't cracked on the word, but one thing, at least, hadn't changed—even without seeing her, Beni had always been able to hear her emotions in her voice.

They wrapped an arm around Savina's shoulder. "You don't need to worry about me. Or about Nicolau," they whispered. "I've been working with him while you and Reka were back in Chrr. He's smart. He knows what he's doing. And—" they paused, and squeezed Savina's shoulder. "And so do I. You've always had to take care of both of us. But we're going to be fine. So just … take care of yourself, alright? I'll see you when this is over."

And then they, too, slipped out of the cabin.

Savina closed her eyes, leaning against the table. She was fighting back tears, which would have made more sense if anything had actually happened yet.

She opened her eyes as Joska pushed back her seat.

Joska studied her, her weathered face softer than Savina had seen it in a long time. "Take care of yourself, Savina. I used to think I didn't have to worry about that, but I've been forced to revise my opinion after your last few heroic episodes." Her tone was joking, but Savina could hear the sincerity under it.

Joska sighed and glanced around the empty council room. "And I suppose we should probably get to our stations." She left the room before Savina could find anything to say.

She wasn't sure what she would have said anyway—Thank you? I'm sorry? It wouldn't have been anything Joska didn't already know.

So instead, she turned to Reka and gave her her most dazzling smile. "Alright. Let's go kill some people."

After their last attack on the yibo military fortification, getting into the city felt almost too easy—they were able to slip inside without causing the slightest bit of alarm, and they let Rafel's group in without anyone seeming to notice. Joska called in a few minutes later to inform them she was in position.

Savina's nerves were on edge, adrenalin humming through her body as they crept down the familiar city streets. Yibos were rushing towards the government building Joska had taken, and in the resulting chaos, it was easy enough to stay undetected. When they reached the other side of the government compound, Savina turned to her crew of criminals and thieves. "You know what to do," she said, showing her teeth in a bright smile. The smiles she received in return would have been disturbing, had they not been exactly what she was hoping for.

The group of newly minted assassins drifted casually into the courtyard and the surrounding buildings.

Savina and Reka followed their crews inside.

She hadn't been lying to Joska—soon there were at least a dozen people tied up in hallways who would have been dead if she'd been doing this entirely her way. Still, she and Reka between them had shot, slit the throats of, or stabbed through the heart five government officials, still without an alarm being raised, by the time the first call came through.

"We're in position," came Rafel's gruff voice. "Beni?"

"We're in position as well. Reka, do you have communication with the yibo military ships?"

Savina glanced at Reka over the bodies of three of Kachik's officials, seeping blood over the clean floor of the small storage closet.

Reka blinked to activate her wavelink. "They're landing their troops right now. They'll be within range of the city gates within five standard minutes."

"Alright, then," said Rafel. "On my signal."

A thrill of excitement pounded through Savina's veins and tightened her stomach.

They might actually pull this off.

An explosion, muffled through the walls of the building, shook the air around them. There were sudden cries of alarm in the government building as yibos streamed out of offices and meeting rooms to see what was going on. Another explosion, and then another, and then Savina could hear voices cracking over the communicator, alarms shrilling.

"I think that's our cue to get out," said Reka.

Savina tapped her communicator. "Good work," she whispered through her crew's line. "Everyone out, don't wait around to find out what happens next."

Reka grinned at her. Then she shoved open the door to the small storage cupboard, and the two of them took off running down the halls as shots buzzed over their heads.

Savina was gasping by the time they made it outside, and she paused a moment to lean against the wall. "You actually enjoy this, don't you?" she said through her teeth.

"I'm sure you'll enjoy it too, with practice," Reka replied in her laconic tone.

Savina swore under her breath. "Don't count on it."

Reka smirked, and then they were running again, out of the compound and into the streets.

The streets were absolute chaos—perfect cover, and Reka slowed to a swift walk, Savina trotting beside her to keep up. "As soon as we get out of the city, we'll—" Reka began.

And then Nicolau's voice came through Savina's wavelink, sharp with panic. "Savina! I can't get a hold of Joska! I've been trying for the last five minutes, but no one in her crew is answering."

Savina turned back towards the government building where Joska was supposed to be holed up. Even from here, she could make out the heavy concentration of soldiers outside.

The sight turned her blood to ice.

There weren't supposed to be that many. Joska was just supposed to be a distraction, Kachik wasn't supposed to have sent that many soldiers.

"We've got to get over there! We've got to save her!" The edge in Nicolau's voice said he was close to tipping over into full-blown panic.

"Savina?" Reka hissed. "We've got to get out of here, the Synod soldiers will be here in a moment. We've got to open the gates for them."

Savina closed her eyes. "You go." Her voice was barely a whisper. "I—have to go back. Joska's trapped, and Nicolau, that damn idiot, is going to go after her. And he's not going to survive it."

Reka watched her for a long moment. There was a tension on her face that was almost unbearable. "I know!" Savina snapped. "I know I'm supposed to put the good of everyone else in front of the lives of my friends, I know, you've told me that! But—" Her voice choked. "But I can't, Reka. I'm not that person. I'm never going to be able to do that. So you go on, open the gates, let the soldiers in. But I have to go back and get Joska."

At last, Reka nodded slowly. She reached out, running a hand gently down Savina's cheek. "I know," she said, her eyes dark and pained. "I know who you are, Savina. I'll take one of my crew, and I think we'll still be able to get to the gates. You go, I'll meet you when this is over."

Savina nodded, blinking back her tears, then turned and started off at a sprint towards where Joska was trapped.

Nicolau was already there by the time she reached it, waiting for her in an alley, along with Beni, Ines, and Rafel. They were all bloody and exhausted—Rafel was limping even more heavily than usual on his prosthetic leg, and Nicolau was holding his arm tight against his chest, and she could tell at a glance it was broken. Her stomach tightened in worry, but he hardly seemed to notice the injury, his face sick with dread.

Savina slowed as she approached.

One look told her it was hopeless.

The soldiers were already setting detonators at the doors. There was no way they were going to get in there, not before the yibos got inside and took down Joska and all her people with her.

Nicolau watched Savina, his expression one of painful, blind trust that somehow she'd find a way to save them all.

"I—" she whispered. "I don't know what to do."

There was a long moment of silence.

At last, Rafel stepped forward. "I do," he said quietly. "I've got enough explosives. If I strap them on under my jacket and get into the middle of them before they shoot me, that will cause a distraction. The rest of you can get in, pull Joska out, and go."

Savina turned to stare at him.

He glowered at her. "Stop it. You've always hated me, and the feeling's mutual. Just get the captain out, that's all I'm asking." Something in his voice though, belied his harsh words.

Savina closed her eyes and swallowed. "Alright," she said, her voice coming out in a whisper. "Alright. We'll do it."

"You—you can't..." Nicolau turned to Savina, his face a mask of horror. "You can't let him do that!"

"I'd like to see her stop me," Rafel grumbled. He'd already pulled out the explosives, and was tucking them carefully against his chest,

Savina swallowed hard.

"You'd best be ready," said Rafel grimly. "We're only going to get the one chance."

And then, above the city, drowning out even the sound of the explosives still echoing from the military compound, there was a roaring boom that shuddered through the force field.

Savina looked up in shock.

The scene around them devolved into utter chaos as another explosion hit the force field, and it flickered violently.

Savina stared around her as the soldiers who'd been surrounding the building scattered, dropping their weapons and fleeing in panic.

"Joska! Joska, if you can hear me, get out! The soldiers are gone, get out!" Savina could hear Rafel's voice in the back of her mind. But she couldn't tear her eyes away from the scene above her.

The force field shuddered again with another explosion, and then, at last, it flickered and died. And above them, arrayed in black-and-red spiked horror, appeared a raider ship, surrounded by countless attack pods.

Joska stumbled out of the building, supported on either side by two Labarinto humans, blood streaming from a cut on her head. From the corner of her eye Savina saw Rafel and Nicolau and Beni run forward to catch her. But Savina was still staring at the raider ship as it descended into the city's main plaza.

It was only moments later that she heard the screams. Even from here, she could sense the terror of the fleeing yibo as the raiders disembarked and stalked forward into the mass of fleeing prey. She could smell the iron, sickly sweet smell of blood, the sour tang of urine and the bitter scent of vomit and feces that accompanied animal death and terror.

"What's happening?" Joska's voice was hoarse and weak.

"We have to get out." Savina heard her own voice, clinical and distant. "There's nothing we can do. The raiders are going to kill everyone. Kachik, our allies, and the humans left in the city—everyone. And we either get out ourselves, or we die with them."

24

Alba

"I don't care what your politics are, standing up for the humans is putting our survival as a species at risk!"

Alba glanced around the advisory chambers, trying surreptitiously to keep track of the number of heads that were tipped to one side in agreement with Tika's outburst.

She could hardly fault the yibo politicians for being upset. If she wasn't keeping an iron grip on her own terror, she'd have been shaking right now, crouched in a corner trembling.

But she didn't have that luxury. And nor did these politicians, much as they might not realize it yet.

"Humans are violent and dangerous. They are, as Kachik says, a foreign species. And we are arming them, and protecting them, and putting yibo lives on the line to do so. Where does it end? You've seen what kind of creatures these humans are—when they came in, we had to send yibo soldiers to rescue them from violence within their own ranks. Right here in our own city, one of them almost murdered another in their refugee quarters we provided, and then tried to pin the crime on the yibo guards who were risking their own safety to protect them. And so I ask again—where does this end?" He threw his arms in a theatrical yibo gesture.

The number of heads tipped in tacit agreement was, alarming, to say the least.

Karri rose to her feet in the box beside Alba. "We have no reason to suspect that the humans will betray us," she said, her voice sharp. "Everything that we've seen to this point suggests the opposite. They're currently risking their own lives to assist us in both neutralizing the threat posed by the Nativists, and protecting our city. And as far as gratitude—it seems to me that saving a yibo village from the ravages of a raider massacre is demonstration enough of their gratitude. We all saw what happened when the raiders attack. Without the humans, it would have been one more holovid of destruction played out for the Advisory Body. And as far as calling humans exceptionally violent—how many yibo criminals have our peacekeepers tracked down in the city this last month? We all know what it is to devour our own. If anything, this proves the humans to be more like us than some of us here may wish to admit."

There was a soft, discontented murmuring from the ranks of advisors around them. Karri cut them off with a twitch of her tail. "At the very least, I say let's continue to provide these humans the support we promised. Our military forces are tracking the raiders' position and trajectory, and it still appears that there will be time to bring the soldiers back here before the raiders attack. If the humans can end the danger of a Nativist insurrection, then as far as I'm concerned, they have proved their usefulness. Do not attempt to fool yourselves, my friends—we all know that matters with the Nativists would have come to a head at some point. All I am asking is that we maintain the aid we promised these humans, in exchange for the aid that they have shown themselves both willing and capable to give."

There was still scattered murmuring through the crowd, but at least Karri's speech had calmed the mood somewhat.

"Advisor Tika. Did you have an advisement to propose?" It was the Master of Readings, and Alba followed her gaze to the young yibo advisor of whom she'd made an enemy not long previous.

He'd been all but powerless when she knew him. But his newfound status as agitator-in-chief against the humans seemed to have given him the support of much more of the antihuman faction then Alba was really comfortable with.

He, too, was glancing around the room, and at last, he turned to the Master of Readings. "I do not, at this time."

Alba's shoulders slumped in relief. But she'd heard the unspoken words behind his qualifier—*at this time*.

He was going to wait until he was certain he had the support to get his motion passed. And Alba was a canny enough politician to understand that that time was coming very soon, should matters on the ground not change.

When she joined Karri in the yibo woman's office after the meeting had ended, the stoic self-confidence on Karri's face had melted, replaced with a weariness that Alba felt in her bones. There were lines of strain written across the light fur of the woman's face that Alba was certain had not been there weeks before, when they'd first met.

Karri gestured with the tip of her tail to a stool, and Alba sat gingerly, fighting back a wince.

"Can your humans do this?" Karri's tone was abrupt. "I don't mean to sound insensitive, but our coalition is breaking. You saw them when Tika made his arguments. If we can't take Chrr quickly and get our troops back here before the raider attack, I doubt there will be anything I or any of us can do to keep the military from pulling the support out from under your friends."

"I know," said Alba. "We should have proof of success within a day."

She hoped, with all her heart, that she was telling the truth.

Karri sighed, her tail twitching uncomfortably. "It would have been better had you humans made less of an issue over the injured man in your ranks earlier. It's done nothing but give Tika ammunition."

"It wasn't one of ours who attacked him." Alba leaned forward over the desk, meeting Karri's eyes. "As I have told you, we have information that Kachik is trying to sabotage relations between yourselves and us."

Karri was watching her, and Alba saw the scepticism in the woman's gaze. "Perhaps you're right," she said at last. "But even if you are—there are yibo guards posted outside your refugee housing, and that of itself is enough to cause ill will, when the same guards could be used elsewhere."

"Then let us make our own guards!" The words came out sharper than Alba had intended, but the strain of the past few weeks had put an edge to her voice that she wasn't sure she could soften if she wanted to. "You know as well as I do that some of the current guards are on Tika's payroll."

Karri leaned back in her seat. "I am doing my best for you. But you are a group of human refugees with uncertain loyalties and reason to hate the yibos." She held up her hands to forestall Alba's protest. "I don't necessarily believe that myself, but that's exactly how Tika will spin it. Sometimes it's best to fight the battles that can be won, and abandon the ground that will be taken anyways."

Alba closed her eyes, biting down on the words she wanted to say.

She'd never realized what a bitter taste that left in one's mouth.

She opened her eyes at last and gave Karri a weary, close-lipped yibo smile. "We may have to revisit this conversation later," she said. "But I'm hopeful that you are right, and that the yibo guards will prevent further incidents." She paused, the words she was about to say almost more bitter than the ones she had bitten back. "I thank you for your help." Her years of political training gave the words a ring of sincerity.

But the truth was, as furious and helpless as Alba currently felt, Karri was putting her entire reputation and career on the line to assist them. And even if the help came with a bitter chaser, it was much more than she could have expected.

Perhaps it was that, more than the years of political training, that added the ring of truth to her words.

Karri sighed and returned the weary smile. "I know it's not what you want, Alba. But I'm doing the best I can."

"I know," said Alba. "And, our differences aside—I hope you understand that I am thoroughly grateful."

Karri nodded again, her smile a little more genuine. Then she sobered. "But you must understand—if your friends cannot pull off this attack on Chrr, we're finished, I as much as any of you. This was a result of me pulling in every political favour I've collected over the past decade, and even then I barely managed it. I'm holding this coalition together based on personal goodwill more than moral persuasion, and that only holds so far."

Alba nodded silently. She knew well enough the truth behind that statement. "We believe that the strategy we've given them will work," she said at last.

Karri tipped her head to one side. "Let us pray that it does," she said, almost under her breath.

* * *

As always, in the busy rush at the end of the day it took Alba an inordinate amount of time to secure space on one of the public transports. She was dropped almost a solid twenty-minute walk away, and when she reached the refugee quarters at last and made her way past the guards, she was thoroughly exhausted.

"Madam Chief Justice. Feliu sent you this message, asking that you attend a strategy meeting." The young woman who'd brought the message glanced at Alba surreptitiously, then added, "Once you've eaten and refreshed yourself, of course."

Alba bit back a weary smile. She must look tired indeed—she was fairly certain the original message hadn't contained that caveat.

Still, the fact of the matter was, if she didn't take a few moments to eat and rest she might very well pass out at the strategy table. This expedition to the yibo system had been the first time she'd ever fainted, and it was not an experience she wished to repeat.

"Thank you," she said brusquely. "You may inform Feliu that I will be there as soon as I have some food in my stomach."

The girl nodded and darted off, and Alba made her way slowly down the corridor to the common eating room, putting out her arm unconsciously to support herself against the wall on the way.

She had barely sat down with a plate of the bland, over-boiled yibo food when there was a commotion at the doorway.

She glanced up to see the yibo guards shoving their way in, pushing terrified, whimpering humans ahead of them.

"Stay where you are!" one of the yibo guards shouted. "No one move from this room!"

Alba stared around her, her mind ticking through the possibilities.

Had there been another assassination attempt while she was away, with the guards taking it seriously this time? Had Tika finally put forth a proposal after hours?

And then there was another commotion, and Jair stepped into the room, escorted between two yibo guards. He was unarmed, and his brown face was pale with shock and horror.

Alba half rose from her seat to meet him, only to be gestured sharply back by a yibo guard, their weapon trained on her.

Jair reached her table and dropped into the seat next to her, as if his knees didn't have the strength to hold him anymore.

"What is it?" she snapped, strain sharpening her voice. "What happened?"

Jair shook his head, as if speech had deserted him. He glanced around, then leaned forward, his voice cracking a little. "It's—it's Karri," he whispered.

Alba frowned. "What about Karri?"

"She's dead."

Alba stared, any words she'd been about to say wiped from her mind. "Dead?" she managed at last.

Jair nodded grimly. "Assassinated. And from the weapon that was used—they're saying it was likely a human who did it."

Alba slumped back in her seat, despair making her sick to her stomach.

The guards made sense now.

Not even Karri had believed her about the assassin sent by Kachik. Even she had spoken of her suspicions of the human refugees. There was no way that anyone in the government, especially anyone who had listened with even half an ear to Tika, would be willing to give them the benefit of the doubt.

"The coalition's over, then." Her words came out hollow.

Jair's face was tight with misery. "The refugee compound has been placed on permanent lockdown. You're not to come back to the

Advisory Council for the foreseeable future. It took me pulling all the strings I could even to get in here to tell you." He hesitated, as if he couldn't quite bring himself to say the next sentence.

"What is it?" Alba snapped.

Jair closed his eyes. "That's not all. It appears ... it appears Kachik misinterpreted the raiders' intentions. They aren't attacking here first. They've landed at Chrr—that's the city their intercepted messages were talking about. It only makes sense, considering the history Sharda has with the city. They're going to destroy Chrr before they come for us, and they'll destroy your friends and all the soldiers the Synod sent with them. And since the Synod sent the soldiers on your word, and since we were the ones who handed them the Nativist intelligence briefings ..."

"They'll blame us for their losses." Alba felt like she'd been hit in the stomach. "Tika won't even have to work to convince them. He'll spin it as a human plot to destroy as many yibos as we can to weaken them before the raider attack."

Jair dropped his head into his hands. "If they don't offer the humans wholesale as a peace offering to the raiders after this, I'll be shocked." His voice was muffled, but Alba could hear the abject hopelessness in it. "I'm afraid we're finished."

25

Aran

Aran wasn't sure how long he sat there, staring at nothing. He heard, at last, a small, apologetic chirp, and looked down to see Ani huddled miserably at his feet, her big eyes staring up at him piteously.

He swallowed back a thick, choking feeling of guilt—he hadn't even thought about Ani after he'd seen what happened to Istvay, she must have been sick or something to not have come when he called her—and behind the guilt, a sharp bite of anger that only made the guilt worse.

Ani climbed up his trouser leg, contrition showing through every line of her body, and plastered herself to his chest. He stroked her gently. "It's not your fault, Ani, I know," he said, the words choking in his throat. "I don't know what's going on with you, but whatever it is, you're doing your best, it's not your fault."

His other hand was still resting on Istvay's chest, and he didn't want to move it, because there was some terror in the back of his head that told him that the moment he moved his hand, the moment he wasn't actively monitoring Istvay's breathing, it would stop. He would turn around, and Istvay would be still, that cold, terrible stillness that had been carved deep into his brain as a ten-year-old boy that morning Istvay's mother hadn't woken up, and had never woken up again.

And he wasn't sure he'd survive it. He wasn't sure he'd ever have been able to survive it, honestly, but now, so close to a solution …

He swallowed back tears.

Outside in the corridor he could hear the shouts of raiders, and for half a moment the part of his brain that was still paying attention to anything that wasn't Istvay snapped to quick alert—had more of the bracelets failed?—But the noises were much too well-organized, and he recognized the shouts as battle commands, not panic.

So they were almost at the yibo city.

There was a soft rustle, and he jumped, staring around frantically before he realized it was something that had fallen from Istvay's closed fingers.

He reached down to pick it up. It was a folded scrap of paper, and he opened it, smoothing it unconsciously against his leg.

The paper was covered in Istvay's spidery handwriting, scribbled and spiky in the way it got when they were excited.

On the top of the sheet, Istvay had scrawled, "Aran, check my calculations, but I think this will actually work! If all my calculations are correct, this should actually get rid of a charak infection for good."

Aran stared at the paper in his hand, and then down at the still form of his friend. The person he loved more than anything in this system or any other.

He should have felt excited, probably.

Instead, he felt sick to his stomach.

He could walk into Krevai's cockpit right now, hand him the cure. And Krevai would use it, and would destroy the yibos, and possibly destroy all of Aran's friends as well, and then he would keep his promise and get Istvay the yibo medical technology, over the torn bodies of the doctors that created it. Aran could save Istvay's life, at the price of everything they held dear.

Or, he could hold the cure back, and the raider-yibo war would stretch on, and he could watch the crew who had treated him as family tear each other apart in vicious, horrifying brawls with their own crewmates as their bracelet slowly failed, and watch Istvay waste away, knowing the whole time that he held the solution in his hands. And in the end, the raiders would kill the yibos anyways. They'd probably kill the rest of the humans in the system as well, and by the time the war was over, even if Krevai was still in a mood to find him the medical tech, Istvay would already be dead.

Ani tightened her tentacles down on his chest, whimpering, and Aran gave her a small squeeze.

"What would you do, Ani?" He managed a small, hopeless little laugh. "You wouldn't have to worry about any of this, would you? Because no one would dare give you that kind of choice. You would just do what you wanted, and they'd have to deal with the consequences. But—I'm not like you, dammit!" Tears were squeezing out through his eyelids. "All I ever wanted was for people to just damn well leave me alone! I don't *want* to save the system. I don't want to be part of any of this, I just damn well want them to leave me alone, and it's never going to happen, and Istvay's going to die and no one in this whole damn system except me is going to care." His voice was choking now, and he had to grit his teeth against the sobs. He brushed his sleeve across his eyes angrily. "If I was just as ruthless as you, or as dangerous, or as—" he stopped, too sick with despair to continue.

"They don't deserve your help half the time, but I've known you for long enough to know you won't stop giving it to them if they need it. So I'm not saying you should. I'm just saying that you have every damn right to insist that at the very least, you do it on your terms instead of theirs." He could still hear the pain in Istvay's voice at the words.

He stared down at the paper in his hand, at his friend's limp body.

"It's not me," he muttered, his voice still so choked he could hardly get the words out. "You're the one who found the cure. You're the one who kept us alive all this time. And they're happy to let you die if they get what they want."

He glanced down at the paper again. Then he looked back at Istvay, something hardening in his chest.

Slowly, he stood. He was still stroking Ani unconsciously. "Dammit, I've been fighting since we got here to convince people that your life is important enough to save—hell, to convince *you* that your life is important enough to save. But they don't care, not unless they need you for something." He glanced down at Ani. "Maybe that's what Pishti meant."

He looked around the cabin quickly, then grabbed an incendiary device out of one of the supply cupboards. "I'm sorry," he whispered, glancing guiltily back the bed. "I hope you're not too mad at me when you wake up—if you wake up." He swallowed hard. "But I'm sick of being the reason for this war. And I'm sick of being the only person who gives a damn about whether or not you live through it." He lit the incendiary and held it up to the scrap of paper, turning his head away as he did so his brain couldn't pick up on any of Istvay's notations as it burned. Finally, he yelped and dropped the last scrap of burning paper to the floor, stomping it out quickly.

For a moment, he stared at the dark ash-smear on the floor, the last remnants of the cure he'd promised Krevai. The last remnants, that was, except for what was in Istvay's head, as they lay on the bed, their breathing so shallow he could barely see it from here.

He leaned over and kissed Istvay on the forehead.

"Ani," he whispered. "I need you to stay with Pishti, okay?" He took a deep breath. "I'm going to go stop a war."

26

Alba glanced around.

The rest of the refugees were being shoved into the room at gunpoint. And every single one of them, as they stepped through the doors, looked first to her, their gaze flicking over to her almost unconsciously.

As if they still believed she could save them.

"Get in there, give up your weapons at the door," the guards were shouting as they shoved the unresisting humans inside. The room was becoming far too crowded—she could pick out Feliu and Yosip across the frightened mass of people, but she couldn't get to them. She couldn't even move to stand up without one of the guards menacing her with their gun.

"What are we going to do?"

She wasn't sure if someone had actually voiced the question, or if it was only her own mind interpreting it from all the looks cast in her direction.

Across the table from her, Jair was still sitting, his face pale with horror, watching her with the same question in his expression.

But she didn't have an answer.

Her entire political career, she'd learned to hoard and hold onto political power. She'd learned to store it for just such an occasion as this, just such an emergency. And to do so, she'd trampled over the people on whose behalf she was making the decisions. She knew that now, and one day she wouldn't be able to run fast enough to keep the sickening guilt from overwhelming her completely.

And she'd sworn to herself, somewhere in the past few unspeakable weeks, that she wouldn't do it again. That she wouldn't cut out the voices of the people she was trying to speak for in order to ensure her own voice was heard.

When she'd come to some semblance of power here, she'd consulted with the yibos who were not in power, and with the human refugees who had no voice, brought their concerns to the debates and fought for them.

And by doing so, she'd branded herself a fanatic. Someone overwrought and emotional, too attached to the people she was supposed to serve to see the bigger picture. The very thing that she herself would have looked at with distaste only a few years previous.

She shook her head wearily, and tried to smile. "I'm afraid, Jair, that in my attempts to be a hero, I've given up my power." Her voice was clear and distant, and somehow much calmer than she felt. "I'm afraid that I simply do not have the political goodwill to get us out of this. I don't regret what I was trying to do. But I'm afraid that I have made more enemies here than I have friends. And our one friend who had the power to help us is dead."

One day, she would grieve for Karri—for everything the yibo woman had done to save the lives of people to whom she bore no obligation. For the fact that she'd died for it. But that time seemed too far distant to contemplate.

Jair's shoulders were slumped in defeat. Alba noticed, once again, the deep lines on his face, the strain and pain and anguish written into his skin.

He had a family here, Yosip had said. A partner, children. He'd survived the almost total massacre of his system, seen most of the people he knew murdered by the yibos, or, worse, killed and eaten by the raiders. He'd never had political power in this system. He'd never had even the small taste of it that Alba had achieved.

But he hadn't stopped fighting, either. Everything she had been able to achieve, she had achieved because he had been willing to put himself on the line to vouch for her. He had been willing, at every step, to risk his position, which must have been hard won, to give her a chance for more. Because he'd never given up fighting for the humans in the system. Because despite all the reasons he had to give up—his lack of power, his own family who'd inevitably be put at risk, his relatively comfortable position as military liaison—he'd never stopped fighting.

And looking around at the terrified human survivors, Alba realized, with a sudden jolt, how common that was, even back in the Joias system—people without a voice, without connections, without any hope, really, of changing things, who stood and screamed in the streets until their voices were hoarse because they *couldn't* give up. Because they cared too much to give up, even when it was hopeless. She could see in her mind's eye the anguish on Istvay's face when they'd berated her for her policies on homelessness, the quiet trauma written into Ines's expression, and the way the girl's eyes had flashed when she'd stood across from Alba at, perhaps, this very table, and snapped, "I wish you'd thought of that twelve years ago."

She'd always, subconsciously, considered herself so much better than them. More educated, more intelligent, more powerful by right. She'd been wrong, of course—she knew that now. But what right had she to stop, when they never had? What gave her the bloody right to sit here feeling sorry for herself, because for once in her damn life she didn't have the respect and deference and privilege she'd grown up with? What in the hell gave her the right to meekly give up when they never had? To give up fighting for them, after all she'd taken from then out of fear, or ignorance, or hubris?

She leaned forward across the table. "Jair."

He looked up, startled, and she made a quelling gesture. "Hush. As I said, I don't have the political goodwill at the moment to get us out of this situation. But—" she glanced around and lowered her voice. "I think I know what might do it. Karri was the one holding the coalition together. But the reason she could do it in the first place was the possibility that humans might be the key to defeating the raiders. And if we can somehow keep that hope alive—it's still possible that we could salvage this."

Jair glanced around him, frowning, and leaned forward as well. "How do you intend to do that? If Savina and Reka can hold off the raiders, more power to them. But I don't see that happening, at least not before the yibo lose an unacceptable number of soldiers."

Alba nodded. "What we need is not for them to hold the raiders off. What we need is for them to get the raiders' attention somehow. And then we need them to demand negotiations." She took a deep breath. "Do you think you could convince your military counterparts to allow me to negotiate with the raiders in an unofficial capacity, if the raiders demanded it? At the very least, it would give you time to coordinate a response. And as I have no political power, and the rest of the refugees are locked up, I can't imagine what harm they could suspect me of doing, beyond what they believe I could have already done."

Jair was still frowning. "And what do you have to offer the raiders in these negotiations?"

"I don't know that it matters, at the moment," said Alba with a bleak smile. "At the moment, what I can offer them is negotiations with a human, which may put them enough off guard that they would be willing to talk. I can offer you and the yibo military, and possibly the humans in Chrr, time. And if things go badly?" She shrugged, hoping that she'd been able to put more nonchalance into the gesture than she felt. "At the very least, the raiders get a meal out of it."

Jair was staring at her. At long last, he nodded slowly. "I won't say it will work," he said. "But—the raiders do admire bravery. And technically, they are at war with the yibo, not you. So putting yourself forward as a third-party negotiator—" he paused. "You know you're not likely to come out of this alive, right?"

Alba snorted. "And tell me how, exactly, that would be worse than this?"

It would be worse. It would be a thousand times worse than this. Even being lined up against the wall and shot by the yibo couldn't possibly hold a candle to the horror of a raider stalking towards you, battle lust in their glittering red eyes, and Jair knew it as well as she did.

But he had the grace to grant her the fiction. "Alright," he said, reaching out and clasping her hand across the table. "If you can get a hold of Savina and Reka, and they agree … I'll put the suggestion forward to my superiors. And I suggest that, if you really mean to go through with this, you be prepared to leave at a moment's notice."

27

Savina

"We're getting her out of here, right now," Savina snapped. "We're getting Joska out, and we'll figure everything else out afterwards."

Nicolau glanced around, his expression tight with indecision, and Savina grabbed him by the shoulder of his uninjured arm. "I've dealt with the raiders before," she hissed. "There is nothing we can do. We need to get out."

Rafel shouldered his way forward and caught the stumbling Joska, then turned towards the gates. "For once in my life, I agree with the damned assassin," he grunted. "Beni, help me. Nicolau, we'll have time to talk this over when we're outside the gates."

At last Nicolau nodded, his face pale with shock. Beni had already come over and maneuvered Joska's arm around their shoulders, and between them and Rafel, they supported her as the small group of them started for the gate.

"I'll cover you," said Savina brusquely. "Just get out."

The panic on the faces of the fleeing people, the screams, the shoving, pushing mass reminded her, horribly and intimately, of the last hours of the diplomatic ship before it broke up. She forced back the memories of those terrifying, claustrophobic last few moments, the sight from the cockpit of the *Dolphin* of a dying ship broken open, spilling bodies across the emptiness of space.

Get to the gates, get Joska and her siblings out. Everything else could be dealt with from there.

The yibo around them were shoving, pushing, knocking people over in their blind attempts to get out before the raiders killed them.

Savina jerked out her knife and slit the throat of a yibo man who was mindlessly shoving people out of his way. Blood sprayed across the crowded street in a bright stream as the man dropped, gurgling. "Stay the hell away from us," Savina growled, her lips drawn back in a rictus grin, and for a moment, their path was clear. Nicolau was staring at her in horror, but she didn't have time to feel guilty for it. She shoved him forward, and he stumbled after Rafel and Beni.

As they got closer to the gates, the press got thicker, and soon even Savina's knives couldn't open a path.

"We're not going to make it," grunted Rafel over his shoulder. Joska had recovered enough that she was mostly on her feet by now. She was casting suspicious glances at the red dripping from Savina's knives, which meant, much to Savina's chagrin, that she was currently holding back from killing anyone who wasn't actively trying to hurt them.

That option, however, might have just ended.

She deliberately avoided Joska's gaze, and turned to Rafel. "I can do my best to cut our way through, but you'd have to move quickly, and I'm not sure I can do it," she said through her teeth.

There was indecision on Rafel's face as he glanced between her and Joska.

"Savina—" Joska's voice was weak, but the censor under it was as strong as ever.

Savina turned on her, suddenly furious. "Listen, damn you, I'm trying to save your Mystery-damned life. You can stop your bloody moralizing, for once."

"And I think you know, Savina, that I would prefer to die if killing innocent civilians was my only other option." There was steel under the captain's tone.

Savina closed her eyes, clenching her fists as they ducked back against the wall trying to keep from being swept off their feet by the panicked crowd.

Damn it to hell! Joska was going to damn every single one of them because she couldn't wrap her bloody head around the fact that sometimes you had to kill in order to stay alive, and sometimes the people you killed might be innocent, and that was just bloody well how life worked.

"I'm not going to hold you here, Savina, you know that. Take your siblings and go, if that's what you'd like. But I won't be coming with you."

Savina could feel tears of helpless anger starting behind her eyelids. "Why the hell does it matter? If I'm going to kill people anyways, why won't you damn well take advantage?"

And then a voice crackled through her wavelink. "Savina! where are you?"

It was Reka.

She could have sobbed with relief. "We're trapped on the east side of the city," she hissed, trying not to let her voice choke. "I'll send you through the coordinates."

"I'll be there." Reka's voice was grim.

Savina let herself sag against the wall for a moment. Then she straightened. "Reka is coming back for us," she said, turning to

Rafel, once again all business. "And if our heroic, self-sacrificing idiot of a captain can wrap her head around it, I think we may actually make it out of this alive. "

Even with Reka's help, it was a close thing. But something about either the government agent's height, or the sheer, unadulterated menace in her glare, made them a path that Savina alone hadn't been able to without resorting to wholesale murder. Within minutes, they were stumbling out one of the city gates along with half a hundred panicked yibos.

Reka grabbed Joska and lifted her as easily as she'd lifted Savina so many times, and gestured with a jerk of her head towards the trees. "We can take shelter back there."

When at last they reached the ramshackle cement storage shed on the outskirts of the jungle, where a handful of the survivors had gathered, and Reka had surrendered Joska to the care of Rafel and Beni, Savina slumped back against the mildewed cement walls of their shelter.

"What next?" she whispered to Reka.

Reka sighed and turned to her, and there was something painfully gentle in her expression. "This is everyone who got out," she said at last. "All of our crews are still on the inside, everyone we brought with us. Everyone except who's here. Alba called in a few moments ago and said there's nothing she can do unless we can get the raiders to agree to negotiate. So ... this is it."

Savina looked around at the dozen or so terrified humans and yibos crouched in the shelter.

She wasn't used to caring about people. She didn't want to care about people, she knew what a bad idea it was.

But she couldn't stop her mind from running over the faces of the people she'd trained. The people who'd followed her, on her assurance that she would keep them safe. Of all the humans and yibos who'd given up their own chance of safety for this one last desperate venture, based on their trust in her and Reka.

"I'm sorry." The sympathy in Reka's voice was almost worse than anything else.

"I don't care." Savina was speaking through her teeth, her fists clenched. "I don't bloody care." She'd straightened without even thinking about it. "They're not my responsibility! I never wanted this. I just wanted to keep my sibling safe, and keep you safe, and keep bloody Joska safe. And here you are! Here we all are! So we win, right?"

Reka was just watching her. The others in the shelter had turned to watch her as well, but she ignored them. "If someone wants to be a hero, they can feel free. But I'm not going to. I never wanted any of this, I never wanted to be a hero, you all knew exactly who I was when you signed on with me."

They were all still just … watching her. And the sympathy on Reka's face, the understanding on Joska's, hurt like a bloody knife through her chest.

"Leave me the hell alone! We're all out safe. We're going to go back to the *Dolphin*, and we're going to fly away, and we're never going to think about this again. As far as I'm concerned, every last damn one of them can be eaten by the raiders, and I won't lose one night's sleep over it." She was breathing heavily, and her cheeks were wet, and she realized with distant surprise that it was tears.

She spun on Reka. "Say something, damn you!"

Reka slid her fingers into Savina's hair and tipped her head back. "Shhhh," she whispered, running the backs of her knuckles along Savina's cheek, brushing away the wetness. "It's alright. I don't expect you to. I told you, I knew exactly who you were when I fell for you. I'm not asking you to be something different."

Savina squeezed her eyes closed, but the tears were running down her face, dripping off the end of her chin, staining her yibo tunic that was already stained with mud and blood.

Reka pulled her forward, and Savina stumbled into her, burying her face in Reka shoulder as Reka stroked her hair. "It's alright. You're right, you never signed up for any of this. It was me and everyone else who pushed you into it, and you don't have to fix it for us."

Even with her eyes closed, Savina could see the raiders' faces. She could feel the icy terror that shot through her entire body at the sight, the speechless, mindless horror at the thought of those creatures grabbing someone she loved, ripping them apart. At the thought of them grabbing her. At the thought of ever having to look into one of those things' faces again, and see the hunger and the hate glittering behind its red eyes.

It wasn't fair. It wasn't fair of Reka to be so understanding. It wasn't fair of Joska to have cared about her when she shouldn't have, and trick Savina into caring about her in return. Savina had lived her whole life on brutality and violence because it was the only way, the only way to survive the brutality and violence that others wanted to enact on you, the only way you protected the people you loved. It wasn't fair that Joska and Reka and Rafel and even bloody Nicolau had taken that away from her. Had made her believe that there was another way, there always had been, that all the awful things she'd done hadn't been necessary after all.

She drew in a long, shuddering breath and straightened, pushing back from Reka's embrace.

The others were still watching her.

Nicolau, damn him, looked concerned. Like he was worried about her. Like he wanted to bloody well take care of her—the baby brother she'd given up everything to save.

"Savina." Joska's voice was quiet. "No one's going to blame you if —"

"Shut up!" Savina snapped, whirling on her. "Shut the hell up! Haven't you bloody damn well done enough already?"

Rafel blinked, his entire face going red with sudden outrage, and opened his mouth, but Savina spun on him. "You too, Rafel, shut the hell up!" She closed her eyes for a moment, then turned to Reka. "Do you still have a line through to Alba?" She had to force the words out.

Reka frowned, and nodded.

"Alright," said Savina through her teeth. "I'm going to need you to call her."

Reka ran her hand down Savina shoulder, down her arm, rested her hand on Savina's elbow, and the gesture steadied Savina more than she'd thought possible. "And what shall I tell her?" Reka asked.

Savina took another deep breath.

This was it. This was her last chance to back out. No one would even blame her.

But in the end …

Well, in the end, it wasn't about them, not anymore. It wasn't about what anyone expected of her, or counted on her for, or needed from her.

She hadn't been lying to Joska, back when the woman had come to save her and Reka on the small moon weeks previous—even if she hadn't known it at the time. For better or worse, she wasn't who she used to be. It wasn't something she'd wanted, or planned for. In fact, she hated it.

But she'd seen too much, since she'd come through the portal. She couldn't just leave people to die, because they'd leave her if the situation was reversed.

Joska and the others hadn't left her. She'd shown them exactly who she was—her crimes, her selfishness, even her religion—and they'd always come back for her anyways.

"Tell her that—that you and I are still here," she said, meeting Reka's eyes. "That we'll go back in. Tell her to damn well be ready, because we're going to get those bloody raiders to negotiate."

28

Savina

"You know there's no way any of us survive this," said Savina flatly.

"We don't have to stop the raiders." Joska put her hand on Savina shoulder. "We just need to get their attention."

Savina whirled on her, shaking Joska's hand off her shoulder. "And how, exactly, do you propose we do that without stopping the raiders?" she snapped.

It wasn't Joska she was angry with, really. It wasn't even Alba, as tempting as that was.

It was the fact that her stupid baby brother with his broken arm, and Beni, and Joska, injured as she was, had all insisted on coming with her and Reka.

She probably could have found a way to be nonchalant about the risk to her and Reka's lives—they both knew exactly what they were getting into. But Joska and Nicolau and Beni weren't trained killers. They were just … people. Good, decent people, the kind of person Savina had never been able to be—had never let herself wish she'd had the opportunity to be, until recently. And there was no way she could think about them walking up to the raiders without every cell of her body freezing up in panic.

Reka crouched beside her, pulling up holorecording of the city. Savina gritted her teeth and tried to ignore the screams of the civilians on the audio as Reka paged quickly through the streets.

"Here," she said, zooming in on the raider ship that had landed in the centre of the city. "It's a warship, not just one of their attack pods, and it's at a strategic location. If we could take that, we'd have the firepower and position to threaten a dozen of the attack pods at the press of a button. They'd listen to us then, I think."

"And you think hijacking a raider ship is going to be just as simple as hijacking a yibo one?" Savina asked sarcastically. Reka, predictably, didn't respond, and Savina studied the map in silence. "I think I know some back ways that will get us close," Savina muttered at last, reluctantly. "I should be able to get us up to the ship without them noticing. From what I can see in the recording, the raiders seem to be sticking to the main thoroughfares to hunt."

Reka nodded. "And once we get there, you and I can keep the raider guards' attention. We have some practice with that. Hopefully that will be enough to let Joska and the others get onto the ship undetected and take the cockpit."

"We're going to have to do more than just take the cockpit." Rafel's voice was gruff, and Savina could tell that he, at least, was as worried about this plan as she was. "They'll almost certainly have some sort of emergency release on the door. And Reka and Savina aren't going to be able to take down a whole crew of raiders."

Savina resolutely fought back a shiver.

Joska was frowning down at the holomap as well. "What about what Reka and Savina did when they were getting the refugees out, and the soldiers on their ship mutinied?" she asked at last. She turned to Beni, who was standing to one side, their ear cocked towards the conversation. "Beni, you don't happen to have specs of the raider ships?"

Beni shook their head. "No, I'm sorry." They paused. "Once I was on the ship, though, I could probably tap into their databases and find something. Considering how long they and the yibos have lived in the system together, I'd be surprised if their technology is all that different."

"Thank you, Beni," said Joska, turning back to the others. "What about this: while Savina and Reka keep the raiders' attention, the rest of us get inside the cockpit and lock it down. As soon as Beni has the ship specs, they can send the information through to Savina and Reka." She turned to Savina. "I'm sure there will be a storage compartment or brig that you could lock down from the outside. We'll just have to find a way to get the rest of the raider crew who are still on the ship in there."

Savina raised an eyebrow in undisguised scepticism. "Ah. We just trick a crew of raiders into their own prison. That's all?"

Joska met her gaze. "We don't have time to make a proper plan, so we'll just have to figure it out as we go. Unless you have a better idea."

Savina scowled. Of course she didn't. That was the whole point, there were no good solutions here. There were no smart plans, except getting the hell out of here, and idiot that she was, she wasn't going to do that.

"I guess we figure it out as we go, then," she grumbled.

Joska gave her a small smile. "Then let's go."

Savina nodded, not trusting herself to speak. She was trying very hard not to focus on the sight of her brother, the brown of his skin pale with fear, his knuckles white around the hilt of his gun, one arm splinted and clasped close to his chest, his shoulder touching Ines's. Once, Savina might have thought his terror would give her an opportunity to talk him out of this. But she knew him much better now—the stubborn courage that hid behind his friendly, open demeanour, the ridiculous loyalty and protectiveness that he felt for his friends and family, no matter how stupid the sentiment or how undeserving the recipient.

Rafel grunted in discontent, and Savina realized, with a quick flash of unexpected insight, that he was probably thinking the same thing about Joska—her head still bandaged, her clothing bloody, but looking mostly steady on her feet, at least—and had probably come to the same conclusion.

At last, with a quick glance around, Rafel stepped out through the tumbledown doorway of the shelter, limping heavily on his prosthetic leg.

By the time they reached the edge of the city, sweat was already trickling down Savina's neck and under her collar, itchy and uncomfortable. She tried to tell herself it was only from the heat of the jungle, but it wasn't. Every time she closed her eyes, even for a moment, she saw the raiders' faces, the gleam of their fangs against their ivory white skin, the bloodlust in their glowing red eyes.

The way her entire body froze at the sight of them, the instinctual, terrified response of prey. Even from outside the walls they could hear the screams from inside the city, the sounds of blows, the harsh laughter of the raiders as they called back and forth to each other amidst the slaughter.

Savina swallowed hard.

Rafel paused at the walls, then tipped his head towards a small back gate, still swinging open. "Here we are," he whispered. "This is as far as I can take us."

Savina drew in a deep breath. Then she stepped around him, through the gate and into the streets of Chrr.

The moment she stepped inside, the sound and the smell and the horror of it washed over her so strongly that she almost gagged. She choked back vomit and, gesturing the others to follow, started down the back alleys.

The city was chaos—even the alleys were crowded with fleeing people, screaming, sobbing, wide-eyed in shock at the violence of their own destruction. Savina stepped past a yibo woman who lay panting against the wall of the alley, holding her intestines in both hands, her eyes wide and glazed with shock. Joska's lips tightened at the sight, but even she didn't suggest stopping to help. There was nothing they could have done, anyway—the woman would be dead in minutes. And what they were about to do was the only chance to stop the slaughter.

As they got closer to the raider ship, the press of fleeing people thinned—everyone in this part of the city must have already either fled or been killed. And from the thick, sticky-sweet charnel scent of the streets, slippery with blood and viscera, Savina could guess at which.

At last she poked her head around the corner of the alley, and saw the raider ship. The sight of it was like a punch to her stomach, making her breath go tight in her throat.

The ship crouched, squat and predatory, in the centre of the city's main transport hub, red and black and angular, still steaming from its dissent through the atmosphere. Savina drew back, and gestured the others closer.

"We're here," she whispered. "I didn't see much of a guard on the ship, but from what I know of the raiders, whoever's left behind will be able to kill us easily."

Reka nodded. "We'll have to assume that there are more of them than we think." She glanced at Joska. "You know what you're doing?"

Joska gave a short, grim nod.

"Good." Reka turned to Savina, the smile on her lips as sharp as a knife and just as deadly. "Are you ready?"

Savina tightened her fingers around the hilt of the throwing knife she'd hidden in the loose folds of her yibo tunic, and smiled up at Reka. "Of course I'm ready!" She fluttered her eyelashes. "I just spent all this time wandering through the streets, completely lost— I'm sure these nice raiders would be happy to give us directions."

Reka's smile widened, just a bit. She turned back to Joska. "Be ready," she whispered. "You'll have to move fast once we have their attention."

Joska nodded again, her face grim, and adjusted her grip on her pistol. Her face was still pale, her clothes blood-streaked, but there was a steady determination in her face that would have made even Savina think twice about crossing her.

As it turned out, attracting the raiders attention was not at all difficult. Savina hadn't really assumed it would be, to be honest. Her wide-eyed little scream when the first of the creatures started stalking towards her was enough to draw the attention of a few of his fellows, and she'd have considered herself a damn poor performer if the rest of her act didn't draw in more.

She backed towards the wall of the alley, making sobbing, whimpering little noises. "Please, please don't hurt me! I just—I just got lost, I was just here in the city, and I got lost, I don't know what's happening—"

Whether he understood her or not hardly mattered. This was about presentation.

"Look at that!" one of the raiders called out in Common Dialect. He laughed loudly. "I suppose this is God's blessing on those of us who agreed to stay to guard the ships—not just any prey, but a human! And it shows up right at our door!"

Savina whimpered, and backed a little farther into the alley.

"Come on, little human," the raider in the lead coaxed in a mocking singsong. "Don't run away, you'll ruin your flavour. Just come nice and easy, it will be over so fast you won't feel a thing."

"I—I don't want to die!" Savina wailed.

The first of the raiders had almost reached her, his long butcher knife in hand. "Come, now, little human." He was still grinning as he stepped forward to close the distance between himself and Savina.

She waited until he was close enough to reach out to grab her. And then, in a quick, practised motion, she stepped forward and slashed the knife she'd hidden in her clasped hands across his unprotected face. He shouted, more in surprise than pain, his hands coming up to staunch the spurting blood, and Savina stepped in closer, grabbed the collar on his armoured suit, and yanked it back just enough to allow her to shove the knife through his jugular.

She jumped back to avoid the hot spurt of blood, and he crumpled with a low gurgle. Two of his companions leapt forward, cursing, and Savina stumbled back, holding up her empty hands with a sob. "I don't know what happened, he was coming for me, and his knife slipped, I think—"

One of them grabbed her by the hair, yanking her around to face him. "We're not stupid, human," the raider gritted through his teeth. "You humans are more dangerous than you look, our war captains have some of you on their crew. So don't you—"

Savina gave him a beatific smile, pulled her hand from behind her back, and shot him between the eyes with the pulse pistol she'd tucked in her waistband.

The raider collapsed, his face a mangled wreck, and Savina slid free of his dying grasp, ducking just in time as a third raider swung his heavy butcher knife at her neck. She went to straighten, but her foot slipped in a puddle of blood. She scrambled for balance, her feet sliding from under her, and landed hard on the concrete, the shock of the fall jolting up her wrists and elbows and into her shoulders and driving the breath from her lungs.

She stared up into the raider's eyes as he lifted his knife for another swing, terror choking her, freezing her muscles and slowing her brain.

There was the quiet, almost inaudible hiss of a rifle. The raider's eyes widened, a small red stain blossoming on the unprotected bit of flesh beneath his collar. Then he stumbled, the knife slipping from his fingers, and the part of Savina's brain that was still functioning made her roll out of the way to avoid being crushed under his body as he collapsed to the filthy pavement.

By the time she'd scrambled to her knees, her hands slippery with blood not her own, half a dozen raiders were charging towards her, shouting in fury.

She glanced behind her to the alley in panic, but there was no way she could outrun them, she'd probably not even make it to her feet before they were on her …

A hand grabbed her under the arm, yanking her to her feet, and she looked up, startled, into Reka's face.

Reka was actually grinning. "I hope you've learned to enjoy running," she whispered, and before Savina could respond, Reka was dragging her down the alley at a dead sprint.

Savina didn't even have the breath to swear, but she could see over her shoulders the raiders coming after them, gaining ground with

every step. She'd thought they looked predatory before, but this …
they were spreading out like a pack of hunting wolves, their
movements fluid and economical and impossibly fast.

"Joska and the others are inside the ship," Reka whispered over
her shoulder. Savina could hardly hear her over the pounding of her
heart. "We just need to keep them busy until she's secured the
cockpit."

"If we damn well survive that long," Savina gasped.

The raiders were close enough now that she could all but feel their
breath on the back of her neck. Her own breath was sobbing in her
throat, her lungs aching, the muscles in her legs burning.

Reka dodged into another alley and pulled Savina after her. The
raiders poured into the alley after them without so much as breaking
stride.

And then Reka sucked in a quick breath, and Savina glanced up
in time to see a raider drop down from the roof of one of the nearby
buildings, blocking their way forward.

"You humans always do surprise us." The raider was grinning, her
fangs glistened in the low light of the alley.

Reka caught Savina's desperate glance at the walls around them
and shook her head, just a fraction. "I wouldn't get up there in time
to throw a rope down for you." She smiled, that dangerous, knife-
sharp smile that Savina had, entirely unwillingly, fallen for months
ago and light-years away. "So, I suppose we take as many of them
with us as we can."

Savina's stomach was tight, horror twisting in her gut. She wasn't
sure if she was more horrified by the fact that Reka could easily get
away and leave her here to die, or … that she was choosing not to.

"Aren't you the one who's always saying that I'm looking for a
glorious way to die?" Reka whispered, checking her pistol.

"A 'glorious way to die' like saving the system," Savina hissed back. "Not like this!"

And then Beni's frantic voice came through Savina's wavelink. "Savina! We're in. I got the specs, and I'll send them through to you. I've marked the compartments that should lock from the outside."

"Get their attention somehow!" Savina hissed. "Or we won't make it back."

"Hold on …" Beni's voice was tense.

Then Nicolau's amplified voice boomed across the open square. "Hey! Raiders! You might want to stop picking on my sister and worry about your ship!"

The raiders paused, frowning and glancing around at each other.

Savina flicked her eyes to the closest raider and raised her eyebrows questioningly. Reka nodded, and, before the raiders had time to react to Nicolau's words, Savina sprung at the nearest of them. Her knife skittered across the creature's body armour until it caught on a small gap beneath the raider's ear, and she jammed it in with all her strength. The raider managed a surprised gasp, and then collapsed to her knees with a choking wheeze. Savina jumped back out of the way, and then Reka grabbed her by the arm and they started for the ship at a dead run.

Savina was swearing steadily under her breath, and Reka glanced at her, her expression still, somehow, amused. "See? All that running we did was good practice."

"If there is any justice in this damn universe, once we get out of this, I will never run anywhere again for the rest of my life," Savina gritted out through her teeth.

Reka actually chuckled.

They rounded the corner of the alley, and once again Savina caught sight of the raider ship.

The hatch door was standing open, but there didn't seem to be anyone on guard—all the remaining raiders must be trying to get at Joska and the others. They must have assumed no one would be self-destructive enough to insert themselves in the middle of the chaos.

"You know, there was a time that I used to have some sense of self-preservation?" Savina hissed at Reka as they sprinted up the loading ramp.

"That must have been before you met me," said Reka, still grinning.

Savina was breathing too hard to answer, so she contented herself with a glare.

"We're inside," Reka said into her wavelink, as Savina collapsed breathlessly against the corridor walls. "Number and position of the raiders still on the ship?"

"My best guess on numbers is half a dozen," Joska's voice was grim. "As for position—I can't be sure, but from the sounds of it, most of them are outside the cockpit door right now."

"Beni, lock down the hatch," Savina snapped, pushing herself upright. "I don't want anyone else inside if we can help it."

A moment later the hatch door slammed shut, the lock clicking, and Savina drooped in relief.

"Let's go," Reka whispered, and they took off down the corridors towards the cockpit. "Get them to follow you, and lead them for the door," hissed Reka as they ran. "If you can get them in position, I've got a percussion explosive. We'll stun them, and shove them inside before they recover."

Savina nodded, too breathless to answer, and then they came around a corner to see the raiders clustered against the door to the cockpit. One of them had their butcher knife in a small gap between the door in the wall, and, to Savina's horror, the door was creaking and buckling as they pried at it.

"What are you doing?" Her voice rang out over the noise, and for a moment, everyone paused in shock.

The raiders turned.

Savina realized, from the corner of her mind that was still thinking logically, that Joska had underestimated. There were at least ten raiders, and they all looked very angry. And very hungry.

She smiled at them. "I hope I'm not interrupting anything …"

The raiders recovered from their surprise with impressive speed.

Reka shoved Savina hard, and Savina stumbled into the corridor wall as half a dozen raider shots cracked past where her head had been. She caught her balance, turned, and took off down the corridor that the blinking direction light in her retinal screen told her was the correct one.

She could hear the raiders pounding after her, and then a shout of pain and more footsteps—she had no idea what Reka had done, but whatever it was seemed to have been enough to get the attention of even the raiders who'd stayed behind to try to get into the cockpit.

She skidded around a corner, then another. She was almost there, just a few more steps—

Claws caught the back of her tunic, and she was yanked off her feet. She scrabbled for her knives, but the raider shook her like a dog shaking a rat, and she lost her grip on her weapons. He shook her again, grinning, his teeth stained red with blood, and with his free hand he drew his long knife.

Savina screamed in real terror this time, writhing ineffectually in his grip.

She was going to die. She was going to die, this time she was actually going to die—

The blade plunged forward, and Savina screamed again, closing her eyes against the expected pain—but instead of a knife, something hit her hard in the ribs, sending her crashing into the wall. The raider's claws tore free of her tunic at the impact, and she landed on the ground, scrabbling for her last pistol. She pulled it out as she rolled, and as the raider grabbed for her again, she shot him in the face.

"Savina," Reka hissed, and Savina grabbed what Reka shoved into her hand. A small corner of her mind noted the explosive was damp with something, but she didn't have time to think about it, just pulled the pin and tossed it into the centre of the group of raiders who'd followed her down the corridor, then dived to the ground, protecting her head with her arms.

The percussive was enough to knock her half dizzy, but she'd been expecting it, and the raiders hadn't, and the open door was right ahead of them. She staggered to her feet and shoved the stumbling raiders through the door, slamming it behind them.

"Reka! The lock!" she snapped. There was no answer, and she swore and scrambled for the control panel, the door bulging and creaking behind her as the raiders put their shoulders against it. She found the panel and hit the lock, and then, finally, her knees gave out, and she dropped to the ground in relief.

"Reka," she gasped. "We did it!"

There was no answer.

Savina rolled over, groaning, and pushed herself up into a sitting position. "Reka?"

Reka lay on the floor of the corridor on her side, her shoulder-length black hair, tangled and bloody, spread across her face. One arm was stretched out, where she'd handed Savina the explosive. And it took Savina a moment to understand that the dark stain across her grey suit, spreading in an ugly, asymmetrical bruise out from her left side, was blood, Reka's blood, and that she was lying far too still, and that under the tangle of mud and blood and the curtain of her hair, her skin was an unhealthy grey, her eyes closed.

Savina stumbled to her feet, her heart suddenly pounding much too fast. "Reka?" she whispered, dropping to her knees beside her. Her fingers were shaking as she rolled Reka over.

There was so much blood. So much blood, and now Savina could see the ugly tear through the grey armoured suit that Reka wore, that must have been from the raider's knife when Reka had shoved Savina out of the way, the blood welling up under it.

"Savina? Savina, are they in?" It was Nicolau's voice through her wavelink, and somehow, she managed to answer … something. Whatever she'd said must have reassured Nicolau, because a moment later there was an explosion she could hear even from the depths of the ship, and Joska's voice over the communicator, calling out, "We've taken your ship, and we have your crew hostage. I'll fire on your attack pods, right now. Or, we can negotiate."

But it all seemed distant, and very far away.

Savina took Reka's shoulders in her numb hands, and dropped her head against Reka's chest, and sobbed.

She wasn't sure how long she stayed like that. But at some point, she heard Joska's voice, a distant, background noise, and felt hands lifting her to her feet, and saw, through the haze of tears, Nicolau and Ines bending over Reka

"Savina? Savina, I need you to talk to me."

Savina blinked dully at Joska, tears seeping from her eyes and dripping down her cheeks, blurring her vision.

Joska shook her, and it startled her back to awareness. "Savina. Listen to me. Reka is alive. Do you hear me, Savina? Reka's alive."

Savina stared at her in incomprehension for a moment. And then she gasped in a breath, what felt like the first real breath she taken since she'd seen Reka collapsed on the floor. "She's—" she began, her voice unsteady.

Joska smiled. "There you are, Savina. Yes, she's alive. I'm not going to say she won't be sore, but her amour turned away the worst of it. I'm no medic, but I suspect she'll recover."

"Are you lying to me?" Her voice was shaking and desperate.

"I promise. You can come see for yourself."

Savina slumped against the walls of the corridor, her entire body gone boneless with relief, and Joska chuckled. "Come on, let's get back to the cockpit. If the raiders don't agree to negotiate, things are going to get interesting pretty quickly."

29

Aran

The moment Aran stepped from his cabin, he knew the battle had already started. Grim-faced raiders jogged up and down the corridors, and he could hear the shouted orders, quickly muffled as he stepped into hearing range with whispers of, "Shhh, it's the human, don't stress our human!"

It only twisted the knife of guilt in his stomach deeper. But he bit down hard on his teeth and forced himself forwards.

When he reached the cockpit, Landru looked up in irritation. Her face brightened when she saw who it was. "Shut up, the lot of you!" she shouted. "Our Aran's here, shut your mouths!"

The clamour in the cabin died abruptly, and again, Aran almost winced at the jolt of guilt.

"Aran!" Krevai glanced up from his seat in front of a vast array of holomaps. "I'm sorry, we're in the middle of a battle, but I doubt it will take us long." He grinned, showing his sharp incisors. "But I'm sure you came out here for a reason. You haven't found a solution to the charaks, have you? Landru told me there's been more incidents of the bracelets failing."

Aran nodded, swallowing hard against the sickness in his stomach at what he was about to say. "I … I didn't, but Pishti—Istvay, I mean —found something that should be able to get them out of your heads entirely."

The gleam of relief in Krevai's face was almost more than Aran could bear. "That's fantastic news! You and your Istvay are truly treasures! I'll tell Sharda that she should be proud of her human. This will mean we'll win the war that much faster, which means we'll get your Istvay taken care of in no time at all."

Aran had to close his eyes for a moment to brace himself. "Istvay —Istvay's unconscious," he muttered. "I—I don't know if they'll wake up again before … before—"

Krevai's face was instantly a mask of concern. "I swear, Sharda and I will get them care at the earliest opportunity. Now, give Dessi your notes on the charaks, and we can—"

"I don't have them." Aran had to force the words out.

Krevai turned to stare at him. "You—"

"I don't have them." Despite his best efforts, Aran knew he sounded just as miserable as he felt.

Krevai was still staring at him. "Your Istvay didn't give them to you before they collapsed? Did they write it down somewhere? How did you know they found a cure?"

Aran looked down so he wouldn't have to look at the captain. "They did write it down," he muttered. "But I—I burned it. I burned it before I knew how they did it."

Now, the entire cabin of raiders was staring at him. "You burned your Istvay's notes?" Krevai's voice was bewildered and hurt, but under it, Aran could hear an edge of danger to his tone. "Aran—"

He wished, irrationally, for the comfort of Ani on his shoulder.

Now that he thought of it, maybe he should have brought her along after all. He'd grown used to seeing the raiders as friends, although he knew damn well they could kill him if they wanted to.

And, he realized, he was now giving them a very enticing reason to want to.

But he could see on the cockpit holoscreens the view of the streets of a city he recognized, abruptly, as Chrr. He could see the yibo screaming and running, the horror on their faces as the raiders grabbed them, snapping their necks or disemboweling them with one stroke of knives or claws. And he remembered the sight of yibo children on those same streets, playing the same clapping games he and Istvay had played as children, Ree, the scientist who'd risked her life to give him information that had finally, finally led him to the cure for Istvay that he'd been searching for his entire life.

He raised his chin and met Krevai's gaze for the first time. "Captain," he said quietly. "I never agreed to this war. Nor did Istvay. We agreed to help you in exchange for medical care for Istvay. You were the one who decided to use our help to kill the yibos. All I'm telling you now is, if you want my and Istvay's help, you'll have it on our terms, or not at all."

For a moment, the cabin was completely silent. Then Krevai rose to his feet, and Aran had to force himself not to take a step back at the menace in the captain's eyes. Krevai stalked over to him, grabbing him by the front of the shirt, and lifted him up to eye level. "How dare you?" His voice was flat and furious. "I took you on as a member of my crew, and you've proved your worth. But how dare you think you can tell me what I will or will not do?"

Aran gritted his teeth and glared back, even though everything in him was telling him to drop his eyes. "I signed on as your crew to help find a cure for Istvay." He tried to force his voice not to shake.

"Istvay and I agreed to find you a solution to the charak infestation in exchange for you getting us medical technology so I could save Istvay's life. You and Sharda were the ones who decided that Istvay's life was secondary to waging your war on the yibo. You said that I'm involved in yibo and raider politics? So fine. I'm damn well involved in your damn politics now. You can call off the war with the yibo and save Istvay's life, and I'm sure the moment Istvay has the strength to sit down at a research table again, they'll happily replicate their notes. Or you can keep your war, and Istvay can die, and eventually those bracelets will fail and your crew will turn on you, and every single raider in this entire damn system will be thrown into war the likes of which you haven't seen before. But you can't use Istvay when you find them useful, and then shove them off, not anymore, and you can't damn well do it to me either. If you don't need me, fine—kill me. Believe me, I understand that you can. But I'm not playing someone else's games, not any longer."

It was strange how steady his voice came out. The adrenaline pumping through his body was probably enough to leave him shaking, the moment it sank in. Some distant, impartial part of his mind was making the calculations of how likely it would be that he'd actually stay on his feet once the crisis was passed, and the numbers it was coming up with were not promising for his dignity.

But he held Krevai's gaze.

"God damn you, human," Krevai snarled.

Oddly enough, the sound of it slowed Aran's racing heart, just a little. He'd never been all that frightened of predators, not really. Not compared with the alternative, the sapient species who were supposed to be civilized.

"I could feed you to my crew right now. They could pull the limbs from your body one by one, and they could do it in a way that you would be alive and conscious the whole time. Believe me, we have practice."

Aran almost laughed, a small, hysterical sound. "Do you honestly think there's anything you could do to me that would frighten me right now?" He asked. "Istvay is unconscious in our cabin, and I don't know how much longer they're going to live. Ani's sick, or upset, or something, and I haven't had two seconds to sit down and try to figure out what's wrong with her. My friends are down there being killed in a war that you started, using me and Istvay as your impetus. Do you honestly believe there is any threat that you could make that would make the slightest bit of difference?"

Krevai stared at him for a long, long moment. At last, he backhanded him across the face with his free hand. Aran hit the wall, hard enough to bruise, and tumbled to the ground, barely catching himself on his hands and knees. Blood was streaming from his nose, and he was pretty sure his lip was split, but he forced his gaze back up to Krevai. "You need me," he said. "Or at least, you need Istvay. And you're not going to get them until they're strong enough to redo their calculations, and Dessi and I have time to get them a cure. After that, you can do whatever you want to me. But not right now. Right now, you use us on my terms, or not at all."

"What's going on in there, Krevai?" Sharda's voice through the holodisplay was sharp and furious.

Krevai stalked over to the screen, and in the back of his mind, Aran heard them arguing loudly.

He couldn't entirely make out the words, and he wasn't sure whether it was because they were arguing in the raider language rather than Common Dialect, or whether he was so lightheaded that his brain had simply given up on assigning meaning to sounds. It could have been either, honestly—the sharp ache at the back of his head told him that he'd hit it hard, and he hadn't even bothered to take stock of the rest of his injuries. They all seemed, somehow, unreal and distant. He thought he might throw up, and hoped, vaguely, that he'd be able to hold it down until he could vomit somewhere that wasn't the middle of a busy cockpit.

At last, Krevai stalked over to him. He could hear the thud of the captain's boots on the cabin floor before they came into view in front of him.

He forced himself to look up.

Krevai was staring down at him, his eyes narrowed in fury. "You say you'll help us on your terms." His voice was thick with sarcasm. "And what, pray, might those terms be?"

"Stop the war," Aran mumbled through swollen lips, forcing back the vomit that was trying to climb up his throat. "Stop the war, negotiate with the yibo to get Istvay medical care until Dessi and I can finish up the cure."

"Ah. And is that all?" Aran winced at the silky anger in Krevai's tone. "You realize, don't you, that Sharda and I can't simply stop a war that's already started. There are two parties to it."

"The yibo are terrified of you." Aran made himself meet Krevai's gaze. "You know that."

"Terrified of us, yes," snapped Krevai. "And with good reason. But do you think that the fact that they're terrified of us will stop them from trying to find some advantage? Kill as many of our crews as they can if they see us simply retreat with no reason?"

Aran squeezed his eyes closed, trying to force his brain to think. Damn it to hell, he wasn't a politician, he'd never wanted to be a politician, this kind of thing was far beyond him.

"Captain!"

He and Krevai both turned at Landru's voice. "Captain, the

humans have called in. They've taken the ship that set down in Chrr, and they want to negotiate. Sharda wants to shoot them down and be done with it, but killing them will mean the loss of several crews."

Aran could feel his entire body slumping in relief. "Negotiate," he said, the words coming out harsher than he'd meant. He turned to Krevai. "Negotiate with them, in good faith. You're right, maybe you can't stop the war single-handedly. But here's an opportunity, and you'd damn well better take it."

Krevai gave him a look that was so full of menace that it would have sent a chill through Aran's entire body if he hadn't already been so far beyond terror that any additional stress response would be irrelevant. At last, though, he stood grudgingly, shooting Aran one last poisonous look. "Put them over the com, find out what they want," he snapped, turning to Landru. "I'll deal with my former human crew later."

30

Alba

"You humans are all the same. And I don't trust any of you."

The raider captain's vicious, snarling face was coming through a holodisplay, but even so, Alba had to consciously stop herself from stepping back from the fury in the raider's voice.

Some part of her knew that the reason she was on a raider attack pod to begin with, rather than having this conversation from the refugee compound in the yibo capital, had much less to do with the physical convenience of the parties, and much more to do with the fact that at the end of it, if the negotiations were unsuccessful, they were fully intending to kill and eat her.

The part of her mind that was still able to see the gallows humour in the situation noted that, at the very least, she would likely be tough pickings.

"You're deceitful, disloyal, despicable—" the raider captain—Sharda, if Alba remembered correctly—was clearly furious. And the raiders on the attack pod, currently surrounding the negotiating table where Alba sat, had obviously picked up on the captain's mood.

"I apologize that I have managed to offend you," said Alba tartly, into the momentary pause caused by Sharda's need to draw breath. "However, I was under the impression that we were here to negotiate, not simply to insult one another."

Sharda was still glaring at her, and Alba recognized the sharp red scar across one side of her face as the remnants of the pulse pistol shot Savina had managed to inflict on the captain, moments after the young assassin had shot Reka in the middle of the street, and moments before Alba had made her first—although unfortunately not her last—flight for her life from a yibo city.

"And why should we negotiate with you?" Sharda leaned closer to the display screen and smiled a deeply unnerving smile, the type of smile that reminded Alba why showing your teeth in this system was considered a threat. "You're hardly a government official, I believe. The negotiation that I'm interested in is which of my crew will get the greatest portion of the meal."

Alba narrowed her eyes. "That is precisely why I'm valuable," she said coldly. "I am not a yibo government official. I am a human. I represent the humans who came through the portal from the Joias system as their legitimate government authority. You have not declared war against us, therefore, at this moment, we are an uninterested third-party. And you agreed to cease hostilities for the duration of the negotiation, in return for my compatriots not firing on your attack pods."

Sharda gave her a thin-lipped smile. "You're right. We haven't declared war on you yet. But you saw fit to attack our ships regardless. That seems in line with the general dealings of your kind." Her voice was tight with anger, but now, at least, it had regained some semblance of calm. "I've discussed this with Krevai.

We agree to cease hostilities for the duration of the negotiations, and we agree to allow you, as a neutral third-party, to act as mediator, and in exchange, your people will not fire on our ships. But none of us are happy with humans at the moment, so best get your yibo counterparts on the line before we change our minds."

It had taken all of Jair's influence, as well as two of the military generals' intervention, to get a representative from the Synod to agree to negotiate. But thankfully, when Alba tapped through to the holobroadcast, his anxious face flickered into view.

The negotiations between the yibo and the raiders were short and to the point. And to Alba's shock, the raiders seemed almost as motivated to strike a deal as the yibos. From the inclusion of access to yibo medical facilities in the peace terms the raiders proposed, Alba had a sneaking suspicion that their eagerness—and possibly Sharda's earlier fury—may have had something to do with Aran, but she kept that thought to herself. No point in antagonizing either party unless absolutely necessary.

"It won't be immediate," one of the yibo advisors was saying, turning to Alba. "We'd have to agree on a guard to let you access the medical facilities, as well as first evacuating the current patients, but I think we can deal with that in a matter of hours, days at most. I believe we can also deal with your requests that we withdraw our outposts from certain of your hunting planets and concede most of the areas you've requested as raider space, and negotiate the withdrawal of intelligence personnel and the opening up of trading relations with raider ships. We would need assurances from your side, however, that hostilities end immediately, and you allow access to medical and emergency personal into Chrr."

Krevai, who'd joined the negotiations, his expression almost as darkly furious as Sharda's, glanced off to the side of the screen as if consulting with someone.

From the set of his body, he was not happy about whatever was prompting the consultation.

He turned back to the screen grudgingly. "We can agree to that," he growled. "But we must have your assurances that there will be no retaliation. I can't promise I'll be able to keep my crews peaceful if you attack us."

"I think we can agree to that, if you can guarantee that your forces will pull out with no further loss of life, and you allow our forces to retreat from Chrr in the meantime," the yibo negotiator countered.

There was a long, long pause. At last Sharda nodded. "We'll agree to those terms for the moment, and call a cease-fire while we negotiate the remainder of the peace agreement," she said briskly.

The release of tension in the cockpit around Alba was almost tangible. She could see it in the yibo as well, through the holoscreens. The yibo negotiator almost sagged with it.

"I propose that representatives from both parties oversee the handing over of the city, to avoid misunderstandings," he said.

"And you, humans. The neutral third party." Sharda's voice was thick with sarcasm. "Will you agree to release our ship?"

Alba cleared her throat. "Of course," she said. "As soon as the city has been evacuated, I shall instruct my associates to release your ship and crew, on the promise that your people will allow them to do so safely." Alba was trying not to think of the irony of her referring to Savina as her associate, or of the laughable absurdity of Alba having authority to instruct Savina to do anything. Still, the raiders didn't need to know how tenuous the human chain of command was at the moment.

"Of course."

Alba managed a bland smile. "I believe we have an agreement, then."

One of the yibo advisors had a screen pulled up, and the raiders pulled one up as well, broadcasting the streets of Chrr. Krevai, offscreen, barked out terse orders, and soon all of them could see the raiders laying down their weapons, and the yibo forces and civilians, bloodied and battered, making their slow, stumbling retreat from the city.

Alba had to bite down hard on her teeth to keep the horror from showing in her face at the carnage in the streets, and the extend and nature of the survivors' injuries, but … there were more survivors than there would have been, had the hostilities gone on for even a few more minutes.

Through her earpiece, she could hear the chatter of the yibo military commands going back and forth, discussing casualties and necessary medical supplies, but she pushed it to the back of her mind.

For now, they'd won.

The thought was a relief so thick that she almost couldn't let herself comprehend it.

The retreat took several hours. Alba was at last forced to either swallow her pride enough to ask for a seat, or risk simply collapsing onto the floor. To her surprise, though, the raiders offered her one without comment.

And then, as the sun began to set on the jungle planet, the last of the survivors staggering out of the city and onto the open plains around them, Alba caught, from the corner of her eye, a glitter of something—a ship, passing into the atmosphere in the jungle close to the city.

"What—" she began.

The yibo military leader saw it as well. There was a shout of alarm, and Alba saw a momentary shock of confusion on Sharda's face.

And then the ship came into full view: a raider ship, diving towards the retreating yibo civilians.

Alba opened her mouth to say … something, ask some question—

And the ship opened fire on the sea of wounded, retreating soldiers and fleeing civilians, defenceless in the open area.

There were shouts in yibo and the raider tongue, cursing, and one by one, the holoscreens flicked off, leaving Alba alone on the raider attack pod, staring in open mouthed horror at the betrayal.

31

Savina

Savina stared out the cockpit window in numb disbelief.

She could hear the gasps from the others around her, Rafel's low cursing, and Ines's half sob. But she couldn't process any of it. All she could do was watch as the shots from the raider ship plowed into the defenceless yibo

She squeezed her eyes shut for just a moment, and when she opened them, her entire body was cold with rage. "Shoot them down," she said quietly, turning to Joska. "Shoot down every attack pod in range, and then shoot down every raider you see. I'll gas the crew in the hold. They'll kill us eventually, but they're going to kill us anyways. We're going to take as many damn raiders with us as we can."

"Savina. That ship is firing, but the raiders here on the ground have dropped their weapons. They're defenceless." Joska's voice was tight with strain, and Savina could hear the unhappiness behind it.

She whirled on the captain.

"What the hell do you want to do, then?" she shouted. "You want

317

to just let the raiders kill everyone? Is that better than us killing them? Sometimes, Joska, you don't get a moral choice. Sometimes all your choices are bad ones, and whatever you choose to do, you're going to come out of it dirty, and there is nothing you can do about it. Maybe it's time that you bloody well accept that."

Joska's face was pale and sick, and for just a moment, Savina felt like she was back in the compound, watching her mother, tears staining her face, lower her baby brother into the shallow grave where he'd be buried alive. Except this time it was Savina, destroying something good and innocent. Her standing there lowering the infant Nicolau into the dirt. Doing nothing to stop what was happening.

Was that how her mother had felt? That she hadn't had a choice? That she was killing her innocent child, not because she wanted to, but because she didn't know what else to do?

But Savina *didn't* have a choice. Either they killed the raiders who'd put down their weapons in good faith, or they let other defenceless people be killed. That had been the story of Savina's whole damn life, and maybe it was time for Joska to learn what the world was really like. Maybe that type of innocence needed to die.

"If there's nothing else we can try—" Joska's voice was hollow and haunted, and Savina knew, somehow, that the captain would never get over something like this. The Joska she knew wouldn't survive opening fire on defenceless people, no matter their species.

"Savina. Wait."

For a moment, Savina didn't react, certain the voice was just her imagination, because Reka was lying on the floor unconscious.

And then she spun. Reka had pushed herself up on one elbow, her face tight with pain and pale with exertion.

"Reka?" Savina managed incredulously.

Reka grimaced and pushed herself up a little more on one elbow. Savina dropped to the floor beside her, supporting Reka's shoulders. "Reka! Reka, just lie back."

"No." Reka's voice was weak, but there was that hint of steel behind it that Savina had grown used to over the last few days. "I've worked with raiders before. This isn't like them. Chances are it's a rogue ship. If you start shooting down the raiders in the city, though, the war captains will cut off the negotiations for good. No raider captain will be able to stand by if their crew is being slaughtered, even if the war captains command it. If we start shooting now, this war is going to play out to the end, no matter what."

"Do you see what's happening out there?" Savina felt, oddly, like crying. "The yibos are going to cut off negotiations anyway if the raiders slaughter their troops, rogue ship or not!"

Reka grimaced again, shifting her weight a little against Savina. "Then stop the ship," she whispered.

"Stop the ship?" Savina's voice was sharp. "How the hell—"

Reka gave her a tired smile. "I remember back in Joias … when I was shooting missiles at an old cargo ship." Her words were slurring with pain and weariness. "And someone shot them down before they could hit. Someone with that kind of aim …" Her voice trailed off, her head slumping back on Savina's shoulder.

Savina stared at her. "We don't have access to the ship's precision weapons. We just have their main guns, nothing for targeted work."

"The raiders we locked in the hold will have access." Reka's voice was barely a whisper.

Savina blinked at Reka, then turned to stare Joska.

This was stupid. The sensible thing to do was to shoot down everyone who could hurt them, before they had time to do it. Trusting that the raiders hadn't double-crossed them, trusting that somehow, if they stopped the rogue ship, the raiders would leave them alive—trusting that she could walk into the hold of the raider crew they'd taken captive, and rather than eat her alive, the raiders would take her to their precision weapons and show her how to use them—was ridiculous, and suicidal, utterly stupid.

But she saw that hint of hope in Joska's face. That maybe it was a way out that didn't involve them either killing innocents, or watching innocents be killed.

They were all watching her.

Gently, she lowered Reka back to the ground and pushed herself to her feet. Her whole body was shaking, and she hadn't been sure her legs would hold her, but somehow they did. "Joska," she said quietly. "Don't shoot, yet. Give me—" she paused, calculating. "Give me five minutes at most. If you don't hear back from me by then, then hand the controls to Rafel. He'll do the shooting."

Joska shook her head, her grin wry and a little sickly. "I appreciate it, Savina, but if we're going to have to shoot, I'd just as soon do it myself. Whether I'm the one pulling the trigger, or I stand by while someone else does, it hardly makes a difference."

Savina managed a small smile in return. "Well then, let's hope you don't have to do either."

"Wait! Savina, what are you going to—" Nicolau's voice was sharp with worry.

Savina didn't wait for him to finish his question. She slipped out the door and sprinted down the corridors towards where they'd locked the raider crew.

For the first time in her life, she was almost grateful for the discomfort of running, because it gave her mind something to focus on other than the horror of what she was about to do. But even that wasn't really enough. The fear was spreading through her body like an ice wash, numbing her muscles, tightening her chest.

The raiders were going to kill her. They were going to kill her, and she was doing this, not to save herself, but—but to keep Joska from doing something that her conscience would never recover from. To keep Reka from the knowledge that they'd started a war that they could have stopped. And somehow, stupidly—that was reason enough.

She reached the door and sucked in a quick breath. Then she raised her fist and rapped sharply.

"Human." The snarl from inside was almost enough to make her rethink her plan. But she forced the words out anyways. "Raiders." She hoped that her voice was steadier than she felt. "I have a proposition for you."

"Does it involve us ripping you into even portions?" The raider's voice was mocking. "Because if not—"

"Shut the hell up," Savina snapped. "You're alive right now because your war captains are negotiating with the yibo. One of your ships has gone rogue, and if we don't stop it, the negotiations are off. I don't think that bodes well for any of us."

There was a moment of silence from inside.

"And what do you want us to do about it?"

From the tone in the raider's voice, Savina guessed Reka had been right. This hadn't been part of the raiders' plan, at least, not the one these raiders had been told.

"I'm a good shot. But I don't know how to use your precision weapons. So—" she had to force the next words out, through the fear clenching her jaw tight. "So you have to show me how."

There were another few moments of silence. "And you trust us to do that?" The raiders voice was cold and amused.

No. She didn't.

But she couldn't live with the look on Joska's face if she had to shoot down unarmed soldiers, and this was their only option to prevent that.

"I think you want this rogue ship stopped as much as I do. Because if we can't stop it, our only other choice is to start shooting down your attack pods and your crews who've given up their weapons. So I'll unlock the door. I'll kill the second raider to come through, so send one out only, one with experience on your precision weapons. And then I will lock the door, and they will take me to the weapons, and we'll shoot down the rogue ship."

This was a terrible idea. This was a terrible idea, and she was going to get herself killed, and for what? There was no reason that she should put her own life, not to mention the lives of the small handful of people she cared about, all of whom were on the ship, at risk for something like this.

"Alright. I will come out, and only I, and you can lock the door afterwards. And then I'll show you to the weapons." The raider's voice was smooth with silky menace, and the fear pumping through Savina's body was so sharp that she almost couldn't force her fingers to hit the hatch lock.

The sound of the lock clicking open was far too loud.

Savina had her pulse pistol aimed at the head of the raider as she stepped out. "Shut it behind you, or I kill you and gas everyone inside," Savina hissed.

The raider chuckled, holding out her empty hands. "We agreed, didn't we? It's just me." She turned and swung the door deliberately closed behind her, and Savina hit the lock with her elbow, not taking her pistol aim off the raider.

"You're damn lucky," Savina gritted through her teeth.

"Follow me, then." The raider still sounded amused. "We don't have time to waste, if you're telling the truth."

Savina thought she might throw up. But she just nodded and followed the raider down the corridor.

They reached a small hatch, and the raider clicked it open expertly and gestured Savina inside.

"You first," Savina growled, and the raider shrugged and stepped through.

Savina followed.

On the other side was a small gun room. She could see where the weapons controls must be, but they were completely unfamiliar.

"Here." The raider put her hands on the controls. "This is your aim, and this is your trigger. Here are the controls for your sights. I'll start it powering up."

Savina gritted her teeth and dropped into the seat.

She had to ignore the soft, padded footfalls of the predator behind her, even though every nerve in her body was screaming in panic, because she needed all her focus if she was going to pull this off.

She closed her eyes and blew out a long breath, forcing her mind blank and calm.

Another job. Just another job, that's all this was.

"It's powered up," the raider woman said at her shoulder, close enough that Savina almost jumped. "Whenever you're ready."

Savina nodded, lining up the rogue raider ship in her sights. It was a long shot, but she'd done worse before.

She drew in a long breath, held it for just an instant, and on the exhale, she pulled the trigger. The guns jumped, the weapon firing three, four, five, six times before she loosed her finger from the trigger.

32

Alba

There was a moment of silence. And then Alba's communicator was buzzing, the holoscreen connecting her to the yibo filled with such a clamour of voices that she almost couldn't hear them. She was so shellshocked that she couldn't have answered any of the shouted questions, even if she'd known what to say.

"—must start firing immediately! We have ships on the way, we can fire on the war captains' ships immediately and the missiles will reach them in a matter of hours. Perhaps then—"

"Humans are working behind our backs—"

Alba closed her eyes for a moment, pushing back the horror of everything she was seeing, the strain, the stress—everything.

"Joska," she whispered through her wavelink. "What's happening?"

"Reka is certain it's a rogue ship. Savina's going to attempt to shoot it down." Joska's voice was grim. "And if she does and the raiders kill us, it means we were wrong," she added, with a weak attempt at humour.

And then there was another voice through her communicator.

"Human. The ship is a rogue ship. It's not responding to commands. We'll have to send in another ship to bring it down, but I'm afraid if you do not reopen communication with your yibo counterparts to let them know our intentions, they'll take the action as hostile. There'll be no going back once they start firing on our warships."

It was the raider captain, Krevai.

"How can I believe you?" Alba snapped, the shock of what had just happened cutting any diplomacy from her tone. "Please. Tell me how I can believe you."

Krevai hesitated. At last, he turned aside and shoved someone forward.

Alba blinked in surprise as Aran stumbled into view on the screen.

She almost didn't recognize him. He looked as though he'd aged ten years in the past weeks, exhaustion and strain written across his face and through every line of his posture. There was an angry purple bruise across his cheekbone and dried blood crusted around his nose and mouth, but he had a calm, ironclad determination under his expression, a steady self-assurance she hadn't seen in him before.

"Aran," she began.

He nodded wearily. "It's true. The ship's gone rogue. I listened in to Krevai's transmissions to call it back—they're not answering at all. I promise, Alba—the raiders are negotiating in good faith this time. I've already staked my life on it. My life, and … and Pishti's, too," he added in a low voice, pain flashing across his features.

Alba studied him, frowning. But she'd spent enough time around the scientist to realize he was pathologically incapable of lying.

"There. Are you satisfied?" Krevai stepped back into the screen.

Alba pulled in a long breath. "I shall do my best. But I can't guarantee the yibos will listen."

Krevai looked grim. "My pet human is very insistent that we reopen these negotiations. But if the yibos are unwilling to talk—" he shrugged helplessly.

"Stay on the line," Alba snapped. "Do not close down the negotiations until I am able to speak with my yibo counterparts."

"I can give you a few minutes," Krevai rumbled. "But that's all I can promise. My people are already restless."

Alba gritted her teeth and reopened her private communication line with the yibo negotiators.

She almost winced at the cacophony of shouting, yelling, cursing voices.

"Silence!" she snapped. "Please!"

No one heard her over the clamour, and she glanced around, picked up one of the chairs the raiders had supplied the room with, and raised it, then slammed it down on the floor again with all her might.

The ringing clash of metal on metal was enough to momentarily pause the chaos.

"Enough!" Alba gasped, wincing at the sharp pain in her shoulder from the exertion.

This time, they listened.

"Alba, you did this!" it was Tika, and this time, it wasn't either hate or scheming on his face—it was pure horror. "You were plotting with the raiders behind our backs—"

"That is ridiculous," Alba snapped, stepping back so that Tika could see the armed raiders surrounding her.

They, too, were staring at her in undisguised shock.

"Had I been colluding with the raiders, it would seem I have put myself in an utterly irresponsible position, considering I left my friends under your power, and am currently being menaced with an entire garden party worth of raider weapons."

There was a long moment, as the veracity of her words sank in to the assembled yibo politicians.

"Now," she said. "Krevai has assured me that this is a rogue ship. He has requested your permission to send in a ship to take it down. I suggest we allow him to do so, as there is no way we can reach the rogue ship before the raiders can. I suggest we take actions to protect ourselves, but I beg of you, please do not end the negotiations and launch missiles until we understand what has happened."

"What is there to understand?" It was another yibo politician, one Alba didn't recognize. But she recognized the anguish in their voice. "What is there to understand, other than that the raiders are slaughtering our people? I suggest we instruct the military to launch the ships immediately."

"No matter how fast the military launches their ships, it won't be in time to stop what's happening!" Alba's tone was sharp. "I know you mistrust humans. It has been made very apparent to me that no matter what we do, there are some of your numbers who will always mistrust us. But please ask yourselves, at least—what benefit would we gain from betraying you to the raiders? If I understand correctly, we are the raiders' preferred delicacy, when they can get it. We are all trying to find a solution."

There was a moment of silence.

At last, one of the yibo said, "Alba. Are you willing to swear to us, on the lives of your companions, that this was not your doing?"

"I swear." Alba hoped that her sincerity showed through her tone. "You may ask any of the humans that you trust to vouch for me."

"Jair has already vouched for you," said another yibo at last. "The moment this came through, he called in, and put his own reputation on the line to assure us that this had not been your doing. The refugees we've been working with did the same. All of them swore to us that this had not been your doing. They put their own lives on the line to guarantee your character. I hope, for all our sakes, that they know you well enough to do so."

Alba turned to the raider who currently had his weapon pointed at her face.

She should be afraid, she knew. Some distant part of her mind was, in fact, terrified, and she knew that if she stopped for long enough to think about it, she might actually faint from the terror.

But she didn't have the leisure for that at the moment.

"Please bring up the line with Krevai," she said.

"Krevai! What explanation do you have for this?" The harshness in the yibo negotiator's tone probably sprung more from panic than bravado, but Alba winced nonetheless.

She could see how Krevai's expression darkened at the tone, but when he spoke, his words were far more conciliatory than she'd dared hope.

"I … apologize. The ship is not responding to commands." The words seem to have been pulled with great reluctance from the raider captain, but he said them nonetheless. "We've been fighting a charak infestation. Our human is working to cure it, but he's not managed it yet." There was a dangerous undertone to his words that did not seem directed at the yibos, and menace in the glance he shot towards Aran. "I suspect the crew of the rogue ship is infected."

From the yibos' reaction, Alba gathered that the term "charak" had some meaning to them that was not apparent to her.

"I'm willing to fire on the ship," Krevai continued, "but I don't have ships in position. We will need to send in something to shoot it down."

Alba could sense the captain's anguish at the words.

"See? This is exactly what Tika predicted. They want to get their ships in position while we're still talking, so they can slaughter their way to victory." The yibo politician turned to Krevai. "How do we know your ship will shoot down the rogue ship, rather than massacre our soldiers?"

Krevai sighed in frustration. "I told my human you yibos would never agree to stop this war," he growled. "All I can give you is my assurance, and it appears that's not enough."

"Wait," said Alba desperately, stepping forward. "Wait." She turned to Krevai. "Put your human on the line."

There was a moment's pause.

At last Krevai nodded and stepped back, and Aran appeared in the screen. "Everything Krevai said is true," he said quietly. "The raiders have been fighting a charak infestation, that's why they haven't attacked in force yet. Istvay and I have been working day and night to find a cure, but what we've come up with so far is temporary at best. We've already had to shoot down an attack pod that went rogue. I'll put my life on it that if Krevai tells you he'll shoot down the ship, he'll do it."

The yibo negotiators were conversing in low tones. At last, one of them stepped forward. "We will allow you to go in and take out the ship, without firing our missiles," said the yibo woman at last. "But if this is another trap—"

She cut off her words abruptly.

On the screen, the raider ship that had been taken by the humans fired, quick flashes of weapons.

One of the yibos gave a half-formed shout of shock, and one of the raiders standing behind Alba started forwards.

The rogue ship exploded.

There was a long moment of silence.

Alba half expected Krevai to cut the holoscreen and plunge everyone back into war.

But he didn't. He closed his eyes, his shoulder slumping in unmistakable sorrow. And then, at last, he straightened, drawing in a deep breath. "It appears the problem has been dealt with," he said heavily. "And so once again, are you willing to negotiate a cessation of hostilities?"

The second round of negotiations went much faster than the first, but Alba was so exhausted she could hardly keep her mind on the matter at hand. All she wanted was to crawl into her small, uncomfortable cot in the refugee compound and sleep for days.

"It will be several weeks at the earliest before we can finalize all the details," one of the yibo was saying. "But we are willing for our physicians to work with yours in order to keep your human alive in the meantime, while the cease-fire holds."

"Understand that if the human dies, the cease-fire is off," Krevai growled. "Take all the time you need a negotiating, but once the human's dead, our incentive not to attack dies too."

Alba could see the relief in Aran's posture, from where he stood behind the raider captain, at the words.

"We understand," the yibo said at last. "We will make the negotiations as short as possible, and in the meantime, if you will allow our physicians on board, we would like to inspect the human's condition ourselves. It will give us some idea of how best to start treatment."

"With sufficient security guarantees, I believe we can allow that,"

Krevai said at last, reluctantly.

And then, at long, long last, the negotiations were done. Alba hardly realized it, until the holoscreens around her began to flicker off.

"Human."

She blinked up stupidly into the face of the raider who had been holding a weapon on her throughout the negotiations.

He looked almost impressed.

"We will take you back to the refugee compound, of course, but in the meantime, I've instructed my crew to prepare you a bed. Krevai has told us that you humans are tougher than you look, but you look like you're going to fall over."

Alba managed a weak smile.

She felt like she was going to fall over.

But the war was over. The humans were not going to be hunted as prey by the raiders, or handed over to the Nativists for slaughter.

And maybe, just maybe, when everything had calmed down, she'd finally be able to re-open the topic of a portal back to Joias. Perhaps, after all, they'd have a chance to save their system from Cavaco. But all that, she would worry about in the morning.

She gave the raider a grateful nod, and let him help her to her feet, and stumbled towards the small cabin they'd prepared for her.

She was asleep almost before the door closed behind her.

33

Aran

Aran had no idea what time it was by the time he dragged himself out of Krevai's cockpit and stumbled down the hallway towards his cabin. During the entire course of the negotiations, the only thing on his mind had been Istvay, alone in the cabin, unconscious. He'd managed, at some point, to signal to Dessi to go check on them, and she'd come back and whispered that they were still alive.

That hadn't been nearly as reassuring as Aran had hoped.

But nor did he dare leave the negotiations, with as tense as they were. He hadn't even had the energy to feel either utter despair at the reluctance of the yibos to promise results for the medical intervention, or tentative hope at the fact that Krevai had specifically pinned the cease-fire on Istvay's life, thereby, hopefully, giving all the parties involved an incentive to keep Istvay alive.

The only thing he could think of was that he was there in the cockpit with Krevai, and Istvay wasn't, and he needed Istvay. And so when the negotiations ended, he could hardly bring himself to bid Krevai farewell, or comment, or thank, or apologize. He just turned and stumbled from the cockpit as fast as he could force his legs to carry him.

He paused at the door to his cabin, his heart pounding unnaturally quickly.

Istvay had to be alright. Dessi had checked on them. Dessi had been monitoring them. She would have told him if something had happened.

He was almost sure she would have told him.

He pushed the door open and stepped inside.

The first thing he noticed was that Ani wasn't on Istvay's chest, where he'd left her … Then he saw that Istvay's eyes were open, and he gave a little half sob of relief and was across the cabin before the door had time to finish closing behind him. "Pishti! Pishti, you're awake. Pishti—" he dropped onto the edge of the bed, careful not to jar them, and took a long breath, trying to bring himself back under control.

"Aran." Istvay's voice was weak and exhausted. "What happened? Did you … Aran, I found the solution to the charaks. Did you see it? We can finally get that thing out of your head …"

Aran sighed and raised his head, running a hand gently over their hair.

"I found your notes. And I—I burned them."

"You …" Istvay stared at him. "Aran—"

Aran shook his head. "I'm … sorry. But I realized something, after you passed out. You were right. Everything we've done has always been political, in one way or another. I always thought it didn't matter how they treated me, as long as I was doing what I loved and as long as I had you. But … it was never just me being hurt when I let people walk over me. All these years, all our lives, really, they ignored you, erased you, gave all the credit to me when we both know you deserved most of it. And I hated it, but I didn't do anything about it, because I told myself I didn't know how." He shook his head, not meeting Istvay's eyes. "And that whole time, I could have. I could have changed things for you, and for me, and for who knows how many other people? I just didn't, because I told myself it was all politics, and I didn't know how to do politics." He looked up, finally, to find Istvay watching him, their expression sad. "I guess—I guess it took you almost dying for me to realize that I'd always had a choice. I never had to just take the terms they offered me. You found them the cure, and they were going to take it and either let you die, or kill hundreds of thousands of people to save you. Those were their terms. So I burned it. No one's getting the cure, not until you're well enough to re-do it. And—and Krevai stopped the war, because I told him that was the only way." He gave a small, humourless laugh. "I've probably made us enemies of the most dangerous creatures in the system now, but it can't be all that much worse than what we've been through so far."

Istvay was staring at him. "You ... you stopped Krevai from—" they began, shaking their head weakly. "Aran ..." they reached up and ran their hand down his cheek before their arm fell back against the bed. "Have I ever told you how incredible you are?"

Aran laughed, a small, wet laugh. "I'm not. I'm an idiot. I can't believe it took me this long to figure it out, when you've been telling me that my whole damn life. I can't believe I let you—" he cut off his words abruptly.

Istvay smiled a little. "You don't need to be sorry. But—but we still need to get that thing out of your head somehow. I—" They were looking around weakly. "Aran, listen. I'm not ... I can't do much right now." He could hear how much it cost them to say the words. "But we have to ... if you get me some paper, maybe I can—"

Aran shook his head, putting his hand over theirs. "No," he said quietly.

The horror of it still choked off his throat if he thought about it too much—the rogue ship exploding into flame, the fleeing yibos, the blood and broken bodies.

Even if he'd given them the cure, he wasn't sure it would have been in time to stop that. But he hadn't even tried.

And as horrible as it was, it was still better than what would have happened if he had given Krevai the cure, and the war had continued.

"I'm not going to let you hurt yourself trying to save me from something that's my own damn fault," he said. "And even if you could do it, if the raiders can't have it, I won't either. Because I don't think I could actually bear that."

Istvay sighed. Their face was still creased in worry, but their expression was soft when they looked at him. "Aran. I'm not sure I ever mentioned how much I love you."

Aran leaned down and kissed them on the forehead. "I love you too." His voice choked on the words. "Just—just hang on, okay? The yibos are going to send doctors, see if they can get you stabilized while they're negotiating getting you into their medical facilities."

Istvay chuckled weakly. "I still can't believe you did it—stopped the war, got the raiders and the yibos to work together."

Aran managed a small grin. "They're doing it to save your life. This is all on you, Pishti." He paused. "You're right. We were up to our necks in politics anyway. It may as well be on our own terms."

Istvay nodded. Their eyes were falling closed.

"Where's Ani?" Aran glanced around the cabin in sudden alarm. "I left her with you, it's not like her to—"

Istvay blinked their eyes open with an effort. "She was here until right before you got here. She stayed the whole time I was out, and she didn't leave until she heard the door crack, and she must've caught your scent. Don't—don't be—" their words trailed off, there head falling back against the pillow.

Aran squeezed his eyes closed against the worry tightening in his chest, and checked the monitors Dessi had set up—their heartbeat was weak, their breathing slow, but steady.

That was the best he could expect, until they got the cure.

He stood, glancing around the cabin. "Ani?" he asked. "Ani, are you alright? What's wrong, sweetheart?"

There was an odd, purring little chirp from the corner where Ani had made her home, and Aran crossed over to it, kneeling in front of the cupboard door. "Ani, sweetheart?" He whispered. "Are you alright in there? Can I open the door?" He tugged on the door handle gently.

When there wasn't any resistance and Ani didn't growl at him, he pulled it open.

It was dark inside, but he could see Ani's bulbous eyes glowing out at him in the reflected light from the cabin, wide and innocent. He reached in to pat her, then paused at an unfamiliar sensation on his fingers.

No, not unfamiliar. But certainly something he hadn't felt in a very long time.

Tiny, delicate tentacles, no wider around than his little finger, exploring tentatively across his skin.

For a moment he just sat there, completely dumbstruck.

"Ani?" he asked at last, his voice cracking a little. "Ani, are you—are these—"

Ani nudged the door open a little wider with one tentacle. In the small space, now lit with the artificial lights from outside, Aran could see a proud, almost smug expression on her face.

And around her …

He counted in his head, his brain somehow still unable to completely wrap itself around what he was seeing.

"Seventeen," he whispered.

Seventeen tiny, wriggling, adorable baby land-devils clustered around Ani.

"Ani!" his voice was choked with emotion. "Are these—are these yours? Sweetheart, are these your babies?" He had to swallow hard, and blink back tears. "They're beautiful! Oh, honey, no wonder you've been hiding away and stashing food." He reached out his hand tentatively. "May I?" he asked.

Ani gave him a sharp look, but she didn't object as one of the tiny infants wriggled onto his open palm.

He stared at it, its curious, bulbous eyes and adorably undersized tentacles, feeling like his heart might actually explode from happiness. "They're beautiful," he whispered in a choked voice. "Ani, they're beautiful! But how did you—" he trailed off, his mind already racing through the research papers he was going to have to write. "Parthenogenesis," he whispered. "Ani! I had no idea—I didn't know you could do that!"

"Aran?" Istvay's voice from the cot was weak and worried. "Aran, what's happening?"

Aran got to his feet in a daze, only remembering, at Ani's irritated squawk, to nudge the infant land-devil gently off his hand before he turned. "Pishti!" he felt actually starry eyed, his entire body almost glowing with awe. "Pishti, it's Ani! She was nesting! That's why she was in such a bad mood and eating everything out of the supply cupboards. She was probably using up all her energy hatching out her eggs!"

"Her ..." Istvay fell silent.

Aran crossed over to them, he wasn't entirely sure how—he felt like he was actually floating, as if his whole body was light as air. "Pishti, did you know that land-devils were capable of parthenogenesis? This is incredible! Can you imagine the kind of information that will give us on land-devil habits? Pishti ..." He was too excited to continue.

"Parthenogenesis ..." Istvay sounded like someone had hit them over the head. "You mean—you mean right now, at this very moment, we are literally inside the nest of an actual land-devil?"

"Yes! Our sweet little girl is a mother!" He glanced over his shoulder to where Ani was herding the tiny land-devils back into their nest. "And there's seventeen of them! Seventeen! I know land-devils generally only have six or seven kits in a litter, and they usually take much longer to hatch out, but maybe this is unique to parthenogenesis—maybe this is what happens when they're trying to repopulate the species!"

"There are—there are seventeen baby land-devils. In our cabin. Right now." Istvay's voice was faint.

Aran turned to them, his grin almost too wide for his face. "Isn't it incredible?"

"I ... could think of some other words," Istvay muttered.

"It's incredible!" Aran couldn't stop grinning. He wasn't sure that he'd ever felt so happy in his life.

The war had ended. Istvay would finally get the cure Aran had spent his life searching for, and they'd survive long enough to get it. And Ani had a nest of *seventeen* baby land-devils. They had seen land-devil parthenogenesis, which no one had even hypothesized was possible.

"I have no idea why, though," he continued. "I mean, she's only—

what, three years old? From everything we know, which isn't really all that much, granted, land-devils usually don't sexually mature until they're somewhere between fifteen and twenty, and they usually only have one litter in the course of their life. If she was getting to the end of her reproductive years without a chance of mating, I could see that triggering whatever gene codes for parthenogenesis, but—" he shook his head. "Do you have any ideas? Because—"

Istvay laid a hand on his arm. "Aran." Their voice was weak, but he could hear their usual fond resignation behind it. "When the raiders kidnapped me—you were upset, yes?"

Aran paused, thrown off his delirious excitement for a moment at the sudden, stomach-turning memory. "I would say that's a bit of an understatement, honestly," he said. "Why?"

Istvay's smile was rueful. "Ani and I might not always see eye to eye on everything, but in one way, at least, we're far too alike. I was frantic when Sharda kidnapped me, not because I was worried about my own damn life, but because I couldn't bear the thought of you being sad." They gave a small, wry shrug. "I suspect it's the same for Ani—I suspect that for her there is absolutely no difference whatsoever between you being upset, and an extinction-level event, any more than there is for me."

Aran blinked at Istvay. Then he turned and blinked at Ani.

"You have no idea how much the two of us adore you, do you?" Istvay's voice was weak.

Aran tried to smile, and had to blink back tears. "Ani?" he managed at last. "Were you really—did you really—"

Ani disentangled herself gently from her offspring and scuttled across the floor on the tips of her tentacles. She swarmed up Aran's leg and wrapped herself around him so that he had to pry her tentacles off his mouth, laughing in a wet, choked sort of way. "Oh,

Ani," he whispered. "Sweetheart, I'm sorry, I really didn't mean to upset you like that—"

Ani chirped and suckered down her tentacles against his chest and back, and again he had to blink back tears, partially from emotion and partially from the pain of a stray tentacle spike in his shoulder from Ani's overenthusiastic affections.

Istvay cleared their throat. "Listen, Aran, this is all very touching, but … what the actual hell are we going to do with seventeen baby land-devils?"

"With … what?"

Aran spun.

Dessi stood in the doorway, her hand half raised, as if she'd been about to knock on the open door.

"Dessi?" said Aran blankly.

Behind her, he could see Krevai and Sharda.

All of the raiders were staring at him.

"I—I knocked a few times, but when no one answered, I thought I'd come in and check on Istvay to make sure everything was alright." There was a distant, shocked tone to Dessi's voice. "I didn't mean to—"

"Sharda?" asked Istvay weakly, a tinge of irritation returning to their voice. "Sharda, what the hell are you doing here?"

"The captains wanted to check on you as well." Dessi's voice was still that shocked, hollow, distant tone of someone who hadn't quite taken in the full implications of what they were seeing or hearing. "I thought that since our chance of getting rid of the charaks, not to mention the entire peace treaty with the yibos, depended on you staying alive, they should both come—" She trailed off again.

"Aran." Krevai stepped past Dessi, his bulk taking up the entire entrance of the cabin. "Aran, what exactly is happening here?"

Aran followed his gaze to the corner, where a mound of wriggling, hissing, tentacled infants were scrambling over each other, their movements adorably awkward. He felt his face relax into a foolish smile. "Ani's a mother!" He rubbed Ani's head affectionately, but she dropped from his shoulder, hissing, and scuttled back over to stand guard between her infants and the newcomers.

"Aren't they beautiful? And there are seventeen of them, which —"

"Seventeen?"

Even through his haze of happiness, Aran could hear the horror in Sharda's tone.

One of the infant land-devils spat, the acid smoking as it ate a hole through the cabin floor. Aran yelped and grabbed for the neutralizer he carried for times when Ani had a fit of temper, and strode over to toss it onto the spot. The tiny land-devils scuttled back from the hissing, steaming hole in the deck, hissing like a huddle of tiny snakes themselves. But the smoke wouldn't harm them, he'd tested thoroughly before he'd started using it anywhere close to Ani.

When he looked up, Krevai and Sharda were staring in a mix of horror and, in Krevai's case, just a hint of admiration.

"There are seventeen of those—those things on your ship, Krevai?" Sharda's voice was sharp. She spun on Aran. "How long before they're dangerous?"

Aran frowned. "The infants are able to defend themselves, obviously, they have to in case of predators or something when their parents are gone, so their acid and venom and tentacle-spikes and poison are fully developed at hatching, although the venom and poison aren't as potent in the babies as they are in the adults. But as far as when they physically mature—" he shrugged. "I can tell you what a normal land-devil's lifecycle is, but this is the first time I've ever seen parthenogenesis, so I have no idea what difference it would make. Ani would usually hatch out five or six eggs, and not until she was much older. It's possible that these infants are genetically coded to mature faster as well. But don't worry, I'll be making meticulous notes, so we should have a solid understanding of what the differences are in their development." He shook his head. "I can't believe how incredibly lucky we are to be able to see this!"

Behind him, he heard Istvay breathe out a long sigh.

"And these things can survive in space. And apparently, they don't need another one of their species to be able to reproduce. So, hypothetically speaking, if one of them got out of the ship—" Sharda turned back to Aran. "Your Ani is three years old, you said?"

Aran nodded, and Sharda turned back to Krevai.

"Three years." Her voice was harsh with panic. "If even half of those seventeen had a litter every three years ..."

Krevai's face had gone even paler than normal. "You saw what one of those things could do, Sharda." His voice was harsher than usual. "The Ani almost took out your entire crew on her own. She wasn't affected by a single one of our weapons. And these ones won't be bonded to our human."

"I'm sure they'll be very well behaved. Ani will be a spectacular mother, she'll teach them all the things that they need to know—" Aran began indignantly.

Krevai spun on him. "All the things they need to know? Like, how to kill an entire crew of raiders if someone offends them?"

"I'm sure they won't hurt anyone unless they're in danger, or—or I suppose, if they're hungry, but—"

Krevai and Sharda exchanged glances. Then Krevai spun on his heel. "Dessi, come on. We're opening up an emergency line of communication to the yibos, right now. They're opening a portal back to our Aran's system, and everything in this cabin is going back through it. I don't think we'll get any arguments on that point."

Then they were gone, leaving Aran and Istvay alone in the cabin with eighteen land-devils.

Aran dropped down on the floor beside Ani and scratched her absently under her chin, then hissed in pain as she nicked him on the finger with a tentacle spike. "Sorry, sweetheart," he whispered, scooting back. "I didn't mean to crowd you."

"A portal." Istvay's voice was still weak, but there was a trace of their old horrified amusement in it. "Well, Aran … it sounds like we just might be going home after all."

34

Alba

"Alba! Human, get up!"

Alba groaned and rolled over, blinking, and tried to figure out whether the voice had been real, or in her dreams.

The fact that there was a raider standing over her cot, his expression frantic, pointed towards it being the former.

"What—" Alba rasped.

"It's an emergency. We need you in the cockpit, now."

The raider had already turned and strode out the door before Alba could organize her thoughts enough to ask what in the Mystery's holy name was going on.

When she reached the cockpit, there were three holoscreens pulled up across the table, and in every one of them somebody was shouting, cursing, or ranting.

She caught the words, "… humans will have to explain—" and, "—get Alba Espina in here immediately!" but in the chaos, she couldn't tell what had actually happened.

At last, she stepped into the centre of the screens so her own face would be broadcast across all of them, cleared her throat, and said loudly, "Would someone be so kind as to inform me what is happening?"

It took a few moments for the noise to die down. Then Tika's furious face appeared in the holofeed from the yibo Advisory Chambers. "The raiders have informed us that you humans have started what could well be an extinction level event in our system! What do you have to say for yourself?"

Alba stared at him. "An extinction level—" She shook her head briskly and addressed the advisor standing at Tika's shoulder. "Advisor Krii. Would you please explain to me what Tika is talking about?"

The yibo woman stepped forward, and Alba could see the shocked horror in the woman's face. "That ... that creature, the one who your scientist brought along. The one who, according to what you told us, saved you from Kachik because it could melt, dissolve, poison, or otherwise destroy a yibo soldier without effort, and was completely impervious to any of our weapons? The one who, we received word from our informants, caused the end of the raider leadership war by all but taking out an entire raider crew on its own? That creature?"

Alba stared.

Horrifying memories flashed across her mind—the young scientist with his soulful eyes and gentle demeanour and the horrifying creature from the depths of a nightmare perched on his shoulder. The way the beast had killed, and then dissolved, the massive felines that had stalked them through the jungle. The smug look on its ugly face as it sat amidst the ashes of a dead yibo soldier, completely unaffected by the weapons.

"Yes?" she said cautiously.

"The raiders told us this … this *thing* has reproduced, somehow. There are babies. Seventeen of them. The human scientist doesn't know how long it will take the infants to become sexually mature, but what we do know is that there is nothing in our system that can kill them, and that one of them is enough to take out a fully armed raider ship, and that they can survive in space without protection."

There was a long moment where Alba's brain struggled with the implications of this information.

She shuddered.

Extinction level event might have been underselling it.

"Due to the urgency of the situation, the raiders have agreed to a complete and utter cease-fire and open cooperation while this is dealt with," the yibo advisor continued. "They suggested that our only hope of living through this is to get the scientist and his creatures back through the portal before that time, and we have agreed. We asked that you be present to give you a chance to voice any objections you may have to our proposed actions. Under the circumstances, I think you do not have to worry about an invasion—Chrr is in ruins and the Nativist's power base mostly destroyed, and I believe everyone involved in this decision has no desire for any further mingling of species after this."

She paused, giving Alba a chance to protest.

Alba's mind was spinning. She couldn't stop to let this sink in, because it would overwhelm her, so she forced her brain to move on to practical matters.

"Who do you intend to send through? Are you going to put the scientist on a ship on his own? And what does this mean for the war?"

Krii shook her head. "The raider ship with the land-devils on it is going through—the human scientist expressed concern that the mother land-devil might become aggressive if anyone attempted to move her hatchlings. One of the war captains, Krevai, will be on the ship. The other, Sharda, will send her first mate through with them to monitor, but she'll stay behind and enforce the terms of the cease-fire in the meantime. We're going to send a yibo ship to monitor the situation as well, and that ship will also serve as a transport for anyone who wishes to travel through to Joias. I believe that after this incident, there will be very little appetite for reopening the portal, so any of the humans who wish to travel through it will go back on the transport, or not at all. I believe earlier you had spoken with Karri and Jair about the possibility of bringing some of the Labarinto humans back into your system—this is your chance to do so, if there are any who are so inclined." She paused. "All parties have an agreement in principle of anti-aggression against the humans in your system, as long as the humans in your system do not threaten them. The scientist insisted on that. I was certain you would request it as well, and we're willing to agree to it—without Kachik, there is little appetite for war. However, I ask that you return to the Advisory Chambers as soon as possible, as we would like some reassurance that our peaceful intentions will be reciprocated."

Alba nodded faintly. "And the war with the raiders?"

"The human who was in need of medical treatment, it appears, can obtain that treatment in your system. It will require some knowledge your scientist acquired while here, which is the other reason a small contingent of raiders will be going through the portal, and we will be sending equipment and people to provide remote medical assistance en route to ensure the human lives long enough to get to the medical facility on your planet. The raider captains have agreed that that, along with our organizing a temporary opening of the portal, will be sufficient to fulfil our agreement, in lieu of our providing medical treatment ourselves here. Once the human is well, they will provide the raiders with a solution for their charak infestation, and that aspect of the terms of the peace treaty will be complete."

"I … I will have to speak with Jair, and with my compatriots in the refugee quarters," Alba managed at last. "I will contact you once I am back."

Krii tipped her head. "We have people starting the portal mechanism. It will take around ten cycles until it's warmed up. You have that long." She turned back to the heated discussion in the Advisory Chamber, and Alba was left standing in the middle of the floor.

She felt as if the ground had fallen out from beneath her.

She couldn't spend too much time worrying about what this might mean politically, for her, for Cavaco, for Jair, or about the reception—and the attendant potential massive diplomatic and security issues—that Aran and … what had they said? Eighteen land-devils? Would receive on Colorida. Those would be yet more things she'd have to deal with as they came up.

Right now, she had to focus on the immediate issue of getting hundreds of humans—perhaps thousands, depending on how many from Labarinto were willing to try their luck in a new system— through a portal with next to no time to prepare.

At last, she crossed over to a corner for privacy and tapped her communicator through to Jair's line.

He answered on the first buzz, his face was gaunt and horrified. "Alba? Is it true what they're saying about these—these land-devils?"

Alba shuddered. "We put out travel advisories for any ship passing anywhere in that entire half of the system if there's a hatching taking place. And that was before we knew they could survive out of atmosphere." She knew her own voice sounded just as horrified as his. "They're the reason that half our system is completely unpopulated."

"And you—you let the scientist just—" Jair broke off, shaking his head.

Alba sighed. "It's rather a long story."

Jair nodded. "I'm going to send word to the human colonies. I assume from what you've told me that your system would be willing to give refuge to Labarinto humans who wish to come through?"

Alba's jaw tightened. "Under normal circumstances, I would say yes. However, I have no idea what we'll be facing when we go back. As you know, there's a possibility that in my absence, there has been progress towards a virtual military takeover of the government. We may be walking straight back into a war." She paused. "But I give you my word that I will use all my influence in government, which, under normal circumstances, is substantial, to provide for any refugees from the Labarinto system."

Jair nodded, his own jaw clenched tight. "They're saying that the portal will be opened, the land-devils and whatever humans wish to come will be deposited through, and, once the raiders get the information they need from the scientist and his friend, the portal will be closed permanently. No one will agree to reopen it now, not with a risk like that on the other side."

Alba nodded grimly. "That is the only assurance I can give you. But I will give you that—if anyone wishes to take their chances, I will do everything within my power to ensure they are given a home in Joias."

"Thank you." Jair's voice was as grim as hers. "I'll pass the word along."

The communicator clicked off, and Alba stared blankly at the device in her hand. At last, she blinked her wavelink through to the line she'd opened between herself, Yosip, and Feliu.

They must have been notified of the crisis as well. They both answered almost immediately, despite the fact she knew that where they were, it was well into the middle of the night.

"Well, Alba," said Yosip. His voice was tired, but there was a twinkle of humour behind it still. "I suppose we're going back home after all."

"We are. Whether we like it or not, it appears." Alba wished that the words didn't sound quite so grim. She paused. "Make sure that the word is been sent out to Joska and Savina. And get everyone ready. We have no idea what we'll be facing once we get back to Joias. But in the meantime, I need everyone awake and considering potential issues that will be caused by opening the portal, and how we can ensure that we don't bring back further danger in the form of raider or yibo aggression, and how to guard against aggression from our side in an uncertain political environment." She shook her head. "It may well be that what will be walking into is more dangerous than anything we've faced here."

"I understand, Madam." Feliu's voice was clipped and sharp, but there was something deeply comforting in the brusque efficiency under it. "Word has already been sent to Joska and Savina, and I'll gather the rest of our council."

"Thank you," said Alba. "I will join you as soon as the raider ship brings me back. And I suppose you'd best tell everyone who's coming with us to prepare for a potentially hostile situation. At least, as much as they can prepare on less than forty-eight hours' notice," she added under her breath.

"Of course, Madam."

"Alba." She glanced over at Yosip's face, creased and wrinkled and warm with compassion, and lit with something that might have been hope. "Perhaps the circumstances aren't ideal, and perhaps we don't know what we're walking into. But Alba—" his voice choked a little. "Alba, we're going home."

35

Savina

"I said," said Savina, smiling sweetly, "you can either be careful with her, or I'll slit your throat."

The human man at the head of the stretcher that held Reka looked vaguely terrified.

He did not, in Savina's opinion, look nearly terrified enough.

"Savina." Reka's voice was weak, but amused. "I'm touched. But I'll be alright."

"He might be alright too, depending on how careful he is," Savina said in her most friendly voice.

Reka laughed, then winced and laid back.

The knife wound was deep, but it appeared Reka was going to live. It appeared—well, it appeared all of them were going to live. And, looking out on the people around them, the cheering, smiling, laughing crowd, Savina realized something else.

These people, who smiled at her when they caught her eye, who'd leapt forward to volunteer to take care of Reka, who'd given Joska and Rafel and the others a hero's welcome when they'd stepped out of the ship—

They didn't know who she was, or where she was from, or what she'd done, and … they didn't care.

For the first time in her life, she didn't have to hide who she was, and no one here hated her for it.

She wasn't entirely sure how to deal with that.

"Savina? Are you alright?" Joska had fallen into step beside her. The woman looked tired, and Savina could still see, under her wry expression, the horror of what they'd all witnessed. But she was smiling. She was smiling in a way that Savina knew, instinctively, she would not have been, if she'd been forced to make the decision between shooting down raiders who'd laid down their weapons, and allowing innocent civilians to be slaughtered.

And Savina found herself smiling back, not in the calculated way she usually did, but out of sheer, probably unearned happiness. "I'm good." She cleared her throat. "I'm good. I'm alright."

They walked in silence for a bit. "I spoke with the doctors," said Joska. "They say Reka's wound is clean. It will take her a while to recover, but she should recover fully."

Savina nodded.

Joska glanced out over the crowd of people, humans and yibo both. "And, I suppose," she said ruefully, "we're not going to be left to ourselves tonight. At least, not from the looks of it."

Savina smiled. "Nicolau will be glad about that. I think he's been craving conversation with someone he's not related to."

Joska chuckled, and they were silent for a few moments.

Savina's wavelink buzzed, and she glanced down at it, frowning.

It was Yosip.

She hadn't expected a call from him, and the sight made something tighten in her stomach. "Go on, I'll catch up in a second," she said to Joska, stepping to one side and blinking to accept the call.

"Savina." Yosip sounded worried. "I'm sure you'll hear soon enough, but I thought I'd best call to warn you. There's ... been a new development."

By the time Savina caught up with Joska, she could tell from the woman's face that she, too, had been briefed.

"You get your siblings together," Joska said when she saw Savina. "I'll get the *Dolphin* ready to go. I think the humans from Labarinto are already in contact with their own people, and working out who's going to come through the portal. In the meantime, Alba suggested that we start for a set meeting point, since we won't reach the city before they leave."

It wasn't more than an hour later that they were on the *Dolphin*. There was a crowd gathered to bid them farewell, but Savina could see the concern on all their faces.

"Safe travels," said the human majordomo.

"And to you," said Joska. "If any of you decide to come back through the portal, we'll see you there."

The woman nodded. Then Beni hit the hatch control, and the loading ramp swung silently into place and clicked shut, the sound of the lock loud in the sudden quiet.

When they were out of atmosphere and their course set, Savina made her way out of her small cabin—the cabin Rafel had pointed her to months ago on a remote moonport—and into the cockpit. The others were already gathered. She'd known, somehow, that they would be. Even Reka was there, sitting up on the makeshift medical bed. Her face had an unhealthy greyish tinge to it, but she was conscious and alert.

She'd been more quiet than usual since learning they were going home, and when Savina sat down beside her and took her hand, she didn't pull away, but she didn't squeeze Savina's hand back, either.

Savina shot her a quick glance from the corner of her eye.

But then, Reka had never really seemed to like public displays of affection. And she must be as shocked as any of them at the sudden turn of events.

Joska turned in the pilot's chair and leaned back, surveying them. They'd all donned mag boots, but after all the time on the yibo ships with their artificial gravity, Savina found herself forgetting, every so often, that if she let go of something, it wouldn't stay where it was put.

"We're going home after all, Captain." Rafel's voice was quiet, and more muted than usual.

"So we are." Joska still sounded shellshocked.

"And you, boy—what are your plans when you get back?" Rafel said at last, turning to Nicolau.

Nicolau gave a small laugh, holding tightly to Ines's hand. "I … I'm not really sure." He sounded lost, somehow, and Savina's heart hurt to hear it. "I—I guess I'll stop by and see my family. My adoptive family, I mean. Maybe stay there for a little while before I look for work again." He tried to smile.

"You, Beni?"

Beni didn't turn their head in Savina's direction, even though they must know where she was. "I … haven't really thought about it." Their voice was quiet, too.

"I suppose you'll be going home, Savina." There was a note of sympathy behind Joska's voice that told Savina that the woman had guessed more than Savina had ever told her.

Savina cleared her throat and nodded. "I suppose I will."

"And where's home for you?" asked Reka.

Savina managed a small smile. "A compound, in the Rim

Mountains. An … an Old Believer compound." The words hurt in a way she hadn't expected.

Her whole life she'd kept it secret. Her whole life, she'd known that if anyone ever suspected who she was, where she'd come from, they'd hate her. They'd try to kill her, not because of what she'd done, but because of who she was. How her parents worshipped. What she believed—or even, what she didn't even believe anymore, but had been taught as a child.

And then she'd met Joska, and Rafel, and … they hadn't. It hadn't even mattered.

Reka stilled. It was something so subtle that, if it had been anyone else, Savina might not have noticed. "An Old Believer compound?" There was an odd note to her voice.

For a moment—just a moment—Savina couldn't move. Every part of her, everything that had allowed her to survive her whole life, was frozen in sudden, heart-stopping terror.

She forced herself to breathe.

This was Reka. Reka, who already knew exactly who she was. Reka, who loved her anyways.

"Reka?" she asked, trying to keep her voice steady. "What's wrong?"

But something had shuttered over Reka's face, that same cold, emotionless expression that Savina had seen there so often before. "Nothing," she said shortly, turning away.

Savina closed her eyes against the ice forming in the pit of her stomach. "Reka?"

Reka drew in a long breath. "It was … the Old Believers fault my family was killed." Her voice was quiet, but her words dropped into the silence like a stone.

The breath seem to catch in Savina's throat. She couldn't speak, couldn't move, couldn't respond, because this … this was impossible. After everything, this couldn't actually be happening.

"And how is that Savina's fault?" Joska's voice was mild, but there was a dangerous undertone to it.

Reka drew in a long breath. "Joska." Her tone was flat, but there was a sharp pain underneath it. "My family died in the uprisings in Swan River. You do not get to tell me how to feel about that."

"I sympathize, Reka." Joska's voice was still calm and dangerous. "I won't tell you how to feel about something like that. But I think I've made it clear that I don't abide bigots on my ship."

Reka snorted, a sharp, hard bitterness to her voice. "It's not bigotry, Joska. Spend some time in the Rim Mountains, you'll understand better. The Old Believers cry about being persecuted, but they're the ones that provoke the government. Living in their compounds, or pretending to blend in in the villages, it doesn't matter. One of the cults, near where my family lived, ten years ago —they were the ones that poked and poked, stirred people up until the government sent in the military. They were the real reason behind the massacre in Swan River. And they scuttled back to the hills and hid while soldiers killed my family, and my friends, and everyone I cared about."

"Again, what does that have to do with Savina? If I understand correctly from what Beni's told me, the compound she grew up in isn't even close to Swan River, and Savina would have been a child anyways."

Reka didn't answer, but the set of her posture told Savina more than any words.

Savina still couldn't quite speak. "Reka?" she managed at last. "Reka, what …" Her voice died out, small and pitiful.

"Savina." Reka was still turned away. "We'll talk about this later."

For a moment, Savina just sat there, still too stunned to react. And then a sudden, sharp anger rushed up around the hurt, flooding through her until she was shaking with it. "No, Reka." Her voice was trembling. "If you have something to say, you can say it here. In front of everyone. You knew exactly who I was, all this time. You were the one who decided to work with me, to …" She broke off, and sucked in a quick breath. "You knew everything about me, Reka, and now, after all of that—where I was born? That's the thing that you can't accept?"

Reka turned to look at her, finally. There was a humorless, mocking half-smile on her face. "You're right," she said. "You're right. Savina. I fell for you, knowing you were an assassin and a murderer. That if you were faced with a choice between what was right and what you wanted, I could never, ever trust that you'd choose what was right over what you wanted. I fell for you, knowing exactly who and what you were, and I knew I was damning myself, and I didn't care." Her voice was low and thick with a mixture of bitterness and shame, and her eyes pinned Savina, so she couldn't move or think. "So you're right. How is this different? I'm not sure how betraying my mother and father's memory would be any worse than what I've already done. Tell me, Savina—are you an Old Believer too, like your family?"

Savina felt like she'd been kicked in the stomach, gasping for breath that wouldn't come. Reka was still watching her, gaze as intense and piercing as ever, and like always, it cut through Savina like a knife, opening up everything inside of her for examination.

And this time, she hadn't even tried to hide it. She hadn't, because for the first time in her life, she hadn't believed she had to.

Her thoughts were spinning, too fragmented for her to grasp any of them, her body buzzing with an odd, shocked detachment like the one that came when you were hurt too badly for your brain to process it.

Maybe she was hurt. Maybe she'd been sliced open and hadn't noticed, somehow, maybe none of this was actually happening and it was all some delirious nightmare.

Maybe she'd wake up to Reka whispering her name, stroking her hair, Reka's lips on her temple, the warmth of her body reminding Savina that everything would be alright.

"I ... I don't—I haven't—" she managed at last. The words choked off in her throat, thin and pathetic, and for just a moment, she was hit with that familiar sharp, desperate ache, nestled under her collarbone, cold and painful, to be anything other than what she was. To be free of her family, her past, her history. To be free of the compound, and of what she'd done to save Nicolau, what she and Beni had done to survive. To be free of the horrible, awful religion she'd been brought up in, the one her great-grandmother had cared about enough to watch her children burn before she'd renounce the faith. The one her mother had believed in enough to bury her own infant alive when the Head Order commanded it.

The one that had made Savina's entire life its own sort of living hell.

She could lie. She could tell Reka it was just a cover, she wasn't an Old Believer after all. She'd dreamed about it for almost as long as she could remember—freedom. She could lie, and never look back.

But it wouldn't change anything. What she'd done to survive the compound, to rescue Nicolau, to get herself and Beni away and safe, couldn't be undone. It was written in blood, and nothing could take that away. She was everything Reka had said she was.

She'd thought, for a moment, that it didn't matter. That she could be loved anyway. That who she was could be forgiven. But the sickness that was the compound had spread its roots through Savina's entire life—through her seven-year-old self, who'd frantically pulled back the dirt covering her baby brother, her fingernails bleeding, horror and fear pounding through her chest, through her twelve-year-old self, who'd bent and lit the fire outside the farmer's abandoned cottage, then stood back and listened to the screams of the people trapped inside as they died, through her decision to kill, and kill, and keep killing, because it let her and Beni escape the compound, even just for a little.

Through the woman who'd tricked Joska into taking her onto her ship, then threatened to kill her for it.

She closed her eyes and swallowed hard. "Does it matter?" Her words came out in a whisper. "Does it matter to you what I believe? After everything I've done, does it even matter?"

She could see, in her mind's eye, vids she'd been forced to watch, over and over, from her youngest memories. The heresy trials, the vicious, gleeful hate in the faces of the crowds gathering to watch the sentences being carried out. Their cheers at the screaming of children being burned alive, drowned, tortured, the frantic sobs of their parents. An infant's screams from a cauldron of boiling water, Savina's own great-great grandmother sobbing and screaming like it was she, along with her child, being murdered.

They'll always hate you, my little Savina. They'll hate you because of who you are. Her mother's fingers, stroking her hair as Savina sobbed, holding her in place as she struggled to turn away from the vid feed. *You need to understand that so you can stay safe.*

And she'd killed and killed and killed and she hadn't even cared, because she'd just wanted to stay safe. She'd just wanted to be safe, and to keep her siblings safe, because no one else in the system would.

And then Joska had forgiven her anyways, cared about her anyways. Loved her anyways. And she'd started to think that maybe, just maybe, the reason she'd done all those things mattered, not just that she'd done them. She'd thought, perhaps, that explaining would make it better.

But it wouldn't. All it had taken to finally condemn her in Reka's eyes was to learn she'd grown up in an Old Believer compound. And so no explanation would matter, in the end. If she was already damned for who she was, nothing else mattered.

Reka's jaw was clenched. "Maybe I can forgive myself if you don't believe it yourself." There was a trace of bitter mockery in her tone, and Savina couldn't tell if it was for Savina, or for herself. "Maybe if you told me you'd left your family and everything they stood for—"

"Then what?" Savina still wasn't sure how she was managing to form the words. "You could maybe forgive yourself for loving me? You could maybe forgive me for the sin of being born into something that I've spent my whole damn life trying to get away from? That's the thing, after everything, that you can't wrap your head around?"

Reka drew in a long breath. "Savina ..."

"No." The word came out steady, somehow, cold and distant. "I was born in an Old Believer compound, Reka. I grew up in the middle of hell. And I'll be damned if I spend one more second with someone who thinks they need to forgive me for that. I'm exactly who you always knew I was. And I disgust you—so be it. So what now? If I prostrate myself and kiss the Orthodox icons and tell you how much I hate my family, you could maybe bring yourself to forgive me for who I was born? You could maybe force yourself to stay with me, even though I disgust you?"

"It's not like that, Savina. I've already given up my damn soul for you, betrayed everything I believe in, and I know that." Reka's voice was low and anguished. "But I lost my family—my entire life—because of Old Believers. If I … if I betray my family's memories like this, without even a second thought … I just want to do the right thing, and I … I don't even know what that is anymore. Don't you see—"

"No!" Savina snapped. "I don't. But then, you and I have always had a difference of opinion on what's right, haven't we? You thought it was right to sell me out after we escaped from Kachik's prison, even after I'd saved your life. You thought it was right for me to leave Joska to die back in Chrr, rather than neglect my duty. Maybe I'm every disgusting, horrible thing you think I am. But where I was born? Who I was born to? What my parents believe? You don't get to judge me for that. You don't get to forgive me for that. You have no damn right."

The cabin was silent

Everything felt almost too clear—the elegant angles of Reka's face, the shape of the cabin around them, the pressure of the mag boots on her feet.

Reka stared at her for a long moment. And then, at last, deliberately, she let go of Savina's hand and pushed herself carefully to her feet. She swayed, and Savina had to hold herself back from leaping up to steady her.

"Joska. If you don't mind, I'm going to the main cabin to sleep. Please let me know if you need me before we arrive."

Her voice sounded far away, and Savina didn't look up to see her face. She was staring at her hand. Her fingers felt cold, without the warmth of Reka's on them.

"Reka, I don't have patience for that sort of bigotry on my ship." There was a sharp anger in Joska's voice. "You'd best—"

"No." Reka's tone was flat. "I'm sorry, Joska. I can't do this."

Savina was still staring at her hand.

There was the sound of Reka's mag boots on the floor, and then the click of the cabin door behind her.

There was utter silence after she'd gone.

Savina could have said … something, but she wasn't sure what to say. Everything inside her felt empty and hollow.

"That filthy bastard."

She looked up, distantly surprised at the anger in Rafel's tone.

"That dirty bigot. If her family was killed in the Swan River massacre, I should be the one she was cursing at, not the Old Believers. I've heard this garbage before in the military, and it doesn't smell any better now than it did then."

Savina almost felt like laughing. It was so absurd, this whole thing was so absurd.

"Savina." Joska's voice was quiet, and Savina … couldn't, not right now. She couldn't handle the woman's sympathy, or her pity, or her kindness.

She stood, shaking Joska's hand from her shoulder. "I'm alright," she said, her voice distant. "I'll be fine."

"She'll be leaving, as soon as we put down on Colorida." Joska's voice was dangerous. "I have no use for those attitudes on my ship."

Savina managed a small smile. "Joska. She didn't say anything I haven't heard before."

Joska was quiet, but Savina could see the anger in her face, and a sharp, helpless pain that she recognized, with an odd detachment, as what her expression must look like when someone hurt Nicolau.

"We don't have time to worry about it anyway," Savina said. "You all heard what Feliu said—we may be going right back into the middle of a war. So we may as well forget about Reka and get ourselves ready for whatever we're going to come back to."

Joska nodded slowly, her face still creased in concern.

There was something wet on Savina's face, and when she reached up to brush it away, she realized she was crying.

"Vina," Nicolau's voice was worried.

"It's fine," she said harshly. "Let's deal with what's ahead of us. We can worry about the rest later. Rafel, why don't you bring up a holomap of Joias and we can figure out where we'll come in? I think they sent through information on where the portal will open."

Reluctantly, Rafel pushed himself to his feet and came over, muttering something uncomplimentary under his breath about government agents and bigots.

Savina bit back her tears, and focused on the map in front of her.

She'd let herself believe, for a little while, the Joska was right— that no one cared what religion you were, or where you came from, or who you'd been born. That they'd judge you on your actions, not your past. That there was forgiveness to be had, and redemption, and that you could always find a second chance if you really wanted one.

But that had been here. That had been on this side of the portal, where no one knew if they'd ever make it home.

And now they would make it home. All the things she'd been running from for so long were coming back. And somehow, she had to remember what it felt like to always be on guard, to not trust anyone, or anything, or ever, ever let yourself be vulnerable.

Because she knew well enough that back in Joias there was no forgiveness, and no redemption, and no second chances. And her life, and Beni's life, and Nicolau's life, depended on her remembering that.

36

Cavaco

"General!"

Cavaco looked up from his paperwork at the young woman standing stiffly at the door, her arm in a tight salute.

"Yes, soldier?" he said brusquely.

"General. I have a report for you." Her posture was so stiff that he could probably have tipped her over by pushing at her shoulder. She was new here, just assigned to him as a junior aide, and he could see the equal parts respect and terror he inspired in her.

He smiled internally, and returned the salute.

"Thank you, soldier," he said, modulating his voice a little. "Report."

He bit back another small smile as she dropped her salute, her hands stiffly at her sides, her jaw clenched, her eyes straight ahead.

His soldiers worshiped him. They'd die for him a thousand times, if they could, and he'd cultivated that loyalty carefully.

"We have received a message, General. My superior officer thought it important that you review it."

"Approach," he said, and she marched stiffly over, holding out a small holodisk in one white-gloved palm.

He took it from her and nodded, and she marched stiffly backward to her original position.

"At ease," he said glancing up with a small smile. "Wait outside the door. I'll read through this, and I'll need you to bring back a response."

She closed her eyes a moment, as if overwhelmed with relief, and stepped into an at-ease position that was almost as stiff as her position at attention, then marched out the door, closing it firmly behind her.

Once she was gone, he tapped the holodisk.

A message sprung up, the face of his second-in-command. "General." The man's face, in the holographic image, was dark with concern. "I thought you should know immediately. We've received word through the newly opened portal." The screen flickered, and then there was a grainy recording. Despite the warping, he recognized the voice at once: Captain Mattin.

"General. I apologize it took us so long to get word back. Alba managed to close down the portal, and it took some time before the yibo opened another. Thankfully, we had been working to set up a message deposit before ..." His voice choked off, and he closed his eyes for a moment. "We were able to open contact with these aliens, and they were amenable to our proposals," he continued at last. "I have sent, in another file, full details. But there is an urgent message you need to know first: there have been ... complications. Our allies were all but destroyed by a group of bloodthirsty creatures, and we barely escaped with our lives. They intend to come back through the portal. They intend to send Alba and the others back as well, and the aliens accompanying them are the same that murdered most of our soldiers and our allies. We will do our best to assist you, and you will find full details on the next recording. But I wanted to ensure you were prepared."

The recording cut off, and the holoimage of his second-in-command's face reappeared. "We're working to open and decode the accompanying transmission," he said. "But I wanted you to hear that immediately."

Cavaco frowned at the still image for a long moment, his mind turning the words over and over.

"Alba Espina," he said thoughtfully. "So you were too bitter a dish even for death, this round."

This was … not ideal. Alba Espina still alive. Hostile aliens coming through a re-opened portal.

But he had long years of practice turning adverse circumstances to his advantage.

And oddly enough, there was a small thrill of something that felt like excitement in his chest at the news.

He'd known, somehow, that it would never be that easy. That he'd have to face Alba himself one day.

And now that day was coming.

And he found he was looking forward to it more than he'd imagined he would.

He was smiling as he pushed back his chair and stood.

"Soldier," he called. "I'd like you to take a message back for me, please."

Thank you for reading!

You might also enjoy The Ungovernable series, also by R.M. Olson.

A mouthy ex-smuggler pilot, a grumpy demolitions expert, a tech genius and a hacker. They're pulling a job on the most dangerous weapons dealer in the System. They're stealing tech that could change the course of history. And every one of them has something to hide.
What could possibly go wrong?
"Spectacular and thrilling! Olson's debut novel is filled with compelling characters and endless excitement." -SD Simper, author of the Fallen Gods series

You can order book one, Zero Day Threat, on Amazon.